Lisa Nowak

Published by Webfoot Publishing
Milwaukie, Oregon

Publishing

Redline

The text of this book is set in 11-point Georgia.

Book design by Lisa Nowak

Cover design by Steven Novak

ISBN-13: 978-1-937-167-20-2

First Edition

DEDICATION

This one's for Elisabeth Miles, who went above and beyond in helping me get it ready for publication, and who consistently bolstered my confidence in a time when I really needed someone to have my back.

ACKNOWLEDGMENTS

I'd like to thank David Frye for letting me use a photo of his '71 Pinto for my cover, Hallie Lichen for modeling as Jess, her mother Pat for helping with the photo shoot, and Steven Novak for putting it all together. (Those of you familiar with Eugene will recognize Spencer Butte in the background.)

Additional thanks go to Dale Silver for reading this book for accuracy regarding alcoholism, and to Todd McCann for answering all my questions about long-haul trucking then checking to be sure I hadn't misinterpreted his good advice.

Special thanks go to Elisabeth Miles, Alice Lynn, and my husband Bob Earls for reading and re-reading this book to help me fine-tune it. Additionally, I'd like to express my gratitude to my editor Annetta Ribken and my copy editors Bob Martin and Carol Sweet.

Finally, I want to show my appreciation for all my beta readers and critique partners: the members of my critique groups, Chrysalis and Wow, Joel Schmitz, Barb Froman, Paula Manley, Karen Champ, Roxie Matthews, Jenny Landis-Steward, Marian Meyer, Kayla Meyer Matsuura, Bob Douglas, Sylvia Potter, Bill and Ruth George, Bobby Shaw, Lois Lane, June Fezler, Laura Marshall, and my sister, Angela Moist.

CHAPTER 1

My first mistake was answering the phone. My second was not hanging up when I heard my mother's voice.

"Jess? Is that you?"

The words sent a surge of octane through my veins, then anger flooded the system. "What do you want?"

"Just to talk to my daughter."

As if that were a reasonable request. As if *I* wanted to talk to *her*.

My fingers constricted around the phone. "You gave up that privilege last summer."

In the long silence that followed, I almost broke the connection, but something made me wait.

"Jess, I know you're mad, and I understand, but . . ."

"You ran out on me, Lydia."

"It's not like you think."

"It's not? You mean you didn't take off without so much as a goodbye?"

"I left you a letter."

Letter? A splinter of laughter caught in my throat. I could see the words clearly—the insinuation that I deserved to have her leave me. The conspicuous lack of signature after four bitter lines. "Would that be the one you hid in your room so I wouldn't find it until you were long gone?"

She snuffled, and her voice tightened like an overstretched rubber band. "I was angry. You acted like you didn't need me anymore. I thought you wanted me to leave."

"Did you think I wanted you to take all my money, too?"

"Sweetie, I'm sorry. I figured you had more stashed away. You always do."

"Not this time."

The line went silent.

"I didn't know, Jess."

"Oh, like that makes a difference?" Another emotion swelled beneath the heat of my anger. I swallowed hard to keep it in check. "Where did you get this number? How did you know I was living here?"

"I didn't. You gave me the number last spring when you started working on your friend's race car."

My stomach seized as I realized what I'd revealed. I rested my forehead against the wall, silently cursing myself.

"I went by the apartment," Lydia continued, "and I saw you weren't there, so—"

"How was I supposed to keep the apartment without any money?"

Lydia stammered, then went quiet, the void of silence drawing out for several breaths. "Well, it worked out, didn't it?" she said at last. "You found a place to stay."

"Only after I lived in my car for a month!" As much as I wanted to rub in the consequences of what she'd done, I couldn't say more than that. Couldn't admit to how badly I'd failed at fending for myself, how I'd almost destroyed my friendships because I'd been too scared and ashamed to ask for help.

"I have nothing more to say to you, Lydia."

"Please, sweetie." The defensiveness vanished from her tone, replaced by the apologetic whine I knew so well. "I messed up. I'm sorry. All I want is another chance."

I hung up, the way I should have in the first place.

It wasn't until I was back at my desk, staring at my calculus homework, that I realized how much the call had rattled me. The scribbles on my paper made no sense, and after reading a problem three times, I still couldn't comprehend it.

C'mon, Jess, get it together. Lydia had done enough to foul up my life before she left. I couldn't let her ruin the good things I had going now. For the first time, I was putting some effort into school and had a real shot at college. Once I got my degree in engineering, I could open my own shop and concentrate on the thing I liked best—building race cars.

I leaned back in my chair and looked out the window. The late afternoon mist should've dulled the rampage of fall colors. Instead, it gave them a surreal glow. Big leaf maples blazed like golden torches between the Douglas firs, and the sumacs at the end of the driveway were glowing embers. My gaze slipped over the familiar features of the Clines' front yard—the barn where we worked on my friend Teri Sue's race car, the alder in which her little brother Rhett had built his tree house, the fire pit where we'd had our cookouts. This place was my refuge, so why did my heart seem to be on the verge of shorting out? It wasn't like Lydia had any authority over me, now that I'd found Dad. Even though his job as a long-haul trucker kept him on the road, I had his blessing to stay with Teri Sue's father and little brother.

But that wasn't the real issue. While Lydia had been gone, I could pretend I was just like my friends, that instead of scrabbling to keep food on the table, or my mom out of trouble, homework and hanging out were the norm. But now . . .

I should've known the idea of being normal was too good to be true.

Monday morning, as I leaned into my locker, a hand pressed gently at the small of my back.

"Hey," said Cody, my best-friend-turned-boyfriend. "You get your essay done?"

"At great expense to my sanity." I found my psychology textbook and turned to meet his world-class grin. No matter how many times I saw it, it always sent a rush of warmth straight through me. "How'd things go with the bodywork?"

Cody's smile twisted back on itself. "I'll be lucky to get it done by Christmas." He'd spent Saturday evening and most of Sunday at his uncle's shop, doing bodywork on his '65 Ford Galaxie to get it ready for paint. I would've helped if I hadn't been stuck home writing an English essay and trying to fit my other assignments around it. I'd always been friendlier with numbers than with words.

"Next time I'll give you a hand," I said.

"I know." His lips perked up, as if itching to kiss me, but I knew he wouldn't embarrass me that way in school. Instead, his fingers sought mine, and his eyes, brown as the Euphoria chocolate he was always sneaking into my locker, said the forty-one hours since he'd last seen me were forty too many. He tossed his head to sweep his dark rooster tail bangs out of his face. "Anything exciting happen while I was so mercilessly separated from you? Alien abduction, maybe? Or a call from Dale Earnhardt begging you to be his next crew chief?"

My hand twitched in his at the mention of a call, and guilt sent my eyes scurrying away.

"What's wrong?"

I'd decided not to say anything about Lydia. Cody hadn't met her, and I wanted to keep it that way. She'd probably never call back, and what was the sense of bringing up something that made me want to crawl under a rock if it had no effect on either of our lives?

"Nothing," I said.

"Uh huh. Then why'd you jump? Is everything okay with your dad?" Cody had always been able to read me. While his sensitivity and intuition had been big factors in winning my trust, he was a born worrier, and I hated to provide him with any fuel.

"Dad's fine. He just had to cancel his visit next weekend."

"Oh." Cody's fingers pulsed against mine. "I'm sorry, Jess."

"It's okay. I can wait another week." Much as I hated the

delay, I was grateful for the excuse it provided. Cody and I didn't lie to each other, not since last summer, when I'd almost driven him away by neglecting to tell him about Lydia abandoning me. Living in my car had scared me half to death, but I'd been even more afraid of getting tossed into a foster home, of being separated from the first friends I'd had in years.

Of course, this wasn't anything like that. I wasn't in danger. I just wanted to spare myself some humiliation, to go on pretending my life wasn't a broken, dysfunctional mess.

Cody closed my locker and circled his arm around my waist, directing me down the hall. "I know I'm no substitute for your dad," he said. "But I'll give you all my free time next weekend, okay?"

"Sounds like a plan."

A year ago, completely lacking in feminine charm, and having the grease under my nails to prove it, I'd never have believed any boy would take interest in me, let alone a cute, sweet, funny guy like Cody.

Now if only I could convince myself I wasn't going to scare him away. Or that Lydia wouldn't do it for me.

CHAPTER 2

That afternoon, I went directly from school to Eugene Custom Classics. Cody and I both worked there on Monday, Wednesday, and Friday afternoons, as well as Saturday mornings. His uncle's fiancée, Kasey, owned the place. She was a wonder with anything mechanical, and once she'd seen the Pinto I'd tricked out with a 351 Windsor, she'd become the mentor I'd never believed I could have.

While Cody was content to do whatever grunt work Kasey threw at him, so he could buy parts for his race car, I wanted to learn everything I could about restorations. Today, she had me working the dents out of the rear quarter panel of a '66 Mustang. It was frustrating, heating and cooling the metal, using the proper hammers and dolleys to coax it back into its original shape. Kasey liked to keep the Bondo to a minimum, arguing there were more elegant ways of handling bodywork.

I tried to lose myself in what I was doing, but for once that didn't work. What if Lydia called back? In the eight years my dad had been gone, she'd rarely considered my best interests. It was always about her. What if she fought Dad for custody? No judge would take her seriously, but everyone would find out. She'd suck me right back into her drama, and this time, she might take my friends along for the ride.

It was almost quitting time when a tow truck pulled up in front of one of the bay doors, which had been left open to let in the last of the good weather. I recognized the name on the door, McCormick Body and Paint. The car on the hook was harder to place. I knew it was a Studebaker, in spite of it being in primer, with the trim removed. But I couldn't determine the year.

"Dad!" Kasey said as a balding tree of a man unfolded himself from the front seat. "I didn't expect you to buy it."

"You said you'd trust my judgment," Mr. McCormick said. "The price was right, and the body's sound. Someone's abandoned project car. They already did a lot of the dirty work."

Kasey showed him where to unload the car then, despite his protests, insisted on writing him a check. She invited him into the office for a cup of coffee, but he declined, saying he had to get back to Cottage Grove.

"Well," Kasey said, glancing at me as the tow truck pulled out of the lot. "What do you say we clean her up? Can you stay an extra hour or so?"

"Sure. Mark doesn't have class tonight. Let me give him a call so he knows I'll be late."

When I got back from phoning Teri Sue's dad, who taught history at the University of Oregon, Cody and his uncle were helping Kasey wash the dust off the Studebaker. With their dark eyes, unruly brown hair, and here-comes-trouble grins, they could've been brothers, in spite of Cody's short stature.

Cody had been living with Race since the end of his freshman year, and the word 'devotion' didn't begin to describe the bond between them. If Race had needed a kidney, Cody would've offered both of his, just in case the first one didn't do the trick. Race had won Cody's trust by appreciating him for exactly who he was, something no other adult in his life had ever done. And it didn't hurt that they shared a crazy sense of humor.

"What year is this thing?" Cody asked, giving the hose a little flick that drenched the back of his uncle's T-shirt.

"1958," said Kasey over Race's startled howl. She tucked a lock of auburn hair under her Snap-On Tools hat.

"It's a Hawk, isn't it?" I wasn't as familiar with Studebakers as I was with some other makes.

"That's right." Kasey glanced across the roof of the car. "Race, don't even think about throwing that sponge."

I took a step back, knowing her warning would do little to put the brakes on the inevitable water fight. Even though Race was in his mid-twenties, he was as bad as Cody when it came to horseplay. Maybe worse.

"This isn't for a customer, is it?" It couldn't be business, or her dad wouldn't have fought her about taking the check.

"No. I've always wanted to do a custom on one of these." Kasey retreated a safe distance from the rainstorm of sponges and hose spray. "The idea is to accentuate the Hawk features. I'll modify the front fenders and add some Mercedes headlights to give it a more aerodynamic look, then replace the hood and deck lid with those from a Commander. They're smoother and swoopier, ironically more bird-like than the stock ones. But the *coup de grace* will be the graphics on the rear fins—ghost feathers."

"Ghost *feathers*?" I'd heard of ghost flames—they were like regular flames, only fainter, and without the pinstripe. But ghost feathers?

"That's a great idea," Race said, abandoning the battle. When a sponge smacked him in the back of the head, he didn't even trouble himself by returning fire. "Too bad I'm not doing graphics any more. I wouldn't mind taking a crack at something like that."

"Maybe you should give it a try," said Cody.

A faint look of weariness creased Race's face. "Let's not start in on that again, all right, kid?"

"Seriously," said Cody. "I read someplace that art isn't in the fingers, it's in the brain. There was this one guy who was totally paralyzed and—"

Race turned abruptly to stare him down over the roof of the Hawk. "It's not my *fingers* that are damaged."

Cody's determination sputtered, but it didn't stall. "Maybe you can still do it," he said, swiping at his bangs with the back of his wrist. "How are you gonna know if you don't try?"

"I don't have to *try* to know." The evenness of Race's tone said he was okay with that, even if Cody wasn't.

"But—"

I grabbed the hose from Cody's hand. "You're wasting water. C'mon, let's finish up before it gets dark."

Cody's eyes stayed locked on Race for one last, lingering moment. Then he wiped his hands on his jeans. "I'm going to Dari Mart. Maybe you guys can work without dinner," he said, patting his stomach, "but this baby gets restless if I don't keep it fed. You coming, Jess?

"No, just bring me a Mountain Dew."

"You got it." He turned and loped off across East Amazon.

Race went to work sudsing up the roof, not seeming the least bit bothered by the exchange. But then Race didn't let much upset him. It was one of the things I admired about him because if anyone had reason for regrets, it was Race. He'd been involved in a wreck at the speedway during the '89 season, almost a year and a half before, and the resulting head injury had affected his fine motor skills, ending his career as a graphic artist. To make matters worse, when he'd gotten out of the hospital, he'd had to swallow his pride and accept Kasey's offer to let him and Cody move in with her. Race never said much about any of it, and what he did say was matter-of-fact or darkly humorous. It was Cody who couldn't seem to accept Race's loss.

As Race, Kasey, and I worked on the car, sharing a comfortable silence, Lydia's call crept into my thoughts. What would everyone think if they knew she was back? Would they expect me to give her another chance? At the very least, they'd be reminded of how pathetic my life used to be and feel sorry for me. I'd had enough of that last summer.

Dari Mart was so close you almost could've thrown a stone and hit it, but the slough stood between it and Kasey's shop, so Cody had to circle up East Amazon and back down West

Amazon to get there. He was gone long enough that we were able to finish washing the car and begin taking inventory of what the previous owner had done.

The Studebaker had a Garibaldi chassis, built to spec from square tubing that was sturdier than the original frame. The rear end held a 4-link solid axle with coilovers, while the front end had been converted to a Mustang II suspension. The crossmember was set up with brackets for a Chevy 350.

"That will have to be changed," Kasey said. "I want to build a Studebaker engine to Avanti R-3 specs."

As she opened the back door of the car to sort through the parts stored inside, Cody returned. His arms were stuffed with junk food, drinks, and a tiny, wiggling kitten.

"Look what I found in the slough," he said, extending his elbow to Kasey, who was a sucker for cats. She unhooked the squalling brown tabby from the crook of his arm and cupped it in both hands.

"Poor baby. He's soaked."

"Yeah, somehow he got himself stranded on a rock. I had to wade in to get him." Cody lifted one of his sodden Converse high tops to illustrate his sacrifice.

"How'd a kitten get in the slough?" Race wondered.

"Someone probably tossed him out of a car," Kasey said. "He couldn't have been there long, or he wouldn't have survived. He's barely big enough to be six weeks old." She picked up one of the towels that hadn't been used on the Hawk and wrapped up the kitten like a burrito.

"I figured you'd take pity on him and give him a home," Cody said.

"Can I have him?" Something about the little ball of fur, with its oversized eyes and ears, was so appealing my fingers itched to snatch it away from Kasey. I'd never had a pet. Lydia was allergic to cats, and even if she hadn't been, we'd had a hard enough time keeping the two of us fed.

"It's fine with me if it's all right with Mark," Kasey said. "I'm sure Winston would just as soon not have the competition."

Her enormous tabby was so mellow, I didn't think he'd notice, but I welcomed any excuse that would make the kitten mine. I held out my hands, and Kasey placed the shivering bundle in them. The tiny mouth opened to let out a squeak. My insides turned to warm pudding, and I pulled the kitten close, mumbling that same obnoxious baby talk I could never handle coming from other people.

Cody tugged at my ponytail where it trailed from the back of my Eugene Speedway cap. "Everybody look out," he said. "Jess's maternal instincts just kicked in."

By the following afternoon, my worries about Lydia's call had faded, but I still hadn't thought of a name for my kitten. Mark had offered suggestions honoring historic figures and characters from the black and white movies he loved, but none of them seemed right. His 11-year-old son, Rhett, wanted to name the cat after one of the Teenage Mutant Ninja Turtles. I didn't like that idea much, either.

"He looks like a Raphael to *me*," said Rhett, using the eraser-end of a pencil to scratch under the brace he'd worn on his left leg since he was six. He was supposed to be doing his math homework, but he seemed more interested in playing with our new baby.

"What about 'Newt'?" he asked, flicking a piece of wadded notebook paper across the kitchen floor at the kitten. "Newts are amphibious, and you found him in the slough."

I stood at the stove, stirring a pot of pinto beans. They were one of the Southern dishes Teri Sue had taught me to cook before she'd gone off to college the month before. "I'm not sure finding him in the slough qualifies him to be an amphibian, but that is a cute name."

11

"Newt," said Rhett. He wiggled a sock, which had slumped down to trail off his toes. "Noot, Noot, Noot," he crooned in that sweet North Carolina drawl of his. "Is that your name, kitty? Owww!" Rhett yanked his foot back, and the kitten, still attached to his sock, came with it.

"You reckon we'll see Teri Sue this weekend?" he asked as he unhooked himself.

"Don't count on it."

Rhett rubbed his punctured toes. "She hasn't been home in weeks. And she only lives a few miles away. It's not like she went to school in New York or something."

"She's probably busy with her classes."

"But she hasn't even come back to work on her race car!"

I peeked in the oven to check the pork roast. "Maybe you should give her a call."

"Yeah, sure. Someone else always answers. Besides, she never calls back."

I could relate to that frustration. Teri Sue's dorm at the University of Oregon had only one phone per floor, and I was never sure whether she was ignoring my messages or not receiving them. She'd asked her dad for a private line in her room, but he said he provided her with plenty of money. If she wanted one that badly, she could pay for it herself.

"Don't worry," I told Rhett. "When your sister gets settled, we'll see more of her. Now what did you get for number five?"

He tossed his red-gold hair out of his eyes and slumped in his chair. "I'm still working on it. Could you show me that trick you did again?"

I sat down with him and went through the steps of converting a fraction to a percentage. "See, it's not so hard."

"Yeah, right. Not everyone's a math genius like you, Jess."

"You don't have to be a genius to know kittens and homework don't mix." I plucked the animal from the leg of Rhett's jeans, where he was doing a Velcro impression.

"Newt," I said, holding him up to my face. I kissed the tiny, brick-colored nose. "Yeah, I think I like that."

Two days later, I was lying on my bed, struggling through the opening chapters of *A Tale of Two Cities*, when the phone rang. I lifted the snoozing Newt from my chest, gently placed him on my pillow, and ran down the hall to answer it.

"Hi, sweetie!"

A shiver of anxiety swept through me. "What part of 'I have nothing more to say to you' don't you understand?"

"Please don't do this, Jess. I know I wasn't there for you last summer, but it hasn't always been that way."

I barked out a laugh. "No, sometimes it was me paying the electric bill when you couldn't, or bailing you out of jail."

Silence numbed my ear. I'd rarely stood up to Lydia before she'd left, so it probably shocked her to hear me doing so now.

"Can you honestly say there weren't any good times?"

"What difference does that make?" I glanced uneasily toward Rhett's bedroom door, then a burst of television gunfire echoed up the steps, and I realized he was downstairs. Mark was off teaching his Thursday night US History class, so there was little chance of anyone discovering my old life had caught up with me.

"We used to be a team," Lydia said. "You and me against the world."

"Sure, once you'd eliminated Dad from the picture." Even now, months after I'd learned the truth, the idea of her deceit made me want to slap her.

"It isn't my fault he left."

"You mean you didn't blatantly lie about him not wanting anything to do with me?"

"I don't know what you're talking about. I never lied to you."

"You're doing it right now!" My throat constricted around

my voice, making it hurt to force out the next words. "I found him, Lydia. He told me how he'd sent the child support you said you weren't getting. And the letters and birthday cards. You threw those away, didn't you?"

"Jess—"

"You stole my father! Then you ran off and left me. How could you possibly think I'd want to talk to you now?" My breath came hard and fast as I waited to hear how she'd write that off. I was ready for her, whatever she had. Let her try to weasel out of this.

"I'm sorry, Jess. But I couldn't handle the way you chose him over me. You always loved him more. By the time I figured out the lies had to stop, I wasn't sure how to un-tell them."

My fist clenched around the phone. "You think that justifies what you did?"

"Of course not. . . . But there's more to the story, you know. Things he's not going to tell you."

"What kinds of things?" The words, thick with skepticism, snuck out almost against my will.

"Well, the drugs, for one."

Uneasiness prickled the back of my neck. "What are you talking about?" She had to be lying. Dad wouldn't mess with that sort of thing.

"It shouldn't be any surprise to you." Lydia's tone oozed snippiness. "Lots of truckers use them. How do you think they stay awake, driving those long hours?"

If she thought I was going to buy into her half-assed attempt to manipulate me, she was in for a surprise. "That's ridiculous," I said. "Dad's not that stupid."

"Don't kid yourself. Every minute he's not on the road is a minute he's not making money. He must've mentioned that by now."

My stomach cramped, and I slumped against the wall. Whenever Dad postponed or cancelled a visit, I heard some version of those words. He owned his rig and worked as an independent contractor for a small company, so he had to hustle every job he could get.

"I know you think it was my fault we broke up, but he put me in an impossible position," Lydia said. "He was never around. All I could do was sit at home and worry—wait for a call that there had been an accident."

It would've been easy to write off her excuse if those same thoughts hadn't hovered at the edges of my mind on a daily basis. While Dad and I talked every week, and he sent lots of postcards, he only made it into town a couple of times a month. It was so hard, being away from him, hoping he was staying safe as he pushed to get those extra miles.

After a long silence, Lydia sighed. "I'll admit it—I was wrong, sweetie. I never should've lied to you. But you need to know your dad isn't the hero you've always thought he was. He's got as many problems as I do."

I rubbed a hand across my forehead, my thoughts and feelings a jumble. "Why should I believe you? You've been lying to me all my life."

"You can believe whatever you want," Lydia said, the nastiness slipping back into her tone. "But deep down, you know I'm right."

"The only thing I know is I can't forgive you. Not ever." I dropped the phone into its cradle and went back to my room, where I scooped up Newt and snuggled his mewing softness against my cheek. But as I settled back down to read my English homework, one thought wouldn't leave my head.

What if she was telling the truth?

CHAPTER 3

I tried to convince myself Lydia was lying about the drugs, but the tiny bit of doubt lingering in my mind made it hard to sleep. What did I really know about Dad's history, after all? I'd been just a kid when he left, too young to pick up on that sort of thing. All I could remember were the fights they sometimes had over him being gone so much. I poured through my memories, looking for clues, as I lay in bed, trying to drift off. Had Lydia seemed worried about him? Had Dad ever behaved in a strange way? I didn't think so, but it had been so long ago.

Regardless, I had no interest in talking to my mother again. If Dad *was* using drugs, it was something I'd work out with him. I didn't need her input. With any luck, now that I'd told her she'd never get my forgiveness, the calls would end.

In the morning, I told myself it was best to keep the whole thing under wraps. And when I got to school and saw the T-shirt Cody was wearing, *My mother is a travel agent for guilt trips*, I knew I'd made the right decision.

Cody's mom was as bad as Lydia. She'd alternated between belittling and ignoring him all his life, and then took off for Phoenix, leaving him with a father who'd never come to his defense. Cody fought back with an act of vandalism that got him shipped off to live with his uncle. For the first time in his life, he'd felt like he belonged, so when his mom tried to uproot him, he'd faced her down. She hadn't spoken to him since. Even if I'd wanted to tell Cody about Lydia being back, how could I? She might be a few laps down in the race for Mother of the Year, but at least she wanted to be part of my life.

At lunchtime, Cody met me at my locker, leaning against the next one over and treating me to one of his famous grins.

"Guess who just aced his trig test, thanks to your awesome

16

tutoring?"

Pride surged through me in a warm rush. Cody's strength was English, not math, and we'd worked hard reviewing formulas until he could apply them flawlessly. "That's great! I knew you could do it."

"Not without you." Cody gave me a sultry look that sent lightning bolts shooting through the zone just below my belly.

"Okay, break it up," said his friend, Quinn, as he slipped out of a crowd of students.

"We weren't doing anything!" Cody protested.

"But you were thinking about it."

"Of course I was thinking about it. I'm *always* thinking about it. And why shouldn't I? You're just crippled by jealousy because I got to Jess before you could."

Quinn laughed and shook his head in that amused sort of way guys do when they're humoring a friend. "That must be it," he said. "Guess I'll have to wait till you screw up so I can have her for myself." He slung one arm around Cody's neck, and the other around mine, steering us toward the cafeteria.

Forcing a smile, I fell into step. I never quite knew what to say to Quinn. He was a nice enough guy, but his friendliness made me uneasy, especially when he said flattering things. How was I supposed to know if he was serious or putting me on? After growing up with Lydia, where every friendship meant the potential of someone tipping off the authorities and getting me whisked out of my home, I figured I was doing well to trust the people I did. I wanted to like Quinn and Cody's other friend, Heather, because I knew he must've had good reasons for hanging out with them. But frankly, I wasn't sure it was worth the stress.

By Saturday afternoon, it looked as if my prediction about Teri Sue was going to prove accurate. She hadn't called, let alone come home to visit. Despite what I'd said to Rhett, I was a little put out. I could deal with the fact that she'd found more interesting things to do than pal around with me, but he was just a kid. He needed her.

At least my mother hadn't called back. Even though it had only been two days since the last time, I had a good feeling about scaring her off. Now if I could just stop worrying about Dad.

Lydia's accusations lurked at the back of my mind as I lay under Teri Sue's Camaro, unbolting the transmission. With the season over, it was time to tackle the labor-intensive projects we couldn't delve into while competing each week. Today, Rhett and I were pulling the engine. Or rather *I* was pulling the engine while he sat in the driver's seat, fantasizing about his debut race.

"I wish Teri Sue would call me back," he grumbled. "I left two messages yesterday."

"Maybe she's not getting them." I didn't want to talk about this any more than I wanted to think about how my dad might be as much of an addict as my mother. The barn was supposed to be my refuge—a place where the scents of oil and racing fuel, mingling with that of hay, helped me get lost in the work I loved. But the truth was, I missed Teri Sue. Everything I had, I owed to her. She'd been the one who'd punched a hole through my personal fortress by offering me a job working on her car last spring. If not for that, I'd never have met the friends I had now or gotten back in touch with my dad. She'd coached me through the early days of my relationship with Cody, explaining things that, as a socially inept tomboy, I'd been at a loss to understand. She'd been the only person I'd ever felt comfortable talking 'girl talk' with. How could she just walk away after I'd trusted her enough to let her in?

"Daddy should get her a phone," Rhett said. "Then we wouldn't have to leave messages."

"Somehow I don't think that's going to happen." I was a

little surprised Teri Sue hadn't given in and paid for one herself. Sociable as she was, not having a phone must've been a serious handicap.

"That figures." Rhett began rocking the steering wheel back and forth, spewing a soundtrack of engine noise and squealing rubber.

"Hey there, Earnhardt. Ease up a little," I said as the back of one of the tires caught me on the elbow.

"Sorry." The motion ceased, and Rhett went quiet. "Hey, Jess?"

"Yeah?"

"What's this red line on the tach for?"

"It's a warning to the driver. If you rev the engine beyond that point, you could damage it, maybe even grenade it."

"Teri Sue didn't do that, did she?"

"No, this engine's just a little tired."

There was a scrambling above me, then a metallic clank as Rhett climbed out the window and his brace banged against the door. He dropped to the ground and crouched to peer under the car. "Are you ready for me to help?"

From almost the moment we met, Rhett and I had shared a special bond. But since the weather had turned, and he couldn't pursue his normal hobbies of building tree houses and digging ponds, he'd been especially eager to keep me company.

"Sure," I said. "Why don't you slide the jack under here?"

Rhett dragged it over to the car and rolled it underneath. Once I got it situated, I had him pump the handle until the saddle was just below the transmission. "Okay," I said after wiggling the three-speed loose from the bell housing, "let her down."

Outside, the familiar rumble of Cody's '65 Galaxie echoed up the driveway. He was just in time to help with the hard part. I wasn't looking forward to manhandling the cherry picker over the barn's dirt floor. Mark had put up insulation, but hadn't yet gotten around to pouring a concrete pad for us to work on.

"All right, Rhett," I said, placing a hand on the tranny to keep it balanced. "Can you pull the jack out?"

"I reckon."

I'd just scooted from under the Camaro when Cody stepped into the barn. Raindrops glistened from his dark hair and leather jacket.

"Hey guys," he said, tugging the door shut and setting his Big Gulp on the workbench. "You ready to pull that puppy?" He extracted two bags of M&Ms from his jacket pocket, handing one to me and the other to Rhett. From the moment Cody had learned of my chocolate addiction, he'd assumed the role of enabler.

"Almost. Why don't you break loose the exhaust while I deal with the radiator?"

With Cody's assistance, we soon had the engine out and mounted on a stand. A race motor doesn't take long to pull. The extraneous components, like the heater and air conditioning, have already been stripped to reduce weight and drag. All that's left is what's necessary to make the car run.

While I began dismantling the engine, I explained to Rhett how the parts fit together, and Cody stood by making stupid jokes.

"Put a sock in it," I finally said, frisbeeing an oil ring at him.

He deflected it with a karate block and slung his arm around Rhett's neck, drawing him close. "So what are you gonna be for Halloween?"

Scowling, Rhett pulled away. "Nothing. I'm not going trick or treating."

"What?" Cody feigned mortal shock. "Dude, you've gotta go. In another year or two, you'll be too old. You need to get in on that free candy action while you still can."

Rhett hiked his shoulders, eyes fixed on the floor. "Teri Sue always goes with me, and she's not even calling me back."

We exchanged a look over Rhett's head. This was something Cody and I had worried about last summer. It was one of the reasons I'd decided to move in with the Clines, rather than staying with Kasey after Cody discovered I was living in my car.

"I'll take you," Cody said.

"And I'll go, too," I added.

This would be a new one. I hadn't been trick-or-treating since my parents split up.

That evening, Dad called. "Hey, honey," he said. "How ya doin'?"

The sound of his voice sent a ripple of worry through me, but I ignored it. What Lydia said couldn't be true.

"I'm good." I stretched out on my bed, bare toes burrowing beneath Newt's chubby kitten belly.

"I'm sorry I couldn't make it home this weekend. I'll be there next week for sure."

"It's okay. I understand."

"Things still working out with Mark and Rhett?" He asked this almost every time he called, as if he thought the arrangement might be too good to last.

"Everything's fine."

So why was my voice stalling out in my throat? I forced myself to keep talking, to sound like a normal teenage girl, happy to be chatting with her dad. "Rhett wants to know if you found any new signs."

He was one of my father's biggest fans, first because of his truck, a red and silver Freightliner, and second, because of his collection. Every time Dad saw a sign that was misspelled, had a double meaning, or otherwise amused him, he snapped a picture and put it in a scrapbook. He'd started the project for me right after the divorce, when he still had hopes of seeing me again. Even though it had been years before that happened, he never quit collecting signs.

"I've got two new ones," Dad said. "'Falling Can Be Deadly' and 'PTA Board Meeting,' with board spelled 'b-o-r-e-d.'"

I laughed, letting myself slip into the easiness I always felt with him. "I'll bet that was on purpose. Where'd you see the first one?"

"A state park up in Washington." He paused as an announcement blared over the truck stop intercom. "Everything okay at the shop? You're not working too much, are you?"

"Of course not."

Newt grunted in his sleep, stretching out and rolling off my foot.

"I'll be glad when I can quit my job and find a local route so I can spend more time with you."

My heart twinged. I wished that could happen, but Dad loved being on the road, and there was no way I'd be responsible for him giving it up. "I don't want you to quit. I'd just like it if you came home more often."

"I'd like that, too. But if I'm ever gonna buy us a place to call our own, I've gotta stay on top of every opportunity to make a buck."

Uneasiness stung me as Lydia's words came surging back— *every minute he's not on the road is a minute he's not making money.*

"We don't need a house," I said, my tone sharp. "I'll be going off to college in two years."

"Well, that's another issue. I've been trying to put away a little bit each month, but there's not nearly as much in your college fund as I'd like."

Why couldn't he stop worrying about that? I understood that between sending child support to my mother, keeping up with repairs and maintenance on his truck, and living out of hotels when he wasn't on the road, there had never been much left of his paycheck.

"Who cares about the college fund? I'll get a scholarship or loan. It's dangerous to push yourself by being on the road so much." The hint was as close as I could come to admitting my real fear, but how do you ask your dad if he's taking drugs?

"That's why there are laws to regulate how many hours a trucker can spend behind the wheel," he said.

The information gave me the smallest surge of reassurance. "Really?"

"Yep. And I promise you, Jessie, I'm not gonna bend those rules."

I wanted to believe him, but Lydia's accusation lingered in my mind, a smoldering ember of doubt. Dad and I had hardly been together in eight years. Our entire modern history consisted of a week-long trip in his truck and four weekend visits. I didn't think he'd lie to me, but how well did I really know him?

CHAPTER 4

Sunday morning, I pulled myself away from obsessing about Dad and went to Race's shop to help Cody with the Galaxie. Kasey had promised him the use of her paint booth on New Year's Day, when her business would be closed, so he only had a couple of months to get the car prepped.

As we applied Bondo and sanded it down, Cody filled me in on yesterday's college football scores. He wasn't a fan of the sport, but Race and Kasey, having attended Oregon's rival state schools, made a point of harassing each other on the topic every weekend.

"The Ducks creamed Stanford, 31-zip. And the Beavers lost again. . . . Of course," he added with a snicker.

I worked a used-up piece of sandpaper out of my sanding block and reached for a fresh strip. "What was the score?" I couldn't care less about football but had an obligation to help Kasey defend OSU, especially since I planned on going there myself.

"Twenty-six to seventeen."

"That's not exactly a blow out. Not like, say, the way the Huskies kicked the Duck's butts thirty-eight to seventeen two weeks ago." It was something Kasey had crowed about. Apparently the U of O's distaste for Washington was almost as intense as it was for the Beavers.

"It is when you've only won one game all season."

The Ducks were having a decent year, winning four out of six games so far, but there was no way Cody would hear me admit it. This was about more than just him taking Race's side. He planned on studying journalism at the U of O and had spent the past month and a half getting a head start on the rivalry thing.

"Maybe the Beavers understand that college is about getting

an education, not screwing around with stupid ball games," I said.

Cody smirked. "You wish."

After spending a couple of hours working on his car, we had lunch at Emerald Country Deli and headed back to my house. I would've been willing to stay all afternoon, distracting myself from the worrisome thoughts about my dad, but Cody had reminded me he owed Rhett a karate lesson.

"I can't let the kid down," he'd said. "Especially after the way Teri Sue's been treating him."

Cody had been studying karate for a year and a half, and three weeks before had moved up to the 6th kyu—a step above green belt. Last spring, he'd started passing his knowledge on to Rhett. He'd also been showing me a few moves.

"You need to be able to defend yourself," he'd told me. But I suspected his real motive was the need for a sparring partner closer to his size.

I wasn't as enamored with the martial arts as Cody and Rhett were, but I loved the way Cody's grin went all lopsided when I executed a move to his satisfaction. "You're such a bad ass, Jess," he'd say. And then the karate would morph into wrestling until Rhett, watching from the sidelines, would start moaning and gagging in protest.

We spent a couple of hours practicing in the barn, then I had to shoo Cody off so I could do some chores and finish my chemistry homework. Rhett followed me inside to resume his efforts to teach Newt to fetch—a losing proposition. So far the kitten's only obvious talent was discovering unique napping places. At night, he preferred sleeping against my head, but we'd also found him tucked away in Rhett's backpack, burrowed into one of Mark's houseplants, and even curled up in his empty food dish.

Despite Rhett's lack of success in educating the kitten, I was glad he'd found a new hobby. The more he played with Newt, the less time he had to obsess about Teri Sue's absence.

That evening, while I was cutting up mushrooms for spaghetti sauce, Mark wandered into the kitchen wearing his Jerry Garcia T-shirt and a pair of baggy hemp pants. He'd spent the afternoon working in his perennial garden, and his hair, the same red-gold color as his son's, was pulled back into a ponytail. He'd been growing it out, something Teri Sue found appalling. She didn't care much for his habit of wearing socks with his Birkenstocks either, though I assured her it was acceptable Oregon fashion.

"You don't have to do this, Jess," Mark said. "I'm perfectly capable of fixing supper on the evenings I'm not teaching."

"I like to help out."

"I know you do, but looking after Rhett while I'm at work is more than enough. Besides, you've already vacuumed and cleaned the bathrooms today."

"You said I was family. Isn't family supposed to pitch in?"

Mark sighed, running a hand through his hair and dislodging a few seeds that had hitchhiked in from the yard. "At sixteen you should be worried about boyfriends and schoolwork, not the responsibilities of running a household. It isn't healthy to be so driven."

Right. I'd been taking charge and pulling my own weight since the third grade. How had it hurt me so far?

"I like doing things for you and Rhett," I said. They appreciated it in a way Lydia rarely had. "Anyway, sitting around doing nothing makes me nervous."

"That's the problem. You need to learn how to have fun." With his interest in Eastern philosophy, Mark was a serious advocate of what Cody called the "chill factor."

"I have fun. I hang out with Cody all the time."

"When you aren't working for Kasey, or on Teri Sue's car."

"But I enjoy those things!" I said, stirring the mushrooms

into the sauce. The rich scent of tomatoes and garlic bubbled up out of the pot.

Mark reached for the spoon in my hand. "Tell you what, let me finish up here, and you go find something non-productive to do."

"I guess I could knock out a couple chapters of *A Tale of Two Cities.*"

"*Non-productive,* Jess."

Sighing, I relinquished the spoon. Why couldn't Mark see it was best to stay busy? That it distracted me from missing Dad and worrying about him?

I was halfway up the stairs when the phone rang. Maybe it shouldn't have surprised me to hear Lydia's voice when I answered, but I wanted to believe I'd run her off for good.

Rhett hung his head out the doorway of his room. "That's not Trevor, is it?"

My heart froze as I realized he could've easily beaten me to the phone. Rhett's own mother was in a psychiatric hospital in North Carolina. Being responsible for the accident that injured his leg and nearly killed him had driven her over the edge. She no longer even remembered she had a son. Rhett was dealing with the loss of his mama pretty well these days, but it had hurt him to see me reunite with my dad. How would he feel if he found out about Lydia?

"It's just somebody from my history class," I said, scooping up the phone and taking it into my room. I hated lying to him, but what choice did I have?

"Lydia," I hissed, "you can't keep calling here. Someone else might answer."

She sighed. "You're ashamed of me."

How clueless could she be? "Yeah. I am. I have a normal life now. I have friends. And frankly, the less they know about the way I used to live, the better." I dropped onto my bed beside the sleeping Newt, who unfurled himself, stretched, and meowed. I wanted to confront her about Dad—to force her to retract her earlier words. But what if she told me something even worse about him?

"Sweetie, you have nothing to be embarrassed about. You did everything right. You were Mommy's Big Girl, remember?"

The old nickname stirred images of me tugging at her limp arm, dragging her into bed when she'd come home blitzed out of her mind—memories of me teaching myself to cook mac and cheese when she was too depressed to do anything but lie on the couch.

"Yeah, I remember. But eight year olds aren't supposed to take care of their parents."

"I know. And I'm so sorry. I've never been strong. Not like you, Jess."

She was crazy if she thought I was buying into her mind games. "You could've tried."

"But I did! Every time I let you down, I tried to fix it. Remember how I taught you to make chocolate chip pancakes from scratch? And how whenever we went for pizza at Track Town, we'd make up a silly name for them to call when our order was ready? And how we'd have our sundae nights, when we'd go to Safeway and pick out those crazy toppings?"

I wasn't about to admit it, but she was right. For all her faults, Lydia had done her best to make things up to me. The problem was, those attempts usually involved spending money we didn't have. And they sure didn't excuse the way she'd been so nasty to me the last time she'd called.

"I know it wasn't easy, Jess. But growing up that way made you tough. You've got it more together than most grownups I know."

That wasn't much of a compliment, considering the company she kept. Anyway, hadn't Mark just lectured me on how messed up I was? At least I'd found something non-productive to do with the past few minutes.

The insight made me realize she'd pulled me into a conversation I'd had no intentions of allowing. "I've gotta go, Lydia," I said. "I have homework."

I hung up and returned the phone to the table in the hallway. But as I went back to my room, I couldn't help wondering. Would I still be the same person if my parents had never broken up?

"Can you stay to help with the Studebaker tonight?" Kasey asked Monday as we were closing the shop. "Race picked up the body parts from the wrecking yard. I could use a hand cleaning them." The Hawk project had stirred an eager-little-kid enthusiasm in her, something I could relate to after my experience modifying the Pinto. But our customers had to come first, so we'd been limited to working on it after hours.

"Sure," I said. "I already told Mark not to expect me for dinner." After Lydia's call last night, I was a little anxious about not sticking close by, where I could intercept future attempts. But I also wanted to get as far as possible from the potential of having to talk to her again. Besides, I was as excited about this project as Kasey. The Studebaker had no deadline, so she was willing to let me do things I hadn't before.

"This will be a great learning opportunity for you," she said as we went out back to her old Dodge pickup. "I can take the time to show you things I've been doing myself or leaving to Jake and Eddie."

Jake, who'd been with her since she started the business, was her painter. Though Kasey had grown up working in her dad's body shop and was experienced in that area, she preferred sticking to the mechanical stuff. Her other employee, Eddie, helped out with general repair. I liked them both, but hadn't connected the way I had with Kasey. Or with Race, whose combination of courage and craziness had made him my speedway hero even before I'd gotten to know him.

The sixty-watt bulb over the shop's door barely illuminated the back lot as Kasey lowered the pickup's tailgate and climbed up to get the parts. Even so, I could tell the Commander hood was sleeker and more rounded than the one on the Hawk. Kasey handed it to me, followed by the deck lid, which tapered smoothly rather than having a chopped-off appearance.

"Okay," I said. "Now I can visualize it." Until then, I hadn't been able to wrap my mind around the avian image she'd described. The front end of the Hawk looked more like a pug dog than a bird of prey. "But why didn't you just use a Commander?"

"It doesn't have fins. I suppose I could bolt Hawk fins on a Commander body, but that would spoil the idea of having a Hawk that looked like a hawk, don't you think?"

"Sounds like a good reason to me."

Kasey hopped down from the pickup. "Race and I were talking about the wedding last night. We've settled on a date."

"And you didn't tell Cody?" If he'd known, it would've been the first thing out of his mouth that morning.

"I thought I'd let Race spring the news tonight."

Cody had been trying to get the two of them together since he'd moved to Eugene. That goal had been complicated first by Kasey's resistance, then the wreck, and finally Kasey's success and Race's lack of it. Though Race was a pretty easy-going guy, he did have his pride.

I leaned the hood against the side of the shop and Kasey placed the deck lid beside it. While she got the hose, I squirted cleaner over both parts, the astringent odor making the inside of my nose prickle.

"So when's the big day?"

"August 4th. A year exactly from the night Race proposed." Kasey smiled, no doubt remembering the spectacle he'd caused by proposing to her on the start-finish line of the speedway. "My sister Brooke suggested it. She thought it would be romantic."

Brooke, the second youngest of six kids in Kasey's family, was my age, but since she lived thirty miles away in Cottage Grove, I'd only met her once.

"Have you decided where you're going to have it?"

"Not yet. I thought we were doing pretty well to set a date." Kasey's lips curved into a shameful grin.

Busy as the shop kept her, I couldn't fault her for that. "One thing at a time, right?" I said. Like everyone who knew Kasey and Race, I was glad to see them making it official. After what they'd been through in the past year-and-a-half, they deserved to be happy.

As we waited for the soap to break up the grease, Kasey gave me a sideways look that told me she was about to delve into darker waters. "It's too bad your father had to cancel his visit."

"Cody told you."

"Only because you didn't."

I sprayed more cleaner on the hood and deck lid. "Complaining doesn't change anything."

"True, but sometimes it helps to talk. Friends confide in each other, Jess. About weddings they have no idea how to plan, and about things that upset them." It was a point she'd made before. But putting my worries into words wasn't something that came easily. Besides, how could I tell her what Lydia had said about my father? I could barely stand to think it.

I stared at the hood, watching the soap cut rivers through the grime. "So I'm supposed to tell you every time my dad disappoints me?"

"No. But you *should* work on your tendency to carry your burdens all by yourself. I know that was your only option when you were living with your mom, but it isn't the case now."

"Are you upset with me?"

Kasey sprayed the hood with a blast from the hose, rinsing off purple suds. "Of course not. Unlearning old habits takes time. I just want you to enjoy being a kid now that you have the opportunity."

I wanted that, too, but Lydia was making it difficult. No matter how badly Kasey might think I needed to confide in others, my mother's return, and the doubts it had stirred up, weren't things I could share with anyone.

When I got home from work, I found a postcard from Dad on the table near the door: *I miss you and can't wait to see you next weekend.*

Well, at least I knew *that* was true. I took the card upstairs and tucked it into a shoebox with the others he'd sent. It was sad, how many of these I had compared to my memories of seeing him. Twice-monthly visits weren't anything. And what about all the important events coming up, like Thanksgiving, Christmas, and the wedding? Would he come home for those?

I just wished he could understand that, rather than a college fund or a house of our own, I'd like to have him here now, if only for a few extra days each month.

CHAPTER 5

On Wednesday, I would've liked to help with the Hawk after work again, but it was Halloween. Even if I hadn't promised to take Rhett trick or treating, Kasey wouldn't have stayed late. She had to get home to help Race hand out candy.

"He spent all last weekend decorating the deck and driveway," Cody told me as we picked up tools. "I swear he's worse than a three year old when it comes to holidays."

"That's hardly accurate," Race said. "No three year old could pull off the sheer artistry of one of my displays." He stopped on his way into the office, hands full of receipts he'd rescued from Kasey's neglect. Along with dealing with the fabrication and welding, Race handled the shop's books. He'd taken some business classes and had a knack for it, which was a good thing, because Kasey had no patience for paperwork.

"Are you bringing Rhett over tonight?" he asked.

"Of course," I said. "How could I pass up your sheer artistry? We'll be there around 7:00 to pick up Cody."

Rhett and Cody had spent the previous afternoon scouting thrift stores for costume supplies. They'd decided to be human versions of the Teenage Mutant Ninja Turtles, the turtle part being too much to deal with on short notice. Rhett would be Michelangelo, with an orange bandana and nunchucks, while Cody would have Raphael's red bandana and sais. Since Cody had taken the costumes home with him to add the finishing touches, Rhett wore his regular clothes when we left the house.

We parked on the narrow lane below Kasey's place then headed up the hill, enjoying that rare occurrence of a clear Halloween night in western Oregon. The breeze held a hint of crispness, and I breathed deeply, inhaling the sweet scent of fallen leaves as Rhett crunched through them. I pulled my flannel-lined denim jacket tight around me, relishing its warmth. Lydia had bought it for me last spring. A surprisingly perfect gift that held the lingering essence of one of her better attempts at drying out.

Even after Cody's heads up, Race's decorations wowed me. Rhett shrieked and I nearly wet my pants when a ghost swooped over our heads on a wire. Dracula and Frankenstein's monster leered from the bushes, bats and spider webs adorned the trees, and a row of jack-o-lanterns lined the steep driveway. Along with the standard Halloween ghoulies, Race had come up with a few of his own. A headless race car driver, a flagman speared through the heart with a black flag, and a skeleton wearing racing shoes, gloves, and a full-face helmet. Moans and howls wavered through the air, and a garland of orange lights spiraled the handrail to the deck.

A couple of little kids, dressed as Bart and Lisa Simpson, tromped down past us as we climbed the steps.

"Arrrrr, mateys!" Race growled. He'd clad himself in pirate garb, complete with eye patch and a stuffed parrot on his shoulder. It was the perfect alter ego for a guy who could slice through speedway traffic, smooth as a swashbuckler in one of Mark's old-time movies. Despite his horrific wreck, Race wasn't afraid to push his car or himself to the limit. And he didn't lord his talent over everyone else, like some drivers. In fact one of the things I liked best about him was his ability to poke fun at himself.

Cody stepped through the doorway in full costume, his rooster-tail bangs hanging down over the red bandana in a dark whorl. Using the tip of an oriental dagger, he gave the bird a flick. "So appropriate for a Parrothead." Cody never missed an opportunity to taunt Race about his Jimmy Buffett addiction. Or about anything else, for that matter.

"Don't be messin' with me parrot, boy, or I'll make ye walk

the plank!"

"Oh yeah?" Cody whistled a few bars of *Margaritaville.*

"The place looks great, Race," I said.

Cody rolled his eyes. "Just wait till you see what he does at Christmas."

"I like the flagman," said Rhett. "And the skeleton with the helmet."

"Well, we wouldn't want our undead to wind up with a head injury," Race said.

Cody grunted. After witnessing the wreck and standing by Race through the most difficult parts of his recovery, it wasn't a laughing matter to him. "C'mon," he said, ducking back into the house. "You need to get dressed."

I thought he was just talking to Rhett until he led us to his room, where two more ninja costumes lay on the bed. Black boots, pants, and blousy shirts provided the foundation, while the weapons, sashes, and bandanas offered distinctive details for each character. "Here's yours, Jess," Cody said, picking up the one with the purple headband. "You're Donatello."

"What do you mean, *mine*? I'm not dressing up."

"Oh yes you are. And you know why? Because Rhett worked really hard on this costume, and if you don't wear it, you'll break his little heart."

Rhett made sad eyes at me and sniffed.

"Fine," I said, holding out my hand. "Give me the stupid costume."

Cody grinned. "You can change in the bathroom."

We drove to a high-income neighborhood in the south hills where Cody's grandma lived.

"You really oughta score here, Rhett," Cody said. "These people have the big bucks."

In that native habitat of BMWs and Mercedes, I was a little embarrassed about the Pinto. While it was pristine under the hood, the red paint was washed out and marred by blotches of rust and primer.

"Gee, I hope nobody thinks your car's abandoned and tows it off," Cody quipped as we left it behind.

I smacked him on the butt with Donatello's bo staff. The Pinto might be ugly, but it was my baby.

Cody was right about the abundance of candy. Unfortunately, with the huge lots and hilly terrain, getting from house to house took effort. Rhett had never been one to complain, and in spite of his brace, he could do pretty much whatever any other kid could, but I knew by the end of the night his leg would be throbbing.

"This neighborhood's too much work," I said, shivering because Cody'd insisted my jacket detracted from my costume and had made me leave it in the car. "Let's go find ourselves a nice apartment complex. Or try the dorms."

"Yeah!" said Rhett. "Maybe we'll see Teri Sue."

"Okay," Cody agreed. "But I want to stop by Grandma's first. It's just up the block."

"She'd better be giving out half-pound Hershey bars. My feet are killing me." The boots Cody had scrounged from Goodwill were half a size too small.

The way Cody talked about his grandmother, you'd think she'd be some sweet, plump old woman who went around in a flour-dusted apron. Instead, she was all prickles and properness. She reminded me of my fifth grade teacher, who wouldn't tolerate slang and insisted on perfect penmanship.

"Well, sure, Grandma's got a hard shell," Cody had said the day I admitted she intimidated me. "But inside there's that melt-away sweetness, just like with M&Ms."

I'd laughed at the idea. Still, I knew she'd done a lot for her son and grandson. Cody said that after the wreck she'd worked hard to rebuild her relationship with Race. *And* to make up for the way she'd let his father bully him when he was a kid. In addition to providing most of the sponsorship for Cody's race car, she was the only person in Race's life who understood art and culture on the same level he did.

Cody rang the bell, and when his grandmother opened the door, shouted, "Trick-or-treat!"

She regarded him with a raised eyebrow. "Aren't you a little old for Halloween?"

"Grandma, at this very moment, your son is pretending to be a pirate. Anyway, Rhett's sister bailed on him, and Jess hasn't been trick-or-treating since she was eight, so I figured I'd help them out."

"I see." Mrs. Morgan held a bowl of full-sized candy bars out to Rhett. He meekly took a Baby Ruth and mumbled, "Thank you, ma'am," in a lilting drawl that brought a smile to her face.

"Would you like one, Jess?" she asked, offering me the bowl.

"Thanks." I took a Butterfinger and slipped it into my pocket.

"You know, I don't believe I've ever seen you without your Eugene Speedway cap," Mrs. Morgan said. "You look quite nice in black. You should wear it more often."

"Yup, Jess was born to be a ninja," Cody agreed, earning himself another steely look. He grinned at his grandma and snagged two candy bars from the bowl.

"Well, we've gotta jet. We're taking Rhett to the dorms so he can see his sister. Oh, and Race says he'll pick you up at ten on Sunday to go to that Monet thing up in Portland."

Mrs. Morgan nodded. "You can let him know I'll be ready."

It was impossible to find parking at the U of O, but we located a spot several blocks east of campus. The warm fragrance of freshly baked bread wafted out of Williams Bakery as we walked to the dorms.

Cody wouldn't let Rhett pass up a single house along the way. And he never said no when the owner disregarded his age and offered him candy. "Score!" he said after a young mother insisted he take two Hershey bars. "I never thought of using a kid to extend my trick or treating eligibility. I'll have to rent me a pack of rugrats when you get too old, Rhett."

When we reached the campus, we went to Collier, Teri Sue's dorm. Normally the main door would've been locked, but tonight the RA sat at the entrance, passing out Tootsie Rolls. Green and yellow steamers bedecked the stairwells, because the traditional Halloween orange and black belonged to OSU. Rhett rushed us straight up to the third floor, where little kids and their parents filled the hall and *Monster Mash* blared from someone's high quality stereo system. I followed, soaking the blessed warmth into my half-frozen body. If there was one thing I couldn't take, it was being cold.

"She's in 308," Rhett said. Eyeballing the numbers, he made a beeline for his sister's room. Teri Sue stood in the doorway, wearing her firesuit as a costume and using her helmet as a candy bowl.

"Hi, Teri Sue," Rhett said, hanging back. He clutched his bag as if he were meeting a stranger.

She looked up from stuffing Tootsie Rolls into a ghost toddler's plastic pumpkin. "Rhett!" Her cheeks bunched up in a grin. "Hey, Sarah, meet my baby brother."

A warning bell clanged in my head. There was something just a little too cheerful about her tone.

"Hi there, baby brother." Teri Sue's roommate, dressed as a gypsy, stepped into the hallway to greet Rhett, while Cody helped himself to a piece of candy.

"Back off! This is for the young'uns," said Teri Sue, snatching the helmet away. She turned toward me. "Hey, Jess. Cute costume. Sorry I haven't been home to work on the car."

It wasn't until she slung an arm around my neck that I

smelled it. Beer. Oh man. Not her, too?

"Rhett's been helping," I said, because I didn't know how else to react. "We pulled the engine last week."

"Great! I'll try to drop by sometime soon. It's just I've been so busy. I've got a pile of homework, and I've been thinkin' 'bout joining a sorority." She let go of me and tucked her arm around her brother's shoulders. "C'mon Rhett, I wanna show you off to my friends."

Teri Sue took us to several rooms on that floor and the others, bragging on Rhett, who ate up the attention, and introducing Cody and me as her racing buddies. Cody smoothly answered the questions this brought, but I hung back, smiling, nodding, and letting him tackle the socializing. Did Cody realize Teri Sue was drunk? Did Rhett? As happy as he seemed, I was pretty sure he hadn't figured it out.

A geeky-looking guy with graphic novel posters plastered on his walls connected our costumes to the Ninja Turtles and engaged Rhett and Cody in a conversation.

Teri Sue shook her head and smirked. "Jamie's such a dweeb, but ya gotta love him. He's from Winston-Salem, so he actually knows what pulled pork sandwiches and sweet tea are."

I took a step back, tugging at her sleeve to make her follow me.

"What are you doing, getting drunk in the middle of the week?" I hadn't intended to go right for the throat, but the accusation spilled out on its own.

Teri Sue laughed. "Relax, girlfriend. It's Halloween—a holiday—remember?"

"And you're passing out candy to little kids. Don't you think their parents are going to notice?"

She shrugged and glanced over her shoulder at one of the mothers leading a kindergarten Spiderman down the hallway. "None of 'em have said anything so far."

I stared hard at Teri Sue. Slowly, the smile melted from her face.

"Aw hell. You're really worried about it, aren't ya?"

"You haven't been home once since school started, and now this?" Didn't I have enough to deal with, between Lydia's calls and my worries about Dad?

"It's no big deal. One of the guys downstairs had some beer, and he gave me a couple. It's not like I'm boozing it up every night."

And how would I know if she was? But I wouldn't get anywhere confronting her about it in public. Besides, it wasn't the most important issue.

"Are you really coming home soon?" I glanced toward the guys clustered in Jamie's doorway. "Rhett misses you."

A shadow flickered in Teri Sue's eyes. "I know. But he has you now, Jess. Anyway, I'll come visit next week. I swear."

CHAPTER 6

The next day, it seemed the only things I could think about were Dad, Lydia's calls, and Teri Sue. By afternoon I was so stressed out I forgot my psychology book and had to drive back to school to get it. *Enough!* I told myself as I stuffed the text into my backpack. *Last night was no big deal. You're over-thinking this because of Lydia. But not everyone who has a couple of beers is an alcoholic.*

By the following afternoon, I felt a little better and stayed after work to help Kasey with the Hawk, a deviation from my normal Friday night dinner-and-a-movie with Cody. He had other plans as well.

"You sure you don't wanna give me a hand with the Gal-axie?" he asked as he headed out the door for Race's shop.

"Hmmm, let's see. Slap mud on your car and sand it down until my brain goes numb, or help Kasey modify the Hawk and actually learn something. Tough call."

Kasey had shown me sketches of how she planned to alter the fenders to accommodate Mercedes headlights and extend the hood to give it a beak-like appearance. The idea of her tutoring me in the art of bodywork left me itching to get started. Next spring, I wanted to paint the Pinto, and so far my experience had been mainly mechanical.

"I can make it worth your while," Cody hinted, slipping his arms around my lower back and drawing me to the warmth of his chest.

"Like you wouldn't do that anyway." I melted into him for a moment, loving the feel of his body against mine, but this wasn't the time or place for cuddling. I kissed him goodbye and promised my assistance the next day.

Having Kasey to myself for another evening sent a little

rush of happiness through me. Until school started, I'd come in early so we could talk before work, but lately it was rare to get time alone with her. Of all my friends, she was the one I felt most comfortable sharing my ambitions with.

"I've been looking over those brochures you got me from Oregon State," I said as we pushed the Hawk into an empty bay.

After I'd told her I wanted to make a career out of building race cars, she'd sold me on the idea of getting a degree in engineering from her alma mater. She'd even said that if I opened a shop, she'd give me a hand getting started. Her commitment had given me the incentive to start taking school seriously. In the past, I'd never cared about getting decent grades, other than in math and science, where they seemed to happen all on their own.

"So what did you think?" Kasey asked.

"It looks like a great college, but you were right about the foreign language requirement." After eight weeks of Spanish, I still resented the idea of taking the necessary two years. The subject didn't come easily with all those backward adjectives, not to mention the masculine and feminine nouns. Fortunately, Cody had also waited until junior year to tackle the requirement, so we were able to study together. As a word-lover he had an annoying knack for the subject.

"Sometimes you have to do things you'd rather not, in order to get what you want," Kasey said, extending a tape measure so she could mark the Hawk's left fender.

"I know that." Growing up with Lydia had made it a daily part of my life. "But what if I do all that work and still can't get in?"

"You will. It's a state school, not Harvard. With the A's you've been getting in math and science, you'll have no trouble meeting the GPA requirement."

"What about the SATs? I'm going to bomb the verbal part,

no matter how much Cody coaches me."

"You'll do fine, Jess." Kasey sketched a line between the marks she'd made.

"But—"

"There's no reason to think you won't. But if a contingency plan would reassure you, you could always go to Lane your first year."

The idea was so far outside the realm of everything I'd considered, it stopped me short. If I attended our local community college, it would allow me to stay in Eugene with Cody. I'd rather go straight to OSU, but this alternative wasn't the worst thing that could happen.

"Okay," I said. "I think I could live with that. Even though it would mean another year of Cody rubbing in football scores every weekend." The U of O's win last Saturday had made him insufferable, especially since it was against UCLA, the team that had beaten OSU the week before.

"Believe me, he's nothing compared to his uncle," Kasey said. Then her lips pursed into a smirk. "Though Race hasn't been quite so bad since I donated a hundred dollars to the Beaver Athletic fund in his name last season."

"Seriously? That's brilliant. Funny, how Cody never bothered to mention it."

"Isn't it, though?" Kasey moved on to the next fender. "So how are things going with Teri Sue? Has she come by to work on the Camaro?"

A chill chased the humor right out of me. "No. I saw her Wednesday when we took Rhett trick-or-treating, but she hasn't been home since she moved into the dorms."

"It must be frustrating, doing all that work yourself."

I shrugged, leaning back to rest my rear end against the hood. Frustration wasn't much of an issue compared to what I'd seen the other night. "Well, Rhett helps, and it's good experience. Of course, I'd rather be building a car from the ground up." My fingers flexed against cool metal as I imagined the possibility. Starting from scratch, designing it all myself, driving. My chest ached with longing, and that longing helped quell my uneasiness about Teri Sue. "Sometimes I wonder if I could swing it. It would take a lot of work and money, but with sponsors, I could pull it off."

Kasey glanced up from her measurements. "While you're going to school, working, and helping with Teri Sue's car?"

Even though it was the same argument I always gave myself, it felt annoying coming from her.

"Building a race car is an enormous undertaking, Jess."

"I know. But since I finished the Pinto last spring, I haven't had a project of my own to work on." I missed the excitement of that, the feeling of accomplishment. Helping with the Camaro was fun, but it wasn't creative.

"There will be plenty of projects in the future," Kasey said, returning the pen and measuring tape to the nearest workbench. "In fact, Race and I have been thinking about building him a new car next winter. You could help with that. The important thing now is to concentrate on your schoolwork. That's the first step if you want to have a shop of your own."

A shop that couldn't even begin to become a reality for at least six years. Six years was forever. My fingers rapped against the hood. "Sometimes I wonder if that's even possible."

"Why?" Kasey uncoiled the air hose and attached it to the nibbler, a tool that would smoothly cut the fenders.

"Because I keep hearing you and Race talk about how hard it is to start a business, and how most of them fail in their first few years. Besides, I don't have any real experience. The only race cars I've worked on are Teri Sue's and Cody's. How can I start a race shop when I've never built a car?"

"The only car I'd restored before I opened this place was my Charger."

"But you worked at your dad's shop for years. And you're

really smart and dedicated." Kasey had graduated from high school as a junior, made it through college in three years, and started Eugene Custom Classics when she was twenty. How could I ever hope to match that level of ambition?

Kasey motioned me off the hood. "You're just as smart and dedicated. My only advantage was having a devoted family who backed me up and gave me the confidence I needed."

And I was supposed to believe that?

"You can do whatever you want to, Jess. Just look at what you've accomplished with no one but yourself to rely on. You have people who care about you now. It's time to take all the energy you used to put into survival and dedicate it to getting what you want out of life."

That idea sounded so simple, but the truth was, I had no clue where to start.

When Dad came into town Friday night, he rented a motel room, as usual. Mark had told him more than once that he was welcome to stay with us, but he always said it was too much of an intrusion.

Because of his late arrival, I didn't see him until Saturday morning, when he picked me up to take me to buy an outfit for the upcoming racing banquet. I hated shopping, but my everyday jeans-and-a-T-shirt wouldn't cut it, and I didn't own anything else.

On the way to Valley River Center, I studied him across the cab of his truck, looking for signs of drug abuse. Weren't speed addicts supposed to be skinny and twitchy? Dad was heavier now than he had been when I was little.

Maybe I should just come out and ask. I took a breath to work up the nerve, but that was as far as I got. All the way to the mall, I phrased and rephrased the question in my mind. Nothing sounded right.

Dad did most of the talking as we parked and went inside.

"You're sure quiet today," he observed.

"Yeah. I guess." *Face it, Jess, you're a coward. Just forget the whole thing and try to enjoy the time you have with him.*

"So how's school going?"

"Pretty good. Cody and I have been studying together. He's helped me get up to speed in English."

The tantalizing scent of Cinnabon made me salivate like a Pavlovian dog as we walked through the food court. Dad would buy me a sweet roll if I asked, but I hated taking advantage of his absentee-parent guilt.

"I worry about you having too much on your plate, what with your job and watching Rhett." Dad scratched at the beard he'd only begun to grow a few weeks before. Along with his Levis and red plaid flannel, it made him look like a lumberjack.

I stopped to consider a cream-colored sweater in the window of The Gap. Appropriately formal, but not too froufrou. Plus, it looked comfy.

"It's not too much. And I don't really 'watch' Rhett, I just hang out with him." I led my father into the store. In so many ways, he was the same old Dad I remembered, but in others he'd changed. The wrinkles, the worrying, the solemn way he studied me when he thought I wasn't paying attention. Even though he hid that look behind a proud grin whenever he caught me watching, I knew those lost years had cost him as much as they'd cost me.

"All the same," he said, "I'll be glad when I've saved up enough to move back home. Then we can be a real family."

I turned to give him a look. "What do you mean, 'real?' We're real. We're just not conventional."

"Maybe that's what I'm trying to get at. For the past eight years, you had to be the grownup. You deserve a good old-fashioned family, with a dad at home, and a dog out in the yard."

The reference to my life with Lydia brought a prickle of

guilt. If he knew she was back, he'd blow a gasket. But I didn't want to think about that. Or about the accusation she'd made.

I searched the rack for a sweater in my size. "We're not that kind of family," I said. "And if we tried to be, it wouldn't seem normal. I'm happy with the way things are." At least I would be, if I could stop thinking about what Dad did to keep himself awake when he was on the road.

He squeezed my shoulder and pulled me close, kissing the top of my head. "Whoever said teenagers are impossible never met you. Now how 'bout one of them Cinnabons? That smell's enough to drive a man crazy."

We dashed across the parking lot through the early November mist and climbed up into Dad's Freightliner, where I tossed my packages into the sleeper berth.

"Where to for lunch?" Dad asked.

"I don't care. You choose." I lifted the folder containing his bills of lading from the dash and leafed through them. Even though his postcards kept me up to date on where he'd been, I liked to retrace his path across the country. Looking at when he'd delivered loads, and remembering what I'd been doing at those times, made me feel more connected to him. This trip, he'd been mostly on the East Coast and in the Midwest. On October 23rd, when I'd taught Rhett how to convert fractions, Dad had picked up a load of car parts in Detroit. And on the 27th, when we'd pulled the Camaro engine, he'd been in Pittsburgh, dropping off a load of—

Shock jolted through me, the way it does when you step on the brake and the pedal travels further than you expect. "You're hauling explosives?" I looked across the cab at Dad, this new threat eclipsing the old one.

He smiled, weathered skin crinkling around his eyes. "It's no big deal, honey. I follow all the safety procedures."

"It's dangerous. You could get killed. There's a reason they call the guys who haul that stuff suicide jockeys."

Dad pulled the file from my hands and tucked it into the compartment in the driver's door. "There's nothing to worry about. The pay's better, and if I do it for just a few more months, I might have enough for a down payment on a house."

"I don't care about a house!"

Dad sighed. "If you take all the proper precautions, it's really no different than hauling any other load."

"Then why are they paying you more?" My eyes locked on his, challenging him. "I don't want you doing this, Dad." Especially not if he was hopped up on amphetamines.

"It's the best way for me to get ahead." He caught my hand and squeezed it tight. "Don't you fret, Jessie. I'll be perfectly safe."

Further arguments failed to sway my father. He couldn't understand why I was so upset, and I couldn't admit my deepest fears. As easy as it had been to yell at him about the explosives, words abandoned me when it came to revealing what Lydia had said. I tried to convince myself he was right, that hauling hazmat was no different from hauling anything else, and somehow we managed to enjoy the rest of our weekend together. But when he left Sunday night, Freightliner taillights winking at me through the darkness, my fear welled back up.

A couple of hours later, the phone rang.

"Jess? It's for you," Mark hollered up the stairs.

I lifted the handset to my ear, expecting to hear Cody's voice. Instead, I got Lydia's. Anger pulsed through me, barely overshadowing my alarm. I strode into my room and pulled the door shut behind me. "What did I tell you about calling here?"

"Relax," Lydia said, her tone light. "He didn't ask for my name."

"Next time he might. And there'll be big trouble when he

figures out who you are."

A chuckle bubbled through the line. "So I'll call back when he's not there. When does he work?"

"That's none of your business."

"You're probably right." Lydia paused. "I guess I'll have to take my chances."

Thunder hammered in my chest. "Tuesday and Thursday nights." As soon as I said the words, I hated myself for buying into her obvious manipulation.

But not nearly as much as I hated the idea of everyone learning she was back.

The next day at school, I could barely concentrate. It took me forever to finish a chemistry quiz that should've been a breeze, and at lunch, I snapped at Cody for no reason.

He raised an eyebrow but didn't say anything until we'd emptied our trays and were heading for our lockers. "So what's up with you?" he asked, bumping gently against my shoulder.

Frustration welled inside me. I wanted to tell him, wanted to give him a chance to say all the right words, but nothing could persuade me to mention Lydia. And that meant I couldn't admit to half my worries about my father. But there *was* one thing I could say. "Dad's hauling hazardous materials. He says it's no big deal, but how am I supposed to believe that?"

"Aw, Jess." Cody looped his arm around my shoulders and gave me a squeeze. "No wonder you're so uptight."

I leaned against him, wanting just for one moment, to let him make everything better.

"I'll bet he's right," Cody said. "Your dad wouldn't shine you on."

"But how can I be sure? I barely even know him."

"Are you kidding? He's a good guy, Jess. Of course you can trust him."

I sighed and pulled away to open my locker. "If you say so."

As much faith as I had in Cody's ability to read people, I couldn't put to rest the uneasiness in my heart.

Now that I'd told Lydia when it was safe to call, I knew she'd take advantage. Sure enough, Tuesday night after dinner, the phone rang.

Heedless of my iciness, she rambled about how she'd spent the past few months in San Diego and Ensenada, as if she'd been vacationing, rather than ditching her daughter. When I responded in grunts, she changed the subject, describing her job and roommate and attempting to chisel details out of me about my life.

Much as I resented the intrusion, something kept me from hanging up. Probably the fear she'd call back when Mark was home. Half-listening, I stroked Newt's soft belly as annoyance smoldered inside me. I hated problems I couldn't fix. It'd been bad enough when it was just Lydia, but now I had Dad and Teri Sue to obsess over.

One by one, all the important parts of my life seemed to be slipping out of my control. Why did leading a normal teenage existence seem to be so much to ask?

CHAPTER 7

I kept waiting for Teri Sue to call or drop by, but by Thursday, she still hadn't made good on her promise. My one consolation was that Rhett knew nothing about it. After dinner, while he vegged with Newt in the living room, reading a book on geology, I went upstairs to tackle my homework. Anticipating another call from Lydia, I scooped the phone from the table in the hallway and took it to my room.

The assigned psychology chapter on nature vs. nurture immediately sucked me in. While some experts believed a person would develop particular traits regardless of how they were raised, others said environment had a more important impact on shaping personality. The argument reminded me of what Lydia had said about me being strong because of how I'd grown up. But the idea of owing that much of myself to my mother's shortcomings depressed me. I thought about how Cody's circumstances had influenced his behavior until he'd moved in with Race. In comparison, I'd never allowed myself to get into trouble, no matter how bad things got at home. Biology had to have *something* to do with who we were.

As I read, I made a few notes about points I wanted to discuss with Cody the next day. He was taking the class, too, partly because he thought it would help with the stories he wrote, and partly because he wanted to avoid any science involving math.

I was halfway through the assigned questions when the phone rang.

"Hi, sweetie," Lydia said. "How are you today?"

Even though I'd been expecting the intrusion, resentment rumbled inside me like lava pulsing through a volcano. "Pretty much the same as when you called two days ago."

She must've gotten used to my hard-edged responses

because she didn't let this one slow her down. "So how are things with the race car?"

A blatant attempt to weasel into my good graces. Lydia had never approved of me working on cars.

"Why would you care?"

"It's a part of your life. I've missed out on so much these past few months."

The plaintive note in her tone drove my fingers to clench around the phone. "When are you going to quit trying to snow me?"

"Jess, sweetie, I know I haven't been supportive of your hobbies. But I want to change that."

Right. I'd given her dozens of opportunities to change, including the biggest, most painful one last summer that led to her deserting me. No way was I falling for that again.

"So insinuating I was gay because I like cars was a mistake?" My crack rated only the slightest hesitation.

"I never should've said that. It's just you're so much like your father, always tinkering under the hood of some junker. You knew how hard that was for me to watch."

Yeah, I did. To her, my automotive interest was proof I loved Dad best, and because of that, I'd taken pains to hide it.

"I've had a lot of time to think since last summer," Lydia continued. "Not having you in my life made me realize how badly I blew it. I should've put you first. I should've loved you for who you are."

The words twisted like a key inside me, moving old tumblers that had long been rusted solid. But I'd be an idiot to let her in.

"Why'd you come back, anyway? Wasn't all that 'sun, surf, and sand' good enough for you? Or did Jimmy take off?" He'd been the one she'd run away with. The one who'd helped her fall off the wagon when it looked like she just might ride it to sobriety.

"I missed you."

"Bullshit. If I meant that much to you, you never would've left."

"I had to go. Everything fell apart."

"That's no excuse." Sure, she'd lost her job and her best friend in AA had moved to Florida. But worse things happened to people every day, and they didn't abandon their kids. "The truth is, you wanted to be with Jimmy."

A hushed sort of whimper pierced the silence left by my accusation.

"You're right." She hesitated, and then with a catch in her voice, continued. "I should've done better. I know that. But Jimmy treated me like I was special. And all you'd done for years is make me feel like a failure."

In an instant, her words sliced through my self-righteous anger, stripping it from the bone. I could deny my part in this all I wanted, but she was right. She'd been broken, desperate for attention, and I hadn't needed her.

Why shouldn't she have left?

The doubts Lydia planted festered over the next few days, leading me to question everything that had happened between us. Could I have brought some of it on myself? Sure, she'd lied, and there was no way to excuse that, but I also knew how badly Dad's leaving had affected her—how it had changed her from a kind and loving mom into a hopeless mess. Would things have been different if, instead of being so strong and cold and independent, I'd given her just a little bit of myself?

Every time my thoughts went down that path, I'd lecture myself about allowing her to suck me back in. I could see what she was doing. Her mind games were so obvious they were laughable. So why was I falling for them? The only logical answer was that in some strange, twisted way, I missed her. And as pathetic as that seemed, I didn't know how to change it.

When Dad called Sunday, I kept my worries to myself, but a subtle tension lurked in our conversation. He told me a funny story about a man who'd scrubbed down his dog in a truck stop shower. I recounted the jokes Race and Cody had slung back and forth at work the day before. Neither one of us mentioned hazmat.

"Well, I need to get back on the road," Dad finally said. "My next run's to Denver. I'll bring Rhett some of that Rocky Mountain hard rock candy he likes, okay?"

"Sure." I tried to drum up the nerve to ask the question I'd balked on last weekend, but once again, I chickened out. "I love you," I said instead, and hung up feeling lost.

By Tuesday, there was still no sign of Teri Sue. When Rhett grumbled about it, I squelched my own concerns. "She'll show up eventually," I told him. "The racing banquet's next Saturday, and there's no way she'll miss that."

The first big storm of the season blew in that afternoon. Rhett and I left the barn doors open as we worked, so the clean, damp scent could sweep in on the breeze. We were both weather geeks, me for as long as I could remember, and Rhett since last summer when I'd showed him how to build a home weather station. It was chilly with the doors yawning out into the storm, but the wail of wind and staccato drumbeat of rain stirred a cheerful restlessness in me that overrode my normal aversion to the cold.

"I'll bet it pours an inch tonight," said Rhett, standing in the doorway.

"Could be. You want to give me a hand? This'll go quicker if you take notes." I was trying to make a list of what the Camaro needed, but recording what I found was slowing me down. Not to mention getting the notebook greasy.

Rhett pulled himself away from nature's tantrum to take over.

"Hey, Jess?"

"Yeah?"

"I need some advice."

I pulled my head out of the fender well to look at him. "What's up?" While we'd talked a lot about his mother, and even Teri Sue, he'd rarely come right out and asked me for help.

His green eyes cut away to study the dirt under his Nikes. "Well, there's this girl at school. Emily."

Uh oh. I was the last person to counsel someone in matters of the heart. "Do you like her?"

"Yeah. But I don't think she likes me."

Already, I had issues with this sixth grade bimbo. "How could anyone not like you?"

Rhett shrugged. "I dunno. She calls me Bubba and makes fun of the way I talk."

"There's nothing wrong with the way you talk!" I knew exactly what was going on here. I'd been through it myself with a boy who tormented me all through seventh grade. "Rhett, there are plenty of girls who are going to love you just the way you are. Don't waste your time pining over some priss who doesn't know a good thing when she sees it."

"But, Jess, she makes my insides go all wobbly."

"That's even worse. Believe me, if she finds out how you feel, she'll make your life miserable. You asked for my advice, and here it is: stay far away from her."

Rhett chewed his lip. Obviously, that wasn't what he wanted to hear.

I went back to checking out the left front suspension, where Teri Sue had taken a hard hit the last race of the season. "Okay, we need a lower ball joint and an outer tie rod end. The fender mounting bracket tore lose from the front hoop, too, so that'll need welding. Not that we have any way of dealing with it."

"Can't you ask Race?"

"I'd rather not." The couple of times we needed something welded last summer, we'd taken the Camaro over to his shop, but I was hesitant to do that now. Race had enough to keep him busy, with his own car and Cody's. Besides, Kasey would need his help with the Hawk soon.

"I'll bet Daddy would buy us a welder."

No doubt, he would. Mark had family in the furniture industry back east, and he'd come into an inheritance a few years before moving to Oregon. Whenever Teri Sue and I had needed something for the car last season, he'd bought it. I felt weird about that, having worked hard for every penny I'd spent on my Pinto, but Mark was pretty easy-going regarding money. He followed the philosophy of Taoism and was more concerned with being content than being rich.

"I'm not going to ask him to do that. Anyway, I wouldn't know how to use it if he did."

"What about getting Race to teach you to use the welder at the shop?"

Not a bad idea. If I knew how to weld, it would be one less thing I'd be dependent on others for. Begging the use of Race or Kasey's equipment wouldn't be as bad as squandering their time.

"Good thinking, Rhett. I'll ask him tomorrow."

That evening, Rhett and I ate dinner in the living room so he could watch the news for his current events homework. The weatherman was as thrilled as we were about the storm, and predicted it would last throughout the night and into Wednesday.

"And in national news, a tractor trailer hauling hazardous materials overturned this evening on US Highway 6 outside of Denver, spilling its load. We'll have details after the break."

A Toys R Us ad flashed across the screen as fear rushed through my body, turning my skin to ice.

"Oh my God." I grabbed the remote and flipped through the channels, hoping another news station would be covering the story.

"What's wrong?" asked Rhett.

"Dad's driving into Denver."

Commercials on every station. I switched back to 13 and dropped the remote. "Hurry up, hurry up!" I muttered at the television. It couldn't be Dad. There were thousands of truckers in the United States. Probably hundreds in Colorado at this moment. What were the odds?

The TV flickered back to the news, and the bubbly, blonde co-anchor smiled from the screen. "On Wall Street today, the Dow—"

"Who cares about Wall Street!"

Rhett got up from the La-Z-Boy and crept across the room to sit with me on the couch. "He'll be okay, Jess. I know it."

His skinny arm looped around my waist. I leaned into him as we sat through the next five minutes of news, my leg jiggling an anxious rhythm against the coffee table.

"Rescue crews and hazmat teams are on the scene sixty miles west of Denver where a semi-truck hauling ammonium nitrate skidded on ice and plowed into an embankment before overturning. We go live now to our affiliate in Denver."

The bright newsroom cut away to a Colorado mountainside, where red and yellow lights flared across snow behind a reporter clad in arctic gear.

"Thanks, Rebecca. I'm standing at 11,990 feet on this twisting section of Route 6 known as Loveland Pass. Big rigs hauling hazardous cargo are diverted to this highway from Interstate 70 because they're not allowed to use the Eisenhower Tunnel.

"The primary concern at this hour is keeping this spill from getting into the waterways. Fish and Wildlife officials fear that this chemical, a common fertilizer, could upset the delicate balance of the local ecosystem. Additionally, ammonium nitrate is used as an oxidizing agent in explosives. Though the powder itself is stable at room temperature, when combined with diesel fuel, it can be extremely volatile. As you can see, traffic is backed up for miles."

Aerial footage flashed across the screen, showing a red snake of taillights winding around the switchbacks of the highway. Then the camera zoomed in on the truck lying on its side, and every muscle in my body went liquid in an instant. The semi-tractor on the screen was a blue cab-over, not a red and silver conventional rig.

"Paramedics on the scene report the driver, 37-year-old Travis Keyser of Memphis Tennessee, escaped with minor bumps and bruises. He was extremely fortunate not to plunge hundreds of feet down the cliffs that flank long stretches of this highway."

My breath whooshed out in a shaky gasp, and I hunched forward, burying my face in my hands.

"It's okay, Jess. It's not him." Rhett rubbed my back, his small hand making comforting circles between my shoulder blades.

As soon as I could move again, I went to the phone and dialed Dad's dispatcher.

"This is Max DeLand's daughter, Jess," I told the woman who answered. "Could you tell him to call me?"

I didn't sleep well, but by morning the shock of the news clip began to wear off. Still, I could only focus half my mind on what was happening in class. The other half kept formulating arguments to convince Dad to stop hauling hazmat.

As I left the school building that afternoon, Cody fell into step beside me, his arm slung across my shoulders.

"You okay?"

"Yeah, sure."

"Then why have you only said five words to me all day? You

were a total zombie at lunch."

Though I could feel him looking at me, I kept my eyes focused across the parking lot. "I guess I've just got stuff on my mind."

"Like what?"

I shrugged under the weight of his arm. Why was it so hard to admit to things that bothered me? I had no doubt Cody would sympathize, but the idea of talking about last night, about the way my heart had clenched when I saw the news, made me feel so vulnerable.

"Y'know I'm going to keep bugging you until you tell me," Cody said.

"I know."

We were almost at my car. I pulled away to dig the keys from my backpack.

"So what is it?" he asked.

I leaned against the trunk of the Pinto, facing him but looking at the ground. "There was a trucking accident last night near Denver."

"Oh, yeah. I was hoping you hadn't heard about that."

It didn't surprise me that he had. Kasey was a news junkie, so Cody and Race were pretty savvy about current events, whether they wanted to be or not. Cody stood waiting for me to say something, but my throat felt so tight I could barely get air through it, let alone words.

His hand slipped over mine, and he turned around to lean beside me, butt against the Pinto's chalky red paint.

"I understand, Jess. Heck, you know how paranoid I get about Race."

My throat cinched tighter. I swallowed to force it open. "I just found him, Cody! I missed out on eight years. Why does he have to do this?"

Cody squeezed my hand. "If it's bothering you that much, you should talk to him."

"He won't listen. He laughed me off the last time I tried."

"Then you need to be more persuasive." His hand left mine, and he tucked his arm around my waist, pulling me close.

"He'll be fine, Jess. You've had enough bad stuff happen in your life. From now on, things are gonna be good."

CHAPTER 8

After work that evening, I asked Race if he'd be willing to give me welding lessons.

"Be happy to, kiddo. You wanna get started tonight?"

"Sure. If it's not too much trouble."

"No trouble at all."

Once we'd closed up the shop, and I'd called Mark to let him know I'd be late, we raided the scrap metal pile out back. Race laid an assortment of pieces on the steel workbench he'd built for fabrication. He told me to put on his welding leathers, which were so big I had to roll up the sleeves before I could slip my hands into the gloves.

"The first thing you need to know about welding," Race said, "is that it's not like gluing stuff, where each object stays solid. You're bonding metal by melting and blending the pieces together. Because of that, it's really important to get everything hot enough that the materials and filler mix together. It's called getting good penetration."

If Cody had been there, he'd have had a suggestive comment to make about the terminology.

Race went on to explain the differences between stick welding and wire feed, which was what we'd be doing. He selected two scraps of angle iron, clamped them to the workbench, and fired up the welder, first turning on the gas, then setting the current and wire speed.

"Here, put this on," he said, handing me a helmet with a lens so dark I couldn't see through it. "I've purposely set the current too low, so we'll get a bad weld." Lightning flashed, and suddenly the two pieces on the workbench were visible. A hot, metallic odor filled the air as Race used a circular motion to lay a molten bead. I could see now why he could weld when he couldn't draw. Maneuvering the gun that held the wire was something he did with his wrist, not his fingers.

"Okay," he said. "Tip your helmet back and take a peek. Nice, huh?"

I nodded. The weld looked like a stack of toppled coins. Absolutely perfect.

Race picked up the steel with a pair of pliers and whacked it against the workbench. The scraps broke apart and one clattered to the floor. Where the two had been joined, the metal looked as if it had never been welded.

"See?" Race said. "It can look great on the outside even when there's no penetration. This is the single-most important lesson you need to learn if you're gonna work on race cars. Someone's life could depend on it. I'll teach you how to adjust the equipment so this doesn't happen. And we'll make a cross-sectional cut through your first few welds to see what they look like inside."

He spent the next hour explaining the basics and letting me practice. At first, it was hard to get used to the dark helmet and long, heavy cord attached to the gun. But as I continued, I discovered something comforting about having my world reduced to a tiny window. And the sizzle of the electric arc soothed me into an almost meditative state where my worries about Lydia, Dad, and Teri Sue didn't exist.

Though Race had made the process look easy, my own welds were sloppy, with inconsistent loops. We didn't bother cutting up my initial attempts because the pieces clearly hadn't bonded. Eventually, I began to figure out how to slow my speed to make the weld penetrate deeper. But when we sliced through the steel, it was obvious I wasn't being consistent.

"All right, that's enough," Race said when the hands on the clock inched past 7:30. "No sense wearing yourself out on the first day."

I tipped back my helmet. The air in the shop was thick with

the smell of burnt steel.

"I'm not worn out. This is fun. Anyway, I can't give up before I lay at least one decent bead."

"Taking a break is not giving up," Race said as he switched off the welder. "I swear, you sound just like Kasey."

I grinned. How could I take that as anything but a compliment?

"How was the lesson?" Mark called from his office to the left of the front entryway, as I came through the door.

"Great. Race is an excellent teacher. His explanations are easy to understand."

"Good. I made up a plate for you. It's in the fridge."

My stomach gurgled in response. I hadn't eaten anything since lunch.

"Oh, and you got a package today." Mark motioned toward the table near the door.

A package? Who'd send anything to me? Dad delivered all his gifts in person. I grabbed the large, padded envelope and glanced at the return address on my way into the kitchen. The cutesy, bubble gum handwriting set klaxons blaring in my head even before my eyes could make out the name. How had Lydia gotten my address?

A quiver of misgiving skittered up my back as I realized Mark had seen this too. *Relax*, I told myself. He didn't say anything, so he must not have noticed who sent it. I lowered myself into a chair and ripped open the package. The T-shirt inside bore the silkscreened image of Ernie Irvin's Kodak Chevrolet. I unfolded the note tucked between the layers of cloth.

> *Dear Jess,*
> *I thought of you when I saw this in a gas station in Salinas. That's Ernie Irvin's hometown,*

you know. I hope you enjoy it.
   love,
   Lydia

The first emotion to hit me was annoyance. Did she really think she could impress me with some random bit of Winston Cup trivia she'd picked up on the road? Then I realized she must've bought this weeks ago. Her comment the other day about loving me for who I was hadn't been some spur of the moment con job.

I stuffed the shirt back in the envelope, the hunger rumbles in my belly now dormant. As anxious as it made me to have Lydia know where I lived, shouldn't I at least give her credit for trying?

When Dad didn't call that night, it surprised me. I knew he was required to check in every day with his dispatcher, so he must've gotten the message. Was he avoiding me, or was something wrong?

Thursday afternoon, I picked up Rhett from school as I usually did when I wasn't working. When we got home, I jogged down the long driveway to check the mail. Now that Lydia knew my address, it wasn't just the phone I had to be paranoid about.

Last year, Rhett had haunted the mailbox, waiting for a response to the letters he sent his mother in hopes she might remember him, but since she'd been readmitted to the hospital in August, he hadn't written her or checked the mail even once. Sad as that made me, it meant there was no danger of him intercepting anything from Lydia. Mark was the one I had to worry about. But today all I found were letters from several non-profit organizations begging donations.

As I climbed the porch steps, Cody pulled up beside the Pinto for his usual Thursday afternoon study session. He followed me into the kitchen, where I hunted through the cupboards for a snack while he and Rhett began unloading their backpacks.

"Jess, I need help," Rhett said. "I've got to do a science project and give an oral report the last week before Christmas. It's supposed to have visual aids, like diagrams or some kind of experiment. And it's gonna be a huge part of my grade."

"So what are you going to do it on?" I asked, setting a bag of Oreos and a carton of milk on the table.

"I dunno. That's what I need help with. I thought maybe I could talk about how we built our weather station and make a chart of all the data I've been collecting, but that doesn't seem cool enough."

"Nah, dude," Cody said, reaching for the Oreos. "You don't wanna quote a bunch of statistics at people. You'll put 'em to sleep."

"What I'd really like to do is something about geology," Rhett said. "But I don't want to be standing up there with a baking soda volcano like some little kid." Ever since I'd hooked him on meteorology, he'd been fascinated by natural phenomena. Last summer it was extreme weather. Now he couldn't get enough of volcanoes and earthquakes.

"How about plate tectonics?" I suggested.

"What's that?"

I sat down beside him. "The engine that powers volcanoes. You know how volcanoes get started don't you?"

"Yeah, there's a weakness in the earth's crust."

"Right. And that's because the surface is made up of these big plates, which are always moving. They create thin spots where they pull apart, but they also cause eruptions where one plate overlaps another. In fact, it's happening right underneath us. The plate of Juan de Fuca, which the Pacific Ocean sits on, is sliding under the North American plate." I held my hands out flat then tilted one and slipped it beneath the other to demonstrate. "As the rock gets shoved deeper into the earth's mantle, it melts and turns to magma. The magma works its way to the surface and forms volcanoes. That's how we got our Cascade mountains."

"Oh, yeah," Rhett said. "I saw something about that in my book."

"Seriously?" Cody asked, his tongue white from licking the middle out of an Oreo. "That's pretty cool."

"Yeah, but the *really* cool part is that even though these plates move very slowly, over time they can travel halfway across the world. In fact, a hundred and fifty million years ago, all the continents were stuck together in this supercontinent called Pangea."

Cody gawked at me. "No way."

"Really?" asked Rhett.

"Yup. Haven't you ever noticed how the east coast of South America looks like it would fit up against the west coast of Africa like a puzzle piece?"

"Hold on a sec." Rhett ran into his dad's study and came back with a globe. "You're right. It does. That's not in my volcano book."

"I'll take you to the library this weekend and help you find some better books. I remember one that had a diagram of where the continents will be in another hundred million years. Baja California was clear up by Alaska."

"Well, *that's* really gonna trash somebody's spring break," Cody said.

Rhett pushed his books aside to make room on the table for the globe. "Hey, Jess, have you got any tracing paper? I want to copy all the continents and see if I can figure out how they fit together."

Cody cast him a look of mock pity and shook his head as he twisted another Oreo in half. "I'm gonna do my next psychology paper on you guys: *How Geeks are Born—the Study of One*

Egghead Passing Her Affliction to the Next Generation."

That evening after dinner, I reviewed Spanish vocabulary while Rhett disappeared up the pull-down staircase to his hideout in the attic. He called it the Rogue's Den and had hung a sign from the trapdoor, complete with skull and crossbones.

I'd made it through my flashcards twice before the phone rang. *Gee, who could that be?*

"Hey sweetie," Lydia said, bubbly as a cheerleader. "Did you get my package?"

"Yeah." I took the phone into my room, struggling to keep my voice level. "How did you get my address?"

"Well, I didn't think you'd give it to me, so I asked the school."

I remembered the small bits of information I'd revealed over the course of our conversations, including the fact that I'd transferred from Springfield High to South Eugene. *Way to use your brain, Jess.*

"So they just gave it to you?"

"Of course. I'm your mother."

But how had she proven that? Her name wasn't in the records. It spooked me that the school would give up student information so easily. What if she'd been a psycho, like that lady Diane Downs, who shot her own kids?

"Did you like the T-shirt?" Lydia asked.

"Uh . . . it was nice."

"I really do want to understand your world, sweetie. I don't think I could stay awake through a stock car race if my life depended on it, but it's important to you, and that's all that matters."

Right.

"Thanksgiving's next week."

My stomach squirmed. "Uh huh."

"I was hoping maybe you'd let me take you out for dinner.

Remember how we used to do Chinese?"

"I've got plans." No way was I going to meet with her.

"But Thanksgiving's a time for family."

Was she for real? "Look, Lydia. I know you're trying to make things up to me, but you can't do it with a T-shirt or a few nice words. We had a chance to be a family, and you threw it away."

She sighed. "When are you going to forgive me for that?"

"I don't know if I can."

"Are you having dinner with the Clines?"

"That's none of your business." Mark had invited Race, Kasey, and Cody over. Dad was even supposed to come into town. I didn't want to breathe a hint about any of that.

"They might not mind having one more," Lydia suggested.

"Forget it. Even if I *was* planning to have dinner with them, you wouldn't be invited."

Only one thing could top the disgrace of my friends finding out Lydia was back—having them actually meet her.

The phone rang only seconds after I hung up. Annoyed, I snatched it from its cradle. "Look, I think I've been pretty tolerant about your calls. If you can't accept that goodbye means goodbye then maybe we should put an end to them."

"Don't you think that's a little extreme, considering you're the one who left a message?"

"Dad!" The hint of laughter in his voice did nothing to put me at ease. Panicked, I scanned my memory to recall if I'd used Lydia's name. No. I was positive I hadn't. My heart wasn't reassured, thumping on like an unbalanced wheel. "I'm sorry," I said. "I thought you were someone else."

"And who's been trying your patience so much that you can't answer the phone with a simple 'hello?'"

"Um . . ." I thought fast. "Just this girl from school. My . . . uh . . . lab partner in chemistry. She's always wanting help with her homework."

Dad chuckled. "I suppose that's the burden of being the smartest kid in class."

I didn't bother arguing that there were plenty of kids who had me beat. He wouldn't have bought it, and I wasn't going to let anything distract me now that I had him on the phone.

"I expected you to call yesterday," I said.

"I wanted to, honey, but by the time I pulled into Austin, I was dog-tired. And the line at the pay phone was a mile long."

"I wouldn't have bothered you if it wasn't important."

"I know, and I'm sorry. So what's on your mind?"

Anger welled up, a hot, bubbling mess. How could he be so flippant? "I saw that wreck on the news. I thought it was you."

Dad sighed. "Honey, I'm sorry. I did tell you I was driving into Denver, didn't I?

"You need to stop hauling that stuff! Where am I going to be if you get yourself killed?"

"That's not gonna happen. If you saw the story, you must've also seen that the driver didn't get hurt."

"That's not the point."

"It *is* the point. I know the public has this idea that hauling hazmat is dangerous, but it's just not so. In fact, statistically, hazmat drivers probably have fewer accidents."

"Statistics aren't going to save you if you wreck a truck that's loaded with explosives."

Dad hesitated before letting out a long, slow breath. "Jessie, listen to me. I've been driving truck for eighteen years. I haven't had a wreck yet, and I don't intend to. I know I'm the only parent you've got. I'm not gonna leave you stranded, okay?"

"No, Dad. It's not okay." I hung up on him. Since I obviously wasn't going to change his mind, there was no point even trying.

CHAPTER 9

"Are you sure Teri Sue's gonna be there?" Rhett stood in my doorway wearing a suit that rendered him adorable, in spite of the fact that the sleeves and pants were about an inch too short.

"Of course. She told your dad she would be."

"You'd think she'd come home to get ready." He reached down to adjust his left pant leg so the material lay more smoothly under his brace.

"She has everything she needs at the dorms. Believe me, Rhett, your sister's not going to pass up the opportunity to accept a trophy in front of a crowd." At any rate, the Teri Sue I knew last summer wouldn't. Now, I wasn't so sure what she'd do, including show up drunk.

I ran a brush through my mousy blond hair and returned it to its perennial ponytail. Teri Sue would give me grief for not doing something else with it, but I had no idea how to. At least my clothes looked decent—the cream-colored sweater and a pair of black slacks Dad had bought me two weeks before. The thought of that shopping trip sent a wild swirl of emotion through me. I wished I'd never paged through those bills of lading. If I couldn't change what Dad was doing, I'd be better off not knowing about it. Especially since there was nothing I could do about Lydia's bombshells.

I turned away from the mirror. "Are you ready?" I asked Rhett. "Let's go."

Mark drove us to the Elks Club in his environmentally friendly Honda Civic. Relief whooshed through me when I spotted Teri Sue's pickup in the parking lot.

"See? I told you she'd be here."

Inside, a country band belted out a Mel McDaniel song I'd heard on the shop radio, and the mouthwatering tang of roast beef and ham reminded me that it had been a long time since lunch. I glanced around at the people I was used to seeing in firesuits and greasy clothes. A few hold-outs still wore shirts advertising their car and team, but most were dressed up for the occasion. Kasey, a dedicated member of the T-shirt and jeans brigade, had transformed herself with a form-fitting sweater the same striking blue as her eyes. Race and Cody both looked sharp, though somewhat starchy, in their suits, and Teri Sue wore a green dress that shimmered under the florescent lights, accentuating her plump but shapely figure. She'd sculpted her strawberry blond hair into a cosmetological masterpiece.

"Nice sweater," Cody said. I turned to see that his eyes were fixed on the upper half of my top. When he noticed me noticing him, he blushed.

"I'll give you a nine out of ten for the outfit," agreed Teri Sue, who appeared perfectly sober. "But the hairstyle only gets a three."

"I *like* Jess's ponytail." Cody gave it a gentle tug as I took the seat beside him, then his hand fell to the back of my neck and lingered there.

Rhett plopped down next to his sister. "Hey, Teri Sue How come you never come visit?"

"Sorry. I was gonna, but those midterms 'bout killed me."

"It *would* be nice if you made it home now and again," Mark said, settling into the chair beside his son. "Or at least returned our calls."

Teri Sue raised an eyebrow at his tied-back hair, but didn't comment on it. "That'd be a whole lot easier if I had a phone in my room. You know how many people I have to fight off for the one in the hallway?"

"I'm assuming a college student is perfectly capable of dealing with the phone company," Mark said.

Teri Sue held her father's gaze for only a second before

melting into her usual cheery self. "Well, Thanksgiving's next week, so I reckon I'll be home. Somebody's gotta cook that turkey."

"You'll be cooking for quite a crowd," Mark said. "I've invited Race, Kasey, and Cody."

Teri Sue shrugged and grinned. "The more the merrier."

Cody had told me Kasey traditionally spent the holiday with her family down in Cottage Grove, and last year he and Race had joined them. But her brother Eric had to work this Thanksgiving, so they'd re-scheduled their festivities for Friday. I could still hardly believe all my favorite people, including Dad, would be together in the same house.

Race's good friend Denny Brisco ambled up behind Kasey and laid a hand on her shoulder. "My condolences about the Civil War game," he said, fighting to keep a straight face.

Kasey sighed. "Please—don't even start."

"Don't tell me Race has been rubbing it in?" Denny took a seat at our table, his wife and kids also finding places among us.

"I consider the Civil War to be in the same category as religion and politics," Kasey said. "Something you don't talk about in polite conversation."

"Especially when you happen to be the loser," Race added.

The showdown between the Ducks and Beavers earlier that afternoon had wrapped up the season, and it hadn't gone well for OSU. But that wasn't anything unusual. According to Cody, except for a win in '88 and a 0-0 tie in '83, the Beavers had succumbed to the Ducks in the Civil War every year since 1975. It wasn't any wonder Kasey didn't want to talk about it.

"The Hawk's more interesting than football, anyway," I said.

"What Hawk?" asked Denny.

Kasey filled him in, getting up to continue the conversation in the buffet line when it opened a few minutes later.

"I needed something unique to put in the Portland Road-ster Show," she concluded as she and Denny filed in behind Jerry Addamsen, runner up to Race in the Limited Sportsman championship. "A car that can act as an advertisement for my business."

"You think you'll have it ready by then? That's only . . ." Denny counted on his beefy fingers, ". . . less than four months."

"Oh, I won't enter it this year," Kasey said. "I can't invest that kind of time. Business really picked up over the summer."

Jerry Addamsen turned to look at her. "That Hawk's a cute idea, but let me show you a real project." He dug out his wallet and displayed a photo of a metal-flake blue '57 Chevy. Even from the tiny picture, I could see it must've devastated his bank account.

"Greeley Restorations up in Portland," he said. "This baby's tricked out with a blown 454 with square-port closed chamber heads, dual 850 Holley double-pumpers, a Crower solid lifter cam, needle rockers, and a Pete Jackson gear drive. She's got a Garibaldi chassis, a beefed Turbo 400, and a Ford 9-inch locker rear end with four-fifty-sixes. And all that's topped off with a custom Big Ben paint job." He listed each item like an exclama-tion point, but nothing registered in my head quite so distinctly as that first, condescending phrase. *A cute idea.*

It must have struck Kasey the same way because she glanced only briefly at the photo before looking Addamsen in the eye. "Nice, but tri-five Chevys are a dime a dozen."

"Oh, ho ho!" said Denny as Cody licked his finger and held it in the air, making a sizzling sound.

Addamsen's weathered features pinched tight. "Go ahead and laugh. But a woman's never taken best of show up in Portland, and believe me, with that project, you won't be the first."

Kasey returned his unwavering stare with the faintest of

smiles. Then the line moved forward, and Addamsen busied himself asking the server for roast beef.

Back at the table, Race leaned close to Kasey. "I know you're itching to make him eat his words. If you want to get that car ready this year, we'll make it happen."

"There's not enough time. The customers have to come first."

"They will," Race said. "We'll just shift some things around. I can handle more of the mechanical stuff to free up your schedule. And with Christmas coming, Jake and Eddie might want to put in a little overtime."

"I can work more hours," I said.

"That's not an option, Jess. You're entirely too obsessive, and schoolwork needs to be your priority." While Dad had given Mark legal authority to act on his behalf, Kasey often took it upon herself to fill that role.

"You need to give this some serious thought," Race told her. "Sure, it'll mean sacrifice, but having a good car in that show is the kind of advertising you can't get anywhere else."

From the faraway look in Kasey's eyes, I knew she was already sorting out a way to make it happen. Getting the Hawk ready in time might be possible, but it wouldn't be easy. She'd barely begun the bodywork, let alone anything mechanical.

The meal exceeded my expectations, and Cody hadn't quite finished his third helping when the awards ceremony began.

"Better wrap that up," Race said. "You'll be first." The presentation would start with the tenth-place finisher in the lowest division, then work upward.

Cody stuffed the last bit of mashed potatoes into his mouth and scrubbed a napkin across his face as the announcer called him up to accept his trophy. The crowd responded with more applause than one might expect for his position in the points. But Cody was Race's nephew, and Race was a track favorite.

Teri Sue's seventh-place acknowledgment came a couple of minutes later. She, too, received a decent response, being one of the few female drivers at the speedway.

Cody and Teri Sue placed their trophies in the center of our table, sneaking looks at them as we watched the rest of the Street Stock presentations. Up next were the Limited Sportsmen. The tenth place driver, Rick DeHoyos, hustled to the stage, looking underdressed in Levis and a T-shirt that promoted his team.

"You'd think these folks would put a little more effort into gussying themselves up," commented Teri Sue.

"Hey, Race, how come you don't have any T-shirts with your name on them?" Cody asked. "I'll bet you could sell a ton in the souvenir stand."

I'd often wondered the same thing. Most every driver in the upper divisions, and several in the Street Stock class, sold T-shirts to their fans.

"I drew up a design a few years ago, but I never had the bucks to get any printed," Race said.

"Maybe you should do it now."

Race laughed. "There are more important ways to spend my money." He was still paying back his mother for his hospital bill and the debts he'd racked up while he couldn't work.

After a few minutes, Denny received the third place trophy, then Addamsen accepted his, and finally it was Race's turn. This championship meant a lot to him because his bid for it the previous season had been cut short by the wreck. As the only person in years to challenge Addamsen's lock on the title, Race had the speedway community's full support. Addamsen might be a brilliant driver, but his on-track aggression and lack of social skills made him the guy everyone loved to hate.

The crowd erupted into chaos so loud it could've drowned out a Super Stock main as Race approached the stage. Ted Greene, the chief steward, placed an enormous trophy in his hands, and Race turned to face the audience with one of his trademark full-throttle grins.

When his expression sobered, the applause died away. For several seconds, he stared out over the crowd, his eyes seeming to touch each one of us in turn.

"All of you know how long and hard the road to this moment has been for me," he said. "In the first weeks after my wreck there were times I thought I'd never sit behind the wheel of a race car again. But you people were pulling for me, helping in so many ways I can't begin to list them. Yes, even you, Jerry." Smiling, Race tipped the trophy at Addamsen, who'd bucked his reputation as track scoundrel by helping him get his car back together.

"Without this community, I don't think I'd be standing here today." Race paused, looking at each of us again. "This isn't just my trophy. . . . It belongs to everyone in this room."

An uncharacteristic wave of emotion made my throat go tight, then Cody elbowed me, jolting me out of my reverence. "Wonder who gets to put it in their trophy case," he whispered.

I smacked his arm. "Try and show a little respect, huh?" But I could see pride peeking out from behind the smirk on his face. This championship meant almost as much to him as it did to Race.

After the Super Stock trophies were presented, the band started up with *Rocky Top*, a bouncy hillbilly tune. Cody pulled me to my feet. "Let's dance."

He practically had to drag me to the front of the room, but once I was able to melt into the crowd, the rhythm of the music wiggled into my bones and took over. I swept Cody around in my very best approximation of folksy dancing, letting myself pretend I was a normal girl having fun with her boyfriend—a normal girl whose father worked a normal job.

"Yee haw," Cody mouthed at me, tossing his head to get his bangs out of his face. His dark chocolate eyes grinned right along with his lips.

I ignored the teasing. I was happy, I liked this crazy song, and I didn't care who knew it.

The next morning, Cody invited me over under the pretense of doing homework. But the second I came through the front door, he grabbed my backpack and tossed it onto the nearest chair.

"You won't be needing this."

"I thought we were going to study."

"Later." He turned, motioning for me to follow. "C'mon."

"Where are we going?"

"On a secret mission."

I trailed him downstairs, through the finished part of the basement where we often hung out, and into the storage room.

"This is where Race keeps the stuff from the trailer where we used to live," Cody said. "I think his artwork is mostly in the boxes here on this end. I need to find his T-shirt design."

"You don't expect me to help?" Race's past was his business. I had no intention of pawing through it.

"What—are you afraid you're gonna come across his underwear or something? Here, take this box." He slid it across the floor to me.

"Cody, I don't think we should be doing this. What if he comes down here?"

"He won't. He's at the shop with Kasey. She decided to take a shot at getting the Hawk ready for the Roadster Show. Anyway, I'm not doing this for my own entertainment. I'm gonna have Kasey get T-shirts printed up for him as a Christmas present."

Okay. That wasn't a bad idea. I wouldn't mind having a Race Morgan T-shirt of my own.

After an hour of digging through boxes, I began to wonder if the plan was so brilliant after all. The deeper we got into the pile, the quieter Cody became, his face growing dark and moody.

I sat back on my heels, watching as he studied a sketch that showed him draped over the fender of the Galaxie. Even upside down and several feet away, the drawing's details stood out. The look of concentration on Cody's face, the hair hanging in his eyes, the knuckles stretching his skin as he clutched a wrench with greasy fingers.

"Cody, if looking at this stuff upsets you so much, maybe we should forget it."

"Who says I'm upset?"

"It's pretty obvious." I reached to take the drawing from him, but he pulled away, moving it to the bottom of the pile in his hands.

"What have I got to be upset about? It's not like I know for sure he can't do this anymore." His eyes met mine for only a second before flitting back down to the stack of sketches. He shuffled through them abruptly. "Here. Check this out." He handed me a drawing of Denny, only not the 40-year-old Denny I knew now. This one looked closer to Race's age. And the Nova in the background wasn't his #9 Limited Sportsman, but his previous car, Big Red, which started life as a Street Stock before Denny modified it for the Sportsman class. He still hauled it out whenever his current ride broke down, and he was famous for loaning it to others.

"Wow, that's been around a while," I said. These days, Big Red had so many dents it was barely recognizable as a Nova.

"Yeah, Race has known Denny forever." Cody dug back into his box and came up with a South Eugene High notebook, which he began flipping through.

"Hey, put that back," I said. "It might be private." If anybody could understand that some things were personal, it should be Cody. Until he'd met Race, he'd never shown anyone the short stories he wrote.

"Relax. It's just notes from his biology class." He turned the book toward me to prove it.

I had to smile at the margins filled with doodles of race cars. "Well, you're not going to put any of that on a T-shirt. Keep looking."

Cody reached into the box for another handful of paper, bigger sheets this time. "Yes!"

The drawing in his hands offered a peek backward in time at Race's '74 Dart with no dings or dents, no gouges from asphalt grating the roof in the rollover.

"C'mon," Cody said. "Let's get this stuff packed up before Race and Kasey get back."

A grin had replaced the straight, sad set of his lips, but it didn't make a very good mask. And as he set the sketch aside, his eyes lingered on it, trapped in an easier, happier past.

CHAPTER 10

The next day, I got to work just as Race returned from dropping off the Hawk's engine at Metzger's machine shop.

"They say they can get it done by the middle of December," he said. "Hopefully there won't be any problems this time."

Kasey had been using Metzger's since her business opened, but recently the owner's son had taken over. In spite of a few problems with work being late or improperly done, she continued to use their services, hoping things would improve, and not wanting to deal with the hassle of finding someone else.

"Jess, I'd like you and Cody to pull the engine in the Roadrunner," she said. "Eddie's taking over the bodywork on the Rambler, so somebody has to cover the things I had him scheduled to do."

"No problem." I smoothed a few escaped wisps of hair up under my Eugene Speedway hat and pulled on a shop coat. "I'm glad you're doing the Hawk. Addamsen could use a reality check."

Kasey laughed. "Even if someone were to give him one, he wouldn't likely notice. But Race is right about the advertising."

"I really want to help, Kasey. A few more hours a week aren't going to hurt my grades. You could even say it was part of my education." I paused a second to let that sink in. "It might be a good thing to put on a scholarship application."

Smiling, Kasey shook her head. "There's no need to keep selling the idea. I've already changed my mind. But the minute your grades begin to slip, or you seem the least bit overstressed, that will be the end of it."

"Deal," I said, grinning.

Though rain was drizzling down outside in a gray, clammy mist, inside the shop it was warm and bright. I lost myself in the rhythm of my work, allowing it to smooth the rough edges off my worries.

Cody helped with that. He was in one of his crazy moods where everything anyone said became fodder for a joke. Usually Race slung it right back, but today he was quiet—the closest he ever came to being out of sorts.

"I wonder what's up with him," Cody said when Race walked away mumbling, rather than responding to one of his quips.

"Maybe you're not as funny as you think you are."

Cody shook his head. "Impossible."

Half an hour later, we went into the office to eat the Subway sandwiches Kasey had bought when she learned we wanted to stay to help with the Hawk.

My six-inch tuna was plenty, but Cody plowed through a foot-long meatball sub, following up with a bag of chips and two cookies. A third one rolled off the desk, as if sensing its fate and making a run for it.

"Hey, where do you think you're going?" Cody ducked down to retrieve it. "Man, it's a mess under here. Dust bunny city. *Someone* hasn't been doing her job."

"I don't know what you're hinting at," I said. "I'm not the only grunt labor around here."

Cody came back up with a crumpled wad of paper in one hand and his cookie in the other. After stuffing the escapee into his mouth, he flattened out the sheet.

"Uh oh." The better part of his cookie broke off and fell to the floor.

"What?"

"Now I know why Race is in such a lousy mood." He handed me the wrinkled page. Rough sketches of the Studebaker covered it—scrawls that might've been a decent attempt for an art class flunky like myself, but were barbaric compared to the drawings in Kasey's basement.

A cold flutter went through my stomach, even though this was nothing I hadn't expected.

Cody looked like he'd just watched his Galaxie roll off a cliff. I reached across the desk to take his hand, and it instantly balled into a fist.

"Hey, c'mon. He's okay with it, Cody."

"He is not! He's totally bummed."

"Right now, maybe, but he just figured it out. You've got to get a grip. If he sees you upset, he's only going to feel worse. Besides, if he wanted us to know, he would've told us."

"How?" Cody's eyes met mine, raw with emotion. "How do you tell people something like that?" He snatched the sketch from my other hand and studied it again, the remains of his cookie forgotten on the floor.

"Cody, he'll be fine." I stood up and circled the desk to give him a sideways hug. "He's accepted the rest of it, and he'll accept this, too."

"Why should he have to? Why can't he ever catch a break?" Cody's shoulders slumped under my arm. He scrunched the drawing into a ball, tossed it in the trash, and yanked free to stride out of the office.

At the banquet, Teri Sue had promised to come home Wednesday night so we could get the turkey in the oven first thing Thursday morning. But by dinnertime, she hadn't shown. She called at eight-thirty. A throb of voices and loud music in the background almost drowned out her words.

"Hey, Jess, I'm real sorry, but I'm not gonna make it home tonight. I'll be there bright and early tomorrow, okay?"

I stifled my irritation. "Since when have you been anywhere bright and early?"

"Hey, no need to rag on me. I think I can make an exception one day in my life."

After a night of partying? Not exactly a realistic time to be turning over a new leaf. "I hope so," I said, resorting to guilt. "I don't have the slightest idea of how to cook that turkey."

"Trust me, it's a lot easier than you think. Unless there's pies to bake. We don't have to mess with any pies do we?"

"No, Kasey said she'd bring those."

"Good. As long as we get that bird in the oven by nine, we'll be okay. I'll be there at eight."

Right. And pigs would start flying at eight-thirty.

The next morning, I got up early and went down to the kitchen, even though there was nothing I could do until Teri Sue arrived. Rhett shuffled in at 7:45, still wearing pajamas. His hair looked like it had been styled by a category five hurricane.

"'Morning," he mumbled, going to the cupboard for the cereal. "Where's Teri Sue?"

"She'll be here any minute."

Rhett sighed. "I wouldn't count on it."

"She's not going to blow us off. She knows I haven't got a clue about that turkey."

"If you say so." Shoulders drooping, he fixed himself a bowl of Cheerios and slid into a chair.

"What's up?" I asked.

"Nothing."

"Yeah, sure." I took a seat across from him. "Spill it, Rhett."

He plunked one elbow onto the table, resting his cheek in his palm. "Well . . . you know that girl Emily I told you about?"

"Yeah?"

"I tried to do like you said and stay away from her . . ." His words trickled to a halt, and he looked down into his cereal bowl.

"Uh huh." I prompted.

"Well, she won't leave me alone." Rhett used his spoon to push a Cheerio under the surface of his milk. When it popped back up, he attacked it again. "Yesterday she stole a brownie right off my lunch tray."

"And what did you do about it?"

"Nothing." He poked another Cheerio.

"Rhett, you can't let people get away with stuff like that. I had a boy picking on me in seventh grade, and when I didn't do anything, he kept at it all year. Next time, you need to stand up for yourself."

"I can't." Rhett looked up at me with pitiful eyes.

"Why not?"

"Because . . ." His gaze dropped back to the cereal bowl, his voice falling along with it. "She might stop talking to me."

"I thought that's what you wanted."

"No. I just don't want her to be hateful."

I snorted. "Good luck trying to change that."

Rhett sighed and continued to torture his Cheerios. "I wish Teri Sue would hurry up and get here. She'll know what to say."

Right. Relationships were her territory, and Rhett obviously didn't want my opinion. "She'll be here soon."

But she wasn't. At a quarter after eight, I called the dorm and got no answer. No surprise there. Everyone had probably left for the holiday.

Well, that turkey wasn't going to wait much longer, and how hard could it be to cook, anyway? It wasn't as if I needed to launch the thing into orbit. I pulled it out of the fridge and set it on the counter. At least it wasn't frozen. Kasey had warned me earlier in the week that it would take several days to thaw in the refrigerator.

There was nothing about turkeys in Teri Sue's collection of hand-scribbled recipes, so I cracked one of her cookbooks. *Take out the giblets, wash the bird, put it breast-up in the pan, and rub it with oil.* No problem. Stuffing was another story. The book implied that if you cooked it inside the turkey and didn't bring it up to the proper temperature, you might poison your dinner guests.

84

"Does Teri Sue put the stuffing inside the turkey?" I asked Rhett.

"Well, yeah." He gave me a look like I'd just asked him whether Oregon was a state. "Where else would she put it?"

"This says I can do it in a separate pan."

"Teri Sue doesn't."

Since I wasn't sure how to fit anything in the oven along with a 23.6 pound bird—the biggest Mark had been able to find—I decided I'd be okay as long as I used a meat thermometer the way the book recommended.

Washing the turkey took more dexterity than I'd expected. By the time I got it into the pan, Teri Sue still hadn't arrived. I located her stuffing recipe and mixed up a batch. It was a simple matter to get it inside the bird, and then there was nothing left to do but oil it up, cover it with foil, and stick it in the oven. I'd missed my nine o'clock goal by forty-five minutes, but I figured moving mealtime up to five wouldn't kill anyone. Except maybe Cody.

Teri Sue breezed in at ten-fifteen, wearing a hung-over look I'd seen far too many times on Lydia.

"Don't hate me," she said, flopping into a kitchen chair. "You don't hate me, do you? I slept straight through my alarm."

"Sur-*prize*, sur-*prize*, sur-*prize*." Rhett drawled, pushing away from the table and stalking out of the room.

Teri Sue peered after him in bewilderment. "What's got his knickers in a twist?"

"Maybe the fact that you haven't been home to see him since September?" Frustration hung heavy in my tone, but it bounced right off her oblivious nature.

"I call all the time!"

"You've called twice. And then it was to talk to your dad. You never make time for Rhett."

Teri Sue stared silently at me for a good ten seconds before looking away. "Okay. I reckon I could work a little harder on my sisterly duties. Tell you what, he loves helping me bake Christmas cookies. We'll whip up enough for the whole damned speedway."

"That's great," I said. "But he's the one you should be saying this to."

CHAPTER 11

Dad showed up at noon, prepared to stay in town the whole weekend, though once again he'd opted to rent a motel room. I itched to take him aside and go at it again about the hazmat thing, but that would only ruin the holiday.

"Did you bring your harmonica?" Rhett asked, crowding into the entryway with us.

"Right here." Dad patted his jacket pocket. Along with his sign collection, the harmonica was something he'd taken up after the divorce. He'd told me its lonesome, bluesy sound had helped him through the sadness of losing his family.

"And the sign book?" Rhett prodded.

"Out in the truck. Go on and get it. The door's unlocked."

Rhett rushed off into the rain, while Dad, Mark, and I sat down in the living room with Teri Sue. When Rhett returned with the photo album, he plopped down beside me on the couch.

"Hey, look Jess, here's a new one: 'Caution, Water on Road During Rain.' Duh!" he flipped the page and snickered. The latest photo showed a sign that read "Eat Here and Get Gas."

We passed the book around as Dad told funny stories about people he'd met on the road, and Teri Sue added a few of her own about kids from the dorms.

A couple of hours later Kasey, Race, and Cody arrived bearing warm and fragrant pies. The scent of cinnamon and nutmeg brought a rush of holiday memories from a time when the word "family" still meant a mommy, daddy, and little girl.

"You'll want to hide these in the kitchen," Kasey said, handing one to me. "It's been all I could do to keep Cody from sampling them on the way over."

"Hey!" he protested. But I noticed Race was guarding the other two.

"Nice place you've got here, Mark," Race said. "I'll bet it would be a lot of fun to decorate an old farmhouse like this for Christmas."

"Don't let him near it," Cody warned. "He spent every night this week in the yard with a trouble light, transforming our place into Elf Central. He's even got the lights timed to come on tonight at sunset."

"And what's wrong with that? Thanksgiving is the official opening of the Christmas season," Race said.

Cody snorted. "If you had your way, Halloween would be."

We settled in the living room with hors d'oeuvres and hot chocolate, a fire crackling in the woodstove, and Mark's favorite soft rock station playing low. Newt galloped downstairs in a fit of kitten frenzy, took one look at the strangers in his territory, and hit the brakes, rear-end skidding across the hardwood floor.

"Wow, he's really grown," Kasey said.

"Yeah," Race agreed, "but he's a little loose. I think he could use another round of wedge."

Rhett scooped up the kitten and placed him in Kasey's lap. "He's real friendly, y'all just startled him."

Newt proved the fact immediately by climbing her sweater and throwing his whole body into licking her face. His rumble of contentment could be heard throughout the room.

"I swear that cat has canine in his lineage," Mark said.

"Not enough," Rhett noted. "I've been trying to teach him how to fetch, but he just doesn't get it."

Dad shifted the mug of hot chocolate in his hands and looked at Kasey. "So, have you two made any plans for the wedding yet?"

"Not really. It isn't until August. We have plenty of time."

Teri Sue chuckled as she spread cheese log on a Wheat Thin. "Isn't that usually the groom's line?"

"Kasey's got a lot on her plate right now," Race said. "She's building a custom car for the Portland Roadster Show."

"Jess mentioned that," Mark said. "Do you think you'll have it ready in time?"

Kasey launched into a detailed report on what we'd accomplished and what we had left to do. She and Dad were discussing the merits of the Avanti engine—something I hadn't even known he was aware of—when Teri Sue excused herself to start the sweet potatoes.

"You coming, Jess?" she called over her shoulder.

Cody followed us, angling to score more cheese and crackers, and Rhett tagged along.

The mouth-watering scent of roasting turkey was stronger in the kitchen. Cody stopped to peek into the oven before proceeding to the refrigerator.

"So where's your Dad?" Teri Sue asked him. "Couldn't he make it down from Portland?"

"He's having dinner with his new girlfriend." Cody leaned into the fridge, rooting around for provisions.

"And they didn't invite you?"

"Believe it or not, I prefer your company."

"Of course you do." Teri Sue grabbed some sweet potatoes. "Okay, you peel these," she ordered, dumping them onto the table in front of me. "And you snap the ends off the green beans." She tossed those to Rhett. "Cody, you can slice up vegetables for the salad."

"Not until I put this baby out of its misery," he said, holding up the remainder of the summer sausage and shutting the refrigerator.

"You'll spoil your appetite," Rhett said.

I snorted. "I don't think that's possible."

Cody reached out with his free hand to tug my ponytail as he passed behind me to take a seat.

Under Teri Sue's direction, Rhett and I prepared the ingredients for her side dishes as Cody sat at the table, slicing off bits of summer sausage and popping them into his mouth. The conversation drifted from racing, to the brutality of high school and college midterms, to Teri Sue's recent experience with a dorky guy who wouldn't leave her alone.

"There's a girl in my class like that," Rhett said. "Only she isn't 'out for my body', and she doesn't look like 'a walking train wreck.'" He filled Cody and Teri Sue in on the things he'd told me about Emily.

"Jess says I should stay away from her," he concluded. "But I don't *want* to."

Cody eyed me sadly and shook his head. "Dude, Jess is totally and completely wrong about this. The reason Emily's stealing your brownies is because she wants to be your girlfriend."

"She teases him about the way he talks!" I said.

"Translation: she thinks his Southern drawl is sexy."

"Rhett, don't listen to him. You're just going to wind up being humiliated. Right, Teri Sue?"

She glanced up from the cheese she was shredding, a little too much amusement in her eyes. "Actually, I'm with Cody on this."

Rhett grinned at his new love coach, who was ever-so-romantically sandwiching sausage and four kinds of cheese between a couple of Triscuits. "You reckon I should tell her I like her back?"

"You might want to start off with a more subtle approach," Cody suggested. "Smile at her."

"*Smile* at her?" I scoffed. "What kind of lamebrain advice is that?"

"It worked on you, didn't it?" Cody zapped me with one of his most alluring grins.

"You're wrong about this. I know what I'm talking about. Andy Kolmanski pulled the same thing on me when I was Rhett's age."

Cody's grin stretched wider. "Fortunately, you were too amorously challenged to figure out his true motives, or I might not be here today."

The turkey came out perfectly, and when everyone lavished praise on Teri Sue, she gave me the credit. "It's all Jess's doing. I couldn't manage to get my sorry behind out of bed to help."

When the sweet potato casserole, green beans with bacon, and cheesy garlic mashed potatoes were similarly praised, she admitted Rhett and I had done a lot of the work.

"Hey, I helped," Cody said.

"The only thing you helped with is keeping Hickory Farms in business."

Race snickered through a mouthful of turkey, nearly choking himself.

In spite of Cody's earlier pig-out, he made his usual dent in the meal. I wasn't far behind. Everything tasted wonderful, the flavor no doubt enhanced by the good company around me. A year ago, when I was watching Lydia get wasted across the table at Lok Yaun, I never would've dreamed I could be part of something like this. I glanced at Teri Sue. Sure, she'd been a flake lately, and her partying wasn't easy to take, but she was the one who'd set all this in motion when she'd befriended me at the track last spring.

As if sensing my gaze, she looked back, and we shared a smile.

After dinner we adjourned to the living room to let our food settle so we could wedge a slice of pie in on top. At Rhett's urging, Dad broke out his harmonica and started in with *Oh, Susanna*. He continued through an assortment of folk songs, taking requests. Just as the last mournful notes of *Amazing Grace* faded away, the doorbell rang.

"What lost and lonely soul would be out and about tonight?" Mark wondered as Rhett got up to see.

Two servings of turkey with all the fixings turned to ballast in my stomach because I knew even before the door swung open.

"Hi there, hon. You must be Rhett! Mind if I come in and visit wi' my little girl?"

My dinner collapsed further on itself, approaching the density of a dying star. Only alcohol could make my mother's voice take on that pathetic sing-song.

Rhett backed away from the door, turning to me, his mouth agape and eyes round as headlights. This was it, the thing I'd been dreading. But never in my worst nightmares had I imagined it would happen is such a perfectly catastrophic way.

"Lydia! What in the name of God are you doing here?" Dad peered at her as if struggling to look backward through the eight years since they'd last seen each other.

She flinched, the shock of running into him flashing in her eyes. "I was out having dinner all by my lonesome on Thanksgiving, and I thought I might drop by to say hello to Jessh." She stepped from the entryway to the living room, stumbling as the toe of her shoe caught on the rug. "Oopshie!" she giggled, grabbing Rhett's shoulder for balance. He staggered under her weight.

Dad stood up from his seat in the far corner. "I think that's about enough."

"I told you not to come!" This couldn't be real. She couldn't be here. Every cell in my body screamed at me to get up and run.

"You knew she was back?" Dad turned to me while Mark jumped up to relieve Rhett and help Lydia to the couch. Teri Sue and Cody slid over to make room.

"She's been calling," I mumbled, unable to look him in the eye.

"Why didn't you tell me?" Dad asked.

"I . . . didn't think it was important."

Mark stood frozen at the end of the couch, as if his slightest move might set off a world-ending chain-reaction. I couldn't bear to glance at either Race or Kasey.

"Now, now," Lydia said, her voice drawing my attention in that unpleasant way a pile of horse droppings draws flies. "Why all the fuss? I just wanna meet yer friends." She shifted sideways with a sloppy grin. "Lemme guess, you must be Teri Sue, and *you*," she hesitated, her smile growing, "must be Cody." Her hand cupped his knee.

Cody's head jerked up, and he shot me a look so full of shock and empathy I wanted to be sucked into the black hole that had replaced my stomach. What was he thinking? What were all of them thinking? I kept my eyes on Lydia, afraid of what I might see on everyone else's faces.

"Lydia . . ." Dad began, but her voice ran over his.

"Jessh, you di'n't tell me your boyfriend was so *cute*! Now I know why you din't want me to come." She shoulder-bumped Cody, who sat stiffly, his expression a car-wreck of emotions I couldn't read. "She's ashamed of me, y'know—but I'm not without my shocial graces. I brought dessert." Her hand dipped into her purse, pulling out a cluster of candy bars and a bag of Nutter Butters. She dumped them on the coffee table, knocking over Kasey's glass of wine.

"Enough!" Dad said.

Teri Sue scrambled to toss a wad of napkins on the puddle. They flared deep red, like my cheeks, as merlot soaked through. I ached to bolt upstairs and never come back down, but some sound, steadfast part of me knew that would only make things worse.

"It's time for you to leave." Dad circled the coffee table, his hand outstretched and his face a mask of fury. "Give me your keys, and I'll make sure you get home in one piece."

"No!" wailed Lydia, jerking away. "I wanna meet the rest of Jessh's friends."

"And I want to spend a nice holiday with my daughter, without her being embarrassed half to death." He grabbed

Lydia's purse and helped himself to her keys. "Let's go."

Race pushed up from the easy chair by the woodstove. "I'll follow and give you a ride back." His gaze met mine before flickering away to allow me a tiny bubble of privacy.

I sat shamed as they escorted Lydia outside. The door clicked shut behind them, loud as a gunshot in the stunned silence. Rhett sank into the chair by the TV, his big eyes piercing me, but he didn't say a word.

After an agonizing moment, Teri Sue hopped up off the couch. "I'm gonna get me some more hot chocolate. Y'all want any?"

"Sure," Mark said, finally moving to stoke the woodstove.

Rhett stole a look at me, as if puzzling out whether or not that would be okay, then nodded at his sister.

"Let me help you with that." Kasey got up and followed Teri Sue into the kitchen.

Now I was down to three of them. Three people who must think I was the most pathetic creature on the planet. I stared at the floor, unable to bear the pity I'd see on Rhett and Cody's faces. Wondering what Kasey and Teri Sue would say about me in the other room.

The couch creaked. Footsteps sounded, but I didn't look up. Someone settled beside me on the arm of the chair, and the scent of Cody's hair gel swept close as his arm encircled my shoulders.

"It'll be okay, Jess."

I sat stiff in his embrace. Mortified. Petrified.

More footsteps. Two small hands, full of kitten, appeared in my line of vision. Without a word, Rhett set Newt in my lap and backed away.

Round golden eyes peered up at me. They held no questions, no sympathy, just the same adoration as always. I pulled the kitten tight against me, feeling his purr radiate through my chest as I drank in the comfort of his unconditional love.

CHAPTER 12

When Dad and Race came back, I couldn't look at either of them. Dad walked straight over and knelt beside my chair, pulling me into an embrace, but I couldn't return it. Finally, he stood up, kissing the top of my head before taking his seat across the room.

The conversation resumed around me. Pleasant topics like the upcoming Christmas season and the tastiness of Teri Sue's homemade hot chocolate. I hardly heard a word. My brain was stuck in high gear, obsessing over what Dad and Race might've talked about on their way back. Had they criticized me for being too stupid to tell Lydia to take a hike? Had they shaken their heads, pitying me? Last summer, Race told me I was his hero—that the way I'd handled Lydia's abandonment had inspired him to put his demons to rest and propose to Kasey. Now he'd seen me as I really was. The screwed-up daughter of a woman who loved alcohol more than her own kid.

Somehow, I bluffed my way through the rest of the evening. Cody helped, wielding his smart-assed humor to keep the others laughing. But even though everyone pretended the interruption had never happened, my stomach stayed in a knot, rejecting even the thought of Kasey's pie.

After ten thousand glances at my watch, the hands finally wound their way to nine o'clock.

"We probably ought to be going," Kasey said. "I have to put in a little time at the shop tomorrow before we visit my family."

I was torn between the desire to join her for a few unscheduled hours on the Hawk, and the need to disappear into a crack in the space-time continuum.

Dad unfolded his body from the La-Z-boy and likewise excused himself, saying the 400 miles he'd driven that morning were catching up with him. He rested a hand on my shoulder, firing off a quick squeeze. "How about a hug for your old man?"

I stood and let him pull me close.

"Come by the hotel at nine. We'll spend the day together, okay?" He gave the top of my head another kiss.

"Sure," I said, backing away.

Kasey hugged me next. "Call me if you need to talk," she said, her voice low and her lips close to my ear.

Cody didn't say anything when he put his arms around me. He just held me tight.

Then they all filed out and, at last, I could escape to my room.

I slipped out of the house the next morning while everyone was still asleep. Since I had time to kill before meeting Dad, I spent it doing one of my favorite things—exploring new neighborhoods. I liked to piece together clues about families by sizing up their homes and yards, the cars in their driveways, and the toys on their front lawns. The nice thing about concentrating on strangers' lives was that it made it easier to forget my own.

Just before nine, I drove to the New Oregon Motel. Dad and I didn't say much as we walked across the parking lot to Deb's Restaurant, where our usual waitress took our orders. While we waited for breakfast, Dad made small talk about his next run, but I knew what was coming. Sure enough, as soon as the waitress placed our plates in front of us, he got to the point.

"How long has your mother been calling?"

I paged back through the calendar in my head, trying to remember the specific day.

"Since around the middle of October."

"You shoulda said something, Jessie," Dad said as he reached for the jam.

"Yeah, and *you* should stop hauling explosives." The words leapt out on their own, surprising me, but I wasn't sorry I'd said them.

"We're not getting into that again, so don't think you can distract me."

I poked at my eggs, which were scrambled together with mushrooms, peppers, and cheddar cheese. It was my favorite breakfast, but it might as well have been dog food.

"Were you trying to protect her?" Dad asked.

"Of course not!" A tiny dagger of guilt needled me. Had I been? "I just . . . didn't want things to change."

Dad grunted. "Well, they've certainly changed now."

Wasn't that the truth. I closed my eyes against last night's humiliation. If I'd known telling him could've averted this disaster, I wouldn't have hesitated to do it.

"How did she find out where you were staying?" He took a bite of jam-slathered biscuit.

"The school gave her my address."

"What? She's not even listed on the paperwork. They oughta know better. I'm giving them a call first thing next week."

Great, just what I needed, my father raising hell with the school office. Why couldn't he understand that drawing un-needed attention to the problem was not going to make things easier? At least he couldn't show up in person. He was due in Sonoma Monday afternoon to pick up a load of pinot noir.

"Okay, here's what we're going to do." Dad leaned over the table and punctuated his words with his fork. "I'll call the police to see about getting a restraining order. There's no reason you should have to put up with that woman invading your life."

"Dad, no! I can deal with this myself." The thought of in-volving the police made my skin flash cold.

"You shouldn't *have to* deal with it. You're sixteen years old. You should be worrying about—" his fork waggled like a conductor's baton "—the prom and grades, not some alcoholic mother hassling you in front of your friends. You deserve a normal life."

Right. Like that was even possible. "How can I have a normal life when my dad is gone twenty-six days a month hauling explosives?"

"I told you, we're not going to discuss that now." Dad's fork homed in on his potatoes, stabbing violently. When it was fully loaded, he shoveled it into his mouth.

"Then when *are* we going to discuss it? When are you going to start listening to me?"

"Honey, I *do* listen." He struggled to speak around the hashbrowns.

"No you don't! You just keep telling me it's safe. But how can it be? Especially if—" I stopped, my worst fear teetering off into silence.

"Especially if *what*?"

I shook my head and looked down at my eggs. Like the pie last night, they had zero chance of making it into my stomach.

"Jess, what are you so worried about?"

Here it was, my perfect opportunity, and I was too cowardly to take it. At least now I knew why. If I didn't ask him, I could go on hoping it wasn't true—that at least one of my parents wasn't an addict.

"Jess, talk to me."

I pushed my eggs around my plate, shoving them into a perfectly symmetrical mound.

"Honey—"

"It's nothing. Just something Lydia said."

With a sigh, Dad laid down his fork and reached across the table for my hand. "What did she tell you?"

I shook my head.

"Jessie . . ."

How could I possibly say it out loud? But I had to. Calling on every bit of my willpower, I forced the words out in a mumble. "She said you were . . ." I drew a deep breath. ". . . taking drugs."

"What?"

"To stay awake on the road. So you could work those long hours." My gaze stayed focused on my plate, my words dwindling to a whisper. "You're always worried about getting enough miles."

"Honey..." Dad's hand squeezed mine. "It's not true. I've never done that, and I never will. Matter of fact, I couldn't if I wanted to. There's a Federal law that makes it so all truck drivers have to take drug tests."

A Federal law? I looked up into a face crinkled by worry lines. "Really?" If he'd said anything else, I might not have bought it. But a law was pretty hard to argue with.

"Yeah, really." He smiled.

Relief rushed in to chase away the fear that had gripped me just moments before. I took a shaky breath, my spirits rising on a sudden euphoric wave. He wasn't taking drugs. Lydia had lied after all.

"Now you can see why I'm so concerned about your mom being back in your life," Dad said. "You can't trust her, Jessie. All she's gonna do is cause you heartache."

Maybe so, but that didn't mean I wanted him getting the school or police involved. "It's not like she'll come back after that performance. Can't we just forget it happened?"

He shook his head. "It's not open for debate. I'm your father and it's my job to look out for you. Maybe I blew that for the past eight years, but things are different now."

Learning Dad wasn't using drugs should've made me feel better—and it did—but I couldn't change the fact that he was still hauling hazmat. And I couldn't erase the Thanksgiving disaster.

The best I could do was avoid everyone else. Dad made that easy, inviting me to spend the day with him watching movies in his hotel room.

Saturday morning, I woke dreading my shift at the shop. Kasey and Race might act as if nothing had happened, but Cody was a different story. He'd probably give me hell for keeping another secret from him. I remembered the hurt look in his eyes last summer, when I'd repeatedly denied that anything was wrong, in spite of mounting evidence to the contrary. He'd forgiven me then, but what if he didn't this time?

The moment I walked in the door, he grabbed my arm. "Hey, c'mere."

I cringed as he pulled me into the office, which Race had strung with Christmas lights and garland. But instead of the confrontation I expected, Cody wrapped his arms around me and rested his forehead against mine. There were no questions, no words of reprimand, only his embrace. As he held me, energy flowed between us, tucking around me, soothing away my shame.

"Aren't you mad?" I whispered.

"No."

Out in the shop, the air compressor switched on, rattling out a hum that surrounded us in a cocoon of noise.

"I get why you didn't tell me," Cody said. "When my mom said she wanted me back, I kept it a secret from Race as long as I could. And when she tried to drag me off to Phoenix, I couldn't stand having Kasey there, watching her humiliate me."

I leaned into Cody, feeling the heat of his chest against mine, the whisper of his breath on my face.

"Your mom might've embarrassed you, Jess, but you've gotta remember something. You're not the one who showed up drunk at Thanksgiving. You don't have anything to be ashamed of."

I knew that, but my mortification had nothing to do with logic. "Everyone feels sorry for me."

"You make that sound like a bad thing."

"It is. I don't want anyone's pity." I pulled back, and he released me from the hug, keeping one arm draped around my shoulders as he steered me toward the couch.

"No one pities you. We care about you. And we don't want to think about you growing up with a mom like that. We're pissed off on your behalf. You can't expect us not to be."

I stared at the floor, trying to force that quibbling difference to be enough. But it wasn't. "The whole thing makes me feel pathetic."

Cody's grip tightened around my shoulders. "Don't let it. All I feel for you right now is admiration. It took guts to stick it out the other night. Just keep your head up like always, and in a few days everything will be back to normal."

Mark was in his office when I got home from work, and Rhett had escaped to the Rogue's Den with Trevor, who'd come to spend the night. Happy for the privacy, I hid out in my room, reviewing Spanish vocab and reading the assigned chapter in psychology. When I could avoid my English homework no longer, I gathered my notes and the thesaurus Cody had given me. He'd been tutoring me in essay writing since my miserable attempts at the start of the school year. But no matter how well I thought I'd constructed my first draft, he always ripped it to shreds and made me revise it before he'd let me turn it in. At least I didn't have to write it by hand. Last year, Mark had bought Rhett and Teri Sue a state-of-the-art Hewlett Packard 386 computer.

As I approached the guest room where it was kept, I heard the electronic music of a video game. Tetris, Rhett's favorite. I opened the door. He was sitting in front of the monitor, absorbed in working the multi-colored pieces into their proper slots.

"I thought you and Trevor were up in the Rogue's Den."

"We were, but he got a stomachache and had to go home."

"Bummer."

"Yeah." Rhett paused the game and spun the chair around

to face me. "Y'all need to use the computer?"

"No. I was thinking about working on my essay, but I can do it tomorrow." I leaned against the doorjamb.

"You sure?"

"Yeah. I'm kind of dreading it, so I don't mind putting it off one more day."

Rhett continued to look at me, pushing against the buff-colored carpeting with one foot to swivel the chair from side to side. I couldn't remember ever feeling awkward around him, but I did now. We hadn't been alone together since Lydia's intrusion. Last night, I'd avoided him, tackling my chemistry homework and finishing the final chapters of *The Old Man and the Sea.*

"I should've told you my mom was back," I said. My thumb rippled nervously across the pages of the thesaurus, but I wouldn't allow my eyes to stray from his. "I'm sorry."

"It's okay."

"I guess I was embarrassed. I mean . . . well . . . you saw how she was."

He nodded. "Yeah."

"And . . . well . . . I was afraid it might make you feel bad."

Rhett had struggled so much in the first few months I'd known him, seeing Teri Sue get cards and letters from their mother and never receiving any of his own. Then, when her condition got worse, he seemed to lose his last bit of hope. He was doing better now, but I always felt a little afraid of saying something that would rekindle all that pain.

"It didn't seem fair for me to get my mom back when you couldn't have yours," I said. "Especially since it would've been easier if mine had just stayed gone."

Rhett stared down into his lap, rubbing the leather band at the top of his brace the way he always did when he was worried or didn't know what to say. "You don't have to protect me like some little kid. Teri Sue used to do that all the time."

102

Oh man. How could I be so stupid? I'd lectured her about that very thing, and now I was doing it myself.

"I'm sorry, Rhett."

"It's okay." He looked at me with eyes that shimmered just a little bit more than usual. "I still feel bad about Mama, but I don't want people to be afraid to talk about her."

"I'll remember that," I said. "But to tell you the truth, I'd just as soon no one ever mentions my mom again."

Cody was right. With everyone but my dad avoiding the subject, the sting of the Lydia incident soon faded. Even Teri Sue, who normally meddled in my affairs with wild abandon, kept her thoughts to herself. But then, I didn't see much of her. She spent most of the weekend either sleeping or out with friends. At least I hadn't noticed any further signs of alcohol.

By Sunday, after Kasey said the police weren't likely to do much to enforce a restraining order, Dad gave up on the idea. Instead, he told Lydia that if she didn't leave me alone, he'd file charges against her for abandoning me last summer. Then, not trusting me, he gave Mark and Kasey the job of letting him know if she broke the agreement. When I groused, Kasey advised me to let it go. "He's right, Jess. You've had to deal with your mother's disruptions for eight years. It's time you got to focus on your own life."

Monday at lunch, Cody's friend Heather set her tray on the table beside me and sat down. She gave me her usual curt nod, tossing jet-black bangs out of her face. Her eyes were ringed with inky mascara, making them stand out shockingly against her skim-milk skin.

"Hi, Heather," I said. I was even more uncomfortable with her than with Quinn. She sat with us once or twice a week, spending the rest of the time with her Goth friends. I hadn't figured out why she bothered with us at all. It would've made sense if she still had a thing for Cody—they'd dated last year—but Heather had another boyfriend now. A freshman at Lane Community College.

Cody sauntered up a moment later, thumping his tray down and whisking a sheet of paper across the table so it came to rest in front of me. "Check this out."

I scanned the document—an award for excellence in editorial from the Oregon Journalism Education Association.

"Is this for that thing you did about the spotted owl?"

"Yeah."

He'd written an op-ed piece for our school paper explaining why this year's hottest state issue was not as simple as both sides claimed.

"That was a killer article," Heather said. "Didn't I tell you words are your art?" She reached across the table to spin the award around, the chain on her wrist jangling. It wasn't the trendy kind they sold in the mall, but one that looked like she'd liberated it from somebody's dog. She nodded and grinned as she studied the certificate. "You did good, Racer Boy."

Why did Cody let her get away with calling him that? What did he see in her at all? The whole Goth thing seemed pointless and self-indulgent, moping around in black, whining about what a trial life was. Life was tough. So what? You did whatever it took to get by. There was no sense complaining about it.

Still, I couldn't write Heather off entirely. She didn't take crap from anyone, and she wasn't afraid to say what was on her mind. My life would be a lot simpler if I didn't care what people thought about me.

CHAPTER 15

Tuesday afternoon, Cody and I sat in the Clines' kitchen, going over the essay I'd written Sunday.

"You're rambling here," he said, tapping his pen on the paper. "These three sentences mean basically the same thing."

I fidgeted with my pencil. His critique sessions had pulled my English grade out of the gutter, but the process was like having someone scrutinize my soul and list all the flaws. "Yeah. I can never figure out how I want to say something the first time around."

"That's why it's called a rough draft." Cody slid the paper across the table. "Look those over, circle your strongest ideas, and put them together to make a good, solid topic sentence."

It wasn't the first time he'd given me that advice. And no doubt, it wouldn't be the last.

The front door creaked then clicked shut.

"Rhett?" I called. What was he doing home? He'd gone to Trevor's to conspire over how best to impress Emily and wasn't due back until 5:00.

"Nope, it's me," said Teri Sue.

Cody and I exchanged looks. Twice in one week? She stepped into the kitchen, carrying a textbook.

"What's up?" I asked.

She dropped *Introduction to Biology* on the table with a thud. "I need to borrow your brain, Jess."

"Take a number," Cody said, "she's borrowing mine at the moment." He leaned back in his chair, folding his hands behind his head so the lettering on his T-shirt pulled smooth across his chest. *National Sarcasm Society. Like we need your support.*

"This is urgent," said Teri Sue. "I've got finals coming up in two weeks."

"Why should Jess care? You've come around—what—like, *once* since school started? And now you think she's gonna fall all over herself to help you study?"

Teri Sue slumped into a chair. "Why's it any of your business?"

"Because she's my friend, the same way she's supposed to be yours."

"Enough!" I derailed Cody's sarcasm train with a glare. "I'm perfectly capable of giving Teri Sue hell on my own. In fact, I already have."

"Yup," she agreed, shooting him a "so-there" smirk.

"Whatever." He got up to pillage the fridge.

I bounced the eraser end of my pencil off the biology book. "So what do you need?"

"A ten minute crash course in the theory of evolution." She pulled the text toward her, opened it, and took out a midterm branded with a glaring red C minus. "Check it out."

I scanned the multiple-choice answers then the essay questions. "Looks like your biggest hang-up is with natural selection."

"Yup." Teri Sue drummed her fingers on the tabletop and shook her head. "But I thought I had that stuff cold—there's some kinda threat in the environment, and an animal evolves in order to survive. Like those moths that turned gray during the Industrial Revolution so birds wouldn't eat them."

"The moths didn't *turn* gray," I said, "the species evolved to *become* gray."

Teri Sue gave me a squint-eyed, sideways look. "Isn't that what I just said?"

"No. You're implying each individual changes to overcome the threat. What actually happens is the individuals at risk die out, leaving only the mutants to reproduce. Over time, the mutation is passed on until the majority of the species has the new trait."

"Even *I* know that." Cody sat back down with a massive turkey sandwich that must've wiped out the remainder of our leftovers.

"Maybe I should just tell my professor I'm a creationist," said Teri Sue.

"Won't work. Evolution isn't just about whether man shared a common ancestor with apes. It's about the small mutations that occur every day. Anyway, I'm sure he's heard that a million times."

We spent the next hour going over the questions Teri Sue had missed. I jotted down notes so she'd have something to study.

"Well," she said when we were finished, "guess I better get going."

I got up to turn on the oven. "Why don't you stay for dinner? Rhett will be home in a few minutes. He'd be glad to see you."

"He saw me last weekend."

"Teri Sue, I don't think you spent a total of twelve waking hours here."

She folded her test and slipped it inside the biology book. "I've got a date. But look, maybe we can get together this weekend. There's a party Saturday night. Why don't you and Cody pick me up, and we'll go together?"

A party. Right. That was exactly how I wanted to spend my time.

Now that Kasey was determined to get the Hawk done for the Roadster Show, things had changed between us. Her mind seemed too full of project details to spare room for idle conversation, and rather than giving me her sharply focused attention, she directed it at the car. I was limited to doing grunt work or watching and trying to learn as she sped through jobs, ticking them off her list.

I missed her mentorship, but my welding lessons with Race helped take my mind off the disappointment. We'd been getting together twice a week since the middle of November, and after five sessions, I could lay a basic bead that looked impressive and held together.

The Wednesday after Thanksgiving, Kasey didn't need my help, so when I finished with work, I went into the office to see if Race had time for a lesson. Green and red lights winked from the window and bookshelves, while Jimmy Buffett's *Ho, Ho, Ho and a Bottle of Rhum* played softly on the tape deck. Race sat slumped forward, his arms folded across the desktop and his eyes riveted on the computer screen.

"Kasey has things covered tonight. Would this be a good time for some practice?"

"What?" Race looked up, startled. "Uh . . . sure, kiddo." The chair squeaked as he leaned back and sighed, rubbing his forehead.

"If you're busy, we can do it another time."

"Nah, I'm about done here."

He followed me into the shop to help move our "project." After the first lesson, Race had hit upon the idea of welding the scrap pieces together to form one big structure. "That way you can practice welding in various positions," he'd said.

It had been a great idea. Flat welds were easy, but verticals took more skill, and overhead was something I didn't think I'd ever be good at.

The structure we'd built was getting big, and therefore heavy. Race had fabricated a wheeled base so it could be rolled into a corner, since Kasey, who called it "that monstrosity," didn't want it taking up valuable shop real estate.

We dragged it across the floor to the workbench.

"How 'bout we work with different weights of steel today?" Race said.

"Sure." I went out back to find some sheet metal and

brought it to the bench.

"The trick is heating the thick piece more than the thin one," Race explained. "Keep the gun aimed at the heavy stuff and quickly dart over to the light. If you hold it there too long, you'll burn right through." He demonstrated, making yet another perfect weld, then flipped up his helmet and massage his temples with the thumb and middle finger of one hand.

"You okay?"

"Yeah, sure. Just a headache." He motioned toward the workbench. "Give it a try."

"If you want to go home, we can do this some other time."

Race's headaches weren't as frequent as they used to be, but when they hit, they could sideline him for hours. And they always set Cody on edge. Fortunately, he was at Race's shop doing bodywork on the Galaxie.

"I'm fine," Race said, tipping down the visor. "Let's see what you've got."

I pulled on my gloves and picked up the welding gun. When I looped onto the sheet metal, it glowed like magma. Slag dripped away, leaving a gaping hole. "Arrrrr!"

"Happened to me, too, at first," Race assured me. "This is one of the hardest things to master."

"Worse than overhead welding?"

He laughed. "Just wait until I make you weld different thicknesses overhead."

I worked for another half hour, with Race's comments coming less and less frequently. When I stopped for a break, he pulled off his helmet and set it on the workbench.

"Y'know, kiddo, I think I'm gonna sit down for a while. Keep practicing. You're starting to get the hang of it." He'd gone pale, the muscles in his jaw as hard as the steel we were working with. I didn't even want to think about what Cody would say if he found out I'd let this lesson continue.

"Maybe we should call it quits."

"There's no reason for you to pack it in early. Just practice until you get tired, then come get me to take a look."

"But—"

"Jess, if you keep fussing, you're gonna sound like Cody."

"Okay," I said, tilting my helmet forward.

I kept at it for another hour, letting myself get lost in the work. Over the past two weeks, I'd learned that the more attention I paid to the sight, feel, and sound of the process, the better my welds became. As an added benefit, the deep level of concentration temporarily wiped out my troubles. Lydia was only the beginning. Almost as annoying was the way everyone felt they had to protect me: Dad, Mark, and Kasey forming a defensive line, Cody bawling out Teri Sue. The only people who hadn't interfered were Rhett and Race. Maybe they understood it was best to accept your damage and move on.

By 7:30, I'd made some improvements but still burned through at least once on each weld. I wouldn't overcome that tonight, and I had to get home to re-write my essay, so I decided to wrap it up.

When I went to the office, I found Race sprawled on the couch, Christmas lights providing the only illumination. He glanced at me, pulled a hand down the length of his face, and drew a deep breath.

The Little Drummer Boy caroled from the tape deck.

"This is one of my favorites," I said, wanting to give Race an excuse to lie there a few more minutes. "I like how the boy doesn't have a fancy gift, so he gives the thing that makes him who he is."

"And it's exactly right."

"Yeah."

We shared a smile as Race pushed himself into a sitting position, still looking shaky and washed out.

"It's good to see I'm not the only one who appreciates Christmas," he said.

"It was my favorite time of year before my dad left." I rested my butt against the front of the desk. The faint holiday glow, along with Race's intuition about my comment, somehow made me feel confessional. "Back then, Lydia was a real mom. We baked cookies every year. Not just the easy ones, but fancy stuff, like frosted gingerbread men and those candy canes you have to braid together."

Race's eyes caught mine, full of that deep knowing I saw so often in Cody's. "It's gotta be tough, having everyone hassle you about her."

The words sent a bolt of lightning straight through my heart. "People don't understand," I said, looking away. "But then I don't, either. I should hate her."

"Nah, nobody should hate anyone."

My fingers curled around the edge of the desk, gripping tight. "I wish everyone would stop running interference for me. It's not like I can't take care of myself."

"Well, that's an area where I happen to have a little experience." Race gave a slight, sad shake of his head. "Cody's been slaying dragons for me ever since the wreck. And if Kasey'd had her way, I never would've gotten back in a race car."

"She didn't want you to drive again?" She was so solidly in his corner I could hardly believe that.

"Not at first. That was one of the dragons Cody had to slay." Race managed a tired grin. "The thing is, Jess, you can't stop people from worrying. You've just gotta grit your teeth and muddle through."

"It's not only the worrying. Everyone's trying to make me into someone I'm not. Dad and Kasey keep talking about how I need to be a regular kid. That isn't going to happen."

"Yup." Race nodded. "I know exactly what you mean. Look at Cody. He's more worried about what I can do with a pencil than I am."

"Doesn't it drive you crazy?" Exasperation honed my words

to an edge.

Race sighed. "What drives me crazy is how much it hurts him that I'm not who I used to be."

The regret that slipped over his face made me instantly sorry. "He wants to erase what happened," I said.

"Yeah. And the ironic thing is, I don't."

Even though I knew Race had made peace with his challenges, the statement surprised me. The headaches, the memory gaps, the loss of talent. Who wouldn't want to escape all that? "You mean if you could have a do-over, you wouldn't change things?"

Race sat forward on the couch, running a hand through his hair. "Does that seem crazy? I guess I see what I've lost as a trade off. Before the wreck, Kasey kept me at arm's length and Cody was so full of rage he lashed out at anyone who looked at him funny. You might say slaying my dragons helped him put a leash on his own. So . . . no, I wouldn't take the do-over."

I blinked at him for several long seconds, too amazed to speak. Finally, I nodded. "Me either. With my mom, I mean. Otherwise, I wouldn't have you guys." I gave him a cautious half-smile. "I just wish people could see I'm okay with things as they are. Being normal doesn't matter."

Race grinned as he used the arm of the couch to lever himself to his feet. "Kiddo, you *are* normal. Your norm is just different than it used to be. Same as mine."

CHAPTER 14

The Thursday after Thanksgiving, Lydia called. I should've hung up immediately. Any rational person would've. And yet I didn't.

As I stood in the hallway, bombarded by apologies, a whirlwind of conflicting emotions raged inside me. Lydia had shamed me worse than I'd ever been shamed in my life. I couldn't let her off the hook for that. But no matter how much she'd hurt, failed, and embarrassed me in the past eight years, she was still the mom who'd taught me how to bake Christmas cookies. Whether or not I talked to her was *my* decision. Not Dad's or Kasey's or Mark's.

I glanced guiltily at Rhett's bedroom door. He was busy with another of his projects—a model Camaro he was painting to look like Teri Sue's race car for her Christmas present. But even if he overheard, he wouldn't blame me for my weakness.

Damn. I picked up the phone and took it to my room. Lydia's voice continued to wail in my ear, sober and properly mortified. When the torrent of "I'm sorrys" finally tapered off, I still hadn't said a word.

"Jess? Are you there?"

I sank down on the bed beside Newt, my fingers automatically reaching for the soft fur under his chin. "Yeah, I'm here."

"I'm not going to ask you to forgive me. I know I don't deserve it."

No doubt about that. So why was I even letting her talk to me?

"Sweetie, please. Say something."

"Why? To let you off the hook?" I fell back against my pillow, staring at the ceiling, where a spider lay in wait for its next meal. "You humiliated me, Lydia. In front of my friends. In front of the people I work for and live with. People I have to face every day."

A whimper escaped her. "I-I know. And I don't blame you for hating me. I shouldn't have come without calling."

What? My confliction vaporized in a heartbeat. Why was I wasting time on her? "You shouldn't have shown up drunk! You're an alcoholic, Lydia. That's why you're an embarrassment. That's why I don't want you around the people I care about."

A muffled sob shook her voice. "You're right." The whimpers that followed obscured her words, and my fist clenched. Above, the spider sat patiently. It had all day.

At last, Lydia pulled herself together enough to speak coherently. "Sweetie . . . when I woke up Friday morning and . . . and realized what I'd done, I knew I'd blown my only chance. So I called AA. I've gone to meetings every day this week, and I haven't touched a drop. I'm going to change, Jess. This time, I'm going to make it work."

Right. Just like she did last summer. The smart part of me, the part that aced chemistry and calculus, said this was one more wishful lie. But the foolish part only saw my mother's hands guiding my three-year-old fingers to frost a gingerbread man. And that part couldn't let go of the maybe.

I drew air deep into my lungs, calling up the strength to say what needed to be said. "I'm glad you're getting help, Lydia. But you shouldn't call back."

She sniffled. "I understand. . . . You need time. But I'm going to prove it to you, sweetie. I'm done with being an embarrassment."

"I haven't been to a party in almost a year," Cody said as he turned left onto 17th.

Teri Sue hung over the back of the Galaxie's seat, her red-gold hair expertly styled and her makeup applied with the precision I reserved for assembling engines. "Heck, I've been to eight in the past month," she said.

What a surprise.

I'd *never* been to a party, the combination of alcohol and rowdy strangers being my idea of hell on earth. But I figured the only way I was going to get a chance to spend time with Teri Sue was on her terms.

Cody cruised past the party house and through the surrounding neighborhood several times before finding a parking spot three blocks away. As we started up the sidewalk, I huddled in my flannel-lined jacket, tucking my hands into the sleeves. We were having an early cold, dry spell—uncommon for our waterlogged half of the state—and if you asked me, freezing weather without snow was an utter waste.

Teri Sue threw an arm around my shoulders, the scent of her perfume a familiar comfort. "Are you ready for some fun, girl? I'm glad you came. It's about time you did something frivolous."

"Frivolous?" Cody asked. "Oooh, I'm impressed. Is that a new vocabulary word, Teri Sue?"

She took a swipe at him, but he easily darted out of reach.

The music became audible a block and a half away. Some heavy metal group I couldn't have named if faced with a firing squad. Cody's head bobbed to the beat as we got closer. Unlike me, he possessed a mental encyclopedia of current musical hits.

"This is it," said Teri Sue, stopping in front of a rundown ranch house. As if the thump of bass and the barefoot, shirtless guy puking on the front lawn weren't enough of an indication.

The volume jumped to an uncomfortable level as we stepped through the door. Inside, the house was a gloom of darkness broken only by the light from a lava lamp and three strings of clear Christmas bulbs. Cigarette smoke hung hazy in the air, and over the music, I heard that garbled sort of throb that occurs when a lot of people talk, but you can't make out individual voices. I glanced at Cody, feeling as though I'd brought a Street Stock to the Southern 500. Maybe he'd take me home. But he was facing the other direction oblivious to my efforts to drill through him with my gaze.

"C'mon," said Teri Sue, "we'll find someplace for you to toss your coat." She'd left her own in the car.

"I think I'll keep it," I said. If I let go of it, I might never see it again.

Teri Sue dragged me through the mob in the living room. "Let's get a drink." She plowed her way to the kitchen, where the music seemed marginally quieter, but voices made up the difference. College kids crowded the bright room, mixing drinks, jamming chips and Cheetos into their mouths, and filling blue plastic cups from a metal cylinder on the table, which I assumed must be a keg. Behind it, two guys arm-wrestled, capsizing a cup of beer when one slammed the other's hand to the tabletop.

"Hey, Dave," said Teri Sue, nodding at the victor as she stepped into the keg line. "These are my racing buddies, Jess and Cody. Y'all, meet Dave. He's in my bio class. This is his place."

"Well, mine and about forty roommates'," Dave clarified.

"I hope you've got a better grip on that whole natural selection thing than Teri Sue," Cody said.

Dave laughed. "Everybody's got a better grip on natural selection than Teri Sue. But at least our girl knows how to party."

My stomach tensed as Teri Sue tipped an imaginary hat at him. When she offered me the cup she'd just filled, I shook my head. "I'll have a Coke or something."

"The stuff for lightweights is in the fridge," Dave said as Teri Sue took a long pull from the cup I'd refused. I was a little worried the comment might persuade Cody to pour himself a beer, but instead, he followed me to the refrigerator.

For the next half-hour, I shadowed Teri Sue, watching her get progressively more sloshed as she mingled and introduced me to her friends. Cody stuck with us, filling in with a joke whenever I failed to spike a comment someone lobbed across my net of silence. This was stupid. It was torture. Why had I agreed to come?

A girl whose beauty depreciated my looks to the level just above "undead" tucked her arm around Teri Sue's waist. "You absolutely have to see the dress Jennifer's wearing," she whisper-shouted in her ear. "It's hideous!"

"I'll be right back, y'all," said Teri Sue.

Half an hour later, she still hadn't returned. If Cody hadn't been there to navigate the sea of wasted college students, I'd have taken up hiding under the couch.

"Hey." He bumped my shoulder. "Will you be okay a sec? I need another Coke."

He was abandoning me?

"I'll be right back," he said, apparently reading my panic. "You want anything?"

I shook my head.

"Relax. You'll be fine."

Take me with you, pleaded the coward inside me. But my calmer self reasoned he'd only be a few yards away, and hadn't I already proved myself enough of a social reject?

As Cody disappeared into the swarm of people, I forced myself to smile so I'd look like I was having a good time. When I realized no one cared, I gave it up. Maybe I could just stand here until Cody came back and everyone would ignore me. I glanced at my watch and realized I hadn't checked it when he left. At most, a minute had passed. I'd give him five. That should allow plenty of time to grab a drink and say hello to whoever was standing around the table. I would've given him three, but knowing Cody, he'd stop to refuel on Doritos and Lit'l Smokies.

Sweltering in my jacket, I shifted my weight from one leg to the other. Music throbbed around me until I was sure my heart had changed its rhythm to keep up with the beat. Why did everyone within five years of my age think loud equaled good? If I had to damage my hearing, I'd much rather it be hanging over a fender, tuning a race engine. At least then I'd be having fun.

A couple of guys, who'd been arguing about whether the Ducks could win the Freedom Bowl, started roughhousing. I backed away, my legs screaming to sit down. There was a tiny wedge of space on the couch, but by the time I wound my way to the spot, someone else had taken it. Wonderful. Maybe I should go to the kitchen and find Cody. He'd been gone—I checked my watch—eight-and-a-half minutes now.

I squeezed past a guy in a Ducks football jersey, who was sitting on a bench near the stereo. He reached up and caught the sleeve of my jacket.

"Hey, babe, where you goin' in such a hurry?"

"Um, excuse me," I said, pulling away.

"Heyyyyy, don't look at me like that. I won't bite."

My heart revved to outpace the tempo of the music. "I've got to find my friend."

"Nah, siddown!" He gave the kid beside him a shove, toppled him to the floor, and patted the vacated bench.

"She looks a little young for you, Jay," the guy said as he hefted himself to his feet.

"I-I'm in high school." Maybe that would throw a scare into him.

Jay leered. "That's okay, I don't mind breaking 'em in young." He grabbed my elbow and drew me close, his other hand groping for my chest.

My reaction was so spontaneous, it surprised even me. Suddenly, Jay was on the ground, clutching himself and groaning. I stared down at him, unable to recall the karate moves I'd used by instinct.

Cody was there a second later, turning me around to face him, his expression a daze of worry and admiration. "You okay?"

"Yeah." Had I just leveled a football player?

Cody nudged the writhing mass of Jay with his toe. "Consider yourself lucky Jess took you out before I could get to you." His fingers twined around mine, and he pulled me toward the kitchen.

I hung back. "Cody, I want to go home."

"No problem. I just need to find Teri Sue."

He led me through the house, his hand tight around mine, until we tracked her down, buzzed, but not sloppy drunk, in the garage.

"We're ready to take off," Cody said. "How about you?"

"I'm gonna stay, but I can find a ride." She turned back to the people she'd been talking to, as if we were acquaintances, rather than the friends she'd invited.

Outside, the calm of the night enfolded me in a cool embrace, but my ears continued to buzz, and I was redlining on adrenalin.

"I'm sorry, Jess," Cody said. "I shouldn't have left you by yourself."

"It's not your fault. I was stupid to come. I don't know why I didn't tell Teri Sue to forget it. I hate being around drinking." I crunched violently through the last of the fallen leaves, staring down at the sidewalk.

"Yeah, I guess you would," Cody said. In my jittery fog, I hardly heard him.

"I thought I'd get to hang out with Teri Sue. Shows how ignorant I am. As if you could have a normal conversation with someone in a zoo like that. I'm such a moron. I'll bet I'm the only teenager in America who doesn't know how to party."

"Nah, there's probably a few Amish who'd be just as lost."

The joke bounced off my bubble of raw current, leaving the smallest crack. I stopped and turned to stare at Cody. "I just took out a football player."

"Yeah," he said, grinning, "you did." His arms circled me, and his kiss soothed away the last of my fluster.

"Don't worry, Jess," he said softly. "You've still got the rest of us."

An anthill of emotion swarmed inside me Sunday afternoon as I tinkered with the Camaro. Why was I even bothering with Teri Sue's stupid car? Okay, so she'd been distracted by the newness of college. I could overlook that *and* her running off with friends during the holiday weekend. But how could she ditch me at a party? She knew I had all the social skills of a day-old donut.

"What's wrong?" Rhett asked when I slammed a handful of tools down on the workbench.

"Huh?" I looked his way, startled out of my stewing. "Uh . . . nothing." Cody and I had kept quiet about the party, partly because I didn't want Rhett to feel worse about his sister's neglect, and partly because we knew it wouldn't go over well with Race, Kasey, and Mark.

"But . . ." Rhett didn't finish his thought, probably assuming my mood had something to do with the mother I didn't want anyone to mention again.

That was fine. He could keep on thinking it.

Tuesday afternoon, Rhett sat across from me at the kitchen table, doodling little volcanoes around the edge of his science project notes.

"Hey, Jess?"

"Yeah?"

"Do you reckon Cody and Teri Sue were right about Emily?"

I glanced up from my psychology textbook. I might've been steering Rhett wrong, but I didn't particularly want to admit it. "Maybe. They seem to be more on top of that sort of thing than I am. Why? Is she still stealing your brownies?"

"No." Rhett stared down at his notes. "She's sort of being

nice to me now. I guess on account of how I've been smiling at her, like Cody told me."

"So what's the problem?"

Rhett's shoulders bunched up in a shrug.

"You must have some reason for asking."

His pencil moved across his paper, darkening the centers of the o's. "Well . . . what if I tell her I like her and she laughs at me? She's real pretty. She could have any guy in sixth grade."

"So why wouldn't she pick you? You're not half-bad looking yourself, you know. Plus you're smart and funny and interesting."

Rhett scowled at his notebook. "But I've got this stupid brace."

He hardly ever mentioned it, and up until now, I hadn't even known it bothered him. "Rhett, any girl worth your time isn't going to care about that."

"How do you know?" His chin jutted up and his eyes bored into me. "Kids get teased all the time because they're different. Why would a girl like Emily want a cripple for a boyfriend?"

My breath caught in my throat, the brutality of his question hitting me like a slap. Was that how Rhett saw himself?

"You're *not* a cripple. That's a terrible word to use. Just because someone can't do things the way other people can doesn't mean they're not as good as everyone else. Anyway, you can do just about anything you put your mind to."

"Except walk without a brace." Bitterness dripped from his words.

"Rhett, what's this all about? Is somebody bullying you?"

He shook his head, attention riveted once more on the pencil in his hand.

Oh man. What was I supposed to say? I didn't have any more experience with this sort of thing than I did with flirting. "Maybe you should talk to Race. Cody says he had a hard time, too, right after he got hurt. He thought he wasn't good enough for Kasey."

Rhett looked up in surprise. "Race thought that? But he's, like, the coolest guy ever."

"Some people think you are, too."

"Yeah, right." He rolled his eyes. "Anyway, Race's problems don't show."

"Maybe not, but they cause him more trouble than that brace causes you. And Kasey doesn't care one bit. When you love a person, things like that don't matter. You don't see them anymore. If you want to know the truth, most of the time I forget you even have that brace."

Rhett sank back in his chair, the scowl slowly melting from his face. "Really?"

"Uh huh."

"And you seriously think I'm the coolest guy ever?"

I smiled. "Well, you might have to share that title with Cody and Race."

Thursday after school, Cody showed up to study, bearing two medium Track Town pizzas. One for Rhett and me, and the other for himself.

"I figured we could get more work done if you didn't have to cook," he said.

"Is that why you brought this?" I tapped the small box from Premier Video that sat on top of the pizzas.

"Well, we might have to take a *teensy* study break." Cody balanced the boxes on one arm while holding the index finger and thumb of his other hand a millimeter apart.

"Do I smell pepperoni?" Rhett thundered down the stairs in stockinged feet, Newt riding in his arms with both paws hugging his left shoulder.

"I really do have to study tonight," I said. "I only got a 'B-' on that last essay."

"That's because you were busy going ninja on a football

player." Rhett passed Newt off to me so he could launch a barrage of punches at the La-Z-boy. He'd been following me around like a superhero sidekick since he'd overheard Cody talking about what happened at the party.

"Get your backpack, Rhett. You could stand to brush up a little on your math. And Cody, go ahead and put those pizzas in the kitchen."

"Yes, teacher," he said, trading a smirk with Rhett.

We ate and studied until 7:00, at which point Cody announced school was over. While he led Rhett into the living room to start the video, I cleaned up napkins and pizza crusts. I was wiping down the table when the phone rang. Tossing the sponge toward the sink, I made a grab for the receiver. "Hello?"

"Hi, sweetie."

Oh man. Not again. My eyes darted to the doorway where I could see the back of Rhett's shirt as he leaned forward in the La-Z-boy. The opening score of *Total Recall* sounded from the TV.

"I told you to stop calling. You made an agreement with Dad." He'd admitted it was a bluff, that the cops wouldn't trouble themselves over a months-old child neglect case, but she didn't know that.

"He doesn't have to find out."

"He's got Kasey and Mark keeping an eye on me."

"I thought Mark worked Thursday nights."

"He does, but Rhett's a smart kid. He'll know who I'm talking to. And he doesn't lie to his daddy." With the phone clamped between my shoulder and ear, I yanked open a drawer and pulled out a roll of foil for the leftover pizza.

"Jess, I'm sorry, but I've got to talk to you. It's one of the things I'm supposed to do in AA. Make a list of everyone I've hurt and tell them I'm sorry."

I'd read the 12 steps, and I knew there were plenty that came before that one. Soul-searching steps you couldn't breeze through in a few days if they were to mean anything.

"Is Dad on your list?"

Lydia went silent.

"Are you going to apologize to him anytime soon? Like maybe for lying about how he was taking drugs?"

She sighed. "I don't think I'm ready for that."

"Then maybe you need to go back to the earlier steps and concentrate on them a little harder." I unrolled a swatch of foil and tore it free.

Lydia let out another martyred breath. "I know you don't trust me. But I really am going to make this work. One of my friends found a low-cost counseling program for me. She thought it might be easier to stop drinking if I talked to someone about the problems that made me start."

Huh. That idea had some potential. The depression that had plagued Lydia since Dad left had led to lost jobs, ruined friendships, and an eviction from our house near the University. She'd make a little progress when things were going her way, then the second something went wrong, she'd slip back into a self-destructive funk. Maybe counseling would break the cycle.

"I hope it helps," I said.

"It will, sweetie."

For a moment, I hesitated, wondering what it would be like if the couple of weeks of sobriety she'd managed last summer could stretch out for months or years. *No.* I wasn't falling back into that trap. "Look, Lydia," I said. "I've gotta go." Without giving her a chance to protest, I hung up.

As I snatched the foil off the counter and turned around to wrap the pizza, I nearly jumped into my next lifetime.

Cody stood right behind me in the entry to the kitchen.

CHAPTER 16

"You need to tell your dad, Jess," Cody said for the fourth time as his tray hit the table Friday at lunch. I'd hoped my refusal to discuss the matter last night and this morning would've dissuaded him, but I should've known better.

My fingers tightened around my fork, and I gave him a steely look. "I can take care of this myself. She knows I don't want to talk to her. She won't call back."

"That's not how it sounded last night."

Heather pulled out the chair beside Cody and sat down. "What's up, kids?"

I'd said no more than a dozen words to her in my life, but I couldn't help blurting out my frustration. "My alcoholic mother, whom I've been forbidden to talk to by my dad, called last night. Cody overheard, and now he thinks it's his duty to protect me from her evil wiles."

Cody snorted, savaging his roast beef sandwich and speaking around it. "Yeah, that's exactly how it is. Jess's mom shows up wasted at Thanksgiving and embarrasses the hell out of her, and when I try to help, I'm the bad guy."

Heather's heavily shadowed eyes darted back and forth between us, gleaming with something suspiciously like amusement.

"It's none of your business," I told Cody as I ripped open my milk.

"You shouldn't have to put up with her bothering you."

"I don't want to talk about it."

"Why not? After what she did, I should think you'd be glad to get rid of her."

Heather smacked her hand on the table, gloss-black fingernails stark against the white Formica. "Jess is right," she said, skewering Cody with her don't-give-me-any-crap look. "This is none of your business."

"I'm just trying to help!"

"Yeah, Jess is some poor defenseless waif who can't take care of herself." She shot me a glance that somehow combined eye-rolling with respect. For the first time, I felt a flicker of affection for her.

"It's not like that!" Cody protested, forgotten sandwich clutched in one hand. "It's just—"

"Look, Racer Boy, did your girlfriend knock a college football player's nads up into his throat the other night, or did she not?"

Cody gawked at her and then me, finally rendered speechless. After a long and awkward silence, he stuffed his stymied mouth full of roast beef.

I gave Heather only the slightest nod, but inside I was shouting hallelujahs.

Cody didn't bring up the subject for the rest of the day, but he also didn't say much of anything else. After work, I went home alone, something I rarely did on Friday nights. I fixed myself a sandwich and took it to the living room, where Mark was watching one of his black and white movies. Newt, detecting tuna, jumped into my lap, nose aquiver.

"Where's your other half?" Mark asked, not glancing away from the screen. *To Kill a Mockingbird.* I recognized Scout and Atticus from when we'd watched it in ninth grade English.

I shrugged as I gently pushed Newt away from my sandwich. "I think he's annoyed with me."

"Oh?"

No wonder he was surprised. Only once had Cody allowed anything to come between us.

"Yeah," I said. "He feels like he has to butt into the situation with my mother, just like everyone else." I was careful to leave the statement vague. I didn't need Mark knowing about her recent calls.

"Well, if you could stand some commentary on the subject, I think everyone's taking this thing a little too far."

"Really?"

Mark pulled his attention away from the TV. "I promised your daddy I'd keep an eye out concerning your mama, but I don't agree that it's necessary. You're the one who's lived with her for the past eight years. You understand the situation better than any of us. Besides, she's your mama. You can't be expected to voluntarily sever that tie, no matter how poorly she might've behaved."

"I thought you were in the 'Jess-deserves-a-normal-life' camp."

"I suppose I am. But I also recognize that your norm isn't the same as other people's."

Whoa. *Deja vu.* "Have you and Race been talking? That sounds like what he said."

"He'd have some insight on that, wouldn't he?" Mark tapped the remote, shutting off the TV. "I enjoyed the conversation I had with him on Thanksgiving. He's an intuitive Taoist."

"You mean because he's so 'go with the flow?'" I fed Newt a bit of tuna, smiling as his tongue darted eagerly over his nose and whiskers in search of anything he might've missed.

"Exactly." Mark nodded. "By going with the flow, he emulates the principles of *P'u*—the Uncarved Block—and *wei wu wei*—doing without doing. The idea is that things are most powerful in their natural state. By being attuned to that, you accomplish more than by forcing things that don't come naturally. Take water, for example. It's weak and formless, and yet it can carve a valley through stone."

My brain struggled for a finger-hold in the mountain Mark had thrust in front of me. "And here I thought Race was just an easy-going guy."

"Being easy-going is his nature. Because he's in tune with his deepest self, life goes more smoothly for him."

True. When I compared Cody's struggle to Race's acceptance, it was clear who had the easiest time of it.

"So you think I can learn something from trying to be like him?"

"No." Mark shook his head. "I think you'll be happiest being yourself."

"Then how come you keep bugging me about how I like to help out around here? Maybe that's my true nature."

Smiling, Mark leaned back in his chair. "There's something to be said for balance. You are who you are in part because of your experience. But circumstances have changed, Jess. You don't have to take charge anymore. I'm not suggesting you should try to become as mellow as Race or myself—that's not your nature. But you might want to take some time to consider your motivations. Why do you like staying busy? Is it because you enjoy it, or because you feel something terrible would happen if you stopped? Do some soul searching. Hang on to whatever it is that works for you, but don't be afraid to explore other aspects of who you might be."

I looked down at Newt, who'd begun doing happy feet on the front of my sweatshirt. I could see what Mark was saying. Mostly, I did the things I did because I enjoyed them, but sometimes I felt compelled by the very thing he'd described— the feeling that my whole world would fall apart if I lost control for even a minute. "Maybe you should be teaching philosophy instead of history," I suggested.

"As a matter of fact, I sometimes do." Mark motioned toward Newt, whose paws were busily kneading. "He looks so serious when he does that. Like he's mending the universe. Knitting it back together with his paws."

I glanced down at the kitten on my chest. His eyes were

half-closed in feline bliss, and he'd drooled a wet spot on my shirt.

"That's an awfully big responsibility for such a little kitty."

CHAPTER 17

The next morning, I went with Mark and Rhett to pick out a Christmas tree. Mark had called the dorm several days before, leaving a message for Teri Sue to join us, but she hadn't responded. As we entered the lot, Rhett dragged his feet and complained it wasn't right to buy a tree without her.

"Douglas fir, grand fir, or noble?" Mark asked, putting an arm around Rhett's shoulders and directing him toward the rows of fragrant evergreens leaning against two-by-four support racks.

"Don't they have any Frasers?"

"Nope." I tipped up the collar of my denim jacket to ward off the rain. "You're in Doug fir country now."

"I like the nobles." Rhett gravitated straight for a 9-footer, the buzz of the tree lot coaxing him out of his gloom.

"I think that one's a little too big for the house," suggested his father.

"That's what you said last Christmas, and we went home with a tree that was shorter than I am."

Mark laughed. "Not hardly."

"Anyway, we've got a taller ceiling this year."

"True enough. How about you, Jess?" He turned to pull me into the conversation with a smile. "What kind do you like?"

"I'm okay with whatever you guys want." Lydia and I had always made do with a puny little three-foot Douglas fir, the cheapest available. And we waited until a few days before Christmas because that's when the man at the tree lot knocked prices down in a desperate attempt to unload them.

Rhett and Mark disputed the virtues of several trees before settling on a 7-foot noble, which we tied to the top of the Civic.

Back home, Mark and I hauled boxes of decorations down

from the attic while Rhett got silly, dancing lopsidedly around the living room with Newt in his arms as he crooned *The Twelve Days of Christmas*. He'd been in a crazy mood since Emily's friend Kirsten had told his friend Trevor that Emily thought Rhett was the cutest boy in sixth grade.

"I don't think the cat is enjoying that," Mark said.

"Aw, Newt *loves* to dance."

Actually, he seemed perfectly happy, eyelids heavy with contentment as he gripped Rhett's left shoulder. It was always left shoulders with Newt. If you tried to scoop him up to the other side, he'd scramble to rearrange himself.

Rhett waltzed backward, straight into the tree, and sent it swaying.

"Enough!" Mark said.

"Sorry." Rhett deposited Newt on the couch. "Can I put the lights on this time?"

Mark raised an eyebrow. "You want to take away my favorite job?"

"I'll bet Jess got to help with the lights when she was my age."

Most years, I'd decorated the whole tree because by the time we got it set up, Lydia was on her third glass of eggnog and could hardly see straight.

"You can't take away your dad's favorite job," I said, dodging the issue.

Rhett sighed as if he'd been given three weeks of KP and resigned himself to unpacking decorations. The perfumed scent of artificial pine and cinnamon wafted up out of the boxes. "Here's one I made in kindergarten," he said, pulling out a Styrofoam ball coated in red glitter. "And Teri Sue did this one in second grade." He held up a star constructed from gold-painted Popsicle sticks. "She should be here. She always helps us put up the tree."

Not much I could say to that. I'd given up making excuses

for her. If she wanted to party her way into alienating her family and all her old friends, that was her business.

I'd been tempted a couple of times to talk to Mark about the drinking, but I knew it would destroy whatever tenuous friendship Teri Sue and I still had. And even though I'd witnessed some troubling things, there were other times she'd passed up opportunities to get wasted. The wine at Thanksgiving, for example, or the night of the party, when she'd had sense enough to stop drinking after a few beers. Cody seemed to think her partying was nothing unusual for a college student. When I compared it to Lydia's behavior, I suspected he was right. But that didn't mean I wanted it in my life.

Rhett continued to unpack the box, placing each item on the coffee table until he came to a package of delicate glass angels. "These were Mama's favorite," he said, taking one out and stroking the wings.

My annoyance splintered into sadness. Poor kid. At his age, Christmas should be happy.

"Maybe you should be counting your treasures instead of your troubles." Mark reached behind the tree to wind lights around the back. "Remember, this year we have Jess."

Rhett sighed and grabbed a strand of bead garland. "Yeah, okay." As the string rattled over a flap of cardboard, Newt flashed across the room to attack the trailing end. "No!" Rhett hollered, hoisting it above his head. The kitten scampered away, darting up the Christmas tree. A few seconds later, his tiny tabby face peered between the branches.

"I'll get him," Rhett said.

"No." I caught his sleeve. "Let him do it himself. You'll mess up your dad's lights if you try to pull him out."

Rhett's lips bunched skeptically, but after a few minutes, Newt backed down the trunk.

I helped unpack ornaments and set up the nativity scene then sat back and watched Mark and Rhett decorate the tree.

Somehow, it didn't seem right to be putting up someone else's family memories.

When I'd moved out of our apartment, I'd been limited to keeping only what would fit in my Pinto. That meant leaving most of our Christmas things behind. All I'd saved was a small box of special ornaments wrapped in newspaper. Maybe I could string them up in my bedroom windows.

"Why don't you give us a hand here, Jess?" Mark asked.

"That's okay. I think I'll go warm up some of that apple cider you brought home yesterday. You guys want a sandwich? It's almost lunchtime."

"Sounds good," Mark said.

I headed for the kitchen, trying to shake my sudden melancholy. What did I have to be bummed about? The house smelled of wood smoke and evergreen, The Chipmunks squeaked from the stereo, and even Rhett, who had good reason to be sad, had perked up. Compared to all those dismal Christmases I'd spent with Lydia, things were great.

When I returned to the living room with sandwiches and mugs of freshly pressed cider, Mark and Rhett had almost finished with the tree.

"This one's bigger than what we're used to," Mark said. "I don't suppose you managed to save any of your family ornaments?"

"Uh . . . yeah. I've got a few." The words wobbled a little as they fought their way around the narrowing in my throat.

I set the tray on the coffee table and went upstairs to get them.

That afternoon I sat at my desk, staring out the window and contemplating my psychology homework. Newt lay across my notebook, providing as good an excuse as any to put off answering the questions. When I stroked the underside of his chin, he sighed and stretched, kitten toes flexing.

Headlights flashed through the glass. I looked out to see Cody's Galaxy snaking up the driveway. He pulled alongside the Civic. No reason to get up. Mark would let him in and tell him where I was. I rolled my pencil back and forth across the desktop as I heard the knock, the exchange of pleasantries, and the footsteps on the staircase. A few seconds later, Cody rapped at the doorframe.

"Hey," I said, turning in my chair. Though the sky was just beginning to take on the bluish hue of evening, the room behind me lay in shadows.

"You always do your homework in the dark?" His tone was easy, as if our argument the day before had never happened.

"Only when I'm trying to avoid it."

"Looks like Newt's helping with that."

"Yeah, he's good that way."

Cody parked himself on my bed, slouching forward so his arms rested on his knees and his dark hair hung in his eyes. He studied the carpet as if the answers to next week's trig quiz lay imbedded in the fibers. After a long silence, he spoke. "I'm sorry for blowing you off yesterday." He fidgeted, fingers splaying and pressing together at the tips. "I've been thinking about what Heather said. I was out of line."

True, but it would be rude to rub it in. And I couldn't tell him it was okay, because it wasn't.

"I know you can take care of yourself," he continued, glancing my way. "I just don't want you to end up like me. I spent my whole life hoping my mom would start caring about somebody other than herself. I kept giving her chances, but no matter how many times she blew it, I couldn't get it through my head that she wasn't gonna change. Finally, Race told me something that sunk in. He said when you've got messed up relatives, sometimes the best thing you can do is walk away."

I cut him a look. "Did he say you *had to* walk away?"

"Of course not. Race wouldn't do that."

"Then it's not the same."

Cody's eyes slunk off to focus on his hands again. "I know. I shouldn't have hassled you. I'm just worried she'll hurt you again."

I stroked the fur between Newt's ears, firing up his motor. "She probably will, but that's my problem. Everyone wants me to tell her to get lost, and maybe it's what I want, too. But it has to be my decision. When people try to force the issue, it makes things more confusing."

"I'm sorry, Jess."

His deep brown eyes fixed on me again, full of apology.

I didn't give in to them. "I'm not going to tell my dad. And I don't want you to, either. He'll just make a big deal out of nothing. Either Lydia will get her act together, which is highly doubtful, or she'll decide I'm too much trouble and get on with her life. Whichever happens, it's not going to kill me."

Cody nodded. "Okay."

"Okay, what?"

"Okay, I won't say anything." He got up and crossed the room to pull me into a hug.

Kasey finished the Hawk bodywork and exhaust system by the end of the first week of December then began the wiring. She'd used a worn out engine to dummy up the engine compartment while the real one was being machined. On Tuesday, the day she was supposed to get the original back, Metzger's called to say it wouldn't be ready for at least another two weeks.

The next day, Kasey's work on the Hawk involved jobs she had to do herself, which meant another welding lesson for me.

"You're good enough now that you can handle the non-structural stuff on the Camaro," Race said. "But I want you to hold off on anything that has to do with safety, okay?"

I agreed as we wheeled our welding structure to the workbench. Though I wouldn't have admitted it, the idea of working

136

on anything that important intimidated me.

Kasey ducked around us on her way to the Hawk. "That thing gets to be more of a monstrosity every week."

It stood six feet tall, now, and included a variety of discarded car parts.

"It's not a monstrosity," said Race. "It's art." He'd placed many of the pieces himself while demonstrating different techniques, so the structure had a certain balance.

Cody studied it, his lips puckered in thought. "It kind of looks like one of those metal sculptures you see in the park."

"It's an open invitation for a tetanus shot," said Kasey, taunting Race with a smile.

The shop's door groaned on its hinges. "Oh, good, you're still here. I was afraid I'd have to run by the house." Kasey's mom, Peggy, bustled toward us. With her plump figure, cheerful smile, and endless supply of sweatshirts adorned with frolicking kittens, she was the antithesis of Race's mom. Every time she visited, she brought baked goods. Cody was considering adopting her as a third grandma.

She eyed the welding project. "Is that some sort of metal sculpture?"

Race flashed Kasey a triumphant grin, which she dodged.

"Mom!" she said, a little too brightly. "What brings you to town?"

Peggy waved a dismissive hand in the air. "Oh, that little quilting shop in Cottage Grove doesn't have nearly the variety of the one up here. I like to support them when I can, but sometimes they don't carry what I need. And, since I'd already made the trip, I thought we could have dinner and discuss your wedding plans."

Kasey's smile twisted into an apologetic grimace. "I wish I could, but evenings are the only uninterrupted time I have for the Studebaker."

"Baby, you haven't done a thing to prepare. That wedding

isn't going to plan itself, you know."

"The wedding isn't until August. This car needs to be ready by the end of February."

"So you're going to leave everything until then? Isn't that cutting it awfully close?"

"Tell you what, Peggy," Race said, placing a hand on his future mother-in-law's shoulder. "I can help with the planning. Give me a few minutes to get Jess set up, then we'll go in the office and do some strategizing."

"Jess, I'm at a point where I could use some help with the wiring on the Hawk," Kasey said when I walked into the shop on Friday.

"Great!" It had been over a week since she'd asked for my assistance, and I'd really missed working with her. "Just let me make sure Race is okay with it. He said he'd bring some round tubing from his shop today so I could practice welding roll bars."

"Oh, I don't think he'll have a problem." The quirk of amusement in Kasey's tone piqued my curiosity.

"What's up?"

She smiled. "Go see for yourself. Over by the welding bench. He was here later than I was last night."

I scooted around a '68 Olds to have a look. The metal base Race had constructed from plate steel wasn't anything special, except that each cut and weld looked as if it had been made by a robot, rather than human hands. That alone sent a tendril of envy curling through my insides. But the perfect foundation was only the beginning. On top stood replicas of two human lower legs, fashioned from discarded engine and transmission parts. Rocker arms formed the toes, push rods had been cut to size for the longer foot bones, and camshafts represented tibias. Lifters, gears and other small parts fit together to form the rest of the feet and ankles. A couple of photocopies of a human skeleton sat on the workbench, along with a page of notes scribbled in Race's unsteady handwriting.

"He's got a ways to go," Race said, noticing me and pulling himself away from the innards of the '71 Javelin in the next bay.

"A sculpture."

"Yup. Cody gave me the idea the other day. I figured we could put him outside the shop. I call him Mr. Gearhead."

"Are you going to actually put gears inside his head?"

"That's not a bad idea." Race sidestepped the sculpture to add to his notes, greasy fingers gripping the stub of pencil.

"He's really cool," I said.

"Maybe I should make him interactive. Have it so you could turn the gears and watch him think." A grin stretched across his face. "Of course he might wind up with a brain that works better than mine."

I laughed. "Well, I doubt he'd be able to come up with anything as clever as this."

CHAPTER 18

Teri Sue's term concluded a week before mine, so when I got home from work that night, I found her stretched out on the couch watching CMTV. Rhett sprawled nearby, belly-down on the Oriental rug, his chin propped on his elbows and Newt curled up in the small of his back. Rhett wasn't a fan of anything that didn't involve spaceships, screeching tires, or blazing battles, so he was obviously there for the company rather than the entertainment.

I should've been annoyed at Teri Sue. I hadn't heard a thing from her since the night of the party. But the angry part of me couldn't get past the little kid part that was thrilled at the prospect of spending the next few weeks with one of her best friends.

"Hey, you're home," I said. "How'd your finals go?"

"Eh," said Teri Sue, holding a hand out horizontally and waggling it.

"If you want your bed back, I can set up the cot." My bedroom had been Teri Sue's before she'd moved out. When she'd learned how much I loved her full wall of south-facing windows, she'd insisted I take it over.

"That's okay, I threw my stuff in the guest room. I might be coming in late, and I don't wanna bother you. Besides, you know how I like to sleep in."

"Yeah . . . sure." My effort to make the words sound casual didn't impress Rhett, who cast me a glance over his shoulder. But Teri Sue's eyes stayed riveted to the Garth Brooks video, so I'd apparently gotten it by her.

I hung up my jacket and went to find something to eat. It was no big deal. Sure, it had been fun to lie awake half the night giggling those few days we'd shared the room in September.

But anyone with two working brain cells could see those times were over.

Rhett was determined to hold Teri Sue to her promise of a cookie-baking marathon. He wanted to get started Saturday afternoon, but she told him it was too early. "Let's wait until next week, or they'll be stale by Christmas."

"When next week?" he asked, trailing her to the hallway.

"I dunno, maybe Wednesday."

"How about Tuesday?" I asked as Teri Sue wiggled into her coat. "That way I can help."

"Sure thing. We can talk about it when I get home. I've gotta meet a friend downtown at two." She stepped through the door, pulling it shut behind her.

Rhett sighed and went to look out the window, something he'd been doing every ten minutes because it was supposed to snow that evening. Cold air had been hovering over the state all week, and now a moisture-soaked low-pressure system was moving in from the west.

"Nothing yet," he reported, flopping on the couch. "Oregon's a rip-off. Everyone back home told me we'd get snow here."

We generally received at least a sprinkling once or twice a year, but mostly our winters consisted of bone-chilling rain interspersed with occasional spells of cold, dry weather. Snow events sometimes happened in the transitions.

"I think there's a good chance," I said.

"Yeah, and Teri Sue might actually bake cookies with me," Rhett grumbled, picking up the remote to turn on the Weather Channel.

The promised snow hadn't arrived by the time we went to bed, but the next morning I woke to Rhett shouting, "Woo-hoo!"

That could only mean one thing. I rolled over to look out

the window where fat, white flakes drifted down in spirals. Excitement ricocheted through me, firing every nerve, and I scrambled out of bed. Snow blanketed the grass, trees, and split-rail fence.

"Woo-hoo!" Rhett hollered again, pounding down the stairs. The door slammed, and a moment later he appeared coatless in the front yard, boots and brace on over his pajamas. He clomped to the fence, where he plunged a ruler into the snow and crouched to squint at it.

I yanked up one of the double-hung windows and leaned out into the icy air. "Hey, get in here and put on a coat before you freeze."

"It's over two inches deep!" Rhett's voice was sharp in the hush of falling snow.

"Yeah, and it'll still be there after breakfast. C'mon back inside."

Rhett parked his hands on his hips, the ruler jutting out at an angle. "Aww, Jess. You sound like Teri Sue."

I laughed. "No, if I sounded like Teri Sue, I'd be snoring."

After breakfast, Rhett and I built a huge snowman before splitting up to begin construction on enemy forts. The snow continued to swirl down in giant flakes. By the time the front door opened and Teri Sue poked her head out, it had reached a depth of four inches.

"A weather geek's paradise," she said, shaking her head. Teri Sue had never understood my fascination with meteorology, and because of that, I knew she wouldn't give me the satisfaction of admitting she liked the snow. "Hey, Jess, Cody just called. He's on his way over."

"Come out and play with us!" shouted Rhett.

"The only place I'm going is back to bed."

Half an hour later, the Galaxie crept cautiously up the driveway, its oxidized yellow paint now blotched with huge patches of primer.

Cody got out of the car wearing his leather jacket and an Oregon Ducks stocking cap he'd undoubtedly swiped from Race.

"Good thing you put chains on," I said. "If this keeps up, you might get stranded here."

He smacked himself on the forehead. "Now why didn't I think of that? You and me, snowbound together. . . . Do you think there's still a chance if I take 'em off right now?"

"Maybe, but you'd have to put up with three chaperones."

"Bummer." Cody stepped close and tapped the bill of my Eugene Speedway hat. "You know, this thing's not exactly rated for arctic weather."

"It's the only hat I've got."

"No wonder you're always cold."

Ironically, I wasn't at the moment. Somehow, snow never felt as miserable as a 40-degree rain.

Cody traded hats with me, tugging the green and yellow Ducks cap down over my ears. "There. That oughta warm you up. And if it doesn't, this will." He leaned forward to thaw my icy lips with his warm ones.

"Hey, get a room!" Rhett hollered, a split second before a snowball exploded against the side of Cody's head, short-circuiting our kiss.

Cody staggered back a step, shook the snow from his face, and turned in Rhett's direction. "There *will* be repercussions!" he yelled, thrusting a fist in the air.

After a quick lunch, we persuaded Teri Sue to come outside. I aired up the inner tubes Rhett had used at his pond last summer, and we took them across Fox Hollow to the neighbor's pasture, which sloped away from the highway. We only had three tubes, so Cody and I had to share.

We sledded until we were numb and exhausted, and still

the flakes fell, tiny crystals now. I paused near the highway, resting from my trudge up the hill. Air rasped raw in my throat, my cheeks burned with cold, and I could barely feel my feet, but the rush of winter-storm excitement hadn't dimmed at all.

I looked out over the valley, soaking in that muffled stillness that could only come with snowfall. Beside me, Teri Sue huffed to a stop. She secured her tube against a tree and leaned over to catch her breath, hands planted on her thighs. "I'm goin' in."

"Aw, c'mon!" Rhett protested. "It hardly ever snows. Stay out here with us."

"I hate to break it to you, dude, but I'm ready to call it quits, too," Cody said.

"Oh, man! You guys are no fun."

"One more run," I said, climbing onto the inner tube. "We'll race you."

Rhett leapt for his tube, stomach-first. Cody jumped on beside me, launching us at a crazy angle so we careened into Rhett before shooting down the hill. Between Cody's spontaneous leap and our rapid plunge, he never got a good seat. Hanging half off the tube, he clung to me as we spun around backward. I shrieked out laughter, fighting to keep from being dislodged by Cody's unbalanced weight.

Down the slope we sped, a little spooked by not being able to see where we were going. Then—whump—the tube bounced off of something. Cody and I spilled into the soft powder, showered by clumps of snow from the alder we'd hit. Laughter paralyzed me. I lay on my back, giggling and staring into the swirling whiteness until Cody crawled over to hover above me, eyebrows coated with a rime of white.

"That was awesome," he breathed. Then his mouth came down on mine. Warmth unfurled inside me, rushing along my spine and limbs to heat my whole body.

"Not again," Rhett groaned.

Cody pulled away to reveal him standing over us, smirking.

"It's completely necessary," Cody said. "I'm resuscitating Jess."

"Yeah, sure."

In a nanosecond, Cody yanked him off his feet.

"Stop, stop!" Rhett screamed, gasping at the handfuls of snow being stuffed down his shirt.

At last, Cody relented, sitting back on his heels and grinning down at his victim. "I told you there'd be repercussions."

Rhett had high hopes it would snow until Christmas, in spite of reports to the contrary, but by dark, the flakes had warmed to a drizzle. School was cancelled the next day due to the slushy mess on the roads. As we stared gloomily out the windows at our melting dreams, Rhett badgered Teri Sue to get started on the cookies. But she had plans with her friends and said it wouldn't kill him to wait until the next day.

Tuesday afternoon, Cody followed Rhett and me home from school, unable to stomach the idea of a cookie slipping by him un-tasted. We walked into the kitchen to find Teri Sue elbow deep in ingredients. The table lay buried in an avalanche of newly purchased sugar, flour, butter, nuts, chocolate chips, and candy canes.

"Woo-hoo!" shouted Rhett, lobbing his backpack into a corner. I began folding up the paper bags Teri Sue had tossed on the floor. Cody glanced at the candy canes. Catching Teri Sue's evil eye, he reached for the door of the refrigerator instead.

"Just make yourself at home," she said.

"Might as well. I'm here more often than you are."

"Burn!" said Rhett, slapping Cody a high-five.

Teri Sue assigned me the task of putting things away while she and Rhett sorted through recipes, deciding what to make first.

"You just stay out of the way," she told Cody.

"No problem. I'm here strictly in a taste-testing capacity." He slid a chair away from the table, tipping back on two legs as he dug into the ham and cheese sandwich he'd assembled.

The first M&M cookies were fragrantly plumping in the oven, and Teri Sue was starting a batch of gingerbread men, when the doorbell rang.

"I'll get it." Rhett darted into the living room. He came back with a tall, dark, and twenty-something who looked like he should be posing for the cover of a romance novel.

"Andy! You said you weren't gonna be here till seven." Teri Sue slipped across the room to give him a hug only slightly hindered by a bottle of molasses in one hand and a measuring cup in the other.

"I thought we might catch dinner before we went to the movies. There's this great new Italian place up in Santa Clara."

"But we're baking cookies," Rhett said, looking as though he'd led 499 miles of the Daytona 500 only to get a flat on the last lap.

His sister glanced at him, the grin slipping from her face.

"Oh, I'm sorry," Andy said. "I didn't realize you'd be busy. I can come back later."

"No," said Teri Sue. "We've got a good three days worth of baking to do. I'm sure Rhett can spare me for one evening. You'll take over, won't you Jess?" She handed me the cup and bottle.

"Sure," I said, glancing at her little brother, whose expression hadn't quite settled between disappointment and outrage. I studied the recipe. "Rhett, how about getting me the salt?"

Andy sat down while Teri Sue rushed off to primp. He smiled at us but didn't say a word until she came back.

"We'll bake more cookies tomorrow, Rhett," Teri Sue said as Andy held her coat so she could slip into it. "I promise."

"Yeah, like I haven't heard that before."

I sent Cody to the living room to fire up some Christmas music and put Rhett to work measuring and mixing while I tended the oven. When the timer dinged for the second tray, I checked the cookies and stuck them back in for another minute.

"Hey, you're baking them too long," Cody said. "I like my cookies *al dente*."

"*Al dente* means 'to the tooth.' In other words, something that has firmness to it. If that's how you like them, I should be baking them longer."

"Well fine, Miss Latin Scholar," Cody said, pulling my ponytail. "But obviously the analogy made sense or you wouldn't have known what I was talking about." He snatched a cookie from the cooling rack and took a bite.

"How is it?" I asked.

"Puw-feck."

"Then stop the backseat driving."

"Wouldn't that be backseat cooking?" asked Rhett.

"Backseat cookie-ing," Cody said, and the two of them busted up.

At 6:30, when Cody left for his karate class, Rhett and I whipped up some quick sandwiches so we wouldn't have to stop baking. Next on the list were candy cane cookies.

"I used to make these with my mom," I said as I blended butter and sugar together.

Rhett cracked an egg and added it to the mixture. "I really miss Mama this time of year. She always made Christmas special. She's the one who taught Teri Sue how to cook and bake." He measured out the milk, squatting down to be sure the liquid lined up perfectly with the mark on the cup. "Do you miss your mama?"

"Sometimes. I know things were weird at Thanksgiving, but she wasn't like that when I was little."

"It's the same with my mama. She used to take me and Teri

Sue caroling at all the neighbors' houses." Rhett poured the milk into the bowl, a little at a time as I stirred. "Maybe we could send her some of these cookies," he said. "Not from me—I know it upsets her to hear about me—but from Daddy and Teri Sue. Christmas is important to her."

I reached for the baking powder. "I think that's a great idea, Rhett."

CHAPTER 19

The thump of a butt settling onto my bed woke me from a dead sleep.

"Jess, are you awake?" hissed Teri Sue.

"No."

"Is Rhett really mad?"

"Ask him yourself." Good Lord, just because she was a night owl didn't mean she had to keep everyone else awake.

"I didn't mean to blow him off, but I was afraid if I didn't go out with Andy, he'd dump me."

"What?" I rolled over, waking Newt, who gave me a 60 grit kiss. "Don't be stupid. What kind of guy dumps a girl just because she keeps a promise to her little brother?"

"Have you looked at him?"

"Yeah, he's totally hot. So what?"

"So I'm not."

"Are you serious?"

She slumped forward, shoulders sagging. "I'm a big, fat redhead. I have no idea what he ever saw in me."

Wouldn't you know it, when I finally got my girl time with Teri Sue, it had to be at two in the morning.

"Look, there's plenty of stuff for guys to like about you," I said. "You're cute, you've got a great smile, and that drawl of yours probably sends them into a swoon. Besides, your hair's not red, it's strawberry blond. I'd kill for your hair."

Teri Sue turned to peer at me through the darkness. "Seriously?"

"Well, maybe I'd maim."

She shook her head. "I'm still fat."

"So you're not a starving twig. So what? Andy seems like a nice guy. He felt bad about dragging you away from Rhett. I could tell. A guy like that isn't going to break up with you just because you tell him he's interrupted your plans. And frankly, anyone who would isn't worth your time."

Teri Sue rested a hand on Newt's neck, scratching him behind the ears. "You're so logical," she said, her eyes locking on the cat. "I miss our talks."

My throat jammed tight with three months of lost friendship. "Me too."

"I'll try to do better, Jess. I know I haven't been around much. But I'll make it up to you."

I stared at the ceiling, where the hall light cut a rectangular path through the darkness. For Rhett's sake, I hoped she made good on that vow.

I didn't expect much change from Teri Sue, but over the next couple of days she put forth a maximum effort. When Rhett got home from school, she was in the kitchen, ready to bake. And she gave him her full attention, asking about Emily, who now exchanged smiles and spoke to Rhett whenever he could get up the nerve to talk to her. It was Teri Sue who suggested a box of homemade cookies after Rhett admitted he had no idea what to give Emily for Christmas.

"Wrap 'em up pretty and tell her you made them special just for her."

Rhett eyed her sideways. "You think she'd like that?"

"You bet. Girls love a guy who knows his way around the kitchen. She'll think it's romantic."

I was shocked when Teri Sue set up the cot in my room. For the next two evenings, she went to bed at a reasonable hour, and we lay awake reminiscing about the previous racing season. The late nights made getting up for school a trial, but it was worth it. At least there were no tests that week, the teachers being smart enough to know we wouldn't be able to concentrate before winter break.

At the shop Friday afternoon, I put in my regular hours but didn't stay for a welding lesson or to help with the Hawk. Cody had other plans. Race had told him where to find the best Christmas light displays, and he was taking Rhett and me to see them. Miracle of all miracles, Teri Sue volunteered to come along.

"We can deliver the cookies," she said. She'd baked enough for half the people in the Street Stock class.

Rhett hurried down from his room as Teri Sue and I began packing red and green tins into shopping bags. "Guess what?" he said, hiding his hands behind his back.

"*Finally.*" Teri Sue rolled her eyes. "He's got some secret, and he's been making me wait until y'all got here to tell me about it."

"What's up?" asked Cody.

"Emily gave me a Christmas present." Rhett pulled his hand from behind him to reveal a giant Hershey's Kiss, big as a baseball.

"Oooh, how symbolic," said Teri Sue.

Cody laughed. "Like you'd know anything about symbolism."

"It's a kiss, duh! You don't have to be Shakespeare to know what that means."

"Hmm," said Cody. "And here I thought it was just some chocolate." He angled a look at Rhett. "I don't suppose you'd be willing to share?"

"Forget it. Maybe if you're really nice, Jess'll buy you one for Christmas."

"Maybe she'll give me a *real* kiss now." Cody planted one on me before I could object to having an audience.

"So what did Emily think of the cookies you gave her?" asked Teri Sue, ignoring Cody's grandstand play.

"She got this big smile on her face and wouldn't let her friends have any."

Teri Sue gave him a smug grin. "What'd I tell ya?"

"What I want to know is how you did on your science project," I said. Rhett had been one of the last kids to give his presentation.

"I got an A+," he bragged, high-fiving me. "And Emily said it was the most interesting one of all."

"That girl definitely has the hots for you. C'mon, we'd better get going." Cody scooped up the bags and hustled us out to the Galaxie.

Wanting to add to the mood, Rhett brought along his stash of Christmas music. "You can be DJ, Jess," he said, leaning over the seat to set the shoebox beside me.

I sorted through the tapes, squinting at the labels in the dark as we drove down the driveway to Fox Hollow.

"Hey, Cody, what's your favorite Christmas song?" Rhett asked.

"Anything that's not being sung by Jimmy Buffett."

"I like that Elton John one, *Step into Christmas*," said Teri Sue. "Put that on."

Rhett elbowed her across the back seat. "You're not the DJ. What's *your* favorite, Jess?"

"Oh, I don't know," I hemmed, because there was no way I'd tell the three of them what I'd said to Race that day in the office. "Maybe *The Heat Miser Song*. Have you got that one?"

"What kind of drugs are you on, girl?" said Teri Sue. "That's not a real song."

"Sure it is," said Rhett. "It's from *The Year Without a Santa Claus*. Heat Miser and Snow Miser are Mother Nature's sons. They control the weather."

"Ah, now it makes sense," said Cody, glancing at me with an indulgent grin.

"You're making that up," said Teri Sue.

"I am not!"

"Are too."

Rhett began to sing.

"Nooo!" yelled Cody

The crooning continued.

"Don't make me stop this car," Cody warned.

Rhett giggled out the next words, hindered neither by the threat, nor his sister reaching across the seat to muffle him with a hand. Singing on through her fingers, he didn't even stop when she tackled him, straining against her seatbelt to pin him down.

I figured he could use some back up, so I joined him for the last line. "... *I'm too much!*"

"That's for damn sure," said Cody as Teri Sue rubbed her knuckles in Rhett's hair.

I smiled over the seat back at my friends, happy that things were back to normal. Christmas might still be four days off, but I'd already received the only present I needed.

CHAPTER 20

Over the weekend, Teri Sue split her time between her college friends who lived in the area and us, but I was willing to share so long as she didn't ignore me completely. I put in extra hours at the shop, helping Kasey with the Hawk and learning how to weld roll bar tubing.

Saturday afternoon, I got home to find Mark in the kitchen, watering his houseplants. He owned enough to establish a small jungle and fussed over them as if they were children, now that it was too cold and wet to work outside. The oldest was a wandering Jew he'd had since Rhett was a baby. He called it Moses.

"There's something from your mama in the living room," Mark said. "I'm sure your father would like to know about it, but I can't see interfering with a mother's Christmas gift to her daughter."

"Thanks, Mark." I grabbed a few cookies and went to take a look. This package was smaller and heavier than the last one Lydia had sent. I took it to my room where I could open it in privacy.

With the door safely closed, I sliced the end of the padded envelope and tipped out a present. The crinkly red foil tore away to reveal a used paperback: *The World's Number One, Flat-Out, All-Time Great, Stock Car Racing Book*. A Post-it note clung to the front.

> *Merry Christmas, sweetie. Don't worry about me showing up and ruining things for you again. I've learned my lesson.*
>
> *love,*
> *Lydia*

Despite the order to leave me alone, she'd called twice since the night Cody had overheard our conversation. But she'd kept things brief, reporting that her counseling was going well and she still hadn't taken a drink. Even though she'd been on her best behavior, I'd been worrying about what might happen on Christmas. The note didn't do much to reassure me. All it would take was one beer to undo all the progress she'd made.

I flipped the book over and scanned the back cover. It was billed as one of the most comprehensive, entertaining accounts of the history of the sport. Where Lydia had found something like this, I had no idea, but her efforts impressed me.

I flopped on my bed and began to read.

Dad managed to wrangle four days off, beginning Christmas Eve. He arrived late in the afternoon as Rhett and I were tucking presents under the towering noble fir.

"That's some tree you've got there," he said, stepping closer to admire it. He fingered one of the glass snowflakes I'd saved from the apartment. "You know, we used to have some just like this."

"Actually, those are yours," Mark said. "Jess had them stashed away, and we had plenty of room on the tree."

The words brought a soft, misty look to my father's eyes. The one that always made me think he was about to cry. Dad turned to glance at me briefly before focusing a look of gratitude on Mark. "That was very thoughtful."

"You and Jess are family, Max. It's only fitting."

Rhett helped Dad carry in his gifts, then after dinner Mark stoked the fire and we gathered in the living room to sing along as Dad played carols on his harmonica.

The evening was a new experience for all of us—Dad and me because we weren't accustomed to being around so many people for the holidays, and the Clines because they'd never been around so few. This was their first Christmas in Oregon.

Back home, they'd gathered with grandparents, aunts, uncles, and cousins for a big, noisy celebration. I could only imagine what that must've been like. Just having Dad and the Clines was enough for me.

Christmas morning, Rhett bounced on my bed to wake me. When Teri Sue threw a pillow to shut him up, he stole the covers from her cot.

"C'mon you guys! It's time to open presents."

Since there was no hope of getting him to leave us alone, we got up.

Downstairs, Mark had the tree lights plugged in, Burl Ives on the radio, and a fire burning in the woodstove. The scent of crackling cedar curled around me, like a cozy blanket that almost banished my fear of Lydia showing up.

Teri Sue and I settled on the couch while Rhett examined tags on the presents beneath the tree. When an engine sounded in the driveway, my heart pounded for a split-second until I realized it belonged to a Freightliner.

Moments later, Dad came through the door and pulled me into a rib-cracking hug. "Merry Christmas, baby." The morning chill clung to his jacket, and the smell of aftershave, fresh and sharp, sent a ripple of love shivering through me.

I settled on the couch beside my father, feeling like I'd been transported into one of Mark's old-time movies. Compared to the one-gift holidays I'd spent huddled around a Charlie Brown Christmas tree with Lydia, this was surreal. The only thing that could make it more perfect would be if Dad were to tell me he was going to stop hauling hazmat. But I knew that was too much to wish for.

Rhett assigned himself the job of handing out gifts. From Teri Sue, I received a pair of designer jeans, which looked like they'd fit a lot more snugly than the ones I usually wore.

"Just wait'll Cody sees you in those," she said.

In exchange, I gave her four cases of Sundrop, her favorite soda, which could only be purchased in North Carolina.

"Where'd you find this?" she demanded, gaping at the bright green boxes in pure delight.

"I had Dad pick it up the last time he went to Charlotte."

"Girl, you're too smart for your own good. And that's why I keep you around." Teri Sue dug out a can, popped it open, and took a swig. "Ahhh. You don't know how long it's been since I've had one of these." She grinned. "It's perfect, Jess. Thanks."

I gave Mark a copy of *The Sunset Western Garden Book*. A lady at Smith Family Bookstore had insisted it was a must for any gardener newly transplanted to the Northwest. Mark had a vast collection of books on horticulture, and since winter had hit, he'd spent a lot of time paging wistfully through them.

For Rhett I'd found a book on geology packed with full-color diagrams, photos, and illustrations. Dad was more difficult to buy for, since he spent most of his time on the road. I'd made him a mix tape of all the car songs I'd been collecting since he and Lydia split.

"Now you open something," Rhett said, handing me a package I knew he'd wrapped himself due to the abundance of Scotch tape.

I tore off the paper to find a pair of welding gloves, which seemed a little odd, since the ones at the shop worked just fine. But remembering how much he'd struggled over his gift for Emily, I figured it must've been hard for him to pick something out.

"Thanks, Rhett. These are great."

I reached for my present from Mark, but Dad stopped me. "You've gotta open this one first." He handed me a large manila envelope. I slit the flap and pulled out the instruction manual for a Millermatic 35 welder.

"What?" I slanted a look at Dad.

"No way was I gonna wrap that sucker," he said with a grin.

"It's out in the barn. I'm sorry it's not new, but Race said it's a good machine. I figured if you're gonna build race cars, you'll need some decent equipment."

I stared at him, completely unable to believe the words coming out of his mouth. How could anyone spend that kind of money on me? "Dad, this is too much. It must've cost a fortune."

"Honey, you haven't gotten a Christmas present from me in eight years. This doesn't even begin to make up for that. Anyway, if it makes you feel better, Race got me a good deal on it at an auction."

I was trying to figure out whether that made a difference when Mark piped up. "Okay, now you can open mine."

Once I did, I understood Rhett's gift. Mark had bought me a set of welding leathers. "We sort of had a theme going," he said.

"Not me," said Teri Sue. "Somebody's gotta teach this girl it's okay to work on cars and still be feminine."

My voice shook as I thanked everyone, but nobody seemed to notice. These gifts—well, they were the best things I'd ever received. But the real present wasn't something that could be wrapped in paper. My father and friends had just proven they believed in my dreams. As long as I had that, I could take whatever life threw at me.

Mark fixed his traditional holiday breakfast—buckwheat pancakes with applesauce and sliced banana stirred into the batter—then Dad and I went over to Cody's.

As we drove, fog shrouded the leafless, moss-draped oaks that lined the highway. The steering wheel felt like ice under my gloveless hands, and I shivered, waiting for the engine to warm up enough to provide some heat. In the passenger seat, Dad softly hummed *White Christmas*. Suddenly, he stopped.

"You know what this baby deserves?" he asked, patting the Pinto's dash. "A good paint job."

"I'm saving up for one. Kasey said she'd teach me how to use the equipment. We might be able to make it happen after the Roadster Show." A glance at the instrument cluster showed the needle of the temperature gauge inching above the "C," so I turned on the fan, blasting us with a torrent of lukewarm air.

"You need a donation for the paint fund?"

"No! Dad, you just bought me a welder. Anyway, we're too busy at the shop right now."

"Well, you just let me know if you need any help." Dad reached over to squeeze my knee.

When we got to Kasey's, Cody greeted us at the door wearing a freshly silkscreened Race Morgan T-shirt. The scent of orange peel and cloves enticed us inside, where we were plied with shirts of our own, along with cookies and hot chocolate too delicious to refuse. Kasey always made cocoa from scratch, rather than using the powdered stuff.

Cody's dad had driven down from Portland. He was a quiet man who didn't look much like his son beyond his height and build. I'd only met him a couple of times, and Dad had never met him at all. The two of them seemed to hit it off, no doubt sharing their respective offspring's most embarrassing moments.

Cody and I avoided potential humiliation by concentrating on the gift exchange. My present to him was an AP Stylebook to launch his journalistic career. I'd tucked it inside a T-shirt that read, *Five out of four people don't understand fractions.* He gave me a box of Euphoria truffles and a video of the movie *Heart Like a Wheel*, the story of drag racing legend Shirley Muldowney.

"It was Kasey's idea," he said. "I've never even heard of this Muldowney chick."

Neither had I, but after reading the back of the box, I wanted to know more.

Cody and I had pooled our money for Race and Kasey's

gift—a certificate for a night at the coastal hotel they'd visited last January. In return, they presented me with a welding helmet to go along with the rest of my gear.

"I know that welder's a little different than what you've been using at work," Race said. "But it's just like the one at my shop. If you have any trouble figuring it out, let me know."

We spent the afternoon watching a marathon of Christmas specials on Nickelodeon before going home to Teri Sue's prime rib dinner. And although I quietly worried the whole day, Lydia never put in an appearance.

As I climbed into bed that evening, with the gentle strains of *Silent Night* playing on the radio and the rosy glow of the outdoor lights reflecting through my windows, an end-of-Christmas melancholy slipped over me. I hadn't experienced anything like it since I was little. The past month had been filled with a kind of magic I couldn't believe would ever happen to me.

I wasn't ready to let go of it.

Peace on earth lasted until exactly 3:04 p.m. on December 26th when Mark checked the mail. As he hustled through the front door, his face reflected a thunderous indignation that made me want to slink upstairs and hide. He stopped in front of the couch, blocking Teri Sue's view of CMTV.

"Two C's and three D's?" Mark demanded.

"Is that my report card?" Teri Sue shot upright, snatching it from his hand and examining the envelope. "This is addressed to *me*. You had no right to open it!"

"I'm paying for your education, Teri Sue. I have every right to know if you're flunking out."

"You work there. It's hardly costing you anything! Anyway, I didn't flunk any classes, and fifteen credits is too much."

Mark closed his eyes and inhaled deeply. When he spoke, his voice had resumed its normal, measured tone. "If you're struggling, you find a tutor or drop a class. You don't just give up."

"It was too late to drop!"

"The college allows six weeks to withdraw from classes without penalty. That's over half the term. Are you saying it didn't get difficult until after that?"

"Maybe it didn't!" Teri Sue stood up, ducking around her father. "You know what? I don't care what you think. You've got no business getting in my face like this. You've got no business opening my mail!"

"As long as I'm supporting you, it's my business. You may get a tuition break, but I still have to cover your books and housing. And frankly, I don't buy your excuses. The reason you did poorly is that you were too busy partying and hanging out with your friends to study."

"That's not fair!" Teri Sue's fists clenched at her sides. "It's *hard* adjusting to college. It's not like high school. Nobody reminds you when stuff is due. The teachers don't even care."

Mark's expression showed no sympathy. "That's right. They're not babysitters. They expect you to be independent—to take responsibility for your own education."

Teri Sue glared at him, arms crossed over her chest. "I don't have to listen to this. I had an invitation to stay with friends over break. I turned it down to be with my family. But that's not good enough for you.

"So you don't want to pay for my education? Fine. Then don't. But I'm not gonna hang around listening to this crap." She turned and strode from the room, her feet pounding up the stairs. A minute later, she clomped back down with her suitcase and duffle bag, heading straight for the front door.

At the last second, she spun around and caught my eye. "Sorry, Jess," she said with a finality that made my stomach sink. Then the door slammed shut behind her, breathing a cold gust of air over us.

I sat staring at the entryway, trying to make sense of the whole scene. What the hell had just happened?

The engine of Teri Sue's pickup roared and the tires spun, spitting gravel as she peeled out of the driveway. Mark sank to the couch. He couldn't have looked more stunned if she'd slapped him.

No doubt, my expression echoed his. Teri Sue had never done anything like this.

CHAPTER 21

When Rhett found out Teri Sue was gone, he blamed the fight on his father. "She was finally doing stuff with me, and you ruined it!"

"I'm sorry," Mark said, reaching out to grip his son's shoulder. "I'm upset about this, too."

Rhett shrugged him off and dashed upstairs to slam his bedroom door.

"I'll talk to him," I said. But my efforts to explain that Teri Sue was equally at fault only resulted in Rhett snubbing me as well.

Things remained grim in the Cline household for the next few days. My loyalties pulled me in opposite directions, and I wanted to throttle Teri Sue for letting self-indulgence trump her family. Why couldn't she see how lucky she was to have one?

Once Dad was back on the road, I avoided the mess by spending time at the shop. Kasey needed my help, now that she'd finished the Hawk's wiring and begun routing brake and fuel lines. Besides, the holiday had left us behind schedule on customer jobs, so she was allowing me extra hours to cover the load.

On the 29th, the Ducks lost the Freedom Bowl by a single point, and Race was still mourning the defeat two days later.

"Get over it, already," Cody said. It was his seventeenth birthday, and he wasn't about to let anyone spoil the festivities.

Later that afternoon, his grandmother stopped by the shop. "I know you'll have your own plans for the evening, but I wanted to give you this," she said, extending an envelope. As Cody reached to take it, her gaze drifted past him. "What's this?" she asked, stepping toward Race's sculpture. It had grown to include upper legs, hips, and half a rib cage constructed from thin strips of leaf spring.

Cody turned to look over his shoulder. "You mean you haven't been introduced?" He gestured between her and the metal figure with a flourish. "Grandma, meet Mr. Gearhead, Mr. Gearhead, meet Grandma." With a conspiratorial whisper he added, "Forgive him if he doesn't shake your hand. He doesn't have any yet."

A delighted smile spread across Mrs. Morgan's lips. "This must be my son's doing."

"Yup, he's gonna put him out front to welcome all the customers. Pretty cool, huh?" Cody returned his attention to the envelope and ripped it open.

"Excellent," he said, grinning as he showed me the $150 check he'd found inside the card.

"I'd have preferred to get you something more personal, but I thought you could use the money for your race car."

"Or to fill up the Galaxie," I said. In spite of the V-8 in the Pinto, it got better mileage than Cody's gas-guzzler—something I took pleasure in taunting him about.

"Thanks, Grandma." Cody tucked his arm around her shoulders, and she stiffly accepted the embrace.

After work, we both went home to change. I slipped into the jeans Teri Sue had given me and the sweater I'd worn to the banquet before driving over to pick up Cody. He'd washed the Galaxie that afternoon and left it in the paint booth to dry so we could get right to work sanding it the next morning. Even though the plan had been in place since October, he felt a little guilty about it now, knowing how much Kasey needed every spare minute to work on the Hawk.

"Whoa," Cody said as he followed me back to the Pinto. "Are those new jeans?"

"Yeah, Teri Sue gave them to me for Christmas."

Cody lifted the back of my jacket to get a better look at my behind. "I knew there was a reason I liked Teri Sue."

"Hey, behave yourself!" I whipped around to face him.

Cody rested his arms on my shoulders, curling them around my neck as he pulled me close. "If you didn't want me looking, why'd you wear them?"

"Good question," I said, and gave him a kiss.

I'd told Cody I'd treat him to dinner at any restaurant he wanted, but he directed me to Track Town Pizza, his idea of haute cuisine.

As we walked through the door, he inhaled deeply, sucking in the zesty zing of pepperoni and tomato sauce. "Mmmmm. I love that smell."

"Just so long as you don't buy me any pizza-scented perfume."

Cody's face lit up as if he'd stumbled upon a Volkswagen-sized Easter basket. "They make that?"

"Only in your dreams."

I placed our order and gave the cashier my name while Cody stood at the end of the counter under the green-and-gold-clad U of O Fighting Duck, watching the guy assembling pizzas. If his journalistic dreams ever fell through, he could always get a job working here.

I collected our pitcher of root beer and led Cody into the seating area. The dark wood paneling, adorned with photos of Steve Prefontaine and other track legends, gave the place a cozy feel. We chose a booth, sliding in on either side of the heavy wooden table.

"Y'know," Cody said as he reached for the root beer, "whenever Race tells one of the new guys his name, they raise an eyebrow like they think he's making it up."

"That's what Lydia used to do when I was little. One time she said she was Cleopatra."

Cody poured me some soda then filled his own glass, glancing at me briefly over the pitcher. "Is she still calling you?"

The forced note of casualness in his voice left me fighting back a smile. "Yeah. Maybe once a week. She doesn't say much, just that she's still on the wagon. She's the one who sent me that book I told you about." The down-home, unwashed look at the lives of drivers like Tiny Lund and Curtis Turner had provided such entertaining reading that I'd told my friends about it.

"Seriously?" Cody asked. "I thought she didn't like you messing with cars."

"She doesn't. That just proves how hard she's trying."

Cody jammed a straw into his drink and used it as a swizzle stick, rattling the ice cubes against the glass. His mask of acceptance barely covered the doubt underneath. It was the first time we'd spoken about my mother since the day he apologized.

"I know I'd be a fool to trust her a hundred percent," I said. "But she really is trying. This is one of her longest stretches of sobriety. Maybe she'll make it this time."

Cody looked up from his drink. "You know what, Jess? I hope she does."

The next morning, I met Cody, Kasey, and Race at the shop early. Even with four of us, painting the Galaxie would take most of the day.

"Y'know, we don't have to do this right now," Cody told Kasey. "If you'd rather put in some time on the Hawk, I totally understand."

"I made a commitment, and I intend to honor it," Kasey said.

"Yeah, but things have changed since then."

"One day isn't going to make or break the project."

Kasey tackled the masking and put the rest of us to work with sanding blocks. When we finished late in the morning, she shot the primer, transforming the Galaxie from pale yellow to flat gray. An hour later, the car was ready for a second round of sanding. This one required more precision because any defect in the primer would show through in the paint.

It was after three before Kasey could begin shooting color. Race excused himself to work on his sculpture, but Cody and I stuck around to watch. With any luck, I'd be doing this to my car in a few months, and while Cody was happy to let Kasey take charge, I intended to paint the Pinto myself.

"Always start with the roof," Kasey said, twisting the lid of the gun into place. "Otherwise you might drag the hose through fresh paint."

The sweet pungency of acrylic enamel filled the booth as she began covering the gray with a bright, here-I-come red. Step by step, she explained her technique. Much as I itched to give it a try, I didn't ask. I was sure I could do it—I'd had decent results the time I'd touched up a fender on Teri Sue's car—but I didn't want to risk making a mistake.

We finished up by six, with the Galaxie coming out perfectly. Race and Kasey both wanted to stick around to put in more time on their projects, but Cody seemed pretty burned out.

"You wanna go grab a pizza or something?" he asked. Cody could eat pizza seven days a week and never get tired of it.

"Again?"

He rocked forward on his toes, hands jammed in his pockets. "I guess we could do Mexican or something."

"I can't. I'm supposed to have black-eyed peas with the Clines tonight. It's a Southern tradition. If you eat them on New Years Day, you'll have good luck all year." I didn't mention that Teri Sue usually cooked them, and with her incommunicado, Rhett had convinced himself she'd be stuck with twelve months of bad luck. "You could come eat with us," I added. "I'm sure Mark made plenty."

"Sure. I could always use a little luck."

We let Race—who was finishing Mr. Gearhead's ribcage—know about the plan before heading out to the Pinto.

"That sculpture's really looking good," I said as I slipped behind the wheel.

"Yeah. It's cool that Race found another way to be artistic."

I glanced across the seat at him. "You're okay with that now?" While Cody bragged about Race's sculpture to anyone who would listen, he hadn't said much else on the subject.

"I still think it sucks that he can't draw. But yeah, I'm glad he has this."

The starter whined as I turned the key. "It bothers him that you're so upset about his art."

"I'm not upset. If you think this is upset, you shoulda seen me a year ago." Cody turned to look out the window, his foot bouncing lightly against the floorboards. "I used to keep track of the monthly anniversaries of the wreck. I'd watch his improvements and wonder how much more he was gonna get back. And if that's not screwy enough, when I finally forgot to, I felt guilty for it."

"That's not screwy," I said, pulling out onto East Amazon. "I'll bet a lot of people do the same kind of thing."

Cody snorted. "Maybe. Anyway, the whole deal doesn't mess with my head like it used to. I just hate that Race got screwed. I mean, Grandpa's an asshole, Mom's a bitch, and up until I moved down here, I was a total jerk, but it's Race who wound up losing everything."

"He didn't lose everything. He gained Kasey's love and your trust. And he sees that as a pretty fair exchange."

"He should've gotten those things anyway."

"But he didn't." I took one hand off the wheel and reached for Cody's. "Race is happy. He has a family, and that means more to him than anything."

Cody sighed and let his head fall back against the seat, his dark hair shadowing his eyes. "I know you're right, Jess. And I do feel a lot better. I just can't stand to think about bad things happening to the people I care about."

"Then think about good things. Maybe Race will enjoy doing metal sculpture even more than he liked drawing."

CHAPTER 22

School resumed without a word from Teri Sue. But when Mark checked with the registrar's office, he learned she'd enrolled for winter term and had gone back to the dorms. That was pretty much the only positive thing I could say about vacation ending.

One of the bonuses of putting in all those extra hours during break was that it had added a fat cushion to my bank account. Not that I was hurting in that regard. While I'd told Dad I was still saving to paint the Pinto, I actually had enough and more. It made me feel secure, knowing I had money in the bank.

That first Thursday in January, Lydia called again. I hadn't heard from her since receiving her gift, probably because she'd been afraid to risk it, with both Mark and Teri Sue out of school. She started with her usual sobriety and counseling update then asked how my Christmas had been.

"Pretty good. Dad bought me a welder." I waited to see what she'd say to that—if she truly was willing to accept me for who I was.

"That's wonderful, sweetie. I'm sure it's something you'll put to good use. Did you like the book I sent?"

"Yeah, it's great. Thanks, Lydia." I hesitated, reluctant to give her more. But she'd done everything right, even kept her word about staying away. "I appreciate how hard you've been trying."

Her laugh managed to sound lighthearted, despite its sad undertones. "That's not something that's easy to get across in a few minutes over the phone." She paused, and silence stretched out between us. "My therapist said I should ask if you'd be willing to talk in person. She suggested someplace neutral, like a restaurant."

A storm of conflicting feelings churned through me. On one level, I wanted to agree. Lydia had been doing her best. But she'd only been working at it for six weeks. Nothing had tested her resolve, and she was famous for crashing hard when she ran into a challenge.

"I don't think I can do that."

"Sweetie, I want to talk to you face to face."

I let out a long breath. "Do you know what Dad would say if he found out?"

"It's not fair for him to keep us apart."

A bitter thought fired through my head—*why not? You did*—but I kept it to myself. "You didn't exactly impress him at Thanksgiving."

Lydia's sigh rasped in my ear. "Jess, I know I've let you down. A whole lot. I don't ever want to do it again, and that's why I need your help. You've always been so good at holding me accountable."

If there was one thing I'd figured out, it was that acting as her conscience was not my responsibility. "I'm sorry Lydia. I can't help you with this. You've got to learn to be accountable to yourself. Otherwise, you'll never be able to stay sober."

I knew that wouldn't be the end of it, and it didn't surprise me when Lydia called back the following Tuesday.

"I've thought a lot about what you told me, sweetie. I talked it over with my sponsor, and she said you were right. If I'm going to stay sober, I need to do it for myself."

Not knowing where she was going with this, I stuck to a neutral statement. "Sounds like your sponsor's pretty smart."

"Oh, she is. But I still want to talk to you, even if it's just on the phone."

"I guess that's okay," I said, relieved she'd given up on getting together. "Rhett's in his room reading, and Mark won't be home for another two hours."

Taking that as permission, Lydia didn't hesitate, she just launched straight into a nervous spiel. "Well, the first thing is—I didn't want to leave you. Not in my heart. I know I wrote that terrible letter and took your money, but I've been working on this with my counselor, and now I understand why I did those things."

At least one of us did. I scooped up Newt and sank onto my bed, stroking his silky fur.

"Sweetie, I had to blame you. If I could believe it was your fault, I could let myself leave. But it wasn't your fault. Not at all. I was just so scared. I'd blown it at work, my friend Judy was leaving, and Jimmy was talking about taking off, too." Lydia paused only long enough to gulp a breath. "I couldn't let that happen. I've had lots of boyfriends, but never one I loved as much as your dad until Jimmy came along. He might've been a little rough around the edges, but he treated me like a princess. After he said he'd leave without me, I knew I had to go."

The deluge ended abruptly, leaving me wordless. There was no point reminding her how wrong it was, how selfish she'd been to put herself before her kid. She obviously knew, and besides, it wouldn't change anything.

Probably the saddest thing was that I finally got it. Lydia didn't just want Jimmy. She needed him. She was such a weak, pathetic creature, she'd given in to her cravings even though she'd known better. I'd never be okay with what she'd done. But at least now I understood why it had happened.

"I'm sorry I'm not a better mother," Lydia continued. "I don't expect you to forgive me. I just wanted to say that no matter how bad it was to leave, it was even worse to make you believe it was your fault. I might not ever be able to make it up to you, but I'm going to pay back the money I took. Every cent."

Even though I knew she was right—that she'd been the one at fault—my heart couldn't quite extinguish a last whisper of guilt. If I'd been more understanding, if I'd spent time trying to connect, if I'd just once said that I needed and loved her, maybe she wouldn't have been so dependent on Jimmy.

"I'm glad you told me," I said, pulling Newt to my chest and soaking in the comforting throb of his purr. After all the effort she'd made, I couldn't let her think I didn't understand.

"There's more," Lydia said. "I've always given you a hard time because you seemed to love your dad the best. But I never told you why that was so hard on me. . . ." Her words trailed off, and she drew a quivering breath. "All I ever wanted, from the second I knew I was pregnant, was to have a little girl who'd love me the way I loved my mom."

My heart almost thudded to a standstill. Lydia had never once mentioned my grandparents, and every time I brought up the subject, she'd told me to drop it.

"What was your mom like?" I leaned back against my pillow, pulling Newt onto my stomach.

Lydia let out a sigh, and then after a long, lingering silence, spoke. "She was my best friend. She'd grown up in a little bitty Nebraska town and couldn't stand to stay in one place for long, so we traveled a lot. Just me and her. When I was young, I didn't mind. It made life feel like an adventure."

I tried to imagine a little-girl-Lydia, drifting from town to town with a mother she adored. "Where was your dad?"

"I didn't have one." She laughed. "Well, I guess I must've, but I didn't know who he was. I don't think Mom did, either."

"Wow," I said, fascinated to finally be getting this family history. "Wasn't that hard back then?"

"Sure. But it could've been a lot harder. Mom was so fun—so spontaneous—she got away with things no one else could. Everywhere we went, people loved her." A rare buoyancy filled Lydia's tone, so powerful that for a second I could almost see this woman who meant so much to her. "She worked as a bartender, and she really knew how to have a good time. Our house was always full of people. The men adored her, even though she wouldn't commit to any of them. And the women—well, they were lining up to be her friend. But even with all those people to love her, she made me number one in her life." Lydia's words faltered, and suddenly I knew beyond a doubt that this story didn't have a happy ending.

"What happened to her?"

"She died." The statement was so abrupt, it hit me like a sneaker wave. "Alcohol poisoning," Lydia continued, the life seeping out of her voice. "I was only seventeen. She must've been an alcoholic, but she was so good at holding her liquor, I never suspected."

Oh God. Of all the things I'd been through with Lydia, the emotions good and bad, I'd never felt so much compassion for her as I did in that moment.

"I was alone," she said, "and not nearly as strong as you. But a friend of hers found me a job waitressing at a truck stop. That's how I met your dad. The way he loved fast cars and Southern rock, he reminded me of one of Mom's sweeter boyfriends. One I'd hope she'd stick with. By that time, I was sick of traveling. I'd lived in fourteen states, and I wanted a real home. I was a fool to think twice about getting involved with a truck driver, but I fell in love."

"So that's why you had such a hard time with him being on the road."

"That's why." Lydia heaved a trembling sigh. "He promised me he'd settle down, and I was stupid enough to believe it. But he came from a long line of truckers. It was all he'd wanted to do since he was a little boy. I tried to pretend it was okay, and when he took me on the road with him, it was. But then you came along. Being a mom was a lot harder than I expected. I missed your dad so much. I couldn't stand that I was the one staying home with you, doing all the hard stuff, but you loved him best."

At last, the pieces all slipped into place, forming a picture

I'd never been able to see. Lydia wasn't just my mother. She was a real person.

"If you still want to get together," I said. "Just name the place."

CHAPTER 25

My fingers refused to stop tapping the steering wheel as I drove to Lok Yaun, the restaurant where Lydia and I had celebrated so many Thanksgivings. In spite of how forgiving I'd felt last night, I couldn't help wondering if I was making a mistake. Talking on the phone was one thing. I was in charge and could dispatch my mother with the click of a button. But meeting her in person—that was a commitment.

After finding a parking place, I closed my eyes and took several deep, calming breaths, the way Cody did before a race. *There's nothing to worry about.* Lydia hadn't had a drink since Thanksgiving. That was almost three weeks longer than she'd ever made it in the past. And this time she was getting counseling. The things she'd said last night proved she'd worked out some of her problems, or at least come to understand why she had them.

I repeated the *nothing to worry about* mantra as I crossed the parking lot and reached for the door. Inside, the dim, noisy restaurant was rich with the scents of fried rice and sesame chicken. I spotted Lydia at a booth in the corner. As I approached, she stood up, edging out from behind the table. The normal weariness in her eyes had given way to radiance. I couldn't remember her ever looking so peaceful and healthy.

"Sweetie, I'm so glad to see you," she said, wrapping her arms around me.

"You look great, Lydia."

"Thanks." She stepped back, squeezed my shoulders, and smiled. "I remember when I gave you this jacket. Is it keeping you warm enough?"

"Yeah. I love it."

I took a seat, unable to stop staring. How could this be the same person who'd disgraced herself in front of all my friends?

Lydia nudged the menu that sat in front of me on the table. "Order whatever you want. But I'll bet I can guess what it'll be. A Number 15, right?"

I grinned. Then, at the same time, we both said, "With a side of barbequed pork."

Laughter rippled out of Lydia. "I've missed you, sweetie." Her hand slid across the table to rest on top of mine.

And then a man stepped up beside us. A man whose tattooed arms and neck made it clear he wasn't the waiter.

Lydia smiled at him. "Jess, this is my friend Alan."

"Good ta meetcha," he grunted as he tucked himself into the booth beside my mother.

It was only then that I noticed the third menu on the table. My stomach bottomed out as Lydia pulled her hand away from mine and let Alan wrap it in his. "I thought you wanted to talk to me."

"We can still talk. But Alan's been wanting to meet you, and I thought this might be a good time."

"You should've mentioned you were bringing him."

Lydia's eyes darted away. "I was afraid you wouldn't come."

She had *that* right. I studied Alan, looking for anything that might be the least bit reassuring. Everything I saw alarmed me. His arms bulged muscle and bore enough tattoo ink to print a dozen New York City phone books. A scar slashed across his left cheekbone. Even with him seated, his chin came to the top of Lydia's head.

"Your mom's told me a lot about you," he said. A smile broke over his lips, and some of my apprehension faded. His body might be intimidating, but his eyes were kind.

"Sorry, but she hasn't said anything about you." I didn't mean it as an insult, just a matter-of-fact comment. It wasn't Alan's fault my mother hadn't thought their relationship important enough to mention.

"Oh, we're not officially a couple," Alan said. "AA frowns on members getting involved until they've been in recovery for at least a year. We're just good friends."

Uh huh. Was that why he kept looking at her with the same wistful expression Cody used on me?

"I'm sorry, Jess," Lydia said. "I met Alan at one of my meetings. I didn't tell you because I thought you'd hold that against him. But he's been sober for almost two years, and if it weren't for his encouragement, I probably would've given up in those first few weeks." She tilted her head, beaming at him in a goofy, junior high way.

Okay, I could understand that. And I was willing to give Alan the benefit of the doubt. He'd made it farther than Lydia ever had. But none of that changed the fact that this was supposed to be our time, Lydia's and mine. Our chance to connect after all the mistakes. If she expected another moment like the one we'd shared last night, she shouldn't have brought an audience.

"I'm glad you found someone supportive," I said. An honest, non-committal statement. I wasn't sure getting involved with another alcoholic was the smartest thing she could do, but at least Alan was dealing with his problem, unlike the other guys she'd dated.

"Alan understands the realities of being in recovery," Lydia said, drenching him in another lovesick look.

"I guess that would have its benefits."

As if she couldn't, or didn't want to, sense the distance between us, Lydia began chatting about her experiences in AA and the things she'd discussed with her therapist. She stopped only when the waiter came to take our order. Alan didn't say much, simply offering a comment or response when Lydia asked for one. I couldn't believe she was dredging up her most personal baggage in front of this guy. I wouldn't have wanted anyone knowing those things about me.

All I could think about was escaping, but the only respectable option was to stick it out. The meal couldn't last forever.

Finally, the food arrived, and at least that didn't let me down. I made it halfway through my subgum chicken chow mein before Lydia realized I'd said less than Alan had.

"What's wrong, sweetie? You don't seem happy."

My fingers closed around my water glass, the condensation cool and wet against my skin. Did she really want me to answer that? I took a long gulp so I wouldn't have to.

"It's because I brought Alan, isn't it? He's a nice guy, Jess. Honest."

I set my glass back down. "I can see that."

"The trouble is, I shouldn't be here," Alan said. "This dinner should've been between you guys."

My eyes flew to meet his. He'd just earned himself some big points with that observation.

"Nonsense." Lydia patted his meaty forearm. "You're a part of my life. I want all my favorite people to get along."

Focusing on my plate, I poked stray grains of fried rice with my fork. "Getting along isn't the issue. Alan's right, I wish you'd waited for another time to introduce us. But it's too late to do anything about that now."

Lydia met my comment with a silence that lasted so long I had to look up.

"Well, then," she said, forcing a smile. "I guess we've got that sorted out. We'll just chalk it up to poor judgment on my part and put it behind us, right?"

When she took up where she'd left off, detailing her latest therapy session, I tried to follow, but it was all beginning to sound the same. My mind drifted to the calculus assignment that was due tomorrow and the English essay I hadn't even started.

". . . and so that's why I want you to come with me."

This last snippet wiggled in through a crack in my thoughts.

"What?"

"I'd like you to come to counseling with me. My therapist thinks we need to work things out together."

Cold tendrils wormed their way through my belly. She wanted me to tell some stranger about our problems? "I don't think so."

"But sweetie, if we ever want to have a healthy relationship, we should talk."

"We don't need a therapist for that. We were doing just fine last night."

She sighed. "It's not the same. With a trained professional—"

"I'm not going to do it, Lydia." Sure, counseling was a good idea—for her. She didn't know how to deal with her problems, and it was clear they'd contributed to her drinking. But I didn't share her issues. I had no trouble figuring things out on my own.

"Sweetie . . . please. I need this."

"No." I leveled a hard look at her. "If you want to talk, that's fine. But not with some therapist refereeing the conversation."

The serenity began to fade from Lydia's expression. "Why are you doing this to me?"

"Doing what?"

"I tried so hard. I gave you so much." Her tone disintegrated into a whine and her hands pressed flat against the table. "Why won't you do this one tiny thing for me?"

"Because I don't want to!" Didn't I have enough problems without some shrink poking around in my personal business? The cold tendrils corkscrewed deeper at the very thought.

Alan shifted against the booth cushions, eyes flitting back and forth between us.

"I haven't had a drink in seven weeks!" said Lydia, voice rising. "I stayed away at Christmas, even though the only thing I wanted in the whole world was to be with my little girl."

"And those were really good things, Lydia. But I'm not the

one who's got a problem, and I'm not going to counseling."

"But I've done so much for you!" Tears slipped from her eyes.

Alan took her hand in his, squeezing. "Shhh, baby, don't get upset."

"Why shouldn't I get upset?" Lydia turned to scorch him with a glare. "I worked so hard for her, and she can't be bothered to give me anything. I need this!"

"Your recovery isn't about Jess," Alan said.

"What good is being sober if she doesn't care?"

Oh, for Pete's sake. "I *do* care."

Lydia skewered me with the same look she'd given Alan. "Obviously you don't. You've never cared about anybody in your life." She'd gotten so loud now, people at other tables were staring. "You wanted me to stop drinking, and I stopped drinking. You wanted me to leave you alone, and I left you alone. I even bought you that damn book!" She reached across the table, fingers clenching like vice grips around my wrist. Her nails bit in, the way they had last June in that final fit of temper before she left.

"I appreciate all that," I said, struggling to conceal the fear that wavered through my voice.

"No you don't! You never appreciate anything I do. You don't know how hard I worked! You don't know what it's like!"

Alan had his arms around her now, clucking in a soothing tone, trying to calm her. But it was too late.

"I shouldn't have bothered! I shouldn't have wasted my time." Her eyes blazed, focusing with laser precision on my face.

And then she said four final words. "You're not worth it."

I tried to slide from the booth, but her hand clamped down tight.

Panic kicked in. My heart boomed in my chest. With a twisting motion, I broke away and scrambled to my feet.

Dodging tables filled with gaping people, I dashed through the entryway, out into the rainy parking lot. My keys nearly slipped through my fingers in my haste to get into the Pinto. Once inside, I tugged the door shut and slapped the lock button. When reason caught up, I cursed myself for being stupid. Lydia wasn't coming after me. Even if she tried, Alan would stop her. So why was my heart still slamming against my ribs?

I leaned back against the cool, black vinyl, listening to the rain rat-tat-tapping on the roof. It wasn't until then that I realized what had spooked me so badly. The only time I'd seen Lydia this hateful was when she was drunk. But she wasn't tonight. Even if I'd somehow missed all the signs, there was no way she could fool a fellow alcoholic.

The one thing I'd always been able to count on was that, no matter how bad things got with Lydia, as long as she was sober, I was safe.

So what the hell had changed?

CHAPTER 24

I lay awake late into the night, waiting for sleep to slip in and make everything better. Why did this hurt so much? It wasn't like I'd lost anything new. Yet a deep, welling sadness kept tugging at me, telling me it was over now. If I couldn't trust Lydia to be good to me when she was sober, I couldn't trust her at all.

The hours passed with a haunting sort of wakefulness, sleep not pulling me in as it normally did, but leaving me at the edges, watching myself dream. I woke with a hot kernel of weariness smoldering in the middle of my brain.

As I pulled off my pajama top, the sleeve scuffed across the inside of my wrist, waking the fire in Lydia's nail marks. Purple bruises glared up at me, startling me out of my stupor. If Cody saw those . . . well, there was no way I'd let him. He'd been right about Lydia, same as my dad, but he didn't need to know it. I'd pretend nothing had happened, and later, when it didn't bother me so much, I could tell him things hadn't worked out with Lydia.

I found a sweater in my closet that I didn't usually wear because the extra-long sleeves drove me crazy when they fell down over my wrists. Today it provided the perfect camouflage.

At school I floated from class to class, only half there.

"You okay?" Cody asked at lunchtime when I sat down with him and Heather. Concern filled his dark eyes.

"Yeah, I'm just tired. I couldn't get to sleep last night." It wasn't a lie, so I didn't have to feel guilty. I reached up to smooth my ponytail, which seemed to have developed a mind of its own and was curling stubbornly to one side.

"Well, at least you don't have to work tonight." Cody jammed his mouth full of pizza.

As he wolfed down his lunch, he chatted with Heather, but I barely contributed three words to the conversation. I was still toying with my salad when he glanced at the clock and announced he had to go.

"I've gotta finish a newspaper story," he said, lifting his tray with one hand and looping the other arm around me. "I hope your day gets better."

I picked at my lunch a little while longer before realizing I wasn't hungry. Pushing away from the table, I tossed an offhand "see ya," at Heather.

"Wait up." She dropped the remains of her burger onto her plate and followed as I dumped my tray. *Huh.* This was a first.

"Congratulations," she said as we walked out of the lunchroom. "You sure pulled one over on Cody. That's not the easiest thing to do."

"What are you talking about?"

Heather grabbed my arm, stopping me short, and pulled back my sweater to reveal the bruises.

I jerked away. "How did you . . ?"

"Your sleeve slipped down when you fixed your ponytail."

"Oh crap. Do you think Cody saw?"

"If he did, he would've said something." Heather's voice didn't hold a trace of sympathy. "So what's the deal? You cheating on him with some Neanderthal?"

I turned and started walking. "Don't be stupid."

"No, I guess you wouldn't." Heather trailed me down the hallway. "So what happened?"

"I thought you were all about people minding their own business."

"Usually I am. But Cody's my friend. If this is gonna bite him in the ass, I wanna know about it."

I wasn't sure whether that annoyed or impressed me. "He's not going to get hurt. It was my mom, and I'm done with her. End of story."

Only it wasn't. Against all my instincts, I wanted to talk about this. Not to Cody, who'd fuss and worry, or Kasey, who'd lecture me about using my head, or even Mark who'd turn it into a Taoist lesson. No, if I was going to share this, it needed to be with someone who understood the dark side of people. Someone who didn't care enough to judge me.

I angled over to the edge of the hallway and stopped where I wouldn't block traffic. "I met her at a restaurant last night. Cody doesn't know."

"And she attacked you?"

"Not exactly." I glanced at the kids swarming through the corridor. None of them were paying us any attention, but I still felt like I was on stage. "Look, would you mind if we went outside to talk?"

She shrugged. "It's cool with me."

I led her out into the misty afternoon. Too many people crowded the area around the doorway, banging in and out, so we walked through the parking lot to the path that led along Amazon slough. As we headed south, passing the ball fields, I told Heather everything that had happened with Lydia since Thanksgiving. Staying in motion made it easier to talk.

To Heather's credit, she didn't ask why I was spilling my guts. And that was a good thing, because I wasn't sure I could've explained. But it felt liberating to let it out. Something about summing up the experience helped me get a better grip on what had happened.

"So that's it?" she asked as we crossed 24th into Amazon Park. "No matter what, you're not gonna give her another chance?"

"I've given her enough chances. More than my dad and Cody thought I should. They were right. I need to walk away."

"Sounds like she's staying sober, though. Gotta give her points for that."

I tucked my fingers up into the sleeves of my denim jacket,

hiding them from the January chill. "That's what makes last night so weird. Lydia can get pretty nasty when she's wasted, but once she's sobered up, she's a really gentle person. And I know she hadn't been drinking."

Heather kicked a fallen branch out of the path with one of her combat boots. "Maybe she's a dry drunk."

"What's that?"

"This thing people in AA talk about. Someone stops drinking, but they don't change the stuff that made them suck down the booze in the first place, so they keep acting the way they did when they were drunk. Sobriety's about more than just not getting loaded, y'know."

I halted mid-stride, turning to eyeball her. "Where did you learn this stuff?"

"Biology research paper." She hunched her shoulders and grunted out a laugh. "Half my relatives are addicted to one thing or another, so I figured, go with what you know."

Hmm. Maybe Heather wasn't the shallow, self-absorbed whiner I'd been taking her for. "I see what you're getting at," I said, continuing down the path. "But I don't think that's what's going on. Lydia's been in counseling, and everything she's told me lately makes me think it's helping."

"But you said she's only been working on it for seven weeks. When someone's that screwed up, it can take 'em years to get things figured out."

I looked out over the waist-high dry grass that lined the trail. What she was saying made sense, but it didn't change the fact that I was done coddling Lydia.

"Sounds to me like your mom's actually doing all the right things," Heather added. "If she was my relative, and she'd made it this far, I don't think I'd give up on her yet."

Resentment burbled inside me. "Then you're a better person than I am. I've had enough. I've been dealing with this for almost nine years, and up until last night, I knew what to expect. But now she's changed the rules."

"So you're scared," Heather said.

"Maybe I am. What's wrong with that?"

"Nothing, I guess." She shrugged. "At least you can admit it."

Suddenly, I realized we were near the Amazon Community Center, a good fifteen minute walk from the school. "Oh crap! What time is it?" I yanked back my jacket sleeve to look at my watch.

"About five minutes into fifth period."

I glanced up and found Heather watching me with a raised eyebrow and an amused quirk of a smile.

"Why didn't you say something?" I demanded. "I'm late for calculus."

Her hand flew to her mouth in horror. "Oh my God! Life as we know it will surely cease to exist. Let's run before they send the Math Police."

After school I crashed on the couch, not even bothering with homework. By the time the clink of china on glass woke me, the sky outside the living room windows had gone dark.

"I made you a sandwich," Rhett said. He'd succeeded in holding his grudge against me for only three days, and our relationship was now back to normal.

"Thanks." I sat up and reached for the plate. Rhett had piled Nacho Cheese Doritos around an extra-thick PB and J.

"What happened to your wrist?"

The question jolted me, and a cascade of orange triangles fell to the coffee table. *Damn.* My sleeve must have crept up while I was sleeping. I tugged it back down, my brain whirling through a Rolodex of possible responses. Should I tell him the truth? No. It was way too complicated, and I didn't have the energy.

"A girl at school grabbed me."

"Why?"

Good question. I took a bite to buy time as I scrambled for an answer. "She thought I took her purse."

"What? That's crazy." Rhett plopped beside me on the couch.

"Yeah, well, it was no big deal. We worked it out." I tried to remember the last time I'd lied to him and realized that had been about Lydia, too. Back in October, when he'd asked me if it was his friend Trevor on the phone. In fact, all the lies I'd told, all the trouble I'd had with my friends, could be traced back to one source: my mother. Another good reason to be done with her.

"Did you get enough to eat?" I asked through a mouthful of peanut butter and jelly. "You should've woken me up. I'd have cooked dinner."

"That's okay. I didn't mind fixing it." He reached for the TV remote and spun it on the surface of the coffee table, hunching over and watching it twirl.

"What's up?"

"Nothing. I was just thinking about Teri Sue." The remote spun faster. "You reckon we'll ever see her again?"

"Of course we will. She just needs some time to cool off." Even as the words were leaving my mouth, I realized I didn't fully believe them. The problem with people behaving out of character was that it made you wonder if you could ever trust your instincts about them again.

"I wish Daddy would go talk to her. Or send a letter. Or something." Rhett had stopped giving Mark the silent treatment, but things weren't quite right between them.

"I know you don't want to hear this, but I think your dad's doing the best he can. He's scared Teri Sue's going to mess up her life."

Rhett's hand left the remote, and the whirling dwindled to a halt. "I'm scared of that, too."

188

"I'm not," I bluffed. "Your sister's got her faults, but she's a good person. One of these days she's going to figure things out, and then she'll be back."

Unimpressed by my optimism, Rhett stared at the table.

"Look," I said, setting down my plate and draping an arm over his shoulders. "There's not much we can do about Teri Sue, so let's talk about something cheerful. Like your love-life."

Rhett cracked the smallest hint of a smile.

"So how are things going with Emily?"

"Good." He leaned into me, head tucked against my chin. A spicy scent told me he'd been experimenting with his dad's aftershave. "Yesterday, I asked her if she wanted to go do something with me sometime, and she said 'yes.' Only now I have to figure out how. It sucks that we don't live on a bus line."

Our house sat on the south side of Spencer Butte, so our neighborhood was rural, even though we were only about fifteen minutes from downtown.

"Maybe I can help you out," I said. "Do you think Emily would be up for a double date? You could go to a movie with Cody and me Saturday night."

"Really?"

"Well, we'd have to clear it with your dad, but sure. It would be fun."

Rhett peeled himself out from under my arm. "I'm gonna go call her right now. Thanks, Jess!" He raced upstairs to the phone in the hall.

Well, that was easy enough to solve. Too bad all my problems weren't that simple.

A couple of hours later, while Rhett and I were watching a show about hurricanes on Discovery, the phone rang. When I answered it, Lydia's voice startled me. I seriously hadn't thought she'd find the guts to call this soon.

"Jess, sweetie, I'm *so* sorry about what happened last night."

"You're not the only one."

"I don't know what got into me. I swear, it'll never happen again."

"That's right, it won't," I said. "Because this relationship is over."

I dropped the phone into its cradle and went back to watching the program. Rhett glanced at me once, but didn't ask.

CHAPTER 25

Getting busted by both Heather and Rhett made me realize I couldn't go on hiding my bruises from Cody. Doing so would mean no close contact until they faded, something I doubted I could pull off, even if I wanted to.

After my talk with Heather and a good night's sleep, I felt better, so in the morning I cornered Cody at his locker and confessed. He listened with a stormy expression, but he didn't interrupt.

"I know you warned me," I concluded, fidgeting with my jacket zipper. "And you were right. But you don't have to worry about it any more. When she called last night, I told her it was over."

Cody folded his arms across his chest and leaned against his locker. "What if she calls back?"

"I'll hang up on her."

"You could tell your dad."

"If she doesn't leave me alone, I will. But I don't think it'll come to that." Expecting him to unload on me, I bit my lip and shifted from one foot to the other.

Cody surprised me by dropping his arms and wrapping his fingers around mine, his eyes going gentle. "I'm sorry it didn't work out, Jess."

Yeah, I thought, looking at the floor. *Me too.*

Emily approved the idea of a double date, and her mother called Mark to confirm that both Cody and I were upright, moral teenage citizens, gainfully employed and on the honor roll. Late Saturday afternoon, Cody, Rhett, and I stopped by Emily's house to meet her parents and pick her up for dinner and a movie.

Rhett rang the bell then froze when the object of his affection opened the door. Cute, blond, and perky, Emily looked like the sort of girl I'd given a wide berth in sixth grade. But recent experience had shown me my perceptions weren't exactly reliable, then or now.

"Hi, Rhett," she said, smiling to reveal a mouthful of braces. When he didn't respond, Cody gave him a nudge from behind that almost sent him sprawling.

"Uh, hi, Emily," he squeaked. He turned to gesture behind him. "This is Jess and her boyfriend, Cody. I told you about them."

"Yeah, I remember," Emily said, her smile teasing now. "You can relax. I don't have cooties." She grabbed his arm and dragged him, stumbling, into the room.

"It's nice to meet you, Jess," she said. "You too, Cody." Her eyes lingered on his bright blue T-shirt, which read, *If you choke a Smurf, what color does it turn?*

She giggled. "I used to watch that show all the time when I was little. You won't believe this, but my grandpa looks just like Gargamel."

Cody held up his hands as if to ward off some implied commitment. "I have no idea what you're talking about. I don't watch the Smurfs, I just make fun of them."

"Gargamel's the bad guy," I said, calling on my years of babysitting experience.

Emily shot me a smile of approval.

Once we'd passed parental muster, and Cody had assured Emily's mother we'd have her home no later than ten, we piled into the shiny red Galaxie to head for Track Town. Rhett sat paralyzed in the back seat, too tongue-tied to participate in Emily's stream of sixth grade gossip, despite my efforts through the rearview mirror to signal him to relax.

At the restaurant, he remained quiet, hiding his shyness behind slice after slice of pizza. Emily suffered no such debility.

While we ate, she bombarded Cody and me with questions about the speedway.

"I can't believe you really work on race cars," she said, looking at me the way Newt always did just before I poured food in his bowl. "That is *so* cool. Do you think sometime I could come by when you and Rhett are working on the Camaro?"

"Sure, if you don't mind getting dirty." Her sequined pink T-shirt and designer jeans indicated she was a little more fashion conscious than I was.

"Emily's no sissy," Rhett mumbled, disengaging his attention from his pizza to glance first at me, then her. When the earth didn't rumble to a halt, he continued. "She plays soccer and softball."

Emily smiled, making him melt.

"You shoulda seen her at the end of this game last fall—she was covered in mud. She's the goalie, you know, so she's gotta dive for the ball if it comes at her. Man, you wouldn't believe how fast she is!"

Once Rhett broke through that wall of self-consciousness, the words poured out of him. He babbled on, detailing Emily's soccer genius, while she sat back and listened, giving him the sort of look that could persuade a guy to climb Mt. Everest.

Cody and I exchanged glances over the remaining pizza. No doubt about it. Rhett was a goner.

Sunday afternoon I phoned the dorms to talk to Teri Sue, but the girl who answered told me she was out.

"Would you please tell her to call Jess at home?" I asked. I knew I was wasting my breath, and it didn't surprise me when Teri Sue didn't get back to me.

At work the next day, the Hawk saga began heating up. We'd pulled the body off on Friday so Jake could paint it while we continued work on the chassis, but his customer jobs were backed up, and it would be at least a week before he could get started. The engine still hadn't come back from the machine shop, and the company Kasey ordered the gasket set from had sent the wrong one. To add to the stress, her mother had called that afternoon and grilled her about the wedding plans. Race was off at the wrecking yard at the time and hadn't been able to offer a distraction.

Now he was following Kasey through the shop with a clipboard. "Look, I know it's a hassle," he said. "That's why I'm taking care of it. But I need your input."

Kasey bustled along, picking up tools and jamming them into the toolbox. "I don't care what color the flowers are," she said, pausing to holler at Cody to collect the grease rags. "I don't know who we should hire to cater the event." She stopped to help me balance the Packard exhaust manifold I was installing. "I've got an engine compartment detail that needs to be finished by Friday, Eddie wants two days off to help his mother move, and I just found out the paint I'd planned to use on the Hawk is no longer available. I don't have time to organize a wedding."

Race sighed. "You don't have to organize it. All you have to do is help me brainstorm. You must have some idea of what you want out of your special day."

She stopped abruptly and turned to face him. "No," she said, hands telegraphing her exasperation. "I don't. If you asked my sister Amber about her wedding plans, she could give you a list she's updated weekly since kindergarten. If you asked Brooke, she could detail her top five favorite romance novel weddings. But I've never been the type to dream about that sort of thing. I love you, Race, and I want to marry you, but it doesn't make any difference to me whether that happens in a church or our backyard or a drive-through chapel in Vegas."

Race dropped the clipboard on a workbench and stepped close, taking her hands in his to still them. "It doesn't matter to me, either. I just want you to be happy. But you've gotta understand, if you leave this whole thing up to me, we might wind up saying our vows on the start-finish line at the speedway."

Kasey smiled and drew his cupped hands close to kiss them. "I wouldn't have any problem with that."

That evening as I was sweeping up, Cody's grandma paid another visit, this time to talk to Race. He'd completed Mr. Gearhead's torso and arms and was now detailing the hands.

"That's coming along nicely," said Mrs. Morgan, watching as Race fit segments of push rod for the finger bones. "It looks like you'll be finished soon."

"Yeah, maybe in another couple of weeks. Kasey needs my help on the Hawk, so I'm not sure how much time I'll be able to put into it after today."

I picked up the extra bits of metal and stuck them in the scrap bucket. While Race did all the work on the sculpture himself, I liked to stay to watch. The way he hid his welds in some areas, and used them to compliment the work in others, taught me fine points his initial lessons hadn't.

Mrs. Morgan continued to watch, even when Race began cutting and grinding, a messy process that wouldn't do her tailored raincoat any favors. She stood military-straight, purse clutched in her hands, and didn't flinch at the sparks.

"I have a proposition," she told him when the noise ceased. "I'd like to commission you to do a sculpture."

"Commission me?" Race knelt beside the statue and began checking the length of the cut pieces. "Mom, if you want a sculpture, I'd be happy to make you one, but I hardly think Dad would want one of these in the back yard."

"It wouldn't be for me. I've been volunteering for an organization called TBI Northwest. They fund research and offer services to people with brain injuries. In May, they're holding an auction."

Race glanced up at her. "You think someone would actually pay for something like this?"

"I think someone would pay a great deal. Furthermore, you'd be providing inspiration to others with brain injuries. By finding a new way to express your artistic ability, you've proven success and happiness are possible, even after such a life-altering event."

Race grunted. "I don't know about that. I got lucky—real lucky—there are plenty of people who won't ever be able to talk or feed themselves or even get out of bed again. Do you really think they're gonna be inspired by someone who walked away with hardly a scratch?"

"Yes." Mrs. Morgan's tone was resolute. "There's no doubt you're more fortunate than many TBI survivors, but that doesn't mean you haven't had your challenges. The grace with which you've embraced them will most certainly motivate others. I don't think you're giving yourself enough credit."

Race stared at her, considering, then stood up and nodded. "Okay. I'll make you a sculpture, but if it's going to benefit a charity, I don't feel right about letting you compensate me. It's gotta be a donation, okay?"

"That sounds reasonable."

"Good." Race reached for a grease rag and wiped his hands. "Now what sort of thing are you looking for?"

"I'll leave that up to you. But you may want to consider that this will be a signature piece. The cornerstone on which you'll be building your career as a sculptor. TBI Northwest is in a position to help you promote yourself. That's why I selected them for this donation, rather than any of my other charities."

"My career." Race chuckled and shook his head. "Don't you think that's a little premature?"

"Not at all. Regardless of how you might see yourself, you're an artist." Her eyes pinned his, leaving no room for argument. "It's high time you realized that."

*　　*　　*

Tuesday night, Lydia called. I hung up on her.

"Who was that?" Rhett hollered.

"Wrong number." I trotted downstairs to join him in the living room, where he was watching TV.

"Oh, I was hoping it was Teri Sue. I called the dorms earlier and left a message."

Him too? A tiny flame of anger flared inside me. It was one thing for her to ignore my calls, but how could she blow off her little brother?

"You know what we need?" I asked. "Some cookies. You want to help me bake them, or are you watching this?"

"Nah, it's a re-run."

Rhett turned off the TV and followed me into the kitchen, where we spent the rest of the evening pretending we had nothing more important to worry about than the perfect size and chewiness of a chocolate chip cookie.

The following afternoon, I plotted out my evening as I hurried across the school parking lot through a chilling mid-January drizzle. If the Hawk engine was ready, I'd put in a couple of extra hours after work helping Kasey. And when I got home, I'd write to Teri Sue. Maybe she hadn't received my phone messages, but she couldn't ignore a letter.

I was so absorbed in my thoughts, I had to look twice before I recognized the drowned-rat of a woman leaning against the Pinto's trunk. A jolt of alarm ricocheted through me.

"What are you doing here?" My voice came out sharp and scared.

"I need to talk to you, sweetie."

"Well, I don't need to talk to you." I shouldered past Lydia to squeeze between the Pinto and the mammoth truck wedged beside it.

"Please, Jess, just give me another chance."

I worked my key into the lock, fingers clumsy with cold and the shock of seeing her. "Forget it. I gave you plenty of chances." My eyes strayed to seek out hers, violating a direct order from my brain. Hot wetness welled in them, another mutiny. "I trusted you. I *believed* in you. And you screwed it up."

"But I'm not drinking anymore."

"Maybe not, but you're still acting like a drunk." I opened the door and tossed my backpack inside. "Now leave me alone. Because if you keep hassling me, I'll call Dad and tell him everything. You can trust me on that."

CHAPTER 26

The machine shop had returned Kasey's engine, so things were less stressful at work, but I felt spooked the rest of the day. If Lydia had no qualms about tracking me down at school, where would she show up next?

The edginess stayed with me into the following evening, when Mark had class. Sitting at the kitchen table, I wrestled with my homework, my concentration totally shot. Every car whooshing by on Fox Hollow made my stomach clench. What if Lydia showed up and lost it in front of Rhett? He didn't need that kind of drama, and I wasn't sure I could handle another humiliation.

When he wasn't looking, I got up and quietly locked the door. But even that didn't make me feel safe.

Over the next few days, I heard nothing from my mother. The tension eased as I busied myself with the Camaro and work. At the shop, the atmosphere likewise transitioned from anxious to hopeful as Kasey ported and polished the heads and manifolds then began assembling the Hawk engine. But with less than six weeks to deadline, the project was still slightly behind schedule. It wouldn't take much to throw everything into chaos.

Monday afternoon, as Kasey was finishing up the engine, a customer barged through the door. He looked familiar, but I couldn't have matched his face with a name, or even a car. From across two bays, I felt the frustration shimmering off of him, tensing his posture and balling his hands into fists. His eyes scoured the shop, hunting Kasey. When he spotted her, he blazed a trail straight for her.

"That engine of yours blew in the middle of Franklin Boulevard. Now I'm late for my dinner engagement and I've got no way to get there. You'd better make good on this. That car's gotta make the Roadster Show in March!"

I wanted to slide all the way under the Packard I was lubing and huddle there until the man left, but Kasey recovered from his verbal assault within seconds.

"Is the car here?"

"Of course it's here! The tow truck driver wants to know where to park it."

"Well, whatever's wrong, I'll take care of it." She set down her ratchet and wiped her hands. "Let's take a look."

"I don't have time for that! I was supposed to be at the Hilton ten minutes ago."

"Then let's get you where you need to go. You can call tomorrow to find out what the problem is." She turned in my direction. "Jess, see if Race can give Mr. Ackerman a ride downtown."

Good thinking. If anyone could calm this hothead, it would be Race.

After the customer had been hustled off to his appointment, and the car, a '69 Chevelle, deposited in an empty spot in the parking lot, Cody and I followed Kasey out to take a look.

"Maybe it's something simple," I said. "A bad coil, or a faulty fuel pump."

Reaching through the grill for the release lever, Kasey didn't reply. The hinges groaned as she raised the hood. In the weak and waning late January sunlight, we studied the engine compartment.

"Whoa," Cody said, leaning in for a closer look. "That's messed up," And then I saw it, too. On the right side of the engine, behind the fuel pump, a broken rod poked out through a hole in the block.

I gaped until Kasey, who hadn't said a word, lowered the hood. She closed her eyes and took a deep breath, hands resting on the nose of the Chevelle.

Afraid to say anything, I glanced at Cody. He stared back, owl-eyed. The shop was booked solid through April. Fitting in this job would mean working after hours, time that was now being allotted to the Hawk. Even worse was the effect this could have on Kasey's reputation. A thrown rod was never a blameless error. It could only be the result of a serious mistake.

After a month-long silence, Kasey spoke.

"Jess, go finish that lube job so we can free up a bay. Cody, see if you can locate the work order for this car."

She turned and walked away, leaving Cody and me standing there like a couple of headlight-stunned deer.

I didn't want to make things more embarrassing for Kasey, so even though I was dying to know what had happened to the Chevelle engine, I didn't ask. Instead, I waited for a report from Cody. He called me late Tuesday afternoon.

"The crank broke because the radius between the journals and throws wasn't big enough. It's not Kasey's fault—the machine shop screwed up—but she feels guilty for not catching it when she was assembling the engine."

"Is Metzger's going to guarantee the job?"

"Nah, they swear they double-check that kind of stuff, so they refuse to even take a look. Now Kasey's gotta pay for everything herself *and* find a new machine shop. Because she sure as hell isn't gonna give them any more business."

"Oh, wow."

There was no point even thinking Kasey would allow us to help. Pride would insure she'd complete every bit of the work herself. But at least we could take over on the Hawk. Now that she'd finished the rebuild and had the wiring and exhaust complete, Race and I could install the engine.

"She's pretty bummed," Cody said. "Race keeps trying to tell her it's only natural to trust a machine shop she's been working with for almost four years, but Kasey figures this is gonna be a big black mark on her reputation."

I knew just how she felt. I wouldn't have bought Race's attempt at consolation, either. No matter what Kasey did to fix this, word was bound to get out. And there were plenty of guys who'd happily ignore Metzger's blunder in order to poke fun at a woman trying to make it in a man's business.

I figured things had become about as bleak as they could be for Kasey's project. But Wednesday they got worse.

At 6:00, when Jake and Eddie went home, Kasey and Cody continued with a customer job while Race and I got to work on the Hawk. He'd welded the new motor mounts to the frame when we'd mocked up the engine compartment to fit the exhaust, so I thought it would be a simple matter to drop in the engine and hook up the wiring. But Race wanted to go over the chassis first, something that was much easier now that the body was off.

"I'll let you take a look at the welds to see what you can find," he said, "then I'll check to make sure you haven't missed anything. This will be a good opportunity to put what you've learned to use."

I got out a trouble light and started with the front frame rails. It would've been easier if the chassis hadn't already been painted, but that just added to the challenge. The welds on the Mustang II spring towers appeared smooth and solid at first glance, but when I looked closer, I spotted a problem. Porosity. The tiny bubbles could be caused by two things— contamination by some foreign matter like paint or grease, or a lack of shielding gas. In either case, they compromised the weld.

"Uh, Race, you want to take a look at this?"

He crouched down beside me.

"Ah, shit." He pulled the trouble light from my hand to examine the crossmember and driver's side spring tower.

Continuing toward the back of the chassis, he mumbled as he examined each weld. "Frame rails look good. Body mounts are okay." He hunkered down and ducked his head to check the brackets for the 4-link rear-end. "Crap. This is all gonna need to be redone." Pushing up from the floor, he looked at me. "Whoever installed the suspension should never have been let within fifty yards of a welder."

"I thought this was a Garibaldi chassis. Why would they sell something defective?"

"They didn't. It's been modified. You can see the grind marks where they cut the stock stuff away." He pointed to the scratches on the frame rail. "Coulda been the guy Kasey's dad got it from, or maybe this project has been through a couple of owners. Damn. I shoulda caught this when I welded the motor mounts."

Now he was being just as self-critical as Kasey. The porosity was difficult to spot if you weren't looking for it, and it would've been even tougher to see with the body on. But I would have felt guilty about it, too. Kasey didn't need any more problems right now.

Race sighed and ran a hand through his hair. He glanced across the shop to where Kasey was working the dents out of a Fairlane's rear quarter panel while Cody stripped the interior. "Tell you what, Jess. Why don't you go give Cody a hand? I don't think Kasey's gonna want an audience when I break the news to her."

CHAPTER 27

Thursday afternoon, I picked up Rhett from school, but instead of dropping him off at home as I usually would've, I took him to work with me. After conspiring with Cody the night before, I'd gotten Mark's permission to let Rhett help out two days a week. Cody was going to meet us in the parking lot so we could approach Kasey together and offer our assistance.

"I know she's going to put up a fight," I said as we turned onto East Amazon. "So don't let her intimidate you, okay? We're going to do this, no matter what." I pulled into the lot and parked beside the Galaxie.

Cody got out and circled around to join us, hands stuffed in the pockets of his jeans. "You ready for this?"

"Of course. Just let me do the talking. I know you've got that silver tongue, but selling this will call for somebody as hardheaded as Kasey."

The shrill of the grinder greeted us even before we pushed through the door. Inside, Race lay under the front end of the Hawk, digging away at the defective welds. I marched through the shop, flanked by Cody and Rhett. Kasey was up to her elbows in El Camino. Glancing at us, she raised an eyebrow—a talent I coveted because every time I tried, both of mine lurched upward.

"Shouldn't you kids be at home?" she asked.

I straightened my spine, modeling myself after Cody's grandmother. "No. I think this is exactly where we're supposed to be. The shop's backed up, and you don't have enough manpower. You've been there for Cody and me when we needed you. Now it's time we did something in return."

Kasey smiled as she reached into the engine compartment to loosen a radiator hose. "That's really not necessary. I'm sure things will settle down once I button up the Chevelle."

I shook my head. "There's too much to do if you're going to get the Hawk ready by the beginning of March. Especially now that Race has to fix the chassis."

"If that's the case, I'll wait until next year to enter the Roadster Show. It won't be the end of the world." She fitted the proper socket to a ratchet and began removing the radiator bolts.

"But that doesn't have to happen. You've got us. We know you're worried about our schoolwork, but I promise that's not going to be an issue. We can handle the extra hours, at least for a few weeks until the customer backlog is caught up."

Kasey dropped the loosened bolts into a tin can on the intake manifold and hefted the radiator out of the engine compartment. "You do realize that I can't legally put an 11 year old on the payroll?"

"Rhett doesn't expect to be paid. He just wants to help. There are plenty of things he can do around here: pick up tools, wash parts, sweep the floors. I talked to Mark last night, and he doesn't have a problem with it."

"Well, *I* have a problem with it. I'm not going to take advantage of a little boy's generosity. If he works, he'll get paid."

I bit my tongue, waiting, because that sounded awfully close to a "yes."

"Okay," Kasey said, surprising me with the ease of her surrender. "Tuesdays and Thursdays, 3:30 to 6:00. But that's it. Don't come back to me in a week begging to work Sundays."

"I won't. I promise." I stuck my hand out to shake on the deal.

When Kasey gripped it, her lips were set in a firm, businesslike line, but her eyes shimmered with emotion.

On the way home that night, Rhett and I belted out Beach Boys lyrics until our voices went scratchy. I had no idea whether or not the extra fifteen hours a week would make a difference for Kasey, but the small contribution gave me a feeling of power over the catastrophes that kept cropping up. And Rhett was just plain giddy about the idea of making minimum wage.

When we got to the house, we sat at the kitchen table to tackle our homework. We'd been studying for only fifteen minutes when the phone rang.

"I'll get it!" Rhett said, hopping up from the table. "Maybe it's Teri Sue."

But the past three months had made me an expert at interception, and I already had my fingers on the handset. For Rhett's sake, I hoped it was his sister. He'd been calling her dorm every night. A week had passed since I'd sent my letter, and I was beginning to lose hope she'd get back to us.

"Hello?" I said.

"Jess?" Lydia's voice bit into me, making every muscle go tense. "I need a ride."

In the eight days since she'd ambushed me at school, I'd heard nothing from her. I should've known better than to risk believing she'd given up. But the wave of disappointment crashing over me had such an undertow, there was no doubt I'd convinced myself of exactly that.

"Sorry. I can't help you."

"Please, sweetie. I . . . I've had a couple of drinks. I know I shouldn't, but, well, I slipped. I don't want to drive home."

Was this a ploy to meet with me again, or had she really thrown away nine weeks of sobriety? Either way, I wanted no part of it. And I sure didn't want Rhett getting sucked in. I held the phone against my chest and looked at him. "I need a minute, okay?"

He nodded, and I ducked out the sliding glass door to the patio.

"Look, Lydia," I hissed. "You've spent the past eight years driving drunk. Do you seriously expect me to believe you're

206

suddenly concerned about breaking the law?"

"I was wrong those other times."

Or she was lying now. It wouldn't be the first time she'd fabricated a story to get me to do what she wanted.

"I can't leave. I'm taking care of Rhett."

"Bring him with you."

"To a bar? Are you crazy?" The last thing he needed was to be subjected to one of her meltdowns.

"Jess, please."

I leaned back against the cold, smooth surface of the door. "Call Alan. I'm sure he'll come get you."

"He's in Chicago."

"Well, what about your sponsor?"

"Sweetie, I need *you*. Just come pick me up and we can talk. I'll explain everything."

Yeah, that was exactly what I wanted to get myself into. Cody would strangle me if I fell for such a stupid trick. But if she was telling the truth about the drinking, I had to do something.

"Where are you? I'll call a cab."

"I don't want a cab! I want my daughter." Her whine grated me like sandpaper. Okay, maybe she *was* drunk.

"I'm sending a cab, Lydia. Tell me which bar you're at."

"You're not going to come get me?"

"No."

"Then forget it. I'll find my own way home."

The bang of a slammed-down phone sounded in my ear, and the line went dead.

At nine o'clock, Rhett and I abandoned our homework, broke out a bag of Cheetos, and retired to the living room to watch TV. The fact that Lydia hadn't called back confirmed she'd been trying to manipulate me again. Maybe it was time to get in touch with Dad.

The opening credits of *Cheers* were rolling when someone knocked at the door. Oh man, not again. If that was Lydia, I'd call Dad's dispatcher this minute and leave a message for him.

I opened the door to the crisp January night, but instead of my mother, two Eugene police officers stood on the porch.

"Good evening, miss," said one of them. His breath puffed in little clouds. I glanced at his nametag. Officer Reilly.

"Is this the residence of Jessica Deland?" he asked.

"Uh . . . yeah. I'm Jess." I glanced from one officer to the other. "What's going on?"

"You're the daughter of Lydia Deland?"

A hot river of fear flooded through me. "Yeah." My fingers clenched the edge of the door. "What's wrong? Did something happen to her?"

"Do you mind if we come in?"

I backed out of the entryway. The men stepped inside, pulling the door shut behind them. I hung back as they advanced into the living room, glancing around.

The shorter one, Officer Valdez, turned to face me. "How old are you, Jess?"

"Sixteen." The word came out sharp. Panicked. "Why? What happened?" I searched their rigid faces for a clue. Nothing.

"Is your father home?"

"No. He's a trucker. I live with Rhett and his dad." I gestured toward the couch, where Rhett sat staring, a Cheeto clutched between his fingers. My pulse pounded. What the hell was going on?

"And Rhett's father. Where is he?"

"Teaching at the college!" Why couldn't they just tell me why they were here?

"I think you should give him a call," Reilly said. "I'm afraid we can't release information to a minor."

"He's in class. Just tell me. Something happened to my mom, didn't it? Did she get in a wreck? Did she hurt someone else?" Oh, God. What if she'd killed somebody?

"I'm sorry," said Reilly. "Department policy prohibits me from telling you anything."

His partner, apparently thinking he wasn't going to get anywhere with me, turned to Rhett. "Son, why don't you get me your father's work number."

"Didn't you hear me?" I demanded. "He's not in his office. Tell me what's going on! Is she hurt?"

And then it hit me. If she'd been injured, they'd tell me. If she were lying in the hospital in critical condition, they wouldn't screw around wasting valuable time.

"She's dead, isn't she?"

Officer Reilly glanced at Officer Valdez, but neither one answered.

"Oh God. Oh my God."

The warmth drains from my body, sucked down, down, down until even my feet are numb. She's dead. She called me for a ride and I refused and now she's dead.

I falter backward, letting my weight sink against the sturdiness of the wall, but even that isn't enough to anchor me.

Officer Reilly jumps to catch my arms. "Easy, Jessica. Let's sit down, okay?" His eyes brim with emotion. Bastard. Where was that compassion a minute ago? Why the hell didn't he just tell me?

The room fogs, sitcom soundtrack a strange, riotous roar in my ears. Then I'm sitting, something heavy around my shoulders, skinny arms hugging me, a warm furry blur in my lap. A small hand clasps mine and I hear a soft drawl, but the words don't make sense. Nothing makes sense.

I killed my mother. I killed my mother. She asked for help and I said no and now she's dead.

CHAPTER 28

At some point, the mist began to lift. Another voice spoke, and I realized I'd been hearing it for some time. Feminine. Familiar. Comforting.

Kasey.

She placed something warm in my hands. A cup. Tea. I hated tea, but the heat felt good against my palms. I was a glacier—cold, solid—my thoughts creeping slowly, so slowly, as the weight of them gouged deep scratches that would last forever.

"Drink," said Kasey.

The cup rose to my lips as if it was her voice, rather than my will, that controlled my hands.

Liquid fire on my tongue, trickling down my throat, a tiny rivulet nibbling away the ice. Time still wasn't right because a moment later, the cup was gone and I huddled quaking beneath an avalanche of blankets. Images of Los Angeles flashed across the TV screen. The theme from *LA Law* swam in and out between the words of Kasey and someone else. A man. Mark.

Snippets of the conversation began to penetrate.

". . . no one else involved."

". . . police should've had more sense."

". . . talked to the trucking company . . ."

I realized the only way to get rid of the fog was to force my way through it. I pushed away the blankets, swung my legs off the couch, sat up.

Kasey crossed the room to kneel in front of me. Her hands went to my shoulders. She stared hard into my eyes, as if reassuring herself I was still in there.

"I'm okay," I said.

Kasey reached to stroke my cheek, her fingers warm spots

of sunlight against a pane of cold glass. "I know it's a shock," she said. "It would be a shock to anyone. Especially finding out this way."

Especially being responsible.

"I called your father's dispatcher," she continued. "They're giving him emergency leave. Another trucker will cover his delivery, and he'll fly into Portland tomorrow."

I couldn't remember when Kasey and Mark had gotten there, or the cops had left, but bits of their conversation seemed lodged in my head. Enough for me to know Lydia had crashed head-on into a telephone pole on Main Street, and the police had known where to look for me because of a letter in her purse.

"Where's Cody?" I asked.

"Home, by now. He and Race were at their shop when Rhett called. I suppose I should've stopped to let them know what happened, but the only thing on my mind was getting here. Do you want me to call him?"

I shook my head, though I wanted nothing more than to have his arms around me. Kasey's sympathy made me feel guilty enough. I couldn't handle Cody's too.

"Okay, then let's get you into bed. Sleep's the best thing for you."

She led me upstairs and tucked me in, but sleep didn't come. Not when Newt curled up purring against my neck. Not when the house went dark and quiet. Not when the glowing red display on my alarm clock flipped to two o'clock, then three o'clock, then four.

My mind replayed the phone call, trying to re-write the script. If only I'd said yes. Why couldn't I have looked beyond my anger and distrust for just a few minutes? I should've dropped Rhett off with Kasey, or made him stay in the back seat while I went into the bar. Why hadn't I said yes?

Kasey thought she understood, but she was wrong. She

didn't have all the pieces. I hadn't given them to her, couldn't give them to her. Because if I did, I'd never be able to look her in the eye again.

Around 5:30, I lost track of the flashing numbers. Then the alarm rang and I was irreversibly awake. I got up, took a shower, and went downstairs.

Rhett peered at me from the kitchen table, big-eyed and silent.

"I'm okay," I said.

He pushed back his chair and ran to fling himself at me, his gangly body soft and warm against the iceberg that was my own. He sobbed, and my arms mechanically circled his back.

Crying. That was what was supposed to happen when someone died. I felt moved that Rhett could do this for me because I had no tears.

"I love you, Jess. I'm so sorry about your mama." He pulled away and snuffled, looking up into my face.

People weren't going to understand the numbness. They'd expect some sort of response. I forced myself to give him one.

"I love you, too." The words nearly choked me, even though they were true. "You better eat. Your cornflakes are getting soggy." I turned and got the Cheerios out of the cupboard, pouring myself a bowl.

As I forced a tasteless spoonful between my lips, Mark walked into the kitchen.

"Jess." His hand settled on my shoulder.

I stared at a bubble clinging to the edge of a tiny round "o."

"Just tell me what you need. I can cancel my classes if you'd like me to stay home. Or I can take you to the shop if you'd prefer to be with Kasey."

"I want to go to school."

Mark hesitated. "If you think that will help."

The phone rang, pulling him away. The heat of his hand

lingered on my shoulder for only a second. I stirred my Cheerios into a slow, swirling wave.

"Jess?" Mark said. "It's Cody."

A breathless feeling constricted my chest. "I'll talk to him at school."

"Okay." Mark turned away and said something into the phone, his voice as garbled as the grownups' on *A Charlie Brown Christmas*.

After Mark left the kitchen, I dumped my cereal down the garbage disposal and trudged upstairs for my backpack. As I reached to grab my jacket from the back of the desk chair, an electric current shot up my arm and across my scalp. My hand flashed away, quick as if I'd touch a hot manifold. I froze, staring at the denim.

Lydia's voice pierced my memory.

"It's for you. Go ahead, look."

A huge bag from Sears in my lap.

The self-satisfied glow in my mother's eyes.

Leaving the jacket, I turned and raced downstairs, out into the cold morning rain.

As I unlatched my locker, a pair of arms encircled me from behind.

"Oh God, Jess." Cody's cheek pressed warm against my ear, and the scent of his hair gel, normally comforting, made my stomach twist. "I'm so sorry. I wanted to call you last night, but Kasey wouldn't let me. She said you were asleep."

I stood rigid, the heat of his body steaming against the icy dampness of mine.

"Where's your coat? Jeez, you're practically frozen." He drew me tight against his chest as if to warm me.

"I'm okay."

"Yeah, right."

Holding me must be like hugging an iceberg. Would he notice? Would it upset him when he found he couldn't thaw me?

A conveyor belt of kids flowed by on their way to class. Cody's arms stayed around me as if I was the only thing that existed to him.

"Nobody else knows what's happened with your mom since Thanksgiving, do they?" he asked.

"Only Heather."

There was something else they didn't know. Something even Cody was unaware of. I wondered if he'd still want to hold me if he found out.

After school, I went to the shop.

"Jess," Kasey said, "what are you doing here?"

"I want to work." *I need to work.*

Her hand, fragrant with Lemon Gojo, rose to my face, brushing renegade wisps of hair from my eyes. "I don't know if that's the best thing for you."

I stared at the ground, focusing on a quarter-inch nut someone had dropped. Wondering if it was coarse thread or fine. "It is," I mumbled. "Working is the best thing for me."

Kasey's warm fingers curled soothingly around the back of my neck, but I didn't look up.

"Okay," she said. "Your dad called a few minutes ago. He just got into Portland. He's renting a car, and he'll be here as soon as traffic will allow."

She put me to work cleaning the engine compartment of the El Camino. Race came up behind me as I gathered grease rags and wire brushes. He pulled me into a hug.

"I'm so sorry, kiddo. If you need anything, anything at all, just tell me, okay?"

You'd think things like that would melt through the ice. But they didn't.

*   *   *

Mark invited Dad to stay in the guest room, and this time he agreed. He also said he'd no longer be hauling hazardous materials, but the news barely registered. The two of them hovered all evening, asking how I was, trying to get me to talk. Rhett had been hustled off to stay the night with Trevor, despite my protests, so I had nothing to buffer me from their endless concerns.

After dinner, while we were still sitting around the table, Dad asked what we should do about final arrangements. He and I were Lydia's only survivors. She hadn't known the name of the small Nebraska town where her mother grew up, and she'd never met any of her relatives. Dad's parents had died in a car accident before he'd gotten together with Lydia, and the rest of his family was back East.

"She once told me she wanted to be cremated." I stared down at my nearly untouched mound of spaghetti. "She couldn't stand the idea of being shut up in a box in the ground." I'd been nine when we'd had that conversation. It should've given me the creeps to hear my mother glibly discussing her own death, but by then I'd had a year to get used to Lydia's black moods.

"Even so, there should be a service," my father said.

The absurdity of the statement was enough to draw my attention from my plate. "Come on, Dad. Who'd show up? Her only friends were the people she got drunk with, and I wouldn't know how to get a hold of them."

"Kasey told me she talked to your mama's boyfriend this afternoon," Mark said. "He thought some people from AA might like to pay their respects."

"I think your friends would, too," Dad added.

My eyes drifted down. A splotch of sauce had fallen in the space between my plate and the edge of the table. "The only time they ever met her was Thanksgiving. It's not like she gave them anything to respect."

"It's not about respecting her," Mark said. "It's about supporting you. Alan said he thought we could use the church basement where they hold meetings."

My stomach clenched. No way could I handle a mob of strangers patting my back, telling me how sorry they were. I didn't even want my friends doing it.

"No." I closed my eyes to steel myself against the suffocating idea.

"Jess, people need to say goodbye," Dad said. "*You* need to say goodbye."

My eyes snapped open and I glared at him, heart pounding. "I don't know those people! I'm not going to stand around talking to them about my mother. You guys keep asking what I need and what's best for me. Well, that's not it."

Mark glanced at my father, and then at me, his clasped hands resting lightly in front of him on the tabletop. "It doesn't need to be formal. We could have a small gathering here. That way, if it got to be too much, you could go up to your room." The kindness in his eyes made me look away.

I focused on Dad. "Would I have to say anything? Give a eulogy or whatever?"

"Only if you wanted to."

"I don't."

"Then you don't have to, honey." Dad touched my cheek. "Nobody's going to force this on you, but I think it might be a way for you to get some closure."

After what I'd done, I didn't deserve closure. But I'd already robbed my mother of her life. I couldn't rob her of a memorial, too.

"Okay," I said.

The next morning, as I was trying to decide if my stomach would tolerate a bowl of cereal, Dad walked into the kitchen.

"I thought it might be a good idea if we took a drive together.

216

I called Kasey and told her you'd be taking the day off."

"What? Dad, she needs me. She's only got a month to get the Hawk ready for the Roadster Show."

"I'm not going to argue with you. Get yourself some breakfast and we'll go."

As we headed out Highway 126 to the coast, Dad tried to get me to talk, telling me everything he could remember about my mother. But in the whole fifty miles, I probably said no more than five words. He kept at it as we turned north onto 101, his memories like burning missiles aimed at the glacier. Every single one bounced off and fizzled out.

At Devil's Churn State Park, we pulled into the parking area and walked down the path to the overlook. Waves broke white against inky basalt, booming as they sent up lacey plumes. The signs along the wooden fence warned visitors not to go beyond it. Something tugged at me, compelling me to slip beneath the rails and walk right to the brink of the cliff, but I resisted.

I stared into the swirling cauldron as mist drizzled down, soaking my sweatshirt and making me shiver.

"Where's your coat?" Dad asked.

I didn't answer. Last night, I'd balled it up and stuffed it in the back of my closet. How could I explain that?

He took off his own and draped it around my shoulders. The scents of Old Spice and leather hung close around me, but they didn't stir the normal wave of Dad-love.

My father looked out into the Pacific, where gray clouds merged seamlessly into gray waves. "Do you think you'd like to talk to someone?" he asked. "A counselor?"

Panic exploded in my chest. My breath caught, pain spiking, as a giant fist clutched my lungs. *Why won't you do this one tiny thing for me?*

"No!"

I backed away, stumbling as my heel caught on a root bump

in the asphalt. The reaction startled my father, and he turned to catch my arm, steadying me.

"Hey . . . hey. What's all this about?" He stepped close, hands gently gripping my upper arms as he searched my face with worried eyes.

I looked away, not wanting him to see my fear. A counselor would ferret out the truth in a second. I couldn't bear the thought of anyone knowing what I'd done.

"It's okay, honey." Dad pulled me against his green and yellow Oregon Ducks sweatshirt, beard rough against my cheek. "You don't have to. I just thought it might help."

Maybe it would've, if I'd done it when I was supposed to. Now it was too late. Why hadn't I told Lydia I'd go with her? If I had, she wouldn't have felt like she'd lost me. She wouldn't have gotten drunk. She'd still be alive.

I pushed away from Dad's chest. "I'm okay. Please, just let me deal with it myself."

"All right, Jessie. Whatever you want."

When we got back to Eugene that afternoon, he took me to the mall to get a new coat. I picked out leather, smooth and black. The farthest thing from denim I could find.

CHAPTER 29

Over the following week, the glacier thawed enough that I could do everything necessary to get by. But deep inside, a cold core remained, numbing my feelings. It didn't take me long to learn I could function without them. Robot Jess took over, going to classes, taking notes, showing up for work. She was a perfect cybernetic organism, able to fool everyone and even choke down limited amounts of cafeteria food.

My friends rallied, keeping me close, surrounding me in a web of anxious looks and gentle words. It seemed like everywhere I went, someone was patting my shoulder, squeezing my hand, or giving me a hug. Robot Jess smiled back and said, "I'm okay." It became her mantra, and somehow she convinced them.

Dad and Mark planned the service. I didn't want any part of it. Making it through each day was all I could handle. As long as I stuck to my normal schedule, I could cope, but anything that deviated the least little bit slammed my heart into overdrive and my brain into reverse.

They scheduled the memorial for Friday night. Kasey arrived at seven to help Mark with the food. Then, just before everyone else was due, Teri Sue walked through the door.

I gawked as if a brontosaurus had stumbled into the house. It was the first I'd seen or heard of her since she'd stormed off five weeks before. Beyond that, Teri Sue had no patience for her own mother and considered her breakdown a matter of weakness that should've been overcome for Rhett's sake. If she couldn't excuse the behavior of a mentally ill woman, what must she think of Lydia?

With her face screwed into the I'm-so-sorry look I'd been

getting all week, Teri Sue crossed the room and threw her arms around me.

"How you holding up, girl?"

"I'm okay." I backed out of the hug. "I didn't figure you'd show up."

Hurt flared in Teri Sue's eyes. "Whaddaya mean? I'm your friend, aren't I?"

"And you weren't my friend all those times I called and left a message?"

She looked away. "Let's not get into that."

"You should've come before this for Rhett."

"You let me and him work that out."

"He's your brother, Teri Sue. You can't keep ignoring him."

She sighed and finally met my eye, distress etching her face. "Look, this thing with me and Daddy—well, I'm sorry it's come between us. I know I'm not doing right by you or Rhett, and I'm gonna do better. But I've gotta handle things my own way. The only reason I'm talking to Daddy at all is because of what happened to your mama."

"He's just trying to keep you out of trouble."

Teri Sue shook her head. "I'm not gonna talk about it. Not now."

The doorbell rang, reminding me that she was right about the timing, though I'd much rather hash this out with her than deal with the evening ahead.

People began to trickle in. Race and Cody. Jake and Eddie. Folks I didn't know. The only friend of my mother's I recognized was Alan. Like everyone else, he headed straight for me as soon as he walked through the door.

His hand felt big and steady on my shoulder. "I'm real sorry, Jess. I know your mom had her problems, but she was trying hard. I thought she was gonna make it this time."

My gut coiled tight. *He thought she'd had a chance.* As an alcoholic, he'd seen it all firsthand, and yet he believed she

220

could've pulled it off. What if I hadn't kept shoving her away? What if I'd given her a ride? Would she have stuck with the program and finally gotten a handle on things?

Alan sighed. "It's a damned shame. I didn't even know she was drinking again. But that's how it is with alcoholics. The least little thing might set us off."

Like maybe a daughter telling her mother it's over and hanging up on her.

Alan patted me between the shoulder blades. "I wish I coulda been there when she needed me."

How could he think he had anything to do with this? "It's not your fault," I mumbled. Then I got away from him, fast.

But I couldn't avoid the onslaught of sympathy and the resulting guilt. One by one, the rest of Lydia's AA buddies sought me out. There must have been at least a dozen of them. The hardest one to talk to was Gail, her sponsor.

"Jess," she said, touching my arm with kindly fingers that somehow burned. "I'm so sorry about your mother."

"Alan said she could've made it."

"What?"

"Alan. He said he thought my mom was going to make it this time." The idea was still so fresh, but like a malignant tumor, it wouldn't stop growing. "You were her sponsor. Do you think that's true?"

Gail studied my face and sighed. "I know this must be a terrible time for you, Jess, but it doesn't do any good to second guess what might've happened. In AA we try to take things one day at a time. I'm sure you've heard that. And we don't make predictions about anyone's recovery. But I will say your mom really loved you, and she knew getting sober was the only way she could win your trust. A year ago, she might've lacked the motivation to stick it out, but once she realized how important it was to have you back in her life, I think it changed her perspective."

"So Alan's right."

"No." She shook her head. "As I said, we don't make predictions about other people. I just know your mom cared about you, and I feel confident she was giving it her best shot."

I riveted my attention on a carpet blotch, where Rhett had spilled hot chocolate. Somebody should've tried to get that out. I'd have to tell Mark we needed spot remover.

"Jess? Are you all right?"

I nodded. No matter how adeptly Gail might sidestep, I could interpret the facts. Things had changed with Lydia, and this time around, she'd had a good chance.

"It might help to talk to other kids dealing with alcoholic parents," Gail said. "My children are in Alateen, and they say it's made a real difference."

Maybe for them, but what good would it do me? My mother wasn't drinking. She was dead. I didn't want to hang out with kids who still had a chance of seeing their parents get sober.

"If you're interested, give me a call. Your father has my number." Gail's fingers pressed red hot against my arm, and then she was gone.

I looked up to see Cody casting a questioning glance across the room. He'd been watching all night, holding back enough to allow me some privacy, but constantly keeping tabs. I forced a smile at him.

Don't think about the possibility that Lydia might've beaten the booze. Don't think about the people who would've dropped everything to give her a ride. Don't think about what everyone in this room would say if they knew what really happened that night.

I stuck it out until the group settled down enough to begin sharing stories about my mother. After the first one, I snuck up to my room. Newt, who wasn't much for crowds, looked at me and chirped from his perch on my pillow. I lay down beside him, resting my face in the silky sweetness of his fur. His purr rumbled against my cheek. He'd been extra snuggly all week, as if he knew something was wrong.

The door squeaked open just an inch, allowing a streak of yellow light to slice across the bed.

"Jess?" Cody said. "Can I come in?"

"I guess."

He slipped through the door, pushing it shut behind him. Without a word, he sat down and began to rub my back.

A normal girl would've cried. I lay silent, my fingers caressing the soft fur under Newt's chin.

Cody stretched out alongside me, hands stroking my hair, pulling me in close against the heat of his body.

"Things will get better," he whispered. "I promise." His lips found mine, and he kissed me long and deep.

But even that couldn't melt me.

CHAPTER 50

As the first two weeks of February blew past on a cold, damp wind, Robot Jess kept plodding along. But her batteries were running down.

I continued to work extra hours at the shop, taking Rhett with me twice a week. My commitment to help with the Hawk provided some distraction. Race repaired the chassis, Kasey and I installed the drive train, and Jake tackled the body-off paint job. The car stood a solid chance of making it into the Roadster Show, but only two weeks remained, and we still had a lot to do.

Kasey told me every day that I didn't need to work. That I looked exhausted—no surprise, since I couldn't sleep—and should get some rest. But I said staying busy was the only thing that helped, and that was something she understood.

Eventually, even the comfort of routine lost its power. A tiny voice crept into my head, saying, *what's the point?* I kept doing all the things I was supposed to, school and work, cooking dinner and taking care of Rhett. But I no longer felt the purpose behind any of it. School was the worst. I struggled with my homework, unable to stay on task. I'd look up from a page of chemistry problems to realize two hours had passed and I had no idea where I'd spent them.

Cody helped me study, drilling me on historical dates and parts of speech, but even if I succeeded in getting a bit of knowledge past the locked gates of my brain, I couldn't retrieve it when I needed to. As soon as a teacher placed a test paper in front of me, the doors slammed shut. I knew I was blowing it, that if I couldn't pull it together I'd never get into college, never earn my degree or open my race shop. But none of that mattered anymore.

While Dad stopped hauling explosives, nothing changed with his work schedule. He tried to make up for that by sending postcards several times a week and calling every few days. I listened to his colorful trucker's stories without much comment. Responding with anything more than a few of words seemed beyond me.

Several times, Teri Sue attempted to touch base. She always wound up missing me. I returned the first call, but she was in class. After that I didn't bother. It took too much energy.

Through all of this, I felt nothing. I couldn't cry, couldn't respond to the sympathy everyone offered. I couldn't even feel angry. I was empty. Numb. The closest I came to an emotion was never-ending hopelessness, except late at night, when guilt crept in.

Everyone knew I wasn't myself, but they didn't know the depths of it. Robot Jess was too good at her job. Cody had his suspicions, inspired by my lukewarm response to his embraces and refusal to tell him what was going on in my head. But when I said I needed space and time, he trusted me enough to grant them.

I couldn't talk to any of my friends. They had so much compassion for me, and accepting it seemed dishonest. Oddly enough, the person I felt most at ease with was Heather. I hadn't told her about Lydia's call, but somehow I knew it wouldn't shock her. I understood her now. The dark clothes, stark make-up, and grim music. The talk of pain as the soul's pure expression. It all felt soothing.

Aside from Heather, my only relief was sleep. But that remained elusive. I lay awake late into the night, watching time cycle by in red flashes on my alarm clock. Struggling to re-write two critical scenes.

How could I have fouled up so badly? Okay, sure, the thing at Lok Yaun was understandable. Lydia had scared me. But afterward, when Heather explained her behavior, why hadn't I listened? Why had I hung up on my mother, snubbed her at school, refused to give her a ride? One of the hardest things for an alcoholic to do was hand over the keys. Lydia had humbled herself, and no matter how mad I'd been, no matter how spooked, I should've put my feelings aside to give her what she needed. How could I have been so selfish? So stupid?

The thoughts would gnaw at me until the night was almost gone, and then in the slim hours of morning, sleep would slip in to soothe me. I'd wake exhausted, haul my body out of bed, and force myself to go through the motions one more time.

On the second Thursday in February, the twenty-first day after Lydia's death, I opened my locker to find a bouquet of red roses and a box of Euphoria truffles. Cody stepped up behind me. The heat of his lips warmed the back of my neck.

"Happy Valentine's Day," he murmured.

Oh no. I pivoted away, eyes scanning the halls. The evidence hung everywhere. Paper hearts, red and pink balloons, posters advertising the choir's singing Val-o-grams. How could I have missed all this?

Cody grinned and leaned forward to kiss my frozen lips. When I didn't respond, he pulled away. "What's wrong?"

"I forgot, Cody. I'm sorry. I just . . ."

"Hey, it's no biggie." His hands sought mine, cupping them in a little burst of springtime. The kind that comes too early and gives way to six more weeks of winter.

"I should've bought you something. I can't believe I forgot."

"Shhhh." Cody's fingers pressed tight. "You've had a lot on your mind."

"I'll make it up to you. I promise."

"Don't worry about it. I don't need a card or flowers to tell me how you feel." He leaned in to ceremoniously kiss the middle of my forehead. "I hereby absolve you of all guilt."

Of course he meant it, but that didn't mean I could absolve

myself. For weeks he'd stood by me, enduring my silences, taking no offense to my frigid responses to his affection. And each time he looked at me across the shop, or over the kitchen table as we studied, I saw the pain in his eyes. Sometimes it seemed that my distress burdened him even more than it burdened me.

Words were impossible, and I couldn't force my body to demonstrate how much I cared. The one thing I could've done was buy him a Valentine's card. And yet I hadn't even managed that.

I didn't deserve a guy as kind and thoughtful as Cody.

In chemistry, I blew another test. This time I couldn't make sense of the words. I stared down, reading the same question over and over, but by the time I got to the end, I'd forgotten the beginning. The bell rang. I hadn't even written my name at the top. I left the paper on the desk and walked out.

As I headed for the cafeteria, someone tugged the sleeve of my new leather jacket.

"You look like you just crawled out of a tomb," Heather said. "What's up?"

"I spaced on a test. . . . And I forgot it was Valentine's Day."

"Seriously?" She gestured at the walls. "With this shit everywhere? So you didn't get anything for Cody?"

I shook my head.

"Don't worry, he'll get over it."

"He's not mad. I sort of wish he was."

My feet stalled at the door of the cafeteria. The greasy smell of hamburgers sent a wave of nausea roiling through me.

Heather took several steps before noticing I wasn't at her side. She glanced over her shoulder. "What's the problem?"

"I've gotta get out of here."

"Fine with me." She did an about-face, making for the nearest door.

I stared after her. Cut school? Funny how that seemed like such a sin, even now. But what difference did it make? I followed her to the parking lot, where we got into her '72 Gremlin, a wreck she'd painted flat black with rattle cans. The back end was squashed in from being hit by a school bus. She'd told me she'd bought the car for fifty dollars.

Heather seemed to know every back alley and dirt road in town, and she took me down all of them. Cody or my father would've tried to get me to talk. Heather just blared her macabre music and kept her attention on the road.

It was a relief to hang out with someone who didn't attempt to comfort me. I closed my eyes and allowed the music to carry me to dark places that were soothingly different from my own. A rare warmth slipped over me, drawing me in. The next thing I knew, Heather was poking my shoulder.

"Hey, wake up."

I jumped, blinking at the scenery outside the Gremlin. A 7-Eleven parking lot, but not one I recognized.

"I'm jonesing for some coffee," Heather said. "You want anything?"

"Mountain Dew."

I listened to the tick of the engine cooling as she went inside. A few minutes later, she returned with the drinks and two chili cheese dogs.

"Don't know about you, but I'm starved," she said. "Somebody made me miss lunch."

"Sorry."

"Kidding! Jeez." She handed over my Big Gulp and dog, then ate her own.

I forced down a couple of bites.

Heather licked chili off her fingers before pulling out onto the street. We drove some more, exploring the twisty roads in the South Hills, where I often took the Pinto. The cheese congealed on my hot dog, making it even less appetizing. I let the sweet zing of Mountain Dew fill the void in my stomach. When I finished the drink, I pulled the lid off the cup and stuffed the rest of my hot dog inside. If Heather noticed, she didn't mention it.

We drove on, exchanging only a handful of words. The sky faded to a darker shade of gray. I looked at my watch. 5:27. *Shit*. Not only had I blown off work, I'd also forgotten to pick up Rhett from school.

"Oh God. Mark's gonna kill me."

Heather angled a look in my direction. "What's wrong?"

"I forgot Rhett. You have to take me back to my car."

Since Spencer Butte Middle School was on the way, I made her stop there. Of course, Rhett was long gone.

"Oh, hell. Where is he?"

"He must've called someone for a ride."

"Who? His dad? One of his friends?" The thumping behind my ribs zoomed from zero to sixty, and I sat forward, straining against the seatbelt. "Damn it, Heather, I've gotta find him!"

"Where's he supposed to be?"

"At the shop with me."

"Well then, that's probably where he called. You want me to drop you off there?"

"No." I fell back against the seat, rubbing a hand across my face. "Just take me to my car."

The Pinto sat nearly alone in the student parking lot. A Taco Time receipt had been left under the windshield wiper. On the back, Cody's handwriting screamed, *Where are you?????????? I've got Rhett and I'm taking him to the shop.*

I jumped in my car and sped to work, as if the thirty seconds I saved would make a difference. But when I pulled into the lot, I froze. How could I go inside? Swearing, I rested my head against the steering wheel.

A tap at the window jerked me upright. Cody yanked open the door.

"Where the hell have you been?" With one hand on the roof, and the other white-knuckling the frame around the driver's window, he leaned in toward me. "You scared us half out of our minds!"

I'd seen that raging worry in his eyes once before, and it had been due to my stupidity then, too. I wanted nothing more than to look away, but I couldn't. Not yet.

"Is Rhett okay?"

"Other than being scared shitless?" Cody's eyes flashed disgust. "Yeah, he's fine. He waited at school until four. *Fortunately* there was still someone in the office to let him use the phone when you didn't show."

Thank God. My focus drifted to where my thumb was rubbing the torn vinyl of the steering wheel cover. "Does Mark know?" *Please, please, don't let Mark know.*

Cody grunted. "Are you kidding? Kasey called everyone who might've had the slightest idea where you'd be. She even tried Heather's place, after I told her that's who you'd been hanging out with lately."

I jiggled the flap of leather. "Heather was with me."

"What? Where?"

"Just driving around."

Cody slapped the roof of the Pinto. "I'm *so* gonna kick her ass."

"No!" I turned to face him. "It's not her fault. She was trying to help."

"What—by encouraging you to ditch school? That's not the kind of help you need, Jess."

It was exactly the kind of help I needed. "She didn't know I was supposed to pick up Rhett. Just leave her out of this, okay?"

Cody drilled me with a look. But behind all the anger, all the bluster, I saw fear in his eyes. He pushed back from the Pinto's door and turned away.

"You better get inside."

Once everyone had seen for themselves that I was okay, Kasey led me into the office and shut the door.

"Sit down," she said, sliding into the chair behind the desk.

I dropped to the couch, my leather jacket squeaking against the vinyl.

"Tell me what happened today."

Avoiding her eyes, I shrugged. "Nothing. I had to get away to think. Heather and I were driving around and we lost track of time."

"Jess, skipping school is completely unlike you. And I can't imagine what it would take to make you forget Rhett. I want a real explanation."

I stared at a dusty upside-down footprint that marred the black metal of the desk. It looked like Converse high top tread. Must've been from Cody.

"Did something happen at school?" Kasey persisted. "Cody said you were upset because you forgot Valentine's Day. Is that what this is about?"

My fingers traced the seams of the cushions to either side of me.

Kasey sighed. "I know you prefer to handle things on your own, but death is difficult to process. Maybe it's time you talked to a professional."

"No!" Fear sliced away my lethargy, drawing my eyes up to meet hers. What could I say to get out of this? What would she believe? "Okay. The truth is, I fell asleep in Heather's car. She didn't know I had to be somewhere, so she didn't wake me up. I-I had trouble getting to sleep last night."

"From the looks of you, you've been having trouble getting to sleep for quite a while." Kasey's no-nonsense gaze cut right through me. I couldn't stomach it, so I went back to studying Cody's footprint.

"Sleeplessness is one of the symptoms of depression," Kasey said. "You're displaying others, too. That's perfectly natural, considering the circumstances, but what worries me is that you can't seem to talk to any of us."

"I'm not depressed." Lydia was the one who got depressed. The one who couldn't handle her own problems. I wasn't like that. "The not-sleeping thing is getting better. At first I could hardly sleep at all, but now it only happens once in a while. And I talk to Heather all the time." I stared right at Kasey, faking a look of honesty to back up the lies. "Please don't tell Cody about that. He won't understand."

She laced her fingers together on the desktop. "Heather is the Goth girl he went out with last year?"

I nodded.

"I'm not sure that's the type of influence you should have when you're depressed."

"I'm not depressed! And Heather understands. Everyone else keeps trying to cheer me up, but she lets me cope with things my own way."

Kasey's eyes searched mine. Was she buying it? Would she let it go?

"Okay," she said, shaking her head as if she wasn't quite sure of her decision. "As long as you're confiding in someone."

CHAPTER 3I

I apologized to Rhett the whole way home.

"It's okay, Jess," he said, more than once. But he wouldn't look at me, his eyes locked instead on the barren trees flying past the Pinto. As soon as we got to the house, he went to his room.

When Mark returned from work after ten, he sat me down for a heart to heart. But before he could get a word out, a river of apologies ran from my lips.

"I'm sorry. I really messed up this afternoon. It was stupid and selfish and I wouldn't blame you if you never trusted me again." Rambling on, I berated myself until he held up a hand to stop me.

"Jess, I'm upset, but I'm not angry. I know you'd never intentionally do anything to hurt Rhett. I *am* worried about you, though."

"I'm okay. Honest." I gave him the same story I'd given Kasey, tossing in bits of truth here and there to make it sound good. "Nothing like this will ever happen again. I promise."

Somehow I must have convinced him. He sighed and squeezed my shoulder. "I hope not."

As much as it relieved me to have evaded both Mark and Kasey, I felt I'd gotten off too easily, that there should've been consequences for letting them down.

In bed that night, the "if onlys" swallowed me up. Not just about Lydia, but about Cody, work, and Rhett. Was I ever going to get a grip on myself, to stop complicating the lives of everyone around me? I twisted in my blankets, restless and fidgety. No position remained comfortable for more than a few minutes. The alarm clock glared red, minutes blinking by one by one. A glowing coal burned behind my eyes, and not even the gentle thrum of Newt's purr could lull away my fitfulness.

I remembered my last good conversation with Lydia, when she'd told me about her mother. All she'd wanted was to have that kind of relationship with me—the same thing I'd been longing for.

I missed her. Through all the fog and numbness, I missed her and wanted her back. Even if she never changed. Race might not want a do-over, but I did.

Suddenly, I couldn't take any more of the churning mess in my head. I tossed off the covers and sat up. The house lay dead quiet, its stillness a hand that muffled me and cut off my breath. I had to get out.

I pulled on some clothes and tiptoed downstairs, clicking the door shut behind me. Once in the Pinto, I stuck the key into the ignition. Mark's room sat at the back of the house. Would he hear the engine starting? He was a hard sleeper, but I'd better not risk it.

The driveway sloped gently to the road. I stuck the transmission in neutral and jumped out to rock the car until it began to coast. Hopping inside, I steered silently backward down the driveway, using the brake lights as illumination. At the bottom of the hill, I turned the key. The engine howled in the still night, making me cringe.

After backing out onto Fox Hollow, I cranked the volume on the tape deck and drove. I passed the intersection with Willamette and kept going south, away from town. No stoplights, no other cars, just open highway.

The ever-present February rain had stopped late the previous afternoon, allowing traffic to evaporate tire tracks down either side of the street. The Pinto sooshed over dry asphalt, headlights cutting a brilliant swath across the empty road. On the stereo, Bert Convy and the Cheers belted out the morbidly satisfying *Chicken*. The beat throbbed from the speakers, harmonizing with the growl of the engine until the music, the

Pinto, and I became one.

Squeezing the gas, I rocketed through corners, feeling the rear tires slide then grip as I accelerated out of the turns. A tiny thrill shot through me—the first thing besides guilt and hopelessness I'd felt in weeks. I pressed on, driving, just driving, my world a small tunnel of light through the forest of naked trees.

I'd been at it for maybe half an hour when I thought to look at my watch and the gas gauge. Three-oh-five and a quarter tank. Time to head home. I turned around and retraced my path, creeping up the driveway with the headlights off so Mark wouldn't catch me. In a whisper, I let myself into the house, slunk up the steps, and crawled into bed.

The next thing I knew, my alarm was ringing. Almost three straight hours of sleep. A record.

I was careful not to make mistakes that day, in spite of the fog that descended the moment I got out of bed. I stopped at Albertson's on the way to school to buy Cody a half-pound Hershey bar and a Valentine's card. Inside I wrote *I'm sorry about yesterday. I won't let it happen again.*

When I got to school I slipped the gift into his locker.

Cody caught up with me at lunchtime as I walked into the cafeteria. He was wearing his *Feed Me and No One Gets Hurt* T-shirt.

"I'm sorry, too," he said. "You scared me, but I shouldn't have yelled. The last thing you need right now is your friends turning on you."

"It's okay," I assured him. "I deserved it."

At work, I learned Kasey had run into another problem. She and Jake had spent the past two days putting the newly painted body back on the Hawk, but when they'd tried to move the car that morning, the clutch wouldn't release. The impossible-to-schedule graphics painter had just arrived to tackle the ghost feathers, so it would be tomorrow before they could pull the transmission to find out what was wrong. Kasey had planned to deliver the Hawk to the upholsterer in the morning, a job that had already been postponed. Now, Tuesday was the earliest they'd be able to reschedule, which meant she'd have only a couple of days to button things up before the Roadster Show. And that was if they were able to finish the interior in a week as promised. Tensions were soaring, and I sympathized with Kasey, but at least her troubles deflected the heat from me.

For the next couple of days, I drifted in a stupor, just trying to stay out of trouble. At work Saturday, I learned the clutch problem was due to a broken weld on the throw-out bearing release shaft lever. A simple repair for Race, and one that required no waiting for parts. The ghost feathers looked spectacular, so Kasey was happy, despite being buried in customer work we hadn't yet finished.

Sunday afternoon, as I sat spinning a pencil on my desk and staring out the window, I heard something behind me. I turned to see Rhett standing in the doorway of my room.

"Um . . ." he said, fidgeting with the top of his brace. "You wanna work on the Camaro?"

"Not right now." The barn was cold, and even though the heater would warm it eventually, the whole thing seemed like too much of a hassle. Getting out the tools, making the repairs, putting everything away. Before Lydia died, there'd never been a time when working on a car couldn't cheer me up. Now it just seemed like drudgery. At the shop it was okay because there were other people around to offer a distraction and keep my mind from wandering. But here it was only Rhett and myself, and I didn't know what to say to him any more than he knew what to say to me.

"We haven't done anything to it in weeks," he said. "It's gotta be ready for Teri Sue when the season starts." Though his sister hadn't been home since the memorial, she'd been sending Rhett cards, and that seemed to be enough to satisfy him.

"There's plenty of time," I said.

Rhett stared at me as if I'd morphed into a stranger, which was pretty close to the truth. Thursday might've been the first time I'd forgotten him, but I'd abandoned him in so many other ways. Feeding him peanut butter sandwiches instead of real dinners, leaving him to tackle his homework on his own, drifting through the house without saying anything at all. In the beginning, he'd stayed close, talking to me, offering little gifts, and ambushing me with spontaneous hugs. But I'd slowly frozen him out.

Of all the people I'd kept at arm's length, it was Rhett I felt the worst about. I was failing him, just like his sister had. But even that prickle of guilt could not compel me to get up and go out to the barn.

That night, sleep taunted me again, promising the comfort of oblivion then snatching it far up out of reach. I'd grown to hate the look of my room in the darkness, the restless feel of my bed.

The lonesome highway began to call me. Had it just been a fluke the other night, or would I be able to drift off after a drive? Only one way to find out.

I'd filled the Pinto's tank, just in case, so there was nothing to hold me back. Once I rolled the car to the bottom of the driveway, I re-traced my previous route, south on Fox Hollow and again on the Lorane Highway to Territorial Road. Tonight, I pushed the Pinto harder, feeling a dangerous rush each time the back tires went feather-light beneath me. The thrill compelled me to dive even deeper into the next corner, intoxicating me with the idea that this might be the time I went too far.

Finally, it was. As I surged out of a corner into fog-shrouded pastureland, the back end broke loose, and suddenly I was spinning. Once. Twice. The Pinto looped across the opposite lane, headlights careening over fence posts and brush. It slid to rest facing the way I'd come, one tire on the asphalt and the other three on the shoulder.

Terror pulsed through me in a sharp and perfect wave. For one split second, I felt the punishment I'd been seeking all along. I breathed deep, relishing the thunder in my chest, the sheer amperage racing along every nerve.

My shaking hand reached for the key. I started the engine and gave the car a little gas. Fortunately, there was enough gravel at the side of the road to provide traction. Another few feet, and I'd have been spinning my wheels in the sodden field.

I pulled onto the highway and headed for home. But I drove hard all the way, daring fate to settle up with me.

My late-night drive proved once again to be the perfect sleeping tonic. It worked so well, I didn't wake to my alarm. No big deal for me, but it meant Rhett had to take the bus, something he hated.

Without bothering to shower, I threw on yesterday's clothes and went downstairs to make some toast. Mark stopped me before I could get out of the kitchen.

"Jess, we need to talk."

"I'm late for school."

"I'll write you a note. Sit down." He motioned toward the table, where a bouquet of forsythia branches sprouted brightly from a mason jar. He'd brought them in a few weeks earlier to force the buds.

Abandoning my toast on the counter, I pulled out a chair and fell into it.

"I'm not sure I was acting in your best interest when I let you off the hook the other day," Mark said. "I should be doing more to help you through this."

I looked down at the table top, running my finger along the crack between the leaves. "You're doing fine. And I'm sorry for oversleeping. I know I let Rhett down."

"Rhett's not the one I'm worried about. It won't hurt him to take the bus. But it's obvious you're struggling. I've been thinking about asking your father to take more time off to be with you."

An icy current zipped along my spine, snapping my head to attention. I'd already failed Cody and Rhett, I couldn't let my dad down, too. "Mark, no. Please! He took ten days leave just a couple of weeks ago. It's not going to look good if he does that again. What if they tell him they don't need him anymore?"

"They won't, Jess. His boss will understand that family comes first."

"All they care about is making money. And there's a hundred other truckers who'd be glad to cover his loads." As an independent contractor, Dad should've been free to take time off whenever he liked, but in reality, every time he turned down a run, it made him look uncommitted.

"Jess, I'm concerned. You've been so depressed. I think you need your father right now."

"I'm okay. Really." I plastered a bittersweet smile on my lips. "I mean, yeah, I'm sad. Who wouldn't be? But I'll do better, I promise."

"It's not about doing better." Mark's hand slipped across the table to cover mine. "It's obvious you're doing the best you can."

"Please don't ask him. He's supposed to be home this weekend. Can't it wait until then?"

Releasing a long breath, Mark drew his hand away to run it through his hair. "All right. I won't mention it until his next visit."

I had five days to get it together so Mark wouldn't have to talk to Dad. As I drove to school, I gave myself a lecture. This moodiness had been going on long enough. I didn't know what my problem was, but I couldn't be depressed. I was stronger than that. I could fight the numbness. I just needed to concentrate, to try harder. I'd go to bed earlier, start eating better, force my mind to focus on my homework.

There was no reason I couldn't pull myself together if I just worked at it.

My determination to do better had absolutely no effect on the numbing fog, but at lunchtime I broke through it enough to select a salad and a carton of milk. Getting the food into my stomach proved more difficult. I nibbled at the cucumbers and tomatoes and drank the milk while Cody sat beside me, fretting over every bite.

"Have some of my fries," he said. But even crisp, golden, salt-covered potatoes couldn't tempt me. Most of my lunch wound up in the trash.

That afternoon, I was called out of US history to the counseling office. Something told me it wasn't to verify that I was taking the proper classes to get into OSU.

When I pushed through the door, Mrs. Aimes, a heavy-set woman who must've shared Einstein's hairstylist, smiled at me from a desk piled high with college catalogs, Diet Coke bottles, and Care Bear figurines. "Have a seat, Jess."

She waved at the chair across from her. I sat down trying to look serious and alert—a dedicated student intent on going to the college of her dreams.

Mrs. Aimes leaned back, clasping her hands over the front of her purple and white South Eugene sweatshirt. "I'm a little concerned about you."

Her and everyone else. I kept quiet, afraid anything I volunteered might make my situation worse.

"Your teachers say you're not turning in your assignments. I know you're having a tough time right now. Is there anything I can do to help?"

I slumped back, focusing on a poster of a cat dangling from a rope, the words "Hang in there," printed jauntily below. "Not really. I know I'm a little behind, but . . ."

"You're a *lot* behind. I got a call from your guardian this morning. He's very worried about you."

I drew a deep breath and shut my eyes. His betrayal should've made me furious, yet it registered as a mere annoyance. "There's nothing to worry about," I said. "My mother is dead. . . . Don't I have a right to be upset?"

"Of course." Mrs. Aimes's voice was full of gentle reassurance. "But sometimes talking about our feelings helps us process them."

"And sometimes it doesn't." My eyes snapped open and I glared at her until I remembered my vow. Just because Mark had gone back on his word didn't mean I had to. I forced myself to smile as though I meant it. "I know you're trying to do your job. But I need to sort through this on my own." I looked at her directly, the same as I'd done with Kasey. "If that doesn't work I'll talk to you, okay?"

"You're not fooling me, Jess. Every week I see dozens of kids who have no more interest in sharing their feelings than you do. I've gotten pretty good at spotting a snow job."

Okay, maybe she wasn't going to be as easy as Mark and Kasey. But she still wasn't getting anything from me.

"I understand that you don't want to talk," she continued. "I also know you must be terribly sad, angry, and confused. After years of alcoholism, your mom was making progress. Her death must seem so unfair."

What was unfair was perfect strangers knowing my business and thinking they had a right to make assumptions about my feelings. "If you know I don't want to talk about it, why are you trying to make me?"

"Because the people who care about you are worried. It's my job to try to help." She leaned forward, eyes intent. "I can't force you to talk, Jess, but I *can* make you come in here every week and listen to what I have to say."

That wasn't exactly true. She could lecture all she wanted,

but I didn't have to pay attention.

When I got home from work that evening, I found a funny card from Teri Sue on the table where Mark always left the mail. Maybe I should write to her. Phone calls were too much hassle, but typing up a short note ought to reassure her I was working things out.

I glanced into Mark's study, just off the front hallway, and saw he was grading papers. Stepping closer, I waited in the doorway until he looked up.

"Do you need something, Jess?"

"You said you weren't going to do anything until Dad came home. Why'd you sic the school counselor on me?"

With a sigh, he set down his pen and massaged the bridge of his nose. "What I agreed to was not talking to your father until he got back. Consulting with your counselor was hardly an act of aggression."

"I *told* you—I don't need counseling. What I need is a little space."

"We've tried that. It doesn't seem to be doing much good."

"What do you mean, you've tried? For the last month, everyone's been hovering around me, asking how I'm doing, begging me to talk. How am I supposed to figure things out when I have to keep reassuring people I'm okay?" The words kept flowing, and the more I said, the more realistic it sounded. Like it would all be fine if they just gave me a chance to process things on my own.

Mark waited for me to wind down, watching with a sad sort of sympathy. "I'm sorry if my concern feels intrusive, Jess, but I care about you. Things seem to be getting worse instead of better, and I was hoping your counselor might be able to help."

No one can help, I thought. But I had enough sense not to say it.

*   *   *

After heating up the dinner Mark had left me, I went upstairs to write to Teri Sue. I got as far as sitting down at the computer, but once I opened a new document, I couldn't think of anything to say. The few ideas that swirled vaguely through the outskirts of my mind seemed too ephemeral to nail down in words.

Giving up, I went to my room to tackle my homework. No luck there, either. No matter how many times I tried to force my brain to return to my calculus questions, it kept wandering off to fret over things I couldn't change. Like the fact that, in exactly a week, it would be Lydia's birthday. How was I supposed to deal with that?

I went to bed at ten o'clock and lay awake for six hours, longing to get into the Pinto and take a drive. But I'd sworn I was going to do better, so I didn't allow myself the pleasure.

Despite my resolve, I slept through the alarm again and had to rush to give Rhett a ride, skipping both my shower and breakfast. I fell asleep in chemistry and was threatened with detention. At lunch, Heather asked if I wanted to go off campus to grab something to eat.

"I can't," I said. "I promised everyone I'd get it together."

My good intentions didn't buy me any relief. If anything, the lethargy was getting worse. That afternoon, I forgot the valve stem seals while assembling a set of heads. Kasey pointed it out as I was torquing them to the block.

Shock and embarrassment sent heat flushing across my skin. "I'm sorry, Kasey. I'll stay late and make it right."

"Never mind, I can handle it. You need to take Rhett home and make him some dinner."

Even though the Hawk had gone to the upholsterer that morning, I knew she didn't have time to fix my mistakes. But I didn't argue.

That night, the need to drive was so intense I almost gave in.

244

Keep trying, I told myself, *things are bound to get better*. I didn't sleep at all, so I had plenty of time to shower and choke down a bowl of Cheerios before taking Rhett to school. By lunchtime, I was such a zombie Cody tried to talk me into going home.

"I can't," I said. "I told Mark I'd get a grip on things. If I don't, he's going to ask my Dad to take leave again."

"That's probably a good idea."

"No it's not. I don't want him losing his job over me. I can pull out of this. I just need a little time."

I stumbled through that day and the next, staying awake in class with the help of lots of Mountain Dew.

Thursday night Dad called.

"How ya doing, honey?"

If he had to ask, it meant Mark hadn't talked to him yet. At least he'd kept that part of his promise.

"I'm fine, Dad."

"School going okay? You're not working too hard, are you? The last time I talked to Kasey, she was worried you weren't getting enough sleep."

"I'm fine." Lying was so much easier when I didn't have to look the other person in the eye.

"Good. Listen, honey, I'm up here in Seattle, and I know I'm supposed to be home tomorrow, but the boss has an emergency delivery that needs to go to Kansas City. I really don't wanna turn it down. Not in this economy. There's too many independent truckers just begging for any work they can get."

My relief was purely mechanical. An observation that this would improve my odds, give me more time to reassemble the shambles of my life. "You should take the run."

"You sure? 'Cause if you need me, I'll come home."

"No, everything's fine here."

"All right. I'll do my best to get some time off next weekend, okay?"

"Sure, Dad. I'll see you when you get here."

When Mark came home, I didn't tell him about the call. There'd be plenty of time for that tomorrow.

Kasey intercepted me as I came through the door of the shop the next day. "Let's go into the office for a few minutes."

"Why? What's wrong?" Something told me I should be alarmed, but I was too dazed and tired to care.

"Just come with me."

She took the chair, and I sank onto the couch. Cody's footprint still decorated the front of the desk. I let it mesmerize me. Whatever Kasey was about to say couldn't be good.

"Jess, when I moved the Nova you worked on yesterday, the brakes were pulling. I took off the drums and found you'd put the front shoes on backward."

I cringed. A beginner mistake. The back brake shoe had a much longer lining than the front one, so if you reversed them, the car wouldn't stop properly. The foul-up with the valve stem seals had been bad enough, but this could've hurt someone.

"I'm sorry, Kasey. It won't happen again. I promise."

"You've said that before, and not just to me. I'm sure you believe it, but I don't think it's that simple."

The fog began to swirl and close in, making my head throb. Was she going to fire me?

"I want you to take some time off," Kasey said. "I know you think staying busy is helping, but it's not."

Oh God, she *was* firing me. My eyes snapped up to meet hers, and I rocked forward on the couch. "That's not true, Kasey! Please, just let me keep working. I won't slip up again."

"I'm sorry, Jess." The firmness of her expression told me her mind was made up.

"But you need me! The Roadster Show's next weekend."

"The rest of us can handle everything. The Hawk won't even be back until Tuesday."

Fear swelled in my chest. "That only gives you two days before you have to take it to Portland."

"Jess, I've got it covered."

Maybe *she* had it covered, but what about me? What about all those extra hours with nothing to fill them but "if onlys"?

"You can't do this to me. You know working here is the only thing that helps."

She nodded. "And that's what has me concerned. I've let it go this long because I understand staying busy is your way of coping. But you're not processing what happened. You've been walking around like you're numb to the world. I don't think you've even cried."

"Maybe I don't feel like crying."

"You *need* to cry, Jess. You need to rant and scream and stomp your feet about how absolutely unfair it is to lose your mom. You need to grieve." The resolve in her eyes melted into sympathy. "I know how much this job means to you, so I'll make a deal. If you'll agree to go to counseling, I'll let you come back to work on Monday."

Panic welled up, the way it did each time I thought about anyone learning the truth. "Mark's already making me see the school counselor. Isn't that good enough?"

"Not if you refuse to talk to her."

"Did she tell you that? I thought there were confidentiality laws."

"Yes, and they only apply if you actually say something."

I gripped the edge of the couch cushions with both hands. "Maybe I don't feel comfortable telling a stranger my private thoughts. Anyway, I've been talking to Heather."

"Cody says you haven't. He told me you've been avoiding her all week."

My lungs raked the air, scouring it for oxygen. It felt as though a giant vacuum had sucked every bit out of the room. "Cody doesn't know everything. He isn't with me every minute of the day."

"I'm sorry, Jess. We've tried to do things your way, and it's not working. If you refuse counseling, I can't let you continue to work here. And that's for the customers' well-being as much as your own. If I hadn't caught that mix up with the brakes, somebody could have been hurt."

"I don't have to do brake jobs! I could just wash parts or something." The whine in my voice shamed me.

Kasey searched my face with kind eyes. "Jess," she said gently. "Why are you so desperate to avoid talking to a counselor?"

Because I killed a person. Maybe I hadn't put a gun to my mother's head or pushed her off a cliff, but she was dead because of me.

"Have you even considered it?" Kasey persisted. "It might help. How will you know until you try?"

"Forget it," I said, pushing up off the couch. "If you don't want me to work here, fine. I quit."

I strode out of the office, got into the Pinto, and drove.

A cop stopped me doing eighty-nine on I-5. I glared through the windshield while he filled out the ticket. As he walked away, I tossed it on the floorboards then drove exactly the speed limit to the Goshen exit.

Highway 58 was a gloriously dangerous road once you got through the speed trap of Pleasant Hill and skirted the reservoir. I spilled my rage onto the highway, passing on blind corners and challenging every suggested speed. By the time my anger was spent, I'd made it halfway to Klamath Falls.

I knew Mark would be worried, and I should stop to call him, but finding a pay phone seemed like too much work. I turned around and drove home, pulling into the driveway a little past eight.

"Where have you been?" Mark demanded as I walked into

the living room, to find him sitting in the La-Z-Boy. "Kasey called hours ago to say you'd quit and stormed out of the shop."

My gaze drifted to the floor and I shrugged. "Out driving."

"I've been frantic. Why didn't you call?"

I continued my inspection of the carpet. The hot chocolate stain hadn't disappeared.

"Did you even once bother to consider that I might need to get in touch with you? I haven't heard a word from your dad. He should've been here by now."

My head snapped up. "He's not coming, okay?" I looked straight at Mark, daring him to challenge me. "He called last night and said he had to make a run to Kansas City. And for your information, I was right about his job. He can't afford to take time off!"

Mark gaped as if he'd learned his Sunday school teacher had been moonlighting as a biker. I'd never said a word to him in anger, never crossed him in the slightest way.

He took a ragged breath and let it out in a sigh. "The company your father contracts with will have to understand he's needed at home. I'll call tomorrow and explain the situation."

"No you won't! Dad can't run back here every five minutes to babysit me. Maybe you and Kasey and everyone else should stick to your own damn business and leave me alone!" I bolted from the room, feet pounding the stairs, and took refuge behind my closed door.

When the road called that night, I answered. There was no point fighting it any longer.

CHAPTER 55

I figured I could avoid Kasey until after the Roadster Show, but I'd have to face Cody Saturday morning. He was testing for his next belt in karate. I was supposed to watch, but when the alarm rang, I shut it off and went back to sleep. Each time I woke, I snuggled close to Newt, buried my head under the covers, and drifted into the abyss. Mark knocked several times, but I told him to go away.

Early in the afternoon, I emerged from the cocoon of my room. Outside, I found an envelope Mark must've left. A card from Teri Sue.

> *Hey, girl, sorry I keep missing you. Let's get together sometime, okay? Rhett's worried about you.*
> *love,*
> *Teri Sue*

Right. As if either one of us would bother to make that happen.

I had no doubt Cody would come by after his test—I'd refused two of his calls the night before—so I went downstairs and slunk apologetically into Mark's study. Making amends was my only chance of leaving the house.

"Sorry about last night," I said. "I was out of line. I guess I was upset about what happened at work."

Mark turned in his chair, abandoning the student paper he'd been reading to give me his full attention. "It must've been a real shock to have Kasey give you that sort of ultimatum."

"Yeah . . . ." I fidgeted with the doorknob.

"Jess, I understand how upsetting that was for you, but I

can't have you running off and not letting me know where you'll be. Your father is counting on me to keep you safe. And if I can't rely on you, I'll have to make other arrangements for Rhett when I'm working."

I looked down at my feet. "You can rely on me. It won't happen again."

"That's what you told me after you forgot to pick him up at school."

His words jolted me, stirring an echo of Kasey's. *You've said that before. And not just to me.* Why couldn't I keep a simple promise?

"It was an accident," I mumbled.

"I'm sorry, Jess, but we're going to have to make some changes. Finding someone else to watch Rhett will only be part of it. Kasey and I talked this morning, and we agreed. It's long past time you got some professional help."

A cold wave pulsed through me, making my stomach convulse. Why couldn't Kasey keep her opinions to herself? If I hadn't already quit, I'd tell her what I thought of her meddling.

"You can't do that," I said. "It's Dad's decision."

"When he granted me guardianship, he gave me the power to act on his behalf."

"So maybe you can make me go, but it would be a waste of time. You can't force me to talk to some stranger any more than you can make me spill my guts to the school counselor."

Mark nodded. "That's true. The rest of us can only do so much. It's up to you to help yourself."

As if it were that easy. As if the only thing it would take to make life all roses and sunshine was for me to tell the truth about that night.

Mark continued to study me, his eyes so kind and sad I had to look away.

"I'm going to Heather's," I said. If he wanted to know my whereabouts, I'd tell him. But I was through asking permission.

Surprisingly, he didn't object. "How long will you be?"

"I dunno."

"I want you back by eight."

"Okay."

I high-tailed it before he could change his mind.

I didn't go to Heather's. By now I was sure Cody had recruited her into the "Save Jess From Herself" campaign. Instead I went to the movies, paying for one show then sneaking into another when the first was over. It felt good to lose myself in someone else's story. I was careful to be home by eight, even though I couldn't see how it mattered.

The next morning, I fought off sleep so I could escape the house in the early hours. I wanted nothing more than to slip back into slumber, where the thick haze of despair couldn't get to me, but Cody would be over to hassle me the minute he got up.

I spent the day wandering in the Pinto, too numb to bother with a good, intense drive. When I returned late in the afternoon, Rhett told me I needed to get in touch with Cody.

"He came over last night and this morning, and he's called, like, a million times."

"Thanks," I mumbled as I started for the staircase.

"In case you're wondering, he got his belt," Rhett called after me.

Of course he did.

Mark swooped in from the kitchen, wiping his hands on a dishcloth. "Where have you been? I thought we'd agreed you weren't going to run off like that anymore."

Crap. I hadn't even thought about saying anything when I left. What was wrong with my brain? "Sorry," I said. "I forgot. I was just driving around."

"Sorry doesn't cut it." There wasn't a bit of compassion in Mark's eyes. "No more free passes, Jess. Next time, I'll take away your car keys."

Good thing I had a spare set. After all the ways I'd screwed up, I wasn't sure I could do any better.

Monday morning, getting up didn't seem worth the effort. It was my mother's birthday. She would've been thirty-six. How could anybody die that young?

When Mark came in to check on me at seven-thirty, I told him I didn't feel well.

He sat on the edge of the bed. "I talked to your father last night. He's arranged to take some time off. There's a blizzard in the Midwest, and it's holding up a run to Minneapolis, but he's hoping to be home the first part of next week."

"Whatever." I rolled over and buried myself under the covers. Fighting took too much effort.

For most of the day I dozed, occasionally waking to hunger or thirst, but lacking the motivation to do anything about it. Newt stretched out beside me, ever vigilant, but his purr had lost its healing power.

Shortly after three, I heard the rumble of the Galaxie's engine. I turned away from the door and pulled the blankets over my head. Cody and Rhett's voices drifted up from the front porch. Footsteps sounded on the stairs. And then, without knocking, Cody let himself into my room.

He eased himself down on the bed, sitting in the same spot Mark had occupied that morning.

"Jess? Are you awake?" His hand fell softly on my arm, lighting there like a bird that might fly away at the slightest motion. Was that what I wanted?

"I hate to see you hurting like this. . . . I wish I could fix it." He drew the blankets from my face, smoothing my tangled hair, tracing fingers over my cheek.

I kept my eyelids locked, my body still.

"Please, just talk to me." The heat of his gaze swept me,

studying, waiting. "I know you're awake."

Even if I'd wanted to, I couldn't have forced words through my lips.

"You're scaring me. I know you can't help it. I know you're fighting as hard as you can. But Kasey's right. You need help. You've gotta talk to someone."

My eyes flickered open, and I stared at the texture on the wall. If I looked at it just right, slightly out of focus, I could almost see the face of an old man.

Cody lay down beside me, curling his body around my back, as if by touch alone he could make everything okay. "You've got to stop this. You've got to let us help."

Somewhere far away, I felt regret. It was so wrong to hurt him. A detached sliver of consciousness saw this was a time for tears. But I had none.

Cody gripped me tight, lips whispering at my ear. "Just listen to Kasey. She'll take care of everything. She'll even give you a ride. All you have to do is talk."

His pain fell over me, heavy and suffocating, his love no longer a comfort, but a burden. Why couldn't he just leave me alone? Why couldn't they all just *leave . . . me . . . alone?*

"Please, Jess. If you won't do it for yourself, do it for me. It's killing me to see you like this. I can't stand it anymore."

The words were a magic spell, releasing me from my stupor. I tore myself from his arms, rolling away, scrambling backward into the space between the bed and the wall. "Then don't," I said. "Just get out."

"What?" Cody sat up, his face an exclamation point of shock.

"You heard me. Get out." Maybe I couldn't do anything to stop the shipwreck of my own life, but I didn't have to take him down with me.

"No," he said, his face cementing into the fierce loyalty that had won me over so many months before. "I'm not going anywhere. I love you, and I won't let you destroy yourself."

Damn it, why did he have to be so noble? I sprang forward onto the bed, shoving him off the other side. "Get out of my room. Get out of my life! I got along just fine without you for sixteen years. If you can't stand me like this, then go."

"That's not what I said. It's not what I want!" Cody's voice went high with desperation.

"Well, it's what *I* want. Just get the hell out, okay? I don't need you anymore!"

He stood granite-still, eyes huge and glistening. Then slowly, oh so slowly, his hand reached up and out to me. "Jess . . . ?" The word was a question. A whisper. A prayer.

I grabbed my pillow and threw it at him. "Get out!"

Without another word, he turned and left the room.

CHAPTER 34

The next morning, Mark told me I had to get up and go to school.

I rolled away. "I still don't feel good."

"You're going, Jess. I made some calls and found a therapist, but she can't fit you in until next Wednesday. In the meantime, you need to stick to a normal routine. Lying around doing nothing will only make things worse."

"You can't force me to get up."

"That may be true, but I suspect Kasey can. Do you want me to call her?"

"No." Lethargic as I felt, I couldn't make things difficult for her this close to the Roadster Show. Besides, I wouldn't put it past her to drag me to school in my pajamas.

"You don't have to worry about looking after Rhett or fixing dinner tonight," Mark added. "I've hired a college student to come stay with you in the afternoons."

Shame stirred inside me, a vague, far-away feeling. But I couldn't blame him. He'd given me plenty of chances.

At school I sank into myself, dreading how Cody would respond to my attack. He steered clear, only once glancing in my direction with wounded eyes. I half-expected Heather to give me what for, but she ignored me too.

The college student, Sherry, was waiting in her car when Rhett and I got home. I mumbled something about homework and escaped to my room. When Sherry's bubbly cheerfulness drifted up the staircase, along with Rhett's laughter, I shut my door.

At dinnertime, Rhett came to get me, quiet and solemn. He tiptoed around me these days, not bothering to talk, knowing I wouldn't respond. But his gaze followed me everywhere.

Another thing that might have made me cry if I'd had any tears.

After pushing my perfectly balanced dinner around my plate, I went back to my room, collapsing on my bed to study the ceiling. There was a sort of peace in the numbness if I didn't fight it, if I let myself slip down deep, watching time stream by around me. The trick was to focus on something insignificant, to get so lost I forgot my sense of me-ness.

A car pulled up out front, but not the Galaxie. I would've recognized the engine. A knock sounded downstairs, then I heard a rumble of voices. One lilting, one deep. A few minutes later, someone rapped on the frame of my open door.

"Mind if I come in?"

Race. Another person whose eyes wouldn't stop haunting me.

"I don't care."

He crossed the room, turned my desk chair around, and sat. "The Hawk's back. . . . Interior looks good." He hesitated, as if waiting for a reply. When I didn't give him one, he kept going. "Kasey's scrambling with last minute details. There's a problem with the electric windows, so she stayed late to troubleshoot it." Again, he paused.

Just spit it out, Race. This isn't what you came here to talk about.

The silence lingered for a long, empty moment before he continued. "We've got a few things to wrap up tomorrow, but there's no reason Kasey shouldn't be able to trailer the car up to Portland Thursday morning."

I grunted and went on staring at the ceiling. I should've been glad she'd met her deadline, but the news only registered in a detached, factual way.

"Cody and I will be going up to see the show on Saturday," Race added. "You could come along if you wanted."

Sure, that wouldn't be a bit awkward. I felt him looking at me, but I kept my eyes trained upward.

"I'll be so glad when this weekend's over," Race said. "This project's been a nightmare. The whole winter's been a nightmare." The chair squeaked as he shifted. The spring needed oil, I just kept forgetting to deal with it.

He let out a long, deep sigh that told me what was coming next. "Jess, you've gotta know you're one of my favorite people in the world. But Cody . . . well, I'd do anything for that kid."

Last summer, when I'd worried that a choice I had to make might somehow disappoint Race, Kasey had laughed, saying it wasn't possible. But now I'd managed to do it.

"I know if you won't listen to Kasey or Cody, you're sure as hell not gonna listen to me," he said. "So I won't lecture you on what to do with your life. But I hope you'll think about how you left things with him. Last night was one of the few times I've seen him cry. I know you need your space, but please . . . don't shut him out completely."

I spoke without even knowing I was going to, my words a rough whisper. "He's better off without me."

"You know that's not true."

I closed my eyes and concentrated on the murmur of the TV, trying to guess what Rhett and his new best friend were watching.

Race spoke again, but I didn't hear the words. His voice became a rumble, droning on as time lost meaning.

Finally, he gave up and slipped from the room.

The next morning, Mark woke me again. Why couldn't he just let me be? What difference did it make whether I went to school? I was flunking all my classes.

Newt wound around my feet, purring and calling out with that weird little *myat-at* meow of his. I tripped over him as I went to the closet for a shirt. Rage flared, a tongue of flame suddenly engorged by gasoline.

"Damn it, Newt!" I stepped wide to avoid him, but he ran

straight under my other foot. "Get out of my way!" I stomped hard, once, twice, and again. Newt sprang away, panic in his eyes, and banged into the door in his rush to escape.

Guilt flooded in, drowning the fire. What the hell was wrong with me? How could I torment a poor little animal who'd never shown me anything but love?

I dropped into my chair, wishing I could disappear, that I could go someplace far away. Someplace where I'd never hurt anyone I cared about again.

I slunk through the rest of the week, dreading the next confrontation. But Kasey had taken the Hawk to Portland, Mark seemed to feel his hands were tied until my counseling appointment, and Race and Cody—well, I'd probably scared them off for good.

I went to school because Mark made me, but I put in no effort beyond that. It didn't matter anymore. Once Dad arrived, my secret would be out. There'd be a showdown, then counseling, and finally the disclosure that I'd been responsible for Lydia's death. After that, all sympathy would be recalled as people realized I'd never deserved it to begin with.

It got harder and harder to put up with Mark's interference. In addition to making me go to school, he forced me to sit at the dinner table with him and Rhett, and reprimanded me each time I back-talked, which was frequently because he wouldn't leave me alone.

Saturday evening, while Rhett was off bowling with Emily and some friends, Mark called me to task on my attitude.

"I know you're miserable, Jess, but I won't have you mouthing off to me in front of Rhett. He's beginning to imitate you."

I stared at Mark's collection of gardening catalogs on the coffee table.

"It will only be a few days until your dad comes home. In the meantime, I expect you to show me some respect."

And then what? Mark would throw me out because I was such a bad influence? He'd tell my dad the deal was off, and I'd have to find someplace else to live?

Meanness snarled up inside me, a vast improvement over the stupor. "I thought I wasn't supposed to *try*. I thought I was supposed to do without doing. *Wei wu wei* and all that."

Something flickered in Mark's eyes. Sadness? Disappointment?

"That idea was meant to free you from unrealistic expectations, not excuse you from behaving in a socially acceptable manner."

A technicality. One I had no intention of acknowledging, even though deep inside I knew he was right. "Maybe behaving in a socially acceptable manner *is* an unrealistic expectation. Did you ever consider that? Maybe I'm following my true nature." I threw my hands in the air, revealing my hidden self to the world. "This is me, Mark, the Uncarved Block, bad attitude and all."

"You know better than that. You're purposely misinterpreting what I said."

"What difference does it make? Has it ever occurred to you that if you'd just leave me the hell alone I wouldn't *have* an attitude?"

"Meaning what? That you want me to walk away and give up on you? I'm not going to do that, Jess."

"Then you're wasting your time," I said. "Just like everyone else."

The late drives were the only thing in my life worth getting out of bed for. I'd taken one almost every night for the past week. Sunday, I snuck out a little past one. The earlier clouds had dispersed to reveal the moon, full only a few days before. March had barely begun, but a suggestion of spring hung in the air. Not just in the honeyed scent of blooming Daphne, which brought me up short every time I left the house, but in the buoyancy of the night, and that slight shift in temperature from cool to not-quite-warm. Somehow, all of this edged within the boundaries of my fog.

The drive had become a soothing ritual. Roll down the driveway, crank the engine, stick in a tape, and go. I'd become intimately familiar with every twist and turn, every long straight stretch where I could nudge the speedometer to the end of its range. As I sped south, away from my troubles, the tires would whisper a lullaby to the road beneath. I'd fly along, letting the highway eat up my guilt and spit it out behind me.

I always turned back at the same point, and it always came too soon. But the trip home was a whole different road, the corners reversed, the view unique.

In the two weeks since I'd started my night driving, the landscape had undergone subtle changes, showing flashes of green where there'd been none before. The world was waking up. But it had left me behind.

As I charged through a long, sweeping turn, something rippled the brush at the roadside. And then that something was in front of me. Adrenalin surged, neurons firing, thoughts flashing too quick for words. My foot slammed the brake a split second before the impact rocked the Pinto. The seatbelt bit my shoulder and chest. The steering wheel tore at my hands. A brown hulk bounced off the hood, shattering the windshield before rolling across the roof in a thunder of crumpling steel.

The Pinto went into a skid. Some primitive part of my brain instructed my foot to let up, unlocking the brakes. I wrestled the no-longer-obedient wheel, blinded by the spider web of glass looming in at me. Somehow, I bullied the Pinto to the edge of the road.

The door wouldn't open. I threw myself against it, again and again, panicked. Finally it gave way with a groan. As I stumbled, shaking, out onto the highway, a cloying, metallic potpourri of blood and antifreeze filled my nose. I ran back to the dark mound lying on the centerline.

A deer. I'd sensed it was a deer, but somehow the visual made it oh-so-much more real.

I sank to the asphalt, hands pressing the torn flesh, stroking the velvet nose. How could the body be so warm and yet so broken?

Last time it had been an act of not-doing. Guilt by negligence. But this, this was every bit my responsibility. If I'd stayed home, the deer would've sprung safely across the highway. If my car hadn't been in that exact spot at that exact moment, this animal would still be alive.

A glossy black eye stared up at me, reflecting moonlight.

"I'm sorry," I whispered, "I'm so sorry."

And then my heart shattered. I fell forward onto the warm, brown mass of flesh.

And I wept.

CHAPTER 35

Centuries later, headlights swept over me, rousing me from my grief. A car coasted to a stop. I pushed against the weight of the deer, fighting the stiffness of cold to sit up. Blood, now dry, flaked from my hands. The moon no longer zenithed the sky, but hung halfway to the horizon.

A figure walked out of the light. A well-dressed man: expensive clothes and shoes, million-dollar haircut.

"What the hell? Are you all right?"

I staggered up from the ground, legs shaking. "A deer. I hit a deer."

"You sure did." His eyes flickered over the bloody mess in the road before rising to meet mine. "Are you hurt?"

The thought hadn't even occurred to me. My body ached, but it had done everything I'd asked it to. All the pieces seemed to be there. "No," I said.

He took a step closer. "You sure? There's so much blood."

"It's not mine." I glanced down at the mangled body, tears cascading over my cheeks. *I killed a deer. I killed my mom.*

"I'll call the sheriff and an ambulance."

"No!" My voice stopped him as he turned to his car. "I'm not hurt. We don't need the cops." You didn't have to notify the police if there wasn't another vehicle involved, did you? "Just call a tow truck . . ." How was he going to do that out here? ". . . and—and maybe give me a ride home. Okay?"

I begged him with a look, and he gave a slight nod. "Sure thing," he said, studying my face. "But I think you'd better sit down." He stepped close, draping an arm around my shoulders, and guided me to his car, a 5 series BMW. His hand steadied me as I lowered myself onto the front passenger seat.

I glimpsed a smear of blood on his expensive, buff-colored

jacket. "Oh no!" Jumping up, I frantically scanned the upholstery. Could you get blood out of leather?

"Don't worry about it." He pushed gently on my shoulder, making me sit. His selflessness hit me like a slap. More tears spilled from my eyes.

"Hey now, it's going to be okay," he said. "I'll take care of everything, all right? I'm Nathan, by the way."

I drew in a shaky breath, trying to stop the crying. "I'm J-jess."

"Okay, Jess. Just sit tight." Nathan circled to the driver's side, got in, and pulled a long, black brick from between the seats. No, not a brick. One of those high tech cellular phones, something I didn't think existed outside of TV shows and southern California.

After arranging for a tow truck, he turned to face me. "What's your parents' number?"

"Can't you just take me home?"

"Don't you think they're worried about you?"

I explained my living situation, and how nobody knew I was gone. "If you call Mark, he won't want to leave his son home alone. And Rhett's only eleven. I don't want him to see all this."

"Right," Nathan nodded. "This wouldn't be a good scene for a kid."

He went to put out flares then sat with me in the car until the tow truck arrived. He tried to get me to tell him what had happened, but I couldn't even bear to think about it.

As the wrecker pulled up, lights streaming yellow and red across the trees and brush, I stepped out of the BMW to approach the Pinto. Its one remaining headlight cast a dying glow over the highway. The hood and fenders were twisted beyond repair, the roof concave and streaked with blood. I ran my fingers over the steel, remembering the hours I'd put in, rebuilding, restoring, fabricating. From the age of ten, I'd saved my money for this car, and I'd driven it less than a year. My dream—my vision. Crushed. Destroyed. Totaled.

"You're lucky that deer di'n't wind up in your lap," the tow truck driver said around a mouthful of cigar. He reached inside the car to turn off the headlights, and when he shut the door, shards of glass rained down on the interior.

I stared at the crumpled windshield. One tiny variance in the equation, a bit more speed, a different angle of impact, and the deer wouldn't have been the only victim. Ice sluiced through my veins, but I wasn't sure whether that was due to relief or longing.

The tow truck driver hooked up the Pinto, and then he and Nathan dragged the deer's body to the side of the road.

"Where ya want me to take your car?" the driver asked as he jotted down the information from my AAA card.

Instinctively, I recited the name and address of Kasey's shop.

Nathan insisted on calling to give Mark a heads-up while he drove me home, saying he had no intention of abandoning a blood-covered kid on someone's doorstep. We pulled into the driveway to see Mark waiting on the porch in his robe. As I hoisted myself out of the BMW, he raced down the steps and snatched me into a hug.

"My God, Jess. Are you all right?"

I struggled not to wince. Every bit of me ached. "I'm fine."

Mark stepped back and held me at arm's length, looking me over. *Were those tears in his eyes?*

"It's not my blood," I said.

"I should take you to the emergency room."

"I'm not hurt."

"Better safe than sorry." His eyes met mine, but instead of the anger I deserved, they held only concern.

"Please, Mark. I'm fine. You'd have to get Rhett up and explain everything. Do you think he needs to see me like this?"

Nathan came around the side of the BMW. "I've been with

her for the last hour, and other than being shook up, she seems all right to me."

Mark gave me a final once-over and nodded. "Okay. Go upstairs. We'll talk in the morning."

I turned to say goodbye to Nathan, my vision blurring as I thought of his kindness. How could a stranger etch himself so indelibly into my life?

"Thank you," I said, my voice breaking.

He reached out to squeeze my shoulder. "You take care of yourself."

As he and Mark began to talk, I went inside, stripped off my blood-caked clothes, and fell into a dead sleep.

The phone jangled me awake. For a moment, I couldn't figure out why I felt so sore, and then the memory of the deer crashed into my consciousness. I wanted to go back to sleep, to huddle down into my bed and never leave it. But I couldn't hide from Mark forever, and I didn't want to face him like this.

When I tried to sit up, my muscles shrieked in protest, so I rolled to the edge of the bed and slid off the side, hoisting myself carefully to my feet.

I could barely raise my left arm to fit it through the sleeve of my robe. When I undressed in the bathroom to get into the shower, I saw why. A band of purple, so dark it was almost black, cut starkly across my shoulder just below the collarbone. I'd never seen a bruise like that, edges so sharp and distinct. It angled over the top of my left breast before crossing to the right side of my rib cage. I marveled at it in the mirror until weariness took over.

My body seemed to creak as I stepped into the shower. I leaned against the wall, letting hot water flow over me to loosen the stiffness and carry it down the drain. Too bad it couldn't take the memories as well. It wasn't until the water went cold that I got out.

Drying my hair proved so painful and exhausting, I gave up. I slipped the robe on and returned to my room, sitting on the bed to rest before going to the closet.

No way was I going to get a sweatshirt over my head, and my bra was out of the question. I grabbed a heavy button-down flannel, tossed it on the bed, and wiggled into my jeans because they were the easiest. I'd just gotten them zipped when someone knocked on my door.

"Jess, I'm coming in," Kasey said. Shouldn't she be at the Roadster Show? Wait, this was Monday. She must've come back last night.

"I'm not dressed," I hollered.

"It's not like I'm going to see anything new."

The door opened, and I snatched the shirt from my bed, wincing as I pulled it up to cover myself. But I wasn't quick enough.

"Oh, Jess." Kasey pressed the door shut and stepped close, taking the flannel carefully from my hands as she studied the purple brand across my chest. "Let's get you dressed. I'll run you over to Sacred Heart so we can make sure it's nothing serious."

There was no chance of arguing my way out this time, and I was too tired to try. I let her help me into the shirt and sat down while she put my shoes and socks on for me. She took me into the bathroom to dry my hair, wipe the blood from my leather jacket, and drape the coat over my shoulders.

Mark came out of his office as we descended the stairs.

"I'm taking Jess to the emergency room," Kasey said. "I can keep an eye on her the rest of the day."

Mark nodded. "I appreciate it." He stepped close, raising his arms as if to give me a hug, but when I flinched, he softly touched my cheek instead.

"Call me later with an update?" he asked, glancing at Kasey.

"Of course."

She didn't say anything else until we were safely ensconced in the privacy of her Charger. But as we pulled out onto the highway, she let me have it.

"What were you doing at the end of Fox Hollow in the middle of the night?"

There was no sense lying. If I hadn't already been bound for a trip to a shrink, I surely was now. "I couldn't sleep."

"This wasn't the first time, was it? Rhett told Mark he's heard you leaving and coming in before. Now he feels terrible for not saying anything. He thinks he's responsible for what happened."

My stomach clenched against the burning emptiness inside it. Poor Rhett. I couldn't stand the idea of him being burdened by guilt, too. "It's not his fault."

"That's right, it's not, but convincing him isn't going to be easy." She glanced briefly across the seat, eyes hard. "I know these past few weeks have been terrible for you, but you've got to start thinking about how your actions affect others. Imagine how I felt when I pulled up in front of the shop and saw your car—the hood caved in, blood everywhere. Whose blood do you suppose I thought that was?" She shook her head, her knuckles going white against the wheel. "Thank God Cody wasn't with me."

My gut twisted tighter. I hadn't considered what would happen when they saw the car.

"I'm so angry with you, Jess. So incredibly angry . . ." Her voice trailed off, rough and full of hurt. "You were lucky this time. But if that deer had been a little bigger, or you'd been going a little faster . . ." She smacked the steering wheel with her palm, making me jump. "Damn it! Do you realize what it would've done to us to get a call in the wee hours of the night? To find out you hadn't been so lucky?" Her eyes flashed. "To think you've been doing this for who-knows-how-long, that at any moment you might have slammed into a tree or slid off an embankment and been killed. . . . But then, I'm not entirely sure that wasn't the point."

My brain jumped to hyper-drive, shaking off the stupor of pain and exhaustion. "What?"

"I know what it's like to feel so overwhelmed you wish an accident would happen. Something to make it all go away."

The words stirred a whisper of question in the back of my mind, but I was too caught up in her accusation to pursue it. "You think I was trying to kill myself?"

"I don't think that was your conscious intent. But I believe you're desperate enough to put yourself in circumstances where it might happen accidentally."

Uneasiness rippled through me as I remembered that glorious feeling of fear and punishment the night I'd spun out. "That's crazy," I said, my voice cracking.

Kasey glanced at me, somber now. "I don't think so."

I turned to stare out the passenger window at trees whipping by, green buds swelling in anticipation of spring. "Then why don't you have me locked up?"

"Don't think I'm not considering it. But your father will be here tomorrow. He can decide how to handle this. I'm not letting you out of my sight until then. And in case you think you can snow him the way you've snowed the rest of us, believe me, we'll all be reporting exactly what's been going on."

The emergency room doctor determined I hadn't broken anything and wrote a prescription for pain medication. After Kasey filled it at the hospital pharmacy, she marched me out to the Charger.

"I'll take you back to the Clines' to get some clothes," she said, "then you're coming home with me for a couple of days. I wasn't kidding about not letting you out of my sight."

She didn't say much else as we drove, and I thought maybe she'd finished with the lectures. But a couple of miles from the house, she pulled off Fox Hollow into the Ridgeline Trail parking area.

Shutting off the engine, she turned to look at me, the anger gone now. "I'm sorry, Jess. I've wanted to be there for you since your mom died, but I've let the Hawk get in the way. You have three adults in your life who are supposed to be looking out for you. If we'd been doing our job, things would never have gone this far."

That didn't even make sense. Hadn't they all lectured and threatened me? What did she think they should've done, tie me up and drag me to counseling?

"I'm sorry I wasn't there when you needed me," she continued, "but I'm here now, and I'm not going anywhere. I want you to talk to me. It won't be easy, but you need to tell someone what's happening inside your head."

I swallowed hard and looked away. My hand itched to yank the door handle and escape, but this time there was nowhere to run.

"Talking will help. It may not seem that way, but it's true."

My throat clamped into a tight, aching knot. I shook my head. I could never talk about this. Never.

"Jess," Kasey said, her voice gentle. "Tell me what happened the night your mother died."

I didn't even want to *think* about that night. A violent tremor went through me, and I began to shake.

"Tell me, Jess."

My mouth opened against my will. "I . . . I can't."

"Do you really want to go on like this? Don't you want to feel better?"

I stared down into my lap. "I don't deserve to feel better."

"Of course you do." Kasey reached across the seat, laying her hand on my arm. "Nobody should have to suffer like this."

"I should! It's my fault."

Her hand slid down to grip my icy fingers. "Your mother's

death is not your fault. It was an unfortunate accident, and you're in no way responsible."

"Yes I am!" I twisted abruptly to face her, pain stabbing through my chest and shoulder. "She called. She—she called and asked for a ride. And I told her no!" Tears welled hot in my eyes as I spoke the words that would change everything. "I killed her, Kasey. I killed my mother."

CHAPTER 36

Kasey slid across the seat to draw me into her arms, and I sobbed as long and hard as I had the night before. The world faded around me, receding until there was nothing left but my pain. Then, gradually, I began to notice Kasey wasn't pushing me away. Wasn't blaming me.

Stroking my back, she held me tight and murmured soothing things. I gulped the air, trying to stop the tears. But now that the dam had collapsed, there was no controlling the flood.

At first, the things Kasey said made no sense, but finally, the sounds formed into words. "It's not your fault, Jess. It's not your fault."

I pulled in a deep, shuddering breath. "H-how can it not be my fault? S-she called me, Kasey. She asked for help."

"She had no business calling you. She had a sponsor she could've turned to. And you were watching Rhett. What were you supposed to do? Take him to a bar? Subject him to one of your mother's tantrums? Alan told me about the night at Lok Yaun. I don't blame you for steering clear after that."

"B-but she asked for a ride! You can't turn someone down w-when they're drunk and ask for a r-ride."

"Jess, listen to me!" Kasey took my chin in her hand and gently turned my head until I was looking her in the eye. "This is not your fault. I know you feel guilty. Believe me, I understand. But this is *not . . . your . . . fault.*"

But it was. A series of hiccuppy gasps rocked my body. The tears hit me fresh. I buried my face in her shirt and cried. "S-she's dead, Kasey. She's dead and I could've stopped it. I want my mom. I want my mom."

"I know, Jess."

A torrent of memories flooded through me. Lydia buying

gifts she couldn't afford, singing drunken Christmas carols as I trimmed the tree, asking me to call her by her first name, so we could be like sisters. I saw her weeping after my father left, coming home exhausted from dead-end jobs, telling me what a big girl I was for fixing dinner and cleaning the apartment. As imperfect as she'd been, she'd always loved me.

"A-Alan said she was r-really trying . . ." I gulped, "that she was going to m-make it this time. I took away her last chance."

Kasey's hand cupped the back of my neck, warm and soothing. "No. She gave that up herself. *She's* the one who got behind the wheel of a car when she was drunk. *She's* the one who chose to go to a bar."

"S-she wasn't a bad person, Kasey."

"I know she wasn't. She was your mom, and you loved her. I think we've all done you a disservice by not remembering that."

I pulled away and sat up. "Race understood."

Kasey smiled. "He has a talent for that, doesn't he?" The front of her shirt sagged against her chest, damp and heavy with my tears. She reached into the glove box and pulled out a wad of napkins. "Do you think you might be ready to talk to someone about this now?"

I wiped my face and blew my nose. "That counselor Mark signed me up for?"

Kasey nodded. "I think it will help."

"Lydia talked to a counselor."

"Is that why you don't want to? You think it would somehow mean you're like her?"

When she put it like that, it sounded ridiculous. Still, I couldn't help remembering my mother's weakness. The way she'd let her heartache pull her down until nothing else mattered. Depression could be hereditary. There'd been a big spread about it in *The Oregonian*. What if I wound up like her, escaping into alcohol because I couldn't deal with the bad stuff life threw at me?

"Admitting you need help doesn't make you weak," Kasey said. "You might be surprised to learn I've been to counseling, myself."

Seriously? It wasn't that I thought less of her because she'd talked to a counselor. I just couldn't imagine her needing to. "Was it because of what happened to Race?"

"No." She turned away, looking out the windshield at the Doug firs swaying in the breeze. "We all have our demons, Jess."

I stared, wondering what could possibly be haunting her, but I didn't ask. "Can't I just talk to you?"

She shook her head. "I'm always willing to listen. The problem is, I'm not trained to give you the help you need. Processing grief is hard enough, but guilt's particularly difficult to let go of."

"Especially if you're guilty." Despite Kasey's arguments, there was no denying I was responsible for what happened to Lydia.

"You're not guilty. I know you feel that way, and you can't imagine how anything will ever change. But you'll learn to see it differently. You'll learn to let go and understand you can't predict everything."

My temper flared. "How can you say that? How can you know? You've never killed anyone."

Kasey let out a deep sigh and turned to face me. "No. But for a long time I thought I was responsible for allowing two little girls to be molested."

CHAPTER 57

"It's not easy for me to talk about, even now." Kasey looked away, her eyes betraying a distress I so rarely saw in her. "It started when I was about Rhett's age. My father had a friend we called Uncle Mike. He owned a '59 Impala that I absolutely loved, and he took it to all the cruise-ins and car shows.

"Uncle Mike was on Dad's bowling team. We invited him over for barbeques and birthday parties, so when he offered to take me to a car show, nobody in the family thought anything of it. One show led to another, and after a while, I had my own special grown-up friend—one who indulged my automotive interests. That was something Dad didn't have time for outside of his shop—not with a business to run and six kids to raise." Kasey paused, her gaze fixed on something far away beyond the trees.

"One day, when we were coming back from a cruise-in, Uncle Mike pulled off the highway onto an overgrown logging road. I thought we were going to talk about the show. We'd often had long conversations about the cars we'd seen. But then . . . then he put his hand . . ." She hesitated, fingers running back and forth along the edge of the steering wheel, "on my bare leg, right below my cut-offs."

Dread swelled inside me in a slow, sick wave. It wasn't hard to figure out where this was going. I sat motionless, eyes riveted on Kasey as she struggled to continue.

"As uncomfortable as it made me feel, it would've been disloyal to suspect anything out of line, so I convinced myself the doubts were my imagination." She drew a lingering breath and released it in a sigh. "But it happened again and again. . . . And each time it went a little further.

"I never said anything to my father. I was afraid he

wouldn't believe me. He loved Uncle Mike like a brother." Kasey's voice broke, and she paused for another breath.

"I made up excuses not to go with him, but he was smart. He found ways around my roadblocks. And when I finally drummed up the nerve to say I'd tell my parents, he was ready. He told me it was my fault for wearing skimpy cut-offs and following him around like a tramp."

Empathy and outrage filled me. How could anyone be that sick, that manipulative?

"He said that if I breathed a word, he'd tell my father what a nasty little slut I was, and that *I'd* come on to him. So I kept my mouth shut . . . for five years. Eventually, it stopped. Maybe I got better at making excuses, or possibly I just got too old for him.

"And then one day I overheard my father telling my mother that Uncle Mike had been accused of sexual assault on a minor." Kasey's voice took on a sharper edge. "Apparently he'd molested two other girls after he'd stopped bothering me. The latest one had reported him, but when she learned she'd have to testify in court, she got scared and said she'd made up the whole thing. My father was devastated and couldn't believe the accusations.

"I knew I had to say something, that if I'd only done so years before, I could've saved these girls from what I'd gone through. So I told my dad Uncle Mike had done it to me as well. I can't begin to describe how painful it was to break my father's heart like that. And testifying was a nightmare.

"Uncle Mike went to jail. I hoped that would make me feel better, but it didn't. I couldn't stop thinking about those girls. My parents sent me to counseling, but it didn't help because I wasn't honest with the therapist. The whole thing was too painful, too humiliating to discuss. My counselor knew I was holding out, but she couldn't force me to talk. And once I graduated and moved away from home, my parents couldn't make me see her any more."

Kasey's eyes finally met mine, her composure resurfacing. "I carried that guilt for five more years and learned to function in spite of it. I'd already figured out how to channel my bad feelings into hard work—something you're so good at yourself, Jess. But I was never really whole. One of the side effects of having someone take advantage of you like that is it distorts the way you look at sex. I had a long history of becoming involved with a boy only to get scared and sabotage things."

She sighed. "But then I met Race." The slightest smile pulled at the corners of her lips. "From the first time we spoke, I knew he was different—that he was The One. But I also knew I had no chance of making a relationship work. I couldn't stand the thought of losing his friendship, so I kept him at arm's length. Whenever he showed the slightest bit of romantic interest, I told him I didn't think of him that way. It frustrated us both, but I was determined not to run him off like I had the others.

"And then he got hurt. One glimpse of him in ICU, hooked up to those tubes and monitors, so pale it looked like the life had already left his body . . . well, that was all it took to make me see how foolish I'd been. I swore if he lived, I'd never push him away again. But I knew my problems weren't something I could work through on my own. All those years of failure had proven that. So I found another therapist, and this time, I gave it my full effort."

Kasey forced a smile, eyes moist, but now full of their normal toughness. "I'm not saying it was easy. Especially when I had to tell Race—it wasn't something I'd shared with my other boyfriends. But he was patient, and I was determined. And eventually things got better."

I stared at her in shocked silence. Nothing I could say would be enough. I couldn't imagine how horrifying and degrading it must've been to go through the things that had happened to her.

Kasey squeezed my shoulder and reached to turn the key in the ignition. "It gets better. I promise."

But I could only imagine it getting worse. Especially when I had to admit what I'd done. "Um . . . Kasey?"

"Yes?"

"I know you said it wasn't my fault. But what if everyone thinks it is?"

"They won't."

"I don't think I can tell them." What if Race hated me? And how could I even approach Cody after the way I'd treated him?

Kasey's eyes caught mine. "Would you like me to tell them for you?"

"You'd do that?" I'd expected her to say it was something I had to do myself, part of the healing process.

"Of course." She smiled, gripping my hand a moment before reaching for the gearshift. "Now let's go get your things. You look exhausted."

Kasey dosed me with pain medicine and sent me to bed in the room where I'd slept when I'd stayed with them last summer. The pill knocked me out. When I woke, light filtered dimly through the window and the clock on the nightstand read 5:49.

I rolled out of bed. My body had stiffened, and I ached even worse than I had that morning. While my brain no longer seemed completely numb, I felt drained. Empty.

I cracked open the door and peeked out, hoping Cody was at work. How could I face him? I didn't really want him out of my life, but after what I'd said, there was no way he could possibly forgive me.

The living room looked vacant. I ventured out, toward the kitchen, where I heard activity. Kasey stood at the counter, slicing potatoes.

"Are you hungry? You slept right through lunch."

My stomach growled. "Yeah, I guess I am."

"I'm betting that's the longest stretch of sleep you've had in a month."

"Probably." I pulled out a chair and sat down.

Kasey microwaved a bowl of Chunky Chicken Noodle and set it in front of me, along with another pain pill and a glass of water. Despite my hunger, my stomach seized after half the bowl. Kasey took it away. She put me to work chopping vegetables for salad while she made small talk about cars she'd seen at the Roadster Show.

"How did the Hawk do?" I asked, almost afraid to mention it, because she hadn't.

"It took first place in the semi-custom class. It's not Best of Show, but I won't complain. And I had three people approach me about potential projects." She smiled.

"Really? That's great, Kasey. Why didn't you tell me?"

She shrugged. "There were more important things to talk about. And to be honest, I have mixed feelings about the project. No matter how much business it might generate, it wasn't worth the cost. I put everyone under tremendous stress—compromised my business and my friendships. But worst of all, I wasn't there when you needed me."

"I don't blame you for that. You couldn't have known what was going to happen."

"But I could've let go when the difficulties began to pile up. Instead, I let my ambition become an obsession. The truth is, I'm no longer a college student who's accountable to no one but herself. I'm in a serious relationship—about to be married. And I promised your father I'd look after you."

"But—" The front door opened and closed, interrupting my protest. A few seconds later, Cody appeared in the kitchen doorway. I searched his face, dreading the anger and bitterness I expected to find. But the only thing I saw was relief.

"Jess . . ." He dropped his backpack and pulled me close,

letting go when I yelped. "Oh man, I'm sorry. Are you okay? I saw the Pinto. Race put a tarp over it, but I had to look."

"I'm just sore."

He wrapped his arms more gingerly around me and kissed my forehead. "You have no idea what went through my mind when I saw your car. Race said you were okay, but he wouldn't let me come see for myself because Kasey told him you were sleeping. Like I was gonna yank you out of bed or something." He laughed, but tears hung heavy in his eyes.

"I'm sorry, Cody." I wanted to say more. To tell him I'd been an idiot, that I didn't deserve his forgiveness and wouldn't blame him if he never had another thing to do with me. But somehow, the only thing I could manage was, "I'm sorry."

"It's okay. We'll work it out."

The door squeaked again, and after a moment, Race came into the kitchen. His grin was a sad shadow of its normal self. "Good to see you're still in one piece," he said, stepping close to touch my shoulder, light as a soap bubble. "I wish you'd told us about your mom. That's a helluva burden to be carrying around all this time, kiddo."

I looked away, blinking hard. My face flushed with shame.

"It's not your fault, Jess," Race said. "We're behind you one hundred percent. No matter what, we're gonna help you get through this."

CHAPTER 38

Kasey didn't mention counseling again, but I couldn't stop thinking about it. My secret was out. So why did the idea of talking to someone still scare me so much?

In the morning, Kasey woke me. "I'd like to keep an eye on you today. Do you think you could afford to miss school?"

A stomach-churning rush of anxiety chased away the cobwebs of sleep. *School*. What was I going to do about all those missed assignments and failed tests? I felt a little less desperate than I had before I'd told Kasey about Lydia, but there was no way I could drum up the energy or enthusiasm to crawl out of the hole I'd dug.

"There's something I should tell you," I said.

"And what's that?"

"I-I think I'm flunking all my classes."

Kasey nodded. "That doesn't surprise me. Let's not worry about it right now, okay? We'll get it figured out when you're feeling better. Why don't you come to the shop with me? Unless you'd rather I stay home so you can get more rest."

My muscles and joints ached like they'd developed a layer of rust overnight, but I'd gotten plenty of sleep, thanks to those pain pills. "No, I can go to the shop." I didn't want her to miss another day of work.

When we pulled up in front of Eugene Custom Classics, I saw a bulk under a blue tarp at the edge of the lot. The Pinto. A ghoulish little part of me wanted to go take a peek, but the compulsion to ignore the wreck was stronger.

It had been almost two weeks since I'd been to the shop. The completed Mr. Gearhead now stood at attention by the door. I was glad Race had finally found time to finish him.

Inside, the comforting scents of oil and Bondo stirred a feeling that reminded me of hope. Kasey found me some light work washing parts and picking up tools. After that, I helped Race with the filing. He told me about his plans for the TBI Northwest sculpture he'd just begun. It would be far more abstract than Mr. Gearhead. A towering oval composed of steel panels, which would be contoured into curves to accentuate light and shadow.

In the afternoon, he asked me to give him a hand bleeding the brakes on a Roadrunner. I sat inside, pumping the pedal as he went around to each wheel, opening the bleeder valves. When he finished, I got out of the car and watched him top off the master cylinder.

"I'm sorry about last week," I said. "I should've listened to you about Cody. But no matter how hard I tried, I couldn't get things together, and I knew I was hurting him."

"So what are you going to do now?"

I shook my head. "I don't know. I guess maybe Kasey's right about talking to someone, but it's hard enough having you guys know my secrets. I don't think I could tell them to a stranger. It would make me feel . . ."

"Like someone stole all your clothes and shoved you out on stage?" Race suggested.

"Uh, yeah."

He nodded. "That's pretty much how I felt after my wreck. Of course, spending two weeks in the hospital at the mercy of medical personnel will do that to you." He put the cover back on the master cylinder and flipped the bale. "It was rough at first, but once I realized those people were there to help and not humiliate me, I got used to it. Just like you'd get used to telling a stranger about your mom."

It was the first time he'd even hinted at the idea everyone else had been forcing on me. "So you think I should go to counseling?"

He glanced at me, eyes serious but sympathetic. "I don't want to be just one more person nagging you, Jess. But yeah. It wouldn't be a bad idea."

I stared down at the radiator. "Did you ever?"

"No. . . . I should've, but everyone was knee-deep in my personal business, and I couldn't stand to give up what was going on inside my head, too." He screwed the lid on the brake fluid and shut the hood. "It was a mistake. I put Cody and Kasey through hell while I worked things out on my own. That's something you might want to consider."

"Do it for you guys, instead of for myself?"

He crouched to collect the wrench, tubing, and jar he'd used to catch the excess brake fluid. "If that's what it takes to make the plunge, then yeah, I guess that's one way to look at it."

After school, Cody picked up Rhett and brought him to the shop. Rhett spotted me across the open bay and slunk forward with downcast eyes.

"Are you mad at me?" he mumbled, rubbing the edge of his brace.

"Of course not."

He scuffed a sneaker back and forth on the dusty floor. "Maybe if I'd said something to Daddy, you wouldn't have wrecked your car."

"If you'd told him, I'd have gotten mad at you," I said, resting my hand on his shoulder. "Anyway, you had no idea what I was doing."

"But now your Pinto's totaled."

"Yeah, and that's my own fault. I'm the one who chose to go driving like a maniac in the middle of the night, not you." *Oh, wow.* That sounded a lot like what Kasey had said about Lydia. This wasn't the same thing, not at all. But if I'd gotten killed that night, what would he be thinking now?

"You know what, Rhett? I'm still here. That's the important

thing. So no harm, no foul, okay?"

He nodded. "When are you coming home?"

"I don't know. I guess that's up to Kasey."

"Newt misses you, but I'll take good care of him. I'll make sure he gets plenty of snuggles, okay?"

"Thanks, Rhett." I pulled him into a hug.

"I'm glad you're talking to me again, Jess. I missed you."

Yeah. I'd missed him, too.

Just before 5:00, Dad's red and silver Freightliner pulled into the parking lot. He came through the door wearing a harrowed look that made me wish I could take back every stupid thing I'd done.

"Dad . . ." I said, stepping toward him. "I'm really sorry."

"I'm just glad you're all right." He gathered me into a hug that seemed to last forever before kissing the top of my head and pulling away. "I'm gonna talk to Kasey for a few minutes, then we'll go out and get some dinner, okay?"

I nodded.

While the two of them went into the office, I helped Cody replace the shocks and outer tie rod ends on a Falcon. Half an hour later, Dad called for me.

Subdued by the thought of what he and Kasey must've discussed, I pushed through the door. Dad sat on the couch, face etched with every bit of the sadness I'd been unable to feel for so long.

"Honey," he said, "if I'd had any idea all this was going on, I woulda come home right away. I'm sorry."

I sat down beside him. "It's not your fault. You didn't know. I was lying to you . . . lying to everyone."

He shook his head. "And we didn't even suspect. You're so good at taking care of yourself, so responsible. It never occurred to me to think you could be hiding something this huge."

And that was why it had worked. I stared down at my shoes,

noticing one had a hole in the toe. How long had it been that way?

"Jessie, I'm so sorry." Dad slipped his hand over mine. "None of this would've happened if I hadn't tried to shut your mother out of your life."

That might be true, but it wasn't anything we could change.

Dad's fingers squeezed mine. "Tell me what I can do to help."

He'd already given up hauling hazmat, and that was all I wanted, except maybe for him to come home more often.

But that wasn't something I could ask for.

"Talk to me. I can tell there's something you want to say."

I shook my head.

"Jess . . ."

Hadn't we been through this before? What good would it do to repeat it? "It's just . . . I really miss you."

"Aw, honey." Dad wrapped an arm around my shoulders.

"I-I don't want you to give up trucking," I said. "I know you love it. I just wish you could be home more often."

He pulled me closer. "That really matters to you, huh?"

I nodded. "Yeah."

"Okay. I think I can arrange that. But I want you to do something for me, too."

I stiffened. "You mean talk to that counselor?"

"Yeah. I know you're strong and tough and think you can fix everything yourself. But heartache like this has a way of stretching on forever. Believe me, I know. And I don't want you to go through years of pain like I did. Not if there's something that might help."

The idea still made my stomach clench, but it wouldn't be the hardest thing I'd ever tackled. Maybe if I couldn't do it for myself, I could do it for my friends, the way Kasey had for Race, and Race wished he had for her and Cody.

"Okay," I said. "I'll try."

CHAPTER 59

I spent the next two weeks trying to restore the crumpled wreck of my life. Dad and my friends were supportive, but ultimately I had to walk alone through the door of my counselor's office twice a week and re-live what happened, word by word, in front of a witness.

Her name was Sara. She rode a Harley and sold handcrafted jewelry at biker runs on the weekends—not at all what I'd expected. I kind of liked her.

The sessions hadn't magically restored me to normal, let alone happy. It was still hard to get up in the morning, and I cried a lot, something I'd almost never done before I'd hit the deer. At times, guilt and sadness swooped out of nowhere and I'd begin to shake, my whole body going cold. In those moments, nothing could warm me. But overall, things got easier. I could imagine that maybe someday I'd feel better. It was a start.

I'd been afraid Mark would tell my father to find another place for me to live, but while I was at Kasey's, he came to reassure me.

"I want you to know the past few weeks haven't changed the way I feel about you, Jess. You've been through a rough time and coped as best you could. You're a strong, courageous young woman, someone I'd be proud to have as a daughter."

After a few days, I went back home to him and Rhett, but I continued to spend a lot of time with Kasey. Now that the Roadster Show was over, she had to work double-time on wedding plans, and for some reason, she seemed to enjoy brainstorming with me.

Kasey also served as a personal tutor to help with my backlog of schoolwork, which meant she only let me put in five hours a week at the shop. Fortunately, that didn't include the time we spent stripping salvageable parts from the Pinto. Over the summer, we'd find a car to transplant the engine and transmission into. But for now, I was without wheels.

Dad spent a week with me, then, after purchasing one of those cellular phones, went back to work.

"There'll be a lot of places I can't get service," he said. "But at least you'll be able to leave a message for me directly, instead of going through my dispatcher." He'd also promised to come home one more weekend a month, a real commitment, considering the lifestyle he was used to.

By the time spring break began, things seemed to be inching back toward normal, though I could feel the scars. The worst was with Cody. He hadn't once hesitated to show his love and forgiveness, but the things I'd said to him couldn't be erased. I sensed a distance between us now, as if we were classmates rather than a couple. His kisses had become brotherly, restrained and lacking passion.

I hated it. Yet who could I blame but myself?

I spent the better part of spring break studying, mostly in the shop office where Cody or Kasey would be available if I needed help. My teachers had been understanding, saying I could retake my botched midterms. Two weeks of the quarter remained, and if I hadn't caught up with my other work by then, they'd give me incompletes and allow me to finish it later.

My concentration wasn't up to speed, but getting enough sleep helped, and Kasey and Cody provided a constant stream of encouragement, assuring me the endless stacks of assignments weren't as impossible as they looked.

Friday of that week, I stayed home to work on my history reading, something that was easier where it was quiet. The phone rang in the afternoon, and Rhett answered. After a few minutes, he brought it to my room.

"It's Teri Sue. She wants to talk to you."

He'd sent her a letter about my wreck, and since then, she'd come by the house a couple of times when Mark was at work.

Turning in my chair, I took the phone. "Hey."

"Hey there, girlfriend. You wanna come by and do something tonight?" Teri Sue's voice held the cheerful note I'd gotten so used to hearing the previous summer.

"I don't have a car, remember?" That loss of freedom had been incredibly aggravating. I'd had to depend on Cody for rides to school and work. But I didn't ask Teri Sue to come pick me up. There was no way she'd get within five miles of the house when her dad was home.

"Have Cody give you a ride," she suggested. "Bring Rhett along, too. We'll go to the mall."

"I think Cody's going to work on his race car tonight. The first practice is a week from tomorrow."

"Aww, c'mon. He'll do it for you."

I leaned back in my chair, putting my feet on the desk. "I don't know about that. Things have been a little weird between us lately."

"Then I'll call him and ask. Where is he, at work?"

Leave it to Teri Sue not to take "no" for an answer.

"I think so."

"Okay, I'll get back to you in a sec."

When she hung up, I returned to the chapter I'd been reading. A few minutes later, the phone jangled beside me. "Yeah?" I said as I raised it to my ear.

"He'll pick you up at five," said Teri Sue. "Be sure you bring Rhett. I don't need him gettin' ill with me again."

We stopped to get Teri Sue before driving to Valley River Center, where we detoured through Spencer's Gifts on the way to the food court. Rhett giggled at a fart book while Teri Sue considered the selection of lava lamps and Cody modeled a big, blue Marge Simpson wig. Rhett and Teri Sue busted up laughing, but I could only muster a smile. It had been so long since anything seemed funny.

As we headed off to get dinner, Teri Sue clutching a bag containing a purple and bright green lava lamp, I hung back, hoping to have a private word with her.

"I know you think this is none of my business," I began. "But I kind of feel sorry for your dad."

She shot me a wary sideways look. "This isn't gonna turn into a lecture, is it?"

"No. It's just . . . I can see how much he misses you. I'm sure he'll let you off the hook if you come home. I put him through a lot lately, but he forgave me, and I'm not even his kid."

"Who says I need his forgiveness?" Teri Sue's eyes scouted the stores across the wide aisle.

"You yelled at him and ran off. You've been avoiding him since Christmas."

"Well, he's the one who opened my mail. He's the one who told me I was a screw up. I'm not smart like you, Jess. I can't get straight A's."

"You really think he expects you to?"

Teri Sue's hand clamped tight around the handles of the bag, her knuckles white ridges. "He thinks I don't try. Didn't you hear him? He said the only reason I messed up was because I was busy partying."

I almost let the argument die. For the first time in months, Teri Sue was taking an interest in me. If I pushed too hard, she'd cut me off, the same as she had her dad. But I couldn't stand to see what was happening to her family. "Don't you think there might be the slightest bit of truth to that?"

Teri Sue's jaw twitched. She said nothing as we strode past Montgomery Ward and the Hallmark store.

"Look," I said, "maybe you'll hate me forever for this, but

your dad's got a point. You hardly came home fall term. You kept blowing off your little brother, and the one time we did anything together, you abandoned me at a party."

Teri Sue stared straight ahead. "From what I heard, you took care of yourself okay."

"That's not the point."

We walked past four more stores before she spoke.

"Okay," she said, still focusing on something far ahead of us. "So maybe I coulda done better. But I can't talk to Daddy. It's too embarrassing. I botched it something awful fall term, and I didn't do much better this winter."

"You're still in school. That's what matters."

Teri Sue finally glanced at me, her face pinched by a seldom-seen look of distress. "It's hard, Jess. I don't know how to balance things. I'm just trying to figure out what I wanna do with my life. I oughta be able to do that without Daddy interfering. Or being ashamed of me."

"He's not ashamed, he's worried."

Teri Sue shook her head, her softly curling strawberry blond hair bouncing against her shoulders. I could see how this was going to go. I'd keep arguing, and she'd find ways to put me off. Unless I got real with her.

"Look," I said, "I wouldn't make such a big deal about it, but you never know what's coming. What if something happened to your dad, and you never got a chance to patch things up with him? Believe me, no matter how mad you are at someone, it doesn't mean squat once that person's gone."

Teri Sue stopped abruptly, her bag banging against her leg. Her eyes went wide as a sudden awareness swept the slate of her expression clean.

"My mom did a lot of really bad stuff—way worse than your dad opening your report card or getting on your case for messing up. And it went on for years. But you know what? I'd take her back in a heartbeat just the way she was."

"Jess . . . I'm sorry." Teri Sue reached out, her fingers gripping mine. "I never thought about it that way."

"Neither did I, until it was too late."

We stood in the middle of the aisle, just looking at each other as people ducked around us. I wanted to push for a commitment, but I figured I'd said enough.

"Tell you what," Teri Sue finally offered. "I'll think about giving Daddy a call, okay?"

"Yeah." I nodded.

She released my hand and fake-slugged my shoulder. "So what's the deal with things being weird between you and Cody? Everything seems normal to me."

It wasn't something I wanted to talk about. Not here and not now. But after that conversation about her dad, I owed her. "Mostly he is," I said, starting forward to catch up with the boys. "But something's missing. It's like he doesn't trust me anymore."

Teri Sue fell into step beside me.

"I can't say I blame him," I added. "I was pretty brutal when I told him I didn't want to see him again."

"You're thinking too much. As usual," said Teri Sue. "He just needs some time." She bumped me with her lava lamp bag. "I can't see that guy ever giving up on you."

I sighed and glanced ahead, to where Cody and Rhett were staring through the window of a candy store, probably arguing the merits of M&Ms versus gummy worms. "I hope you're right."

Cody would never abandon me completely, especially now. But what if he thought I was too damaged to risk getting close to again? What if he couldn't handle who I'd become?

When we reached the food court, Teri Sue and I decided on Chinese while Rhett selected a burrito and Cody loaded down his tray with pizza, a German sausage, and a huge order of chili cheese fries.

The smell of a dozen different types of cuisine mingled together, strong and spicy, as we found an empty table and sat down.

Teri Sue plucked a crunchy noodle from her plate of chicken chow mein and popped it into her mouth. "So how are you and Race doing with your cars?" she asked Cody. "Y'all think you'll be ready when the season starts?"

"We've got a few things to take care of, but we plan on making practice next Saturday."

She nodded and munched another noodle. "Cool. You reckon Race is gonna take the championship again?"

Somehow, Cody managed to answer, grin, and tear off a bite of pizza all at the same time. "No doubt about it."

"Your car's ready, too," I said. Even though she hadn't once made it to the house to help with the Camaro since September, I wasn't going to let myself feel bitter about it. Not after the effort she'd been making to stay in touch the past few weeks.

"I 'preciate all the work you did," she said, scooping her fork into the chow mein. "But I'm not gonna be here to drive it."

"What?"

"A couple of my girlfriends decided to go backpacking through Europe this summer. They invited me along. I've still got the money Grandma and Grandpa gave me for graduation, so I figured I'd do it."

"You can't!" Rhett said. "You're supposed to go racing."

I gaped at Teri Sue in total shock. Despite her other delinquencies, I'd never once thought she'd blow off the season. "Rhett's right. The car's ready . . . you've got to drive it. You can't just let it sit there."

She pursed her lips and nodded, the slightest hint of deviltry in her eyes. "Good point. . . . Tell ya what, Jess. How 'bout you drive it for me?"

For the next few seconds, I completely lost command of the

English language. Then, finally, one word worked its way into my brain. "Seriously?"

"Sure. You're the one who did all the work."

"I helped," said Rhett.

"Then you can be crew chief."

He crumpled his burrito wrapper and tossed it on the tray. "I'd rather let Jess be crew chief and have you stay here."

"Sorry, squirt. That's not gonna happen."

The idea of me racing was so far beyond the realm of reality, I couldn't begin to process it. "But I don't have any safety equipment."

Teri Sue shrugged. "Use mine. 'Course you'll have to take in the firesuit, or it'll hang on you like a potato sack."

"You're not *that* fat," said Rhett.

She threw a bean sprout at him.

"Are you sure about this? You're not going to change your mind in a couple of weeks?" I couldn't even begin to let myself think this might be real.

"We already bought our plane tickets."

I looked across the table at Cody. His hand had stopped midway to shoveling a couple of chili cheese fries in his mouth. Orange goop dripped to the tabletop, and he grinned. "Oh, I am *so* gonna kick your ass on that race track."

I let the possibility slip fully into my brain, feeling around the edges to see how it fit.

In a few short weeks, I'd be sitting behind the wheel of a race car.

CHAPTER 40

The following afternoon, Rhett and I went out to the barn to work on the Camaro. Even though I'd been over every inch of it, and wouldn't do anything differently for myself than for Teri Sue, somehow it felt like a brand new car now that I knew I'd be behind the wheel.

The sun hung warm in the sky, inching the temperature into the upper sixties, so we left the barn doors open. Sunlight fell in a bright rectangle on the dirt floor. Last night, Mark had said it was time to pour a slab of concrete, so we'd have a flat surface for setting the car up properly. He'd taken the news about Teri Sue's trip to Europe as though it was nothing more than he'd expected. While she hadn't yet called, I wasn't giving up hope.

"Are you nervous?" Rhett asked as we went over the checklist of repairs we'd completed that winter.

"No." My late night experiences in the Pinto confirmed I could drive competently, and in spite of how horrifying it had been to hit the deer, I didn't think it would hold me back. Excitement was the only thing that came over me when I thought about racing. Pure longing for the way a car felt when I slung it into a corner, rear wheels scrabbling over asphalt.

Rhett found a rag and a tub of polishing compound and began rubbing tire scuffs off the driver's door. "Do I really get to be your crew chief?"

"Sure, if your dad will let you in the pits." It would be an honorary title more than anything else. But many Street Stock drivers did all their own work, so any set of hands, even if they belonged to an 11 year old, would be an improvement.

I heard a familiar throaty rumble in the driveway. The Galaxie pulled up and Cody stepped out, sauntering through the barn doors in that easy way of his that used to make me think he was cocky. He wore a T-shirt I hadn't seen before: *I'm not breaking the rules, I'm testing their tensile strength.* The humor hit sharp and sudden, and laughter convulsed through me, spilling out in a rusty, broken guffaw. Once it began, I couldn't make it stop. I fell back against the Camaro, clutching my ribs, marveling at how something could ache and feel so good at the same time. Tears began to stream, and as I slid to the ground to sit in the dust, my laughter dissolved into sobs.

Cody sprang forward to crouch beside me, pulling me into his arms.

"Is she okay?" Rhett worried, wide-eyed.

"Y-your shirt," I gasped, placing my hand on Cody's chest and looking up into his face. I loved him so much. How could I have ever been stupid enough to push him away?

"Guess they should've put a warning label on it," Cody said with a lopsided grin. "Caution: this shirt may cause excessive mirth and fits of helpless laughter."

Giggles coursed through me. I let my head fall against his chest, where the beat of his heart lulled me with its strong, soothing rhythm. I could have stayed like that forever, pretending things were okay between us, but Rhett was watching, his face wrinkled in concern.

"I'm okay," I told him, untangling myself from Cody's arms and getting to my feet.

Rhett studied me with a dawning look of realization. "I haven't seen you laugh since Christmas."

Could that be true? Oh wow. It was. "I'm sorry, Rhett. I know I haven't been much fun to be around . . . and I wasn't there when you needed me."

"It's okay. I understand." His eyes met mine in a look of hound dog loyalty. "Your life hit redline and fell apart."

My vision went blurry with a fresh round of tears. I opened my arms, and Rhett rushed forward to hug me hard.

We spent the afternoon goofing around and fantasizing about the upcoming season. Finally, Cody told Rhett to scram. "Go call Emily or something. I wanna spend some time with my girlfriend."

He and Rhett shared a grin, a real change from last fall, when the pre-Emily Rhett would have faked a swoon or made smooching noises.

Cody waited until he was gone to take my hand. "C'mon, let's go for a walk." He led me out the door into the sunshine. The sweet perfume of Mark's hyacinths—blazing clumps of violet and magenta—wafted across the yard on the breeze. Cody's hand surrounded mine in a little bubble of hope. Was this his way of telling me it wasn't too late?

He directed me to a path through the woods, sidestepping the muckiest spots. Spring rustled the bushes around us— squirrels coaxed into activity by the warm sun and leaves unfurling in a fresh new brilliance of green. Neither of us spoke until we reached the pond Rhett had dug last summer, where sunlight dazzled the water.

Cody lowered himself to the deck at the dammed-up end and, hand still clasping mine, pulled me down beside him.

A puff of breeze brought the sweet, spicy smell of cotton-wood to my nose, causing a shiver of memory to rush through me. It was crazy how the faintest whiff of scent could take you straight back to a better time and make you feel like everything was going to be okay.

"Nice day," Cody said, glancing at the tender-leaved maples and alders, which shimmered with the energy of spring. "I hope we're this lucky for practice next Saturday."

"Me too." It had rained most of our break, so maybe the weather gods would relent to make up for it.

"Kind of a mixed blessing about Teri Sue, huh? I mean, I know you're gonna miss her and all, but getting a chance to drive her car—wow." He gave me a funny little sideways grin.

"I still can't believe it's happening," I said, shaking my head. "It's really cool of her. She could've just gone off to Europe and left the Camaro parked in the barn."

"Well, she does have her moments. I think she feels bad about not being a better friend. Maybe this is her way of making it up to you."

A pang of regret shot through me, and I glanced away. "She's not the one who should be making things up to people."

Cody's fingers tensed around mine. "You've gotta stop thinking like that, Jess. It's not gonna do you any good."

"I let everyone down."

"Don't you think you had a pretty good reason?"

"No." I stared out into the woods. "There's not a reason in this world that could justify the things I said to you."

"I don't care about that. You were miserable, and you were trying to protect me."

"But you can't let it go, can you?" I turned to search his face. "You don't really trust me now."

Cody sighed. "Okay, what you said hurt. I'll admit, it's hard to look at you and not wonder 'what if she does it again?' But Teri Sue and I talked last night. She told me I was blowing it big time. And she was right.

"Maybe there's a risk you'll push me away again. But when I think about the risks you take every time you walk in that counselor's office, or the one you took last spring when you let me get to know you, I realize the things I'm scared of are nothing compared to what you've had to deal with every day since you were eight." His voice went husky, his words a whisper against my cheek. "You're the bravest person I know, Jess. . . . I'm sorry for holding back."

I closed my eyes to stop the tears that now always seemed to hover just below the surface. How could he believe this was his fault? How could he so willingly give me another chance to break his heart?

"You didn't do anything wrong, Cody."

"Yeah. I did. . . . Can you forgive me?"

The breath caught in my chest. "There's nothing to forgive."

His free hand rose, fingers gently stroking my cheek. His dark eyes caught mine in a look that simmered with an old, familiar passion. "I don't deserve you," he murmured.

"I was just thinking the same thing about you."

He smiled. "Well, I guess we're a matched set."

And then he leaned forward, his lips caressing mine in a kiss so warm, gentle, and full of love it melted the last bit of ice in my heart.

CHAPTER 41

The rain returned the next day, but I was too busy studying to worry about it. I turned in the majority of my overdue homework Monday and stayed after school every afternoon that week, re-taking the midterms I'd failed. By Friday, I was completely caught up, which was fortunate because it was almost time for finals.

Getting back on track at school wasn't the only bit of good luck. We also got a break from the weather late in the week when a high-pressure system pushed over the Willamette Valley to put an end to the rain.

On Saturday, Teri Sue pulled into the driveway just before noon, ready to haul the car to the track for practice.

"Hey, girl!" she said as she stepped out of her pickup. "Happy birthday."

I scuffed a sneaker in the gravel. The last time anyone but Lydia had made a big deal about the occasion was the year I turned eight, and now all my friends—including Heather—insisted on celebrating. "My birthday's not until tomorrow."

"But the party's tonight."

"You're coming?" Dad would be pulling into town that afternoon—he'd said he'd be damned if he'd miss another of my birthdays—but I hadn't expected Teri Sue.

She planted her hands on her hips and rolled her eyes. "'Course I'm coming. What kind of friend do you think I am?"

"But your dad . . ."

Teri Sue waved an impatient hand at me. "Old news. I gave him a call last night and we got it worked out."

"And you didn't tell me?"

"I'm telling you now, aren't I?" She turned away, shaking her head, and walked toward the barn. "Sweet Jesus. Like I'd miss your birthday. I baked you a damn cake, didn't I?"

"You did?" I asked, following her. "Is it chocolate?"

"Does a cat come stock with climbing gear?"

In the barn, Rhett was explaining to Emily how to set up the front end of a race car. I'd finally let her come over to help, and she'd been so intrigued by the idea of girls racing and working on cars that I now had two 11 year olds following me around like puppies.

"Let's get stuff loaded up," I said.

Rhett showed Emily the checklist, and the two of them began piling equipment into the back of the truck. I grabbed one handle of the toolbox, and Teri Sue took the other, so we could lug it outside.

"Until I've gotta leave for Europe, I'll be here every Saturday to haul the car to the track," she said.

I smiled at the admirable, but completely unrealistic, commitment. "I'm not going to hold you to that. Somehow, I can't see you giving up half your weekly party opportunities."

"Okay," Teri Sue grunted as we heaved the box into the bed of the Chevy. "My *truck* will be here every Saturday. And this summer you can use it full time."

I slapped her on the back. "Now that sounds more believable."

We drove to the speedway the way we had so many times last summer, with Teri Sue behind the wheel, me riding shotgun, and Rhett between us. Only this time, Emily was scrunched in beside him.

I looked down at my legs, covered in Teri Sue's firesuit, the same baby blue as her car. It was big on me, but not outrageously so. When Dad had given me his blessing to drive the Camaro, he'd offered to buy me a driver's uniform of my own, and I half expected him to do so for my birthday. But I didn't mind wearing Teri Sue's.

We turned off West 11th onto the dirt road that led into the speedway, and even though this was only practice, I felt a minor tremor in my midsection.

Teri Sue pulled across the track to the infield, where she parked beside Race's van and Kasey's old Dodge pickup. Nostalgia stirred in me as the scent of racing fuel tickled my nose. I'd always thought it smelled like an adventure. The sweet, pungent odor seemed to have the sound of shrieking engines and feeling of vibrating pavement packed right into it.

Race and Cody, wearing Race's team shirts, sauntered up to greet me as I hopped down from the cab.

"You definitely belong in a firesuit," Race said, shooting me one of his full-throttle grins.

Cody stepped forward to gather the material at my sides. "It could use a little adjustment." He pulled the cloth tight against my chest and stomach. "Maybe Grandma could get her tailor to take it in."

"Stop that." I pushed him away, and his face wrinkled into a smirk that made me want to smack him. Embarrassed, I ducked around him to pull down the ramps and unbolt the chains that held the car to the trailer.

"So, are you ready to have your butt handed to you on a platter?" Cody asked, giving my ponytail a tug.

"In your dreams." I climbed through the window of the Camaro and cranked the engine. As I was backing off the trailer, Kasey, who'd been checking something under the hood of Cody's Dart, hollered.

"Hey, Cody? Can you come here a minute?"

"Sure thing." He jogged off to see what she wanted.

Race stood by while I pulled myself out of the car.

"I'd like to be able to offer some advice," he said, "but you've been coming out here since you were—what—around twelve?"

"Pretty much."

"And Cody tells me you were driving long before you had your license."

I leaned back against the Camaro, resting my hands on the upper edge of the door. "That doesn't mean I know my way around the race track."

"Maybe not, but you understand what the flags mean, and where to put the car to make it handle. You've already figured out the stuff I'd tell most beginners." He looked somewhat disappointed about that.

"Race, you're a track legend," I said, allowing my old hero worship to resurface. "I'm sure you have some piece of wisdom to impart to me."

His grin stretched wide. "You're right. I do."

"And what's that?"

"Never surrender."

"Never surrender?"

"Yup. My secret weapon. No matter how bad things get, on or off the track, I never give up. Which is something you're pretty good at yourself, so I don't think you'll have a problem." He started to slap me on the shoulder, then gave me a what-the-hell look and pulled me into a rib-squeezing bear hug. "You're gonna do great, kid. . . . And you'll see, getting out on that track is about the best kind of therapy there is."

As I was checking the tire pressure on the Camaro, Heather's Gremlin pulled into the pits. She parked beside Teri Sue's pickup and sauntered over to stand beside me, infield mud clinging to her combat boots.

"Hey," I said as I fit the end of the gage over the right front tire's valve stem. "I didn't expect to see you here."

She shrugged. "Now that I've got two friends racing, I guess I could make more of an effort to come out and watch."

"Just so long as you don't start calling me 'Racer Girl.'"

Heather laughed. "Nah. I was thinking 'Racer Chick' would sound more bad-ass."

It wasn't the worst nickname she could come up with.

We made small talk as I checked the car over. My two crew members stayed with us each step of the way, Emily covertly eyeing Heather's black attire, and Rhett taking notes on everything I said. I'd have been amused by that if I hadn't remembered all too well the way people had discounted my ambitions before I met Kasey.

Rhett's diligence came in handy, since Teri Sue was too busy chatting up everyone in the pits to be much help. While I was climbing into the car to line up for my first practice, she wandered back and elbowed Rhett aside. "I'll get it from here, squirt."

He gave her a shove. "No way! You made me crew chief, remember?" Reaching between the door and roll cage, he pulled out the window net and clicked the buckles into place. "All set," he told me.

"Damned uppity kid," muttered Teri Sue.

"Well, you *did* make him crew chief."

As I flipped the ignition switch and pressed the starter button, Heather pounded the roof of the car with her fist. "Go show those guys how it's done."

Teri Sue laughed. "I already took care of that last year."

The Super Stocks, the highest division, had been given the first practice, and now Race's class, the Limited Sportsmen, were on the track. I pulled into position with the other Street Stocks at the back pit exit to wait our turn.

Excitement simmered in me as I anticipated a whole afternoon behind the wheel, reliving the sensation of speed that had been so comforting those nights in the Pinto. And after practice, there'd be the party. It was sort of embarrassing to have so many people making a fuss over me, but I liked the idea of a celebration. So much had happened in the past year, a lot of it good, and a lot of it terrible. But I'd survived. I'd taken my licks and come out on top. That seemed like a damned good reason for a party.

As I adjusted the wide rear-view mirror, mounted to give me a clear look to the left rear, I caught a flicker of motion in my peripheral vision. I turned to see Kasey crouching beside the driver's door.

"Somehow," she said, "I have a feeling you're not going to be nearly as nervous as Cody was during his first practice."

"I've got a few butterflies. But they're not too big. Actually, they're more like those pesky little white moths that hover around our porch light. I think after the first race, they'll go away."

Kasey chuckled, a soft smile slipping across her face. "I don't doubt they will. You're one gutsy young woman. I'm continually amazed at how well you cope with everything life throws at you."

"I didn't do so great the last couple of months."

"None of us did." A sadness came into her eyes, whisking away the smile. "With all the people you had looking out for you, one of us should've realized what was going on. You're so convincing, it's easy to believe it when you say things are okay. But I should have known better. Especially since I'm so good at playing that game myself."

I turned to stare out the windshield at the car ahead of me. "And I should've been honest with you. Or at least asked for help. I figured it was something I needed to handle on my own, but I was wrong. It's crazy, because that's what you tried to teach me last summer—to trust people."

Kasey sighed. "One of the frustrating things about life is that we sometimes have to learn the same lesson over and over again."

"Well, that's certainly inspiring."

She laughed and shook her head. "It's good to see your

sense of humor has come back."

In front of me, the Limited Sportsmen screamed by. Addamsen made a bid to pass Rob Davis going into the corner but had to fall back.

"There goes your biggest fan," I said. "Are you going to tell him about the Roadster Show?"

A satisfied smile slipped over Kasey's face. "No, I wouldn't want to deprive Race of the pleasure."

The pack of cars decelerated on their next lap, and Ted Greene, the chief steward, rotated his fist in the air, letting us know it was time to start our engines.

"Have fun," Kasey said as she stood up.

"Don't worry. I plan to."

Ted motioned us forward, and I followed Kit McKenzie's purple #84 Camaro out onto the track. A few cars ahead of me, Cody held a spot in the outside row.

We took several slow laps, warming our tires before we began to pick up speed. At first, I kept a moderate pace, getting a feel for the car and the track. With the Camaro's suspension adjusted so it pulled to the left, it handled nothing like the Pinto. The set-up helped with cornering, but made it necessary to steer slightly to the right on the front and backstretch. Drivability wasn't the only difference between the two cars. The Camaro's seat was also closer to the wheel, allowing my elbows to have more of a bend to increase leverage. Then there was the odd sensation of being so tightly secured against the seat. The racing harness, unlike the belts in a street car, went over both shoulders and had no give.

Once I'd developed a feel for the car, I began testing its limits, pushing harder on each lap as I sorted out how far I could drive into the turns. The Camaro stuck to the track surprisingly well, plowing through the corners at speeds that would easily have sent the Pinto spinning off into the weeds.

While I was still experimenting, Cody flew past, lapping me. Well, if he wanted to turn this into a competition, I didn't have a problem with that. I tore out of turn four, squeezing the gas pedal, and had it flat against the firewall when I pulled onto the front stretch.

The acceleration felt powerful and dangerous and good. I kept my foot in it, and at the very last moment, when it seemed the Camaro was sure to fly off the end of the straightaway, I let off and slung the car into the corner. As I nursed the accelerator through turn two, I could feel the grip of rubber on asphalt with all my fingers and toes. The tires squealed, the engine roared to full-throttle, and then I was out on the backstretch.

A surge of adrenalin raced through me as I tailed Cody down the straightaway and passed him going into turn four, tires spitting out bits of the gravel that lined the top edge of the asphalt. For the first time in months I felt strong.

For the first time in months I felt happy.

"Woo-hoo!" I shouted, the words spilling out of me all on their own. I sped under the flag tower, hope soaring in my heart and one thought burning in my brain.

I could get used to this.

AUTHOR'S NOTE

I have always planned to write a fifth and final book in the *Full Throttle* series. The issue is that, at this point, it's still in outline form. The first four books had already been written before I started this publishing venture, so it was only a matter of revising them. That's how I was able to get four of them (and my stand alone title, *Dead Heat*) out in less than two years.

While I do intend to write this final book, I don't have an excerpt ready, and I can't give you a timeline on when it will be released. I'm working on another project at the moment, so I won't even have a chance to begin the fifth book until at least 2014. If you're looking for another title, you might try *Dead Heat*. Though it's a darker book, it has the same sort of character relationships and emotional appeal as my other stories.

ABOUT THE AUTHOR

In addition to being a YA author, Lisa Nowak is a retired amateur stock car racer, an accomplished cat whisperer, and a professional smartass. She writes coming-of-age books about kids in hard luck situations who learn to appreciate their own value after finding mentors who love them for who they are. She enjoys dark chocolate and stout beer and constantly works toward employing *wei wu wei* in her life, all the while realizing that the struggle itself is an oxymoron.

Lisa has no spare time, but if she did she'd use it to tend to her expansive perennial garden, watch medical dramas, take long walks after dark, and teach her cats to play poker. For those of you who might be wondering, she is not, and has never been, a diaper-wearing astronaut. She lives in Milwaukie, Oregon, with her husband, four feline companions, and two giant sequoias.

Connect with Lisa online:

Facebook: http://www.facebook.com/LisaNowakAuthor
Website: http://www.lisanowak.net/
Blog: http://lisanowak.wordpress.com/
Newsletter: http://bit.ly/LisaNowakNewsletter (sign up to be notified of new releases)